MW01076531

A loud *caw* cuts de air. I free

More *caw caw caws*. A volley of dem, right behind me. I turn—four fiens pop up from a tangle of shopping trolleys. All have dese black ledder bird masks with long crooked beaks. Dey stand stock still, staring.

My weak heart clenches—a puny, shaky fist. I back up, slow... slow... Another *caw* fires off to my side. Three more crows stand just a hundred yards from me. Each one with a metal bar in his hand. My stomach cramps up, my legs nearly give out. Dis is de moment de Wayke loves best. Dat bit of shock before de shatters of pain. Before iron bars beat down, cracking bones, ribs, skull, brain... before de shark's mouth closes... dat split second when de hitchhiker sees de lock go down on de passenger door. Something relishes dat moment, whispering into yur ear, *Told you so. Didn't I say I'd get ya? You claim* me, *sunshine? I'm goan to fucken eat you alive. I'm goan to scrape out yur marrow with wire.*

Can't run, can't stand still. Can't even swallow. I keep backing up in small doddery steps. De crows don't move a muscle. Terror twists in my gut—a fat hairy worm. Den it dawns on me: dey're looking for signs of Gombrich. *Right so, I'll give dem a few.*

"Stay back," I stammer, really feeling craw-sick, as it happens. Start itching, coughing, staggering dis way and dat. "Sick! I'm *sick!*"

Speaking out loud pops a bubble, or maybe dey don't like what I said. Anyway, next thing all de crows are swooping—full speed in my direction.

Copyright © 2022 by Colm O'Shea
Cover Art by James Guinnevan Seymour
ISBN 978-1-63789-858-1
All rights reserved. No part of this book may be used or reproduced in any manner
whatsoever without written permission except in the case of
brief quotations embodied in criticalarticles and reviews
For information address Crossroad Press at 141 Brayden Dr., Hertford, NC 27944
A Mystique Press Production - Mystique Press is an imprint of Crossroad Press.
www.crossroadpress.com

First Edition

CLAIMING
de
WAYKE

Colm O'Shea

Dedication

*For Alma, my guide through the literary scape,
and Marie, my guide through the wayke.*

A Note
on Waykean Language

There is something wrong with this book. Specifically, there is something wrong with the sounds it makes. For a start, it has two narrators, and the first one is in the second-person. To make matters worse, that first narrator (in the second-person) is happening in the machine-enhanced mind of the second narrator, who speaks in the first-person. This second (first-person) narrator is Tayto, and his is the slippery, broken, crude language of the disaffected brute. It's a mish-mash of slang from my own youth growing up in southern Ireland—its own unique linguistic universe—together with elements of an imagined future dialect.

Switching narration styles isn't for everyone. And I'm sure Tayto's salty invective will upset the refined reader. But I appeal to you on Tayto's behalf: underneath this unfortunate and cynical man's surface beats the heart of a poet. I hope you give him—and his strange tale—a fighting chance to win you over. Thank you for keeping an open mind and entering the Wayke.

Chapter 1:Intruder

Already forgetting the soft curled silence of your egg, or how you hatched. Previous lives shed like dead skin. Your length drags over cracked earth. Sun is high. A lizard mind registers the only fact of life: hot. Hot now.

You sense it before you see it: water—a wide mass. Dip your foot. A lizard mind registers: Cool. Slip inside, instantly out of your depth. An ocean of relief: cool now.

Limbs grow longer, stretch deeper. Clawed hands cup the brine, feet become flippers. Gills drink in oxygen. This is where you belong: home.

Shapes loom in the murk: a drowned city. You prowl empty streets. A shark rounds the corner, ignoring you. Just as well for the shark.

An eel twists out of a cave: a subway entrance. Swim down steps, only a few feet deeper but into a world of darkness. What awaits? Your teeth get sharper. Just in case.

A rusted train hulk sits on the tracks. Light glows from a carriage window. Spy inside: a green girl, her back to you. On the walls of the car she assembles bioluminescent starfish into spiral patterns. Her green hair floats like a cloud.

This is a private scape—cocooned. How did she get in?
You pull near for a better look. She starts and spins. Her eyes flash: electric green. She darts off down the train. Is she luring you? So what if she is?

You give chase. But the trail is cold. Perhaps she has surfaced.

Press upward with the lazy kicks of a master swimmer. The shallows brighten, and pressure drops away. Is she up there, waiting for you at the edge of worlds?

You breach. Air shocks your lungs. A storm is gathering. All around, skyscrapers stretch from sea to crackling clouds. Climb toward the storm. Pick the tallest tower for the best view.

Waves slam you against the building. You struggle against the wash. Suckers bulge from your palms and feet, fix to the surface. One hand over another—haul to the top.

Heave onto the roof. Search for that green intruder. Peer from the edge—zoom in. The waters below become vivid, layers of urgent colour. There! She bobs on her back, water licking her slick form. Her hands caress the water, hair spooling into an ocean of weed. You can just make out her smile. Come, it says. Come to me.

The three-note jingle rings. Butler-rabbit burrows up from the roof's concrete. He adjusts his waistcoat, dusts his jacket, and straightens his bow tie. Why does a character so formal not wear pants?
    "Ahem. Beg pardon, sir. May I suggest a brief break? Some refreshment?"

He inspects his long feet, absently brushing flecks of dirt from his toes.
    Twelve hours already? There's no point in arguing—you know that.

"Shall I save your settings as usual, sir? Very good."

Chapter 2:
Home Sweet Home

Waykin is shite. No two ways 'bout it. First, dere's a drop into nottin. Black. You get a sense of space, but dat's it. No light, no sound, no tickles. Den yur bits and pieces remember demselves. Yur lump of a corpse comes creeping back. Fingers and toes tingle at first, den flare into pins and needles. Head, legs, spine, stomach, arse: all pour back into place—pure hangover. You wince into real daylight, which manages de nifty trick of being harsh and dull all at once. Waykin. Likesay, no two ways 'bout it. Tis a balls.

De bare white walls glared at me. Sure enough, my feedbag— de IV drip next to my fancy recliner—was near gawp empty. I'd need to hook up a fresh one. I reached into de cardboard box by my side for a replacement pouch and de twisty movement gave me the gawks. I tried not to spew. *Travel sick in my chair now. Nice wan.* I leaned forward to put my head between my legs. Dat made me want to take a waz.

Freezing my nads off in only my vest and jocks. I'd stopped springing for heat ages ago. My flat was a drafty box. Spose dat's all I wanted. A bonebox to hold me while I lit up. But de winter had snaked up on me. Suddenly it was a different season from yesterday. My breath stalled in front of my face—a midget fog.

It was a five-second trot to de bog, but I couldn't be arsed. If I changed my feedbag and lit up, de cold'd be no matter. On de other hand, I'd likely piss myself. How easy would fake ledder be to wipe down? *Fecksake, I coulduv been dere and back by now.*

Some saints wore nappies, like babies or auld codgers. Or astronauts. Fiens call it goan sumo. I could see de logic in sumo, but dere was something bout wearing a nappy, lying in yur own waste, sometimes for hours… it just reminded me too much of de Gerries. I wasn't ready for sumo. Not yet.

I stood over de bowl for a monster waz. A wall crack over de cistern was dodgier dan I remembered. It stretched all the way to de ceiling, black tongue of lightning in a white sky. Everything's backward here. My mind hopped to a newsflash bout a tenement down by de docks—caved in one day, killing… was it everyone? Well, swatting a bunch. No one does building inspections anymore. Not round here, anyway.

How would you even contact an inspector? I peered into de crack as if my savage engineering skills could divine whether or not de sky was goan to fall. An ant nipped out from the split. He paused, all cagey, sniffing de air or whatever dey do, den scuttled across de dirty cistern. Good luck to you, boi.

Scrubbing my hands in de sink, I glanced into de tiny mirror. I'd forgotten to take off my halo. It was a part of me, like my manky hair. But pure elegant—a spaghetti-thin band arcing round de back and sides of my skull, all mothery-pearly. De only truly beautiful thing in de Wayke, in fact. Tis weird: I'd never seen my own halo lit up. As soon as it was lit and at its loveliest, I was gone—off and scaping. Didn't matter. De way it got me out of de Wayke was de most beautiful thing about my halo in de first place.

De music from next door snarled into life, hardly muffled by de wall. Wondered how loud it'd have to be to damage a building, like, over time. Was it even music? Or a torture device? It was all savage drumbeat and screaming. Aggro. Tribal war. Pure hate ripping through plaster to get at me.

I'd lived in dis hole of a Dublin flat for bout a year—well, "lived," y'knaw? I'd gatch home from work, hit de recliner, and spark my halo till it was time to rise. Den I'd maybe gawk in de sink, and gatch back to work. Doubt I spent more dan twenty minutes a day here conscious. And yet nearly every wayking moment I'd spent here I had dis shitehawk music to deal with. Never saw hide nor hair from anyone next door. For all I knew twas just a machine, set to trigger conniptions whenever I shifted in my seat.

Some saints get deadened after a while. De Wayke no longer feels real to dem, like *really* real, and no amount of hot, cold, noise, stink, thirst, ructions, whadevvor, causes upset. Dis couldn't-be-arsed vibe can make saints grand lads to share a room with, or de worst shower of daws and dossers you were ever afflicted with, depending on whether or not yur deadening up yurself. To me—and I'm only speaking for myself here, now—to me de Wayke still enjoyed a sense of "existential primacy." That's what an auld wan said to me one day at work. It means de Wayke can still kick yur ass up and down de park, so be wide. Be *dog* wide. De Wayke is de bully'll give you a good *funt* up de hole for lookin sideways at him. De Wayke's de shark in a kiddie pool. Take a good look at de Wayke, you see it lookin right back at you, boi, givin you de guzz eye. *I know where you live,* says de Wayke. *I'm comin for you one day, y'little bollox.* De more I hid in my halo, de sterner de Wayke got when I traipsed out in it.

A time back, seems like donkeys ago, I didn't bodder wasting my sad wages on rent. At de end of a shift, I'd find a deserted building (a *relikwery,* is de cant we had for dem), and light up with other saints who'd oathed not to rob each other. Most saints anyway are just gowls like me with hardly a knotty shite to steal between us, so a relikwery oath wasn't axing much.

Dere was a good kwery near de canal, handy enough to my job. I was a regular, on nodding terms with de other fiens. I remember—it might be a bit off topic, but whadevvor—dere was a regular who used to cut his arm or leg, sort of a ritual thing, like, before and after he lit up. Still remember de knife. Small yoke, a kid's penknife—comical. He'd slice a knick into a forearm or shin, den shrug and smile at us. I don't think he was suicidal. If anything I'd say he was enthusiastic, always goan on bout his cathedral. He'd been working on it for yonks. So proud, ranting on about design details. De stained glass! De apses and cornices and whadevvor yur having yurself! I could almost see it. He was all *yeah, c'mon in, I'll give y'de tour,* but I don't visit people in de Scape. Don't understand fiens who do. I mean, you finally get *out* of de Wayke, *away* from all de langers and skangers and scuts of de world… and den you're boddering yur hole to catch up with dem in dere? Will I come visit yur scapesite?

I will *yeaahh* boi.

How and ever, one evening just as I was coming in from work to bed down for de night, I see de same thick gom sit up and roll his eyes de way he did whenever he wayked. He flicks open his little red penknife, and, I dunnaw… somehow sliced an artery in his wrist. He just chuckled when someone offered to help stem de leak. We all just sat dere, motionless, as he watched himself bleed out, easy as bedammed. I lay back and lit up. In de morning him and his mattress were gone, no trace left except a red stain on de tiles. After dat, I said to myself: fair enough. Time to get my own place. No more kweries, no more social, no more incidents. Gobshite neighbour here, true, true. But tis a small price to pay for peace of mind.

I was craw-sick as usual, but most of de nausea was passing. As I slumped back on de recliner, yur man's din from next door cut out. Bit of whisht at last. I peered into de cardboard box next to my drip stand. Only a few feedbags left. I changed de old one, reconnected de drip, and looked about for my halo before remembering de pearl arc was still wrapped round my head. A scream sounded in de street below. Whadevvor was goan on down dere, I'd be no use. Lay back and closed my eyes… ready for de drop.

Resume: Lightning lashes the spire. Leap to the green-blue world below. You walk to the other end of the roof: starter's crouch. Butler-rabbit hops in your path.

"Welcome back, sir. May I say, but that was quite a brief dining experience? Ten minutes. Have you partaken of enough roughage? The human colon requires a certain daily–"

Flatten Butler with your fist—the icon vanishes.

He will be back soon. Go! At the edge in three monster bounds—dive clear of the building—the water whistles toward you. Extend arms to steady your line, and then close your body into a single dart. Here it comes... here it comes.

Three-note jingle. Butler floats into view, tiny wings flapping casually, fluffily, on his back. He circles, notebook and pen at the ready.

"Pardon me, sir. Your shift begins in forty minutes. You need to leave now if you wish to avoid tardiness."

Grab his paw, swing to a hanging pause in mid-air. Hover there, storeys above a raging sea. No sign of the girl. She's been swallowed by chaos.

"It's Sunday," you growl. The base-jump thrill is already ruined.

"I beg your indulgence, sir." With an elegant black fountain pen Butler taps his pad, a meticulous record of your activities. "I believe you will find it is Monday."

Slumped in de recliner again. De gawks were back with a vengeance, and so was de rage machine next door. I stared at my wrinkled Gerries uniform fecked on de ground.

Cramped shower: de water spat at me in fits. Only two settings: scaldy and freezing.

As I got dressed, a scalpel of winter sunlight near blinded me. I stumbled out my door and shuffled along de Grand Canal, de sun finally blunted—thank gawd—by a freezing fog. It drifted in over dead water, swamping all de usual *c'mon lads lets get ta work now* bullshit of de morning. All de harsh features of my walk to de Gerries were sucked up in greyness. Cold crept into my lungs. A cough welled up out of me, a deep, chesty, phlegmy bastard. I'd no coat and my uniform—wafer thin overalls, paper face mask—was comical defense. May as well have been starkers. Still, I liked dis fog. Gentle. Fussed bout nottin. Perhaps it'd deepen, swallow more and more of de traffic signs and thrownaway coffee cups in its big grey mouth, wipe out all de edges and angles of buildings, eat all de pigeons and pedestrians alike. I could shuffle into shapeless soft grey, and never come out.

Turns out it didn't only eat things, dis fog. It coughed up a frozen grey gift right in front of me. I bent over it. Dead squirrel, curled in a hunch, like he was guarding a huge invisible nut. Dunnaw why, but it seemed weird to me a squirrel might die of natural causes—old age, like—and just... drop out of his tree. I gave him an old poke with my shoe. Rigid—an ice cube with a furry tail. Normally wouldn't go near such a thing, but de poor bollox being frozen made it seem cleaner, somehow. I picked him up by his tail, like it was a handle, and tapped his head against de footpath. It felt like one of dem stone-age tools—cavemen could use dis guy to crack a nut. With a quick sconce to make sure no one was looking, I stashed de corpse in my deep pocket.

Reddish streetlights flickered, dying stars. Everything worldly was gone, except for de cold ringing clear as a bell through my sinuses; every tiny crack in my holey skull ached whenever I sniffed to clear my nose, mask making no difference at all. A manky ball of tissue sat crumpled in my pocket. Wasn't puttin dat anywhere near my face. Even de hand sharing a pocket with it kept its distance, like two wary cellmates eyeing each other.

But de fog was no match for de Gerries. Somehow de old folks' home had survived, dark walls only more solid and real in de grey. A big black iceberg floating into view—certainty in de midst of chaos.

I trudged to de main entrance and "submitted to the viral test station," which meant dropping de mask, sticking my hands in metal cuffs dat locked fierce tight around my wrists.

Submit sample, said dat creepy calm synth voice. I blew into de breath collector yoke. Nottin doin.

Please submit a breath sample. Dat ghost voice again. I blew as hard and as long as I could, waiting for a chirpy sound to let me know: *Jolly good old-chap-me-laddy-buck, you're not infected at all at all. Now get on with yur chores ya culchie muppet!* "Huffers" dey call dem in Dublin, because you have to huff and puff like a big bad wolf before it finally goes: *Bleep*BLAARP. *Gombrich Virus—Negative. Welcome to the East-Central Gerontoplex.* Cuffs release, door hisses open, I enter de iceberg. Wonders of modern bleepin technology.

Lift doors parted and I peered out, sketchin round for de floor supervisor, Copperknob. (Or Bosley, if you want to be official about it. I didn't.) No sign of de langball. I didn't recognise de new byor behind reception. Wondered if old Sylvia was dead or taking a personal day. New byor didn't look up from her mess of files as I passed by. She was having a private meltdown, belting her keypad and getting spat back de same electronic squawk. I could translate. Squawk was saying: *Lookit girl, nottin I can do for ya.* No matter how bad she needed it, no matter how urgent it was, tough toffees. *End of de line, Dillinger.* Dis was as far as she was going with de "process she was trying to implement," or whadevvor cant it is receptionists use. *Tis nottin personal, love*, squawk was saying. Squawk didn't give details. Poor byor clawed her fingers through her hair and moaned, giving de ringing phone a deaf ear.

A good meltdown can be engrossing, like. I was so wrapped up in watching dis byor from a safe distance lose her rag I didn't notice tiny, soft-shoed Copperknob creep up behind me like de snakey little prick he is.

"Mr. Tayto." His nasally voice triggered something in de receptionist. She answered de phone pronto, stammering out a greeting. I turned, slow as possible, slow as a pig on a spit, like as long as I don't see him everything's hunky-dory—*so far so good, so far so good...* But dere he stood, big bolshy Belfast head on him, short and baldy, de bit of orangey hair he had cropped in a tight bazzer dat set off his round red cheeks, like a tike just come in from muckin about in snow. From behind, you might take him for a lost child searching de halls for his granny. But den you spy his mean little eyes...

"Just 'Tayto', sir. It's a nickname, like." Soon as I said it I knew it was a mistake. Why correct him now? Was I looking for trouble?

"It says 'Mr. Tayto' on your name tag."

"Yeah, dat's... sortuva joke. Sir."

Running into Copperknob was always like coming face to face with a pixie, or an imp. He was fierce patient today. Usually he'd be shouting by now, wagging his finger in my face, maybe poking me in de chest as he made his point. Instead he took a deep breath.

"Go to HR and get your proper name put on your tag." I nodded, and turned to leave.

"It must be nice," he paused, "to lead such a leisurely life."

"Sir?"

He grasped my wrists.

"Still no watch, I see."

He let go, and I instinctively rubbed de spot he'd grabbed like in old filums when a guy gets out of handcuffs.

"Sorry, sir. I meant to, but, like..." I browsed round for a daycent excuse but de only thing in my head was *Screw you, boi, and yur watch and yur stupid job in dis city I fucken hate almost half as much as I fucken hate you, ya coppery fucken KNOB.*"

I could hear de receptionist byor behind me on de phone, trying to put on a posh accent:

"Certainly, Mrs. Rogers, we can, um, appropriate that, um, expediently. There will be no problem securing that for his birthday at all." She was bangin away on de console again as she spoke, getting de same squawk. Why de fake accent? Why dose words? I wanted to focus on dis baffling crayture sat at our reception desk, but Copperknob prodded a digit in my chest. It was more gentle dan normal—worrying. His low tone was starting to freak me out too.

"I know our clients don't mean much to people like you, but bear in mind every resident here is someone's mother or father, grandmother, grandfather. This organization," he waved his hands around his hips, "is an extension of the love those families feel for their elderly relatives. We are those families' eyes and ears, their hands," he paused again, "even their hearts." He drew close. "When you're consistently late to work, when you keep falling short of working a full shift, what it really amounts to is a failure to love."

I noticed de tip of de squirrel's tail poking out of my pocket and moved my arm to cover his fur. Copperknob drew back, like a drunk who'd blabbed too much and regretted it. His tone toughened up into dat familiar chisel, and I felt more at home again: "We may need technicians around here, but that doesn't mean we're desperate. Get a watch. And use it."

I nodded, acting de cur-with-tail-between-legs, and walked past him to de staff room. Could feel his beady eyes on me with every step—gawd dere was no end to dat feckin corridor—and I cursed de Wayke for its long, slow, gawpin spaces dat couldn't be crossed with a heroic bound, but had to be plodded through, no option. My cheeks burned in spite of myself. Copperknob de magician: he could conjure shame in a saint. Fair duce: he was a man with a gift.

In de staff room I wrapped de squirrel in a spare plastic bag and stuffed him in de pokey freezer over de fridge. It was empty except for a few cartons of choco-chocky-chip ice-cream and a load of ice crusting up de walls. I fiddled de cartons to make room for my squirrel. Den it was on with my white lab coat, which Copperknob said "set a tone of professionalism in the workplace." My white coat always made me feel like even more of a chancer.

I started as usual, working from room to room, greeting residents who pottered round, or sat together playing gin rummy. Most of de codgers were haloed most of de time, tucked up in bed, dropping out of gawd-knows-what pretty paradises and hellish challenges for a bit of daily physio, a weekly inspection from de doc, or a visitor. But visitors were rare. And when dey did show up, you'd wonder why dey boddered. Whenever I was in a room during a visit, doing some dusting in de background, say, or fixing a busted toilet, I got de sense both parties were disappointed to be caught up in such a woeful scenario. Embarrassed even. Codger'd be eager to get back to de halo. Visitor squints up at de clock like he's double-parked. Banter wears out, silence and blankness follow, and den, sudden as a stroke—*sin é*. Visitor remembers de house is on fire, he left de kids riding a wolf who looked hungry, de car turns into a pumpkin in twenty minutes, whadevvor. He rises, all grave reluctance, promises to return once de housefire is snuffed, de wolf is dead, de pumpkin's a pie. And de codger nods, and maybe winks, and as soon as dat door's closed—*without fail*—don't dey light up and leave me to work in peace.

I liked visitors being few and far between—halos everywhere. Made my rounds a straightforward affair. No small talk, no commiserations, no cheerful gabbing. Just change feed drips, empty bog bags. A monkey could do it, honest to gawd. Most clients, as dey were called, had given permission for de techs to wipe dem while dey were lit up. I didn't even need a partner to heft anyone in a bath or shower, I just opened de thin cotton peejays and rubbed each auldy down with some anti-microbials. You'd be surprised how easy you stop thinking of dem as people, or even animals. Twas all de world like servicing floppy machines: cut finger and toenails, trim hair, collect any waste and organic debris, and at end of day dump it all in a bio-haz chute. Sometimes I went from one end of a shift to de other, not a real thought in my head. You might say a monkey *was* doing it.

I rubbed a sponge over dis old wan's torso. Ruth. Her halo was lit, but her eyes were open and goan like de clappers. What was it like for her? We had some clients, retired maths guys and physics-heads mainly, just ditchin any sense of de body and becoming equations. No messin. *Equations*. No auld corpse at all. Nottin to distract. No belly to get hungry, skin to get itchy, back to get sore, neighbours playin shite or bangin away on a DIY job. Just one section of de brain firing to beat de band, tinkering from dawn to dusk in a lightless, noiseless realm of abstract gobbledegook. *Best work I've done since my twenties* one of dem crowed to me while I emptied his bin.

Not dis bird Ruth. She was embodied alright. Bet de farm. Some intense stuff goan on in dat dusty grey noggin. Maybe flowing through a series of bodies, figuring out undreamed-of sex positions with dirty partners... new dimensions of gender... a multiverse of orgasm. And why not? Isn't she owed something for her sacrifice after sacrifice, all for de good of de brood who're now grown strangers? For having survived De Scythe, having lost de world she knew... But what can you guess from a twitch? Sher, maybe she was playing lawn tennis.

I stopped cleaning her to stare at her shrivelled paps. Couldn't call dem "breasts" now, but she'd fed her sprogs with dese once. Tiny, helpless, hairless apes clung to her, sucking de life out of her, right out of dose ancient stone nipples—babies all round her, far as de eye can see, a world quiet except for sounds of sucking... babies twitching, half-dreaming de half-dreams of babies. Now auld Ruth suckled from her own feedbag hanging over her bed, twitching to herself.

I thought of a rotting fruit melting into de forest floor, dreaming it was still on de tree, feeding straight out of de air and earth. I remembered my squirrel fallen out of his tree—plop!—like Newton's apple. What would Newton do with a halo? Disappear into equations? Orgy? Lawn tennis?

I pictured my frozen squirrel in his plastic bag, stuffed between tubs of ice-cream like a pharaoh buried with treasures—better dan a pharaoh—all decay paused for him while I slowly worked my shift, aging myself, washing all dis fallen fruit.

Home Sweet Home. Dere it was, framed on de wall, hung no doubt by some wag with a sense of humour. What kinduv mind would put it here otherwise? Hung in a little glass frame, like a frame could make it official. Real. Like de way our staff doc framed his diplomas for de world to see—a sad little claim to power over all de things a saint knows we'll never get de best of. I'd never noticed it before: *Home Sweet Home,* de little letters looking out on a discombobulating maze with its stink of antiseptic. I clipped Ruth's nails.

Shift breaks are long. Too long. And if you pull a double shift, legal says you have to take a full break. I'd work straight through if I could, go home early, like, light up for de night. But naw, buzzer sounds—break. Break break break. Break up de whole traipsing day, until it's just bits and pieces, draaawwing it out so it drones on and on and... Ever since discovering feedbags here in de home (one good thing to come out of de hole) I don't really do de *bia agus deoch* thing anymore. Stopped munching a few months ago. It happened fairly quickly, dis weaning off solid food. In de relikwery a fien offered me a splodge of pro-V carbo-nosh (de plumpy'nut yokes) but I had de gawks as usual—just couldn't look at it. *Erra naw boi,*

I'm sound, waved it away, and before I knew where I was, it clicked dat I *was* sound. Have feedbag, will travel. A few fibre capsules a week and yer away with it. No bodders. But dey make you take yur break in here, so be wise and bring a project.

De microwave in de staff room is dodgy. Well, what isn't dodgy? But if you wiggle de lead, it'll kick in after a bit. I took de pharaoh squirrel from his tomb between de ice-cream tubs, unpacked him from his plastic, set him on a plate, stuck him in de oven: *Defrost.*

Rota has me on bio-haz, wiping floors, de lot, all while checking on auld wans too. Cheeky bolloxes: Dey can make you do twice de work to get out of paying overtime, but dey still make you take yur break. I'm not even a janitor. I'm hired to be a *physio tech*, fecks sake. Not dat I'm a real physio, mind. Back when I was a gentleman of leisure, I knew a London fien working here, same guy who turned me onto feedbags, said it to all of us at de kwery one night. I think he was sick of stealing bags for everyone and his brother.

—*You lot should get physio gigs at the 'ome. They're desperate for someone to 'andle the derelicts an wash em down an all. Easy money, lads. Eeeasy.*

—*I will yaah boi. Sher I'm not a physio.*

—*Tayto, you nonce! They don't check up on that, do they! You can rub a back here or stretch a leg there. They're gaggin for help. Just show up, you'll walk into the job, you twat.*

True enough. I walked into de job. Yur man didn't even look up from his desk, just *When can you start? Today, sir,* printed out my tag for me. I didn't even bodder with my real name, just gave my nickname without thinking, and bam!—dere I was, transmogrified in an instant. A bright young man of gainful employment. Mr Tayto: Physiotherapist.

A job's a balls, *Yes sir no sir three bags full sir,* but de home was… I dunnaw actually. Was it harder or easier dan de streets? It's called a gerontoplex, so it sounds complex. It's a tangle of halls and corners to me, but den I can't tell—saints lose de way fairly easily. Lit up, we can go anywhere and do anything faster and better dan Superman himself, but out in de Wayke, you forget simple things. I forgot how to open a door once. Was staring at de knob for ages and den it came to me—*turn* it. Where's north? What way is left? How do you tie a shoelace?

All dat stuff takes a while to come back. If you've nowhere to go it's not a bodder, like. Or you can simplify matters into straight lines, de way I follow de canal to work. But in here, jaayz... without de rooms alpha'd and numbered, I'd be turned around like a spinning top. D-32 comes after D-31. Dat much I can handle.

Smell. Antiseptic smell. Dat's maybe de worst of it. No smell in de haloscape—saints live in a no-smell zone. But de Wayke *stinks* to high heaven. De road stinks of tar. De rabble stink of sweat, *I* stink of myself, and de Gerries is stink on stink. Tell ya, when I first started working here I thought cleaning up de lads' shite and wiping into auld wrinkly armpits might do me in—and true enough it nearly did (fecken *disgussssting* I nearly gawked a few times a day in de beginning)—but of all de gawd-awful stuff dat stinks in here, it has to be de stuff we use to stop de stink dat stinks worst of all.

Ping—squirrel was ready. Opened de micro door: blast of stink. How fucken unforseen.

He was more dan defrosted, like. Maybe a bit on de cooked side. Hot round de edges.

Probably still cold in de centre. Be great if he could just get up, brush himself down, go *Cheers for dat, boi, got a bit nippy out dere*, and trot off out. Ah well, odds were against it.

Black marble eyes. Hard as onyx in one angle of light, liquid bubbles of oil in another. I made an incision around where de bellybutton would be, if he had one. Scalpel sliced into fur, cut round to make a wide flap. Inside, a total mess. No clear set of separate parts at all, just a squishy mash of greyish tubes, pink and dark purply lumps and sacks. Madness. It's not like in textbooks claiming a bit of order: heart here, stomach here, kidneys shaped just so, a neat jigsaw... Naw. It's just lumps of stuff piled in or under or round other stuff, wherever dey'll fit, squeezed in together like slippery wet homeless faceless wordless breathless immigrants, bunched up in one tight damp sleeping bag—manky, mucky, squidgy, sucky...

How does anything *work*? How did dis squirrel work? How does a hand hold a scalpel? I'm full of de same stinking mess. Poking into a small, hairier version of myself.

Abeetha opened de fridge door behind me. She's such a big byor, dunnaw why I *never* hear her coming. Always a smile on her except around me, so I'm pretty sure she's a Waker. All *roll-up-yer-sleeves-and-let's-do-it!* Any rate, she knows I'm saintly, and she's not delighted bout it. Dat look every time she sees me, my skinny frame, giveaway pale skin. Dat big warm smile just falls away, cold as de sun dossing behind a cloud. Nearly make you shiver, *if* you gave a flying fudge what Abeetha thought bout anything. She stood dere, ice-cream tub in hand, staring at me hunched over my squirrel, squinting, nose right up in his splayed privates. She grabbed a spoon and left.

Actually, forget bout de smell, and losing yur way, and all dat. De worst thing about de Wayke is spending time with yurself. Dis stupid voice, goan on and on in yur head, babbling away like a muppet, axing questions and explaining shit to yurself all de time, and no one—absolutely *no one*—dere listening.

Chapter 3: First Contact

Resume: Lightning whips the spire.
At the edge in three bounds—dive!
You are a dart, hurtling toward the water.

Three-note jingle. Butler floats into view, tiny fluffy wings flapping casually.

He circles, a solid black rotary phone clutched in his paws, receiver to his long ear.

"Pardon me, sir."

Grab his foot. You hover above the waves.

"What now?"

"I am so sorry to interrupt. You have a call."

"I'm cocooned. Doesn't that mean anything anymore?"

"Quite so, sir. Be that as it may, there is an urgent request for an audience with you from a Dr. Zeke Zohar. He says it regards your brother. Shall I put you through?"

Butler flaps his tiny wings, patient.

Brother? It's a struggle to remember that old life. You nod instinctively.

"Very good, sir."

He spins violently, flinging you from his long furry foot through the side of the skyscraper. The steel and glass swallow you—liquid.

You rocket to a halt in a private booth, facing a jet black figure. Together you sit on the cusp of the mutating dancefloor with its spinning dancers.

"Who are you?" you ask in default voxbox.

"I am Zeke," an identical vox responds.

Neither of you has customized his social voice. Whoever he is, he must be the type who understands a wish for privacy.

"You are a hard man to find," Zeke sips his bright milkshake.

"My profile is cocooned. How did you—"

"I am resourceful." Zeke sips again.

The stranger nods to your massive form filling the booth. You morph down to human scale: a tanned, toned version of your Waykean meat.

"God assigned you a butler," Zeke observes.

Butler-rabbit hops onto the table to declare: "Butlers help halo users live healthy lives!"

Zeke scratches behind the creature's ear. Butler shuts his eyes, foot-thumps the table.

"I blacked out from overplay last month," you say, scowling at the happy bunny.

"So, this is the closest you can legally get to being friendless." The stranger smiles—glowing white teeth. "You know you have a halo problem when God tells you to socialise more."

Your anger flares: "Why are we here?"

Zeke looks to the dancers. They backflip from orbiting floor to ceiling.

"Quadriplegics, ALS and stroke victims," he says. "Here often—I checked the log. But none has a butler. They all manage to regulate themselves, dutifully return to the Wayke, never miss a meal."

"Probably have families that force them."

"Where's your family?"

"None of your business."

"I wish to make it my business. I have a proposition for you. Would you like a milkshake?"

"What flavour is yours?"

"Birthday. Can I order you one?"

"No. Too strong. Had a Homecoming once. Couldn't handle it."

The stranger smiles, trying to set you at ease, with the opposite effect. "You are wise. Milkshakes are a vice."

The Butler lies docile on his back, lightly kicking the air while Zeke tickles his tummy. "What is it like to have a butler?" Zeke asks.

"A dream come true. What do you think? Thing won't leave me be. Keeps asking if I'm lonely. Gives me dietary advice. It's a psych program. Long-eared little rat. Always has a suggestion. I was in the middle of some deep stuff last week. Out of the blue, it suggests I just... wayke. 'Why not do some jumping jacks with a family member or school chum?'"

"Jumping jacks?" Zeke looks at Butler. "Was that your idea?"

Butler scrambles to attention, nods enthusiastically. You find yourself barking at the rabbit: "No one should tell you to wayke! It's unconstitutional! Surely."

Butler lowers his ears.

"God has to cover its ass." Zeke sips calmly. The colours in the glass swirl and rage.

"Yeah well… If I avoid blackout over the next six months they'll take him away and let me get back to my privacy."

"I wouldn't count on it. The world and its legal department is coming around again. The days of unrestricted, unmonitored scaping are over. All the ads creeping in, they're the least of it. Butlers are about to become a permanent feature for every saint. And when you see the new wave of 'personal assistants' that are on the way, let's just say unsolicited diet advice will be the least of your worries. Are you quite sure you don't want a milk—"

"No, Zeke, or whatever your name is. I don't want to call a school chum, I don't want to do any jumping jacks, and I definitely don't want a goddamn milkshake." You grab his glass, slug a freezing, sparkling mouthful, and wipe away the moustache. "Now what is it about my brother you're so eager to discuss?"

"I am a research colleague of his."

"Okay. So? How is he?"

"He is missing."

As he says it, the drink has its delayed impact: the room dulls, dancers slow. The phrase turns in your mind, fizzing: mizzzzz-zzz-zz...he is miizzzinizzzing...Who is? Iz he? He izzzz.

Shake off the shake.

"What do you mean 'missing'?"

"Yogi made a series of breakthroughs at work. He also suffered a nervous breakdown and disappeared. I have been searching for him since, and exhausted all options. Were it not for the record of your blackout and your butler's trail, I probably would not have found you either."

His syllables fizz, become candles burning on a small cake. Two cakes, one for each brother, you and Yogi, born on the same date one year apart. Irish twins. Make a wish! Blow! Yogi's extinguishes in a flash, to applause. But yours is a trick candle. It keeps burning, burning—you're too young to understand, frantically blowing, but the flame keeps dancing, hot tears filling your eyes—why can't you stop it?—until you grab your cake and hurl it at a wall. That was the last birthday before The Scythe. Before everyone and everything went missing.

"Well... what do you expect from me?"

"I want you to help me find him."

The garish dancers speed up again. Their fashions alter, the walls spin—you must escape.

"Yogi hasn't contacted me in a very long time. I need to go."

"Wait."

His word sounds level, but reverberates with hidden power. His eyes lock yours and you freeze like prey.

He turns away, looks into his drink: "Wariness is to be expected, given your psych file."

Spell broken, you feel the anger flash: Why should you help this stranger?

"For all I know Yogi's trying to give you the slip!"

"Yes," he says. "I think Yogi is hiding—from everyone. But if you help me find him... As I said, I have a proposition for you. A compelling one."

Consider the small, matte black figure—eyes bright as a cartoon in the dark. He sits, shadow incarnate, gripping his milkshake. Fractals of colour unfold behind thin glass.

He has drunk over half, yet seems perfectly balanced, as if the storms of nostalgia and childish excitement firing in his synapses are little more than a cup of tea. This entity is even more at home in the Scape than you are. A true saint.

"His last halo trace was located near your childhood home in Cork."

"Off you go, so."

Suddenly Zeke winces, trying hard not to remember something so beautiful it hurts.

"The promise of wrapping paper on presents..." His vox mutates, a foreign accent breaking through. A human voice. You like him better for an instant while his mask slips. Momentarily, the buzzing club is less lonely. Zeke regains focus, and his neutral vox.

"If Yogi is there, he may need to be... reasoned with. Calmed. Your presence might help. And if he isn't there, any files left behind will probably be written in autobiographical code. He used to do that at work. I'll need help from a translator to understand."

"Sounds like he doesn't want you to understand," I say. "Why should I help?"

The stranger pauses, relishing his reply.

"If I told you there was a way to stay lit up—no more wayking—would you be interested?"

What is his game? Hardly a con man. You have nothing worth stealing. A psychoviral, perhaps—those bored demons, worming into your brain, dissolving a saint's mind just for fun.

But certainly he knows of Yogi—golden boy, favoured child, the Elect. That alone is enough to make him fascinating. He must be one of the elect, too. Is Yogi... inviting you to join him? When you thought the door had closed, leaving you behind, alone in the dark?

Perhaps this is what you have been waiting for. Maybe this is how it happens: a stranger arrives, asks for help, and reveals himself: the key, the light, and the way.

Two sexdrones slink up, giraffe-tall on stilt high heels, predators dressed as prey, huge brown deer eyes over full-lipped pouts. They have locked in on you. Insinuating themselves into the booth, the models chant in unison: "Hey there. Don't you two STUDS want to chat with REAL WOMEN about your DEEPEST FANTASIES?"

Feel them slide against you. One drone grasps your hand. Her grip is firm, cool. It is a shock to be grasped by a dead thing, startling and unpleasant. Her partner runs a claw under your chin.

You try to shove them from the booth. The drones block you, stuffing your face into their over-sized cleavage: "GIVE IN! GIVE IN TO WHAT YOU NEED!"

You bark a muffled order from between breasts: "Butler! Deal with them."

Butler springs: "Ladies, follow me please."

He hops off the table and bounds into the club. The drones follow his cottontail, mesmerized.

"Hey there, STUD. Wanna chat with REAL WOMEN about..."

The stranger grasps your hand. His skin is warm, pulsing. It is a shock to be grasped by a living thing. Startling and unpleasant.

"We can't talk here. Arboretum is quiet."

Zeke stands on the table, dives headfirst into the strobing dance floor. His form is swallowed without trace. You stand, crouch to dive. What is this creature after? He drops a few pieces of ancient history and you simply follow?

In the bowels of the club you spy Butler. One of the mesmerized drones massages his tiny shoulders as he devours her partner's face with insistent nibbles. His tail twitches in excitement. Get away from here. Leap. Leap. Leap.

Emerge from a murky pond to towering trees. Zeke waits in the tall grasses by the water, almost invisible in dying light. Narrow as slits, his eyes lock on your crawl from the mud.

Your hands shrink into small, tight paws. Claws peer from the fur, eager for the feel of bark. Your new squirrel-self drops to all fours. The sudden body-lightness is exquisite. Spring a few steps into the woods.

Zeke's skin peels off in black flakes. Underneath, scales glint in the sunset. He uncoils luxuriously, as though he has waited epochs to do so. The creature slithers into the open, pure serpent now, advancing in pulses.

You sprint up a redwood. Zeke spirals up after you, swift, inevitable. Reach a branch, leap into... nothing.

Flaps unfold from your arms—you glide! speeding on air faster than on the trunk, though it feels slower, effortless.

Tilt left, right— zero in on a giant trunk, bracing for impact. Zeke pursues, winding through air—a long curved line of insistence. A message you're not ready to receive. Yet.

A vast moon rises behind him. His silhouette reels, smooth as soundwave. Stars flood the sky. The serpent sends you scrambling for a hole to hide in. There! Dart into that crevice, sensing company inside—to be safe, somehow, in a dark warm hole, with family.

A female squirrel with five little kits squirming. They clamber on her, sniffing everything. Her mind reaches out to them: Now, who can tell me if squirrels hibernate or not? Five tiny heads turn as your snout and whiskers probe their den.

The teacher hops between you and her wards, flicking her tail defensively. Her mind is focused, piercing: This is an animal empathy class: stay-out stay-outoutout! Don't bring the snake to them.

Into the night again, fur bristling at the sense of threat. A pair of saucer eyes blink open. Invisible wings flap nearby. A chilling hoot slices through the mindless buzz of insects.

Life is a clout of pounding heartbeats in a pulsing night, before fangs or talons puncture the rhythm, and cold stars spill into silence.

Another hole! Tight, but you struggle inside. Panting. Outside, a long slender fact slinks down the tree. You can hear the smooth belly tracing the bark.

Don't... breathe.
Through the hole, diamonds glint. Beyond the rim, a hiss—the sound of a tongue, tasting air in stereo.

Zeke's head squeezes in, blocking escape. His jaw dislocates. Slide into the mouth's tunnel, flesh crawling, insane with fear.

Smothering darkness. Then a luminous squirrel skeleton encases you, a canoe of light. In human form again, you rise from the rodent carcass. All around, the walls of a giant serpent belly contract and relax in easy rhythm. A snake at rest.
Zeke is by your side, jet black again, little more than a shadow though his eyes are bright. You sit beside the glowing bones of your squirrel corpse.
"Never died as a squirrel before. Horrifying. Amazing."
"It'll take your butler time to burrow here," Zeke says. "Now we

have a moment's privacy, tell me: have you noticed any suspicious activity of late? Strange characters trailing you? Trying to make friends?"

You decide not to mention the green girl.

"You mean besides you?"

Zeke breaks off two squirrel ribs, sticks a marshmallow on the tip of each. A fire lights between you, flaring out of the carcass.

"You're very oral," you observe. "Milk-shakes. Marshmallows. Squirrels."

"I go through phases. Hardly use my real mouth any more. Do you?" He hands you the second rib—marshmallow topped: "Let's get nostalgic."

Roast your treats over the crackling fire. It's reassuring to be a human ape again, at rest, massive frontal lobes digesting the chase scene calmly.

"It's years since I played hide and seek, or chase," you reflect. "Not since I was a child. In the Wayke."

"Your psych profile says you like scaring yourself. But you don't play with others."

"Hacked my psych profile? Figured a game of chase would make us friends?"

"Actually I think it was the milkshake's influence. I used to play chase as a child too. Coin of the realm, no?"

"I don't know what you're talking about."

"COIN – co-emergent instinctual neuroplay. A fusion of players' desires." He peers at you. "You really never play with others, do you?"

You shake your head, strangely embarrassed.

"That's good," Zeke nods. "Purer. I despise social sites too. That's why I wished to meet in such an awful nightclub. To remind us both of the mire we are trying to escape."

Biting down on his mallow, the eyes roll in his head. You lick your own spongy singed mess. What will happen? Eat.

The effect begins before your teeth sink all the way in. Energy cascades though your nerves, a sense of being invaded, opening a viral file. Grab the slow breathing floor to steady yourself.

Zeke regards his own dose, as if scanning it for secrets.

"They get stronger," he murmurs, almost to himself. "Go slow."

The floor begins to swerve. The snake is awake—advancing again. No way of knowing if he prowls for food, sex, or shelter. None of that matters. He moves. He is original movement.

The marshmallows blaze—geometric flames. Stare into the fire—such intricate order; order within order. Universes of order, spiralling. If you squint it looks like chaos.

Zeke's voice draws you back. You want to dissolve into the patterns, but Zeke just keeps speaking. Does he not see this display? Or is he so used to it that it bores him?

A wave of sadness. You are the chaos that balks at order. You are the squinting eye.

Emotions lurch wildly: self-disgust, anger, then sadness again. You take another large bite. Why do you keep eating it?

"I need to find Yogi," Zeke says. "No one else knows him."

"I don't know Yogi," the words are velvet in your mouth. "Not really."

"But you two are so alike."

That sadness again, cresting now.

"Don't say that." Afraid you'll cry—what is wrong with these mallows?

"It's true," Zeke continues. "He was issued a butler also. Two blackouts in one week. And lo: the clouds part and bestow on him a Cheshire Cat."

The geometric flames briefly form a cat's face. It winks at you.

"Not a friendly monitor like your rabbit. This was a psych program. It really curled into his head. I finally tracked down his butler in the crystal forest."

"The crystal forest? How did you get in?"

"I am not completely uninspired," Zeke smiles, and points to your marshmallow. "And when we're finished this little bonding session, you should know how to break in there too. I've tucked a skeleton-key procedural memory away in this little snack."

And then you have it: a whole route to the NO-GO crystal forest, as if you've always known how to get there.

"I broke off a memory flake to view the last fragments of the

Cheshire Cat's log," Zeke says. "I couldn't record or share it. You have to check it out yourself."

"Well, could you try to put it into words? I know it's old-fashioned, but..."

"The butler's log for the last few micro-seconds monitoring Yogi... zero-point-zero-three seconds, to be precise—runs to over seven hundred experiential hours."

The two mallow flames fuse. Now one interweaving pattern grows between you and Zeke in pulses—an expanding mass of candyfloss, flashing with silent lightning storms. You bite into it, preoccupied.

"So?" you shrug. "Yogi's butler broke."

"Perhaps. The cat's memory may be faulty. But there's another possibility." The candy floss grows larger. Zeke stuffs his face, then chews very slowly, deliberately, as if checking for something in the mass that fills his mouth. He swallows, pauses. "Before the university cut our funding, Yogi and I were working on sensory array stuff. Cognitive amplification. Multidimensional spatial awareness. Temporal distortion. Next-gen halos."

He sees your blank expression, stops to choose more simple words. Anger swells again. Are you stupid? Does he need to draw you a picture?

"We are caterpillars," he finally announces.

"You and me?"

"Everyone. Human minds are like caterpillars: Puny. Slow moving. Incredibly limited. We have synapse technology now, and we can do things previous generations only dreamt of, like accurately record, share, synthesize experiences. But behind all that achievement, we are basically the same neurotic cretins we were a hundred thousand years ago. No matter where we go, or what we learn, or acquire, we're always... us. We cannot break through to the next stage."

"Caterpillars..." you murmur, touching the ground for reassurance. Zeke warms to his subject: "We all crawl through time at more or less the same rate. We meet, rub our antennae together... like we are doing now." Can he see you don't understand? Does he know a cretin when he sees one? "I stupidly believed the object of the game—of our research—was to become a faster caterpillar. Crawl quicker, munch more info, and grow longer feelers. But Yogi— and I don't know how—Yogi turned into something completely different: a kaleidoscope of butterflies."

"You've lost me."

"Well," Zeke smiles, his teeth lighting up, "he lost me too. He lost all of us."

The candyfloss becomes a soft brain, a dome of electrical storms, billions of neurons silently firing—the pyrotechnics of intelligence. It expands and engulfs you both. Zeke sits in one spacious hemisphere, you in the other, surrounded by flashing synapses.

"The root," Zeke announces, pointing vaguely around him. "That's what Yogi called it. Our ancient brain. It holds us back, like a vast anchor. Roots us to time, to a single perspective. Makes us crawl like caterpillars, alone and lonely in the cognitive universe. Yogi wanted something to cut that anchor. He became obsessed with a new halo interface. He called it The Crown. Spent all that time lit up, designing models... If anything, I'm surprised he didn't black out more. It was just a matter of time before the cat came calling."

Inside the glowing neural architecture you feel like a caterpillar yourself, curled in a lettuce leaf, so safe and peckish, the whole world made of food. Eat the leaf. Rip out a ganglion of nerves, devour them. You can taste symphonies, discern on your tongue each note the celestial choirs sing. You can't find the floor anymore.

Brain damage—has this black magician tricked you into eating your own brain? Perhaps. You hope so. Destroy it. Maybe you'll never wayke again.

"The Crown," you whisper, turning the phrase in your mind. The Crown. The more it echoes, the more wonderful it sounds. "How does it work?"

"It didn't work. Two test subjects had psychotic breaks."

Zeke sparks his finger, like a match, off a synapse. It bursts into flame. Inside the small blaze you make out a screaming head. Zeke claps the fire out, clearly startled at the memory. It is striking to see him lose his cool. "Crown research was shelved," he continues. "A liability. That's when Yogi began working on it full time, and became... unpredictable. He vanished soon after that. Some assumed he had quit. There were rumours of a stroke. But now, with the monumental time disparity in the cat's records..."

Eat more, little caterpillar. The more you devour this growing brain shell, the more you feel Zeke's enthusiasm, grasp his intent. His consciousness is breaching yours.

Is it the same for him? Can he sense how small your thinking cap is?

"Ah!" you exclaim, dim Watson to his dazzling Holmes. "You think Yogi pulled it off! He built the Crown. But..."

No need to vocalise the question—he knows what you're thinking now: What does it mean to wear the Crown, to cut this anchor? What does it mean to be unrooted, finally?

The engulfing pattern still unfolds, evolves, and now you float in dazzling geometric infinity.
No centre, no edge—no movement, no stasis.

Are you talking to Zeke, or yourself? No one is speaking, but a dialogue persists, far beyond all narrow notions of a mouth, a head, a brain, a self:
—Are you saying... Yogi might have found a key to heaven?
—I don't know. He could be a vegetable—fried out of his brainpan. Your bodies break into simpler geometric forms, dissolving, absorbing into the flux. There is nothing solid left, no reference point, no embodiment.
—He might be transparent in infinite unspooling consciousness.
—Or he's dead.
—Either way, he doesn't have to wayke... to piss... and change his feed-bag.
—Help me. Let's learn if Yogi is dead, or finally free. Wanna take a trip in the Wayke?
—I'm not ready...   to get into that right now.
—Dwell on it. Take all...
                    the time...
                         you need.

I couldn't make head nor tails of my meeting with Zeke. I wayked with dis massive sense of importance, like Moses with de two big tablet yokes in his arms, about to gatch down de mountain back to de lads. *C'mere bois. Look at de text I just got.* But by de time I was freezing my fanny off in de shower dis Zeke fien struck me as a pure odd bird altogether. Now I felt more like de little pig peering out of his brick house, with a wolf outside saying *C'mere to me a minute, Pork Chops. I've a* mad *interesting thing to show you. Come out of yur brick house dere for two secs. You'll love dis.*

Work was brutal. I traipsed through my shift, forgetting to replace toilet rolls, doing a half-ass job of cleaning into all de auld wans' crevices, making a hames of inserting IVs, y'knaw like, just trying to figure out if I was freaked out or excited or scared or completely unconvinced or what. *Hmm? What's dat Captain Weirdo? Can't find Yogi! Well, sir, dat's de thing with pesky genius types. Dey're skittish. Always disappearing on you when you need dem. Like herding cats! Never fear, I am a fully licensed and bonded savant hunter. I'll follow his trail, give you a full safari tour of my home town, and if we find any renegade neuroscaper knocking around in my dead parents' house, I'll kill and skin him for nottin. Do we have a deal? Spit on it, sir!*

Dat's de strangest thing bout Huge Events dat come into yur life. De plainness of de Wayke can always overwhelm. No matter how mon-u-mental you think a moment is, de Wayke is like an acid, just breaking it down into little pebbles of shut-yur-*hole*-boi. You can be all *Jeez I met dis guy and he might be a mystic or a psycho but he wants to hunt down my brother and we might escape into a different universe*—and de Wayke'll just shrug and go *Naw*. What do you mean naw? *Just naw. Doesn't matter. Dat toilet roll holder is empty.* And tis true. De toilet roll holder is empty. You need to deal with dat now. And no one cares. So shut up with yurself.

De Brigadier, I called him. Doubt he was military, but dere was a bit of stiff-upper-lip about him all de same. No idea what he used to be. School principal, maybe? *What he used to be*, like he's nottin now. Well, I spose he's not much, like most crusties here. A species of ghost. A memory of himself, fading in and out of focus like a gammy camera lens. De saddest thing bout de Brigadier was de way he had no clue he was dotty as fuck. He sneered at de other gerries who didn't know his secret—de same feckin secret he told me every time I entered his room.

"Keep the mind active, Mr. Tayto," he says, tapping an auld book or a crossword or whadevvor little puzzle his day has in store for him. "An active mind! That's the trick!" Oh, *dat's* de trick, is it? I'll have to remember dat. Too bad you can't remember it yurself, next time you take a notion yur grandma is trying to guzzle you up, or enemies are hiding in yur skin.

He's afraid of halos, but every so often he gets curious bout them—bit hard not to, I spose, in evenings near silent with de stillness of saints.

"*What's it like, Mr. Tayto? These... doo-dads,*" he whispers, like it's shameful to ask.

"Dunnaw. Hard to describe, really."

"Yes, I imagine so, but still..." You can see him fumbling for de right question, de one dat will unlock it all, explain why de world has gone and changed so much on him behind his back. "Can one... *talk* to another? Are they... that sort of thing?"

"Well sir, if you talk in de halo, it's like when you talk to yurself. It's like a voice in yur head, de memory of a voice."

"Like reading?"

"Wouldn't know much about dat now, sir."

"Not a big reader, eh?"

"Naw, boi—I mean, no sir. Not up on de books at all. Boring. Take too long, and what do you get out of dem?"

"Ah though, don't you see? That's where we went wrong! Where your generation went off-track. People stopped reading."

Yeaaah, boi. Half de population wiped out in de first month of De Scythe cos people wouldn't stop shopping and goan to pubs— and not having our snouts stuck in a pile of fucken words is where we went wrong.

"And how do they work, Tayto? Eh?" I knew it was coming, his same old round of questions, like a conveyor belt of kiddies axing why de sky is blue. *I don't know, sir. I don't know how they work.* I don't know how anything works! How do *you* still work? Why are you still pottering around, pointing at things and saying "How?" Him and his "active mind." Sher, de brain is more active when it's lit up dan when it dreams. Not to mind reading—such a crap, awkward way of peeking into someone else's head using pictures from yur own. Screw dat.

I can't face "How?" today, so I slink out of de Brigadier's room as soon as I've gone through his exercises with him. He loves his exercises, de Brigadier does. He's de only mothball here who goes mad for our hokey-pokey dance. I just make stuff up and fire it off at him: *touch yur toes touch yur shoulders touch yur right hand off yur left heel now stand on one leg with yur eyes closed—good maaaan yurself!*

Dunnaw why I was in such a rush to be done with de Brigadier. It only hurried me up to deal with de new client in D45. He's another one who never wears a halo, which is a balls already, but dere's more. He's always out of bed when you walk in, which is unnerving for a rake of reasons. First, he's freakish tall and skinny, and he stands in a stoop with his hands drawn up into his chest, like a praying mantis or whadevvor, just waiting to pounce. He's silent, so you mightn't know when he's behind you (he made Abeetha scream de first time she went in to him). But de worst thing is—and dis really is rare in de gerontoplex—he often has a rooster, a stonking great jack, hitching up under his pajama pants. He rubs it a bit, like he's checking it's still dere, and then he draws his hand back to his chest. Doesn't put you at ease, like.

De Mantis was stand-offish at first, but in de last couple days he'd been coming on strong. Hats off to him for still getting it up, like, but hands off me. So today don't I walk into his room and spin fast to see him, looming as usual, behind de door. I'm dreading any physio with dis gowl. He needs a psych tech, not a bluff artist like me. *Alright so, sir. Let's sit you down on de bed over here and we'll… try to do some exercise today, yeah?* He has dis big grin on his face, pure enthusiastic. "Exercise," he says, really quiet but really happy. I get him to sit on de edge of his bed, and I can see de auld pup tent in his pants poking through.

I say to him, raising my own hands to demonstrate, *Okay now raise yur hands above yur head, and we'll try to get them straight up in de sky*—doesn't he shoot out one of his mantis hands and grab my langer. It was only a tap, really, den he whisks de hand back to his chest, a big grin on his face like we're playing a game and he just tagged me. He waits, beaming all over, probably expecting me to tag him back. Nottin doin, I'm just in shock like *What de fuck, bud?* when he does it again. He holds on dis time, and when I knock his hand off he lets a huge laugh out of him like *Oh what fun! Now we're really playing!* I can't believe it. No one's ever grabbed my lad before, not even in de juvenoplex, and dat hole was crawling with Frustrated Freddies. I feel dis huge anger fill me up, like a pressure in my head, and I roar in his face: "What's dis shit about, fien?! Hah?" He just gets coy, lets a series of hiccuppy little laughs out of him, like he's saying *Oopsy! Looks like little Lord Fauntleroy's upset.* Den I see his hand snaking out to do it again, slower dis time, like he's almost axing permission, and before I know it—WHACK! I dawk him right in the face. Not hard, like, but it's right on de button.

I don't know which of us is more stunned. I've never hit anyone in my life before. Even my knuckles are shocked. De Mantis doesn't move for a second, both his hands retracted to his chest. Den a thick line of blood streams from his nose. He wipes it, sees de vivid red all over his grey fingers, and his face goes ashen. He's a little kid who realises he's after taking a fall and it's time to cry now. De features collapse into a wrinkled mess, almost in slow motion.

"I... I'm sorry," I stutter, eye on de open door for any sign of Copperknob. De Mantis gets up and cowers in a corner, like I'm about to thrash him. I hold up my hands to show tis all cool beans, but it only makes him crouch and wail more.

"I'm really sorry, really sorry, I didn't mean to... I'm sorry." He's crying like a baby now, just sobbing like he's lost his mother, and shame burns all over my skin, dat great fire trying to swallow me up cos I'm such a dirty waste of space and air. I don't have a clue bout dis auld lad, or how he got here, or what woeful shite he's been through, or who left him here, or whether he was just dumped by de state. Whadevvor happened to him, it hasn't been good, and I don't know how to make right what I've done, because I'm not used to people touching me, and I don't fucken like it, and now I've done something terrible to someone who really needs people to help him and to just be kind to him for once. So I inch closer, and he twitches but he doesn't shift, and I get near enough to hunker down next to him, and reach out my arm and stroke his back, and he sobs a bit quieter, and I just keep stroking his stoopy hunch of a back, and say quietly again and again, like a lullaby, like a prayer: "I'm really sorry, man, I'm really sorry... really sorry... sorry... sorry," and as de tears fill my eyes, I think he knows dat I am.

I stayed down near de ground with de Mantis, both of us crouched over, for a long time. I couldn't leave till he stopped crying, which he did, but he didn't move from his spot. I figured I'd have to shift first before he'd budge, so dat's how I left him. Next few rooms were all haloed clients, so I just cleaned up, and it helped me clear my head a bit and get back into work mode. Empty bins, replace toilet paper, bio-haz duty, check IVs, wash clients, search for bedsores, check off report. By de time I got to my last room—Ruth's home sweet home—I almost felt like normal again.

Something bout doing de last room in yur shift—some fiens speed through it just to be done, but I tend to slow down. Tis like a breather before I have to brace myself into de night, trudge back to de flat. Even if I'm desperate to leave, I can't seem to rush it. And Ruth tended to be my last room every time, so I came to connect her face, and all her assorted bits and bobs about de place, with decompression from work mode. I did a bit of cleaning and den sat in de visitor's chair next to her. Her eyes were open as usual, twitching away to her haloscape. I usually wasn't curious about de scapes of others, but something bout Ruth… maybe it was her wide-open eyes, like she was trying to tell me something. I just sat back, admiring de speed I'd finished her room in, when her halo went dead. She lay dere, her eyes still rolling, but I knew she must be dropping back into de Wayke. I got ready to spring from my chair and not get caught loitering, but her eyes suddenly pierced into me and I couldn't move. She looked terrified, and tried to whisper, but it was so low I couldn't make it out. I leaned in. *What's dat, Ruth? What can I get ya, girl?* She grasped my hand, surprising strength. De lips were off like de clappers again, but still I couldn't make it out. Put my ear right in. *Come again, Ruth. I'm not getting it.* And just as I was about to give up—my shift was surely over now—I heard: "The shoes…"

"Uh huh. Shoes, right. What about 'em?"

"Those… tight shoes." She squeezed my hand even harder, staring into my eyes so dat I had to look away, down at her nightgown. "Not tight anymore… slipping off…" And with that, her grip relaxed.

Just about every tech has shown up to work to find a cold body in de bed when dey go to change de sheets. Death's as everywhere as de antiseptic smell.

But Ruth's death struck me hard, for some reason. It's not like I knew her—she was super-saintly, after all—but her face was something to me. Always open, a rigid look of surprise. De earthly look of a saint, what Waykers see, not de fine inner picture, just a simple, animal look of *Wow, what kind of new experience is dis now? Should I go into it? Will I go? I will. I will.* Or maybe she was just de last face till home sweet home. Dunnaw. But I checked her vitals, and I had trouble when no pulse answered my fingertips.

Procedure is simple. When you find a bagger, you press de alert button and gurney lads come up to take him or her off yur hands. But I just couldn't press de alert right den and dere. I needed a minute. So I took Ruth's halo, sat down again in de visitor's chair, and since it was pretty much de end of my shift, I decided to do something I'd never done at work before. I lit up.

You are a worm, tunnelling through endless space.
Nothing outside the darkness, no worry of a sky above.
No notion of birds hungry for your flesh.

No fear, no hope. Only a vast feast of dirt.
Transform cool filth into fertile soil.
Enjoy the emptiness of your heart.

I came round and found Copperknob standing dere, eyes boring holes through me. Two big Latvian gurney fiens were wheeling Ruth's corpse into de corridor. I'd half a mind to yank de halo off, defend myself, but something told me to let what was going to happen happen. Copperknob rested his wide hips on Ruth's bed, and folded his hands like an altar boy on his lap.

"You're having quite the day," he inspected his fingernails, "aren't you?"

Still saying nottin, I slowly pulled Ruth's halo off, cradled it.

"Mr. Cavendish is quite distraught," Copperknob went on. "It seems he was physically assaulted during his physio session. He's reluctant to discuss it, but Gardaí may need to be contacted on the matter."

I thought of de Mantis, curled in his cot, wondering what he did wrong.

Suddenly de whole antiseptic maze unfolded in my head: room after room of rotting fruit wishing it was back on de tree. De Brigadier and his puzzles, so proud of his noggin, forgetting his screaming fits. Ruth in de basement, bagged up for de incinerator. De metal door opening, great tongues of flame licking her up into de sky, into a spray of carbon—millions of hard little grains of night. Home sweet home? I think I envied her a bit. No more tight shoes.

"And now we find…" de Knob wags his finger at me like I'm dogshit "—*this* one, relaxing next to a deceased client, enjoying a spot of recreation—with *her* neuroscaping device, no less—on company time, while her death goes unreported." He stared into my eyes so hard and long I figured I had to say something.

"Sir, I know—"

"We could install a hammock room, maybe." He cut me off after daring me speak. "We've been asking too much. We could hire a private masseuse to recuperate you after your few taxing hours of labour."

I didn't feel fear, or even shame now. I just felt heavy, like a lead doll. Lead bones, lead eyelids weighed down with long lead lashes. *Time to go home,* I thought to myself. *Hurry it up dere, Copperknob, let's get dis over with.*

"Hmm?! A nice massage after your tough day."

"I take it I'm fired so—"

"You'd better believe you're fucking fired!" he leaned in to roar, swearing at me for de first time. He must have been storing up dat nice juicy word for an age. Spittle flew into my eye but I didn't wince. Wouldn't give him de pleasure, case he thought he was de hard man or something. Little muppet. I'd a mind to dawk him in de nose too—soften his cough for him. But such heavy hands. Better to save my energy for de walk home. I hauled myself up, placed Ruth's halo on her pillow, and moved to de door.

"Have Linda revoke your security clearance," he said behind me. "And never darken our door again, you lazy, stupid little Cork gurrier."

I traipsed back home along de canal. It was night, but no stars overhead. Fat orange clouds instead. A duck waddled alongside me for a bit. He kept pace for a few steps before stopping to peck at de facemask stuck to his leg. He just couldn't get free of it.

"Arsehole," I said to him, but he didn't look up.

I stepped into de flat, hauled my Gerries uniform off for de last time, and chucked it into a corner. I stood under my single bulb, watching my breath float in de light. I felt my skin tighten, and my ribs jutted out more dan normal.

Glancing into my feedbag box, I saw only one miserable specimen left. It dawned on me dat my last chance to nick a bunch from work had been and gone, and now I'd have to buy dem or something. I should've walked out with a whole box in my arms, feedbags just spilling out over de top. *Night dere, Linda. Be sure to revoke my entry pass, won't you? I am a fucken scumbag, don't forget.*

I was just trying to deal with dis feedbag situation—just process it, like—when de gobshite music from next door, dat putrid storm of hatred, launches in again, scraping at my wall. It was so loud, so sudden. Was like being slapped. All de leaden feeling vanished. My heart was beating again.

I didn't move a muscle. Didn't open my mouth—still as a saint. But inside, I felt something rising to meet dat noise. It swelled, sweeping up from someplace in my gut, squeezed out from all my cramped organs, a whip-round collection of bile spitting back at dat mad evil racket, spurting out through every hole in my body: nostrils, pores, de trackmarks from my feedbags—every little round open thing in dis fathom long body just hissed right back at de claws scraping and pounding at my wall:

SHUT—DE—FUCK—UUUUUPPP!
SHUT—DE—FUCK—UUUUUPPP!
SHUT—DE—FUCK—UUUUUPPP!
…You're not going to destroy me!

Creep along the glacial plane, searching. Stars glint above, snow glitters below.

The reflected moonlight makes you squint. Cartoon and animal butlers stand everywhere, translucent—frozen mid-metamorphosis into crystal trees. The artificial cold pinches, but does not bite.

The crunching of snow behind! Spin! Butler-rabbit stands at your leg, worried.

"Where are we, sir?"

"You startled me," you whisper. A crack appears in a nearby crystal tree. Barely discernible in its trunk, the remnants of a bearded face release a faint groan, a cloud of freezing breath. You look down at Butler and hold your finger to your lips. *Shh*. Butler bows apologetically.

You walk on, Butler hopping nervously around your heels.

"Should we be here?" he whispers.

"Don't worry. A friend of mine gave me the key." Your reassuring words remind you that Zeke is not, in fact, your friend.

"But where is this?" Butler asks, increasingly concerned. "I don't recognise it."

Suppress the smile you feel coming on. Relish the moment—little fellow so rarely asks questions. Crouch down to his eye level.

"This is where programs like you come to disintegrate: something between an asylum and a graveyard. This is where you'll end up some day... *as soon as you're done monitoring me.*"

His ears draw back as he scans the frozen figures arrayed around him. Some newly discarded ones still have a semblance of character: facial features, clothing, fur in fading colours. The older ones are perfect dendritic crystals—faceless, ownerless, clear.

"Oh dear," Butler murmurs, his eyes large and pleading. "Should we really be here?"

"Define 'should.' I need to check something out," you say, rising and striding ahead. "You're free to leave though." Butler hesitates, then you hear his pawsteps quicken to catch up.

"What are you searching for?" he asks. "Perhaps I can help."

The Cheshire Cat still grins, but is almost transparent now, its face a complex of geometric shapes. You stop when you find it, this cat-like crystal tree.

"This is it," you breathe.

"Pardon?" Butler perks his ear.

"*Shh!* Be careful. It's very decayed."

Butler hides behind you as you reach for the cat's crystallized ear. On contact with your fingertips, the tree's face cracks a little along the mouth: *Hello.* Its voice is hollow, a disintegrating synth tone, chilling even in the cold air.

"Hello yourself," you respond quietly. "What secrets have you got for me today?"

This way madness lies.

The cat's answer hardly calms your doubts, which are many. There are penalties for this sort of spying. Nor is it advisable to eat a memory chip in the first place, to surf a condensed wave of someone else's halo memory. A degraded chip is worse—the effects could be unstable. And if this particular chip contains experiences from Yogi's Crown experiment, the results will be completely unpredictable, maybe even dangerous. Above all, you have no real reason to trust the man who sent you here, who tells you this is Yogi's butler.

Perhaps the risk is not worth taking. Who knows what effect it will have on your own neural circuitry?

One more blackout and your butler will be permanent.

Beneath you, Rabbit-butler shakes his head, silently imploring no. As if watching from outside yourself, you reach, gently breaking off the ear. It comes off cleanly—the cat's face cracks a little more.

Crouch. Butler sniffs the fragment.

"You would follow me anywhere, wouldn't you?" you ask. Butler nods, earnest. "Well, this cat was just as loyal to my brother. And look what happened to it. Just think," you smile, "someday you will fall apart." Butler shivers, glances around. There's no pleasure in tormenting it. There's no pleasure in tormenting anything. You consider the flake and go on: "Everything falls apart. What's left of you, when you lose your mind?" Hold it to your lips.

Swallow the shard.

The cat laughs, hearty, then violent, cracking up along its sheer geometric lines.

It shatters, reverberating through a crystal clean universe.

I don't remember wayking. Seemed I'd just been sitting on de edge of my recliner, staring at my empty feedbag for hours. Must've been in shock.

I found it hard to retrace what had happened in de crystal forest—it all seemed so long ago. After I'd swallowed de cat's ear I felt dizzy, so I sat on de snow and held onto de ground like I might fall off. I heard Yogi's butler laughing and shattering, and saw my own butler hopping in circles around me, axing did I "need assistance." *Yes*, I felt like grabbing him by his tiny shoulders and shaking de gomey little bollox, howling: *I need assistance! Get a priest, a doctor—call de coastguard, for feck's sake! I'm in grand trouble here.* But I just lay back on de snow, silent, and watched de world implode, slow at first and den quick, like water down a plughole. It wasn't just a world going down de plughole. Sher, I see dat every time before I waykey-waykey. Dis time I vanished too. Sortuv.

When it comes to dis sort of thing, words are like tools on a dodgy plumber's belt. Say de world is vanishing down a plughole and our plumber's trying to close off de pipe, stop us from losing everything, like, so he looks around for de right size wrench, and when he looks back up at de pipe it's... *a ten-dimensional space...* well, dat same wrench dat was grand for normal jobs is not up to much, you could say. Words to describe de Crown? Like taking a spanner to an equation, or swinging a lump hammer at a void.

Words. It's all just words, and de Crown doesn't fit them. Or maybe it's just me. If I was a poet, or a floppy-haired philosophizer up in Trinity or whadevvor, maybe I could do it some justice. But I'm not, and I can't. Dunnaw. I seriously doubt dose college langers could either. Come off it! Nobody could. Explain colour to a blind man!

I'll say dis: twas de most real, most vivid, most profound experience of my life. You might want to go and say "beautiful," but I'd resist de temptation—wrong direction altogether. "Beautiful" is an awful postcard-y word: de mountains, and flowers, and sunset, *how luvvly*. But what's maazing bout de Crown is how it shows you beauty is a big fucken chain round yur neck. Cos at de end of de day, you still want to *use* beauty, dontcha? You and de beauty, doin a nice line for about two seconds, and den it's all fear it'll leave you, getting frustrated you can't get more of it, or wish you could share it with someone else, or everyone else, maybe, but you can't. Or wish you could fuck it, or eat it, or hold it just for a minute. Dat's de problem, la? You and yur tormentors: beauty, ugliness, fear, love, loss, sickness, health, hunger, happiness. All of dem hanging on you, you you. Can't get away. You're de devil, really, screwing up yur own paradise, winding yurself up in knots. Pull harder away from yurself and wind up deeper up yur own arse. *I'm freeee! Waaait a minute—dis arsehole looks familiar... ahhh shite!* And on it goes.

But with de Crown, all dat takes a rest. I swallowed de cat's ear, and after a moment I was a warm jungle, *and everything in it.* I was a rush hour of ants; I was de spider wrapping her spoils in silk at munchtime. I was de moss on de tree, wishing it was de tree, and also de tree begging up to de sun, and de sun raging out love being all soaked up in de soil and de grasses streaming up and de cow chowing down and fish in de stream bursting out from eggs and flying through weed freer dan liquid lightning, happier dan gods on neurodrome tabs, catching insects and being caught demselves and ripped apart, everything food and eating food, everything just about to be born, and being born, and winning de day, and de terror of loss, and everything dying, de terror and de joy all one and de same, like de sun and de soil, but you can't know dat till de big picture comes into view, come at it from all sides, and you can't do dat when anchored to one body, one perspective, when you're seeing out of yur one set of eyes from yur one little skull, and weighing everything up in yur narrow, scheming, squirming noodle, saying *how is dat for me, now? Do I want more? Less? I want*

my mammy back, I think. I don't like de music next door. What'll happen
when I'm not around any more?

Sher, I was in shock. But good shock. I-see-de-light kind of
shock. Being just one itsy-bitsy, one-thing-at-a-time human mind
was shocking to me now. Embarrassing, almost. Is dat de word?
Naw. Who is being embarrassed, and in front of what? *Clumsy*—
dat's a more likely tool for de job. Sitting in my skin and bones,
on de edge of my chair, staring at my hands opening and closing
when I think to open and close dem, I felt *clumsy*. Like sunlight
dressed up as seaweed on de beach. And now I had to go fucken
shopping.

De Wayke wasn't long tapping me on de shoulder and reminding
me where I was again. At de Forum Galorum's main entrance
some skinny auld wan was trapped in de huffer station, her hands
rattling round like pure bone in de handcuffs. She was going
into conniptions, squirming like a hooked fish, shrieking bloody
murder at anyone she could make eye contact with: *Lord have mercy*
it can't be happening feckin machine is banjaxed let me go I'm not sick
Lord knows I'm not sick! Most people bolted—a handful hung round
on de footpath watching. Dey gave her a wide berth, a mad wide
berth, but dey watched to make sure some cops and a bio-haz team
arrived to cart her away. No one said a word to each other. Just
stood dere, listening as she begged and pleaded.

Weird to hear a plague alarm whining away at de gate like
a dull toothache. There'd been no confirmed Gombrich cases for
yonks, and you could tell from numbers on de streets dat people
were starting to relax a bit—half of dem not even wearing masks!
Sher, maybe she was healthy after all. Huffers can go off sometimes
for no reason—any machine can get banjaxed. But a tech fail's rare
enough with huffers. It's more likely dat auld wan's afternoon was
a nice big cosy shot of something to quiet her down, followed by
a few days naked in a windowless room with a camera trained
on her. And den, if de lads spotted red sores turning black, or de
cough… Well, someone might be due a shot of something stronger,
followed by an acid bath. De sense of relief dat it was her and not
me was wafting round me before I could smother it. How quick I'd
come back to my old small self.

Didn't stick round for de white suit brigade with deir big masks
and scuba tank yokes. I just gatched to de other side door, stuck my

hands in de cuffs, and hoped for an uneventful entrance. Bleep-*blaarp!* I always feel a bit grateful when de huffers let me pass. Like I'm getting a thumbs-up from de world. *Goan so! We'll let you away with it for now, ye ragamuffin ye!* But I felt extra grateful after seeing dat auld wan, writhing fox in a snare, raw fear in her eyes. If she could have gnawed through her wrists I'd say she would. Bloody dentures—not up to de job.

Market wasn't too crowded, considering it was Saturday. Maybe people left when dey heard an alarm. Wasn't it safer in here, where everyone was tested? Folks aren't logical. Cows who learned to walk upright, la. I tried to put de wailing banshee at de gate out of my head, and just root round trying to find a good deal on feckin feedbags. I wandered de maze of pokey stalls, laying out stinking fish on paper, slabs of meat, cheeses, herbs, microchips, booze, and smart drugs. Some stalls were louder dan others: lads and lassies chattering and shouting over each other bout special offers. Everyone beavering away, keeping de head down, scrambling to make ends meet day in, day out. Hauling in de fish, chopping up de cow, some pale fien bent over his make-station, fiddling around with molecules to build de happy pill. All so dey can peddle it off to get cred to buy de crap de other lads are peddling next door. Don't look up, or you'll see de shrieking wan clawing away in handcuffs at de gate. And if you're a good boy or girl, and you dodge all de sharks and knives and bad pills and cheese-and-meat heart attacks and de fucken *plague*, den—maybe!—you can end up a guest of Copperknob in our fair city's gerontoplex, with dashing professionals such as myself attending to you.

Pigeons tucked into a jelly doughnut some skinny little girl had chucked on de ground for dem. She watched a big fat fella bully his way into de circle, shoving his scrawny buddies out of his way. *Peckpeckpeck—mmm, jelly.* De little girl stood by, looking like she didn't ever eat a pick, watching her feast get savaged by Dublin's dirtiest. She clutched a huge fat ginger tomcat in her arms, used to a bit too much munch himself. Despite his paunch, he wanted at dose feathered fellas in de worst way—now freezing in an awkward hunch, now straining about in her arms. He almost looked insulted: *Look at de flapping fools! Don't dey know who I am?* What would he do if she let him go? Pounce, sink his teeth into a pigeon just as it was counting its blessings at finding a jelly doughnut! How could you stomach putting yur mouth on a pigeon? Be like frenching a hobo. Filthy.

Neon prayer beads—half-price! Vendor bawled away beside me. I wondered could I stomach another job. It's either work for rent or go back to a kwery, cadging food, sharing a dodgy crapper with twelve strangers, wiping yur arse with a bare hand, rats sniffing bout in de shadows—endless hassles. Still, part of me watched de stall fiens hustling to wrap fish, count out pills, hawk new halo models from Beijing, and I felt weary as an old man. Dey're all stuck, I thought. Stuck fast, squirming round like de worm on de hook. All stuck in a cramped piece of a puzzle, can't progress. All de world's a marketplace, and if you don't like it, get de feck out. Only... where do you go?

My head swam and de ground tilted off to de side, like riding a whirligig at de merries, and I thought I'd gawk. I hunkered down, touched my fingertips to de cobblestones, waited for it to pass and de *normal* come washing over me again. Get some feedbags sharpish now and you'll be grand altogether. Through all de pairs of legs gatching about, I focused on de scrum of pigeons, still pecking apart lunch. De gawks passed after a while, but de normal was nowhere to be seen. Everyone was grotty apes stuck in small ape minds, shoving and shouting for a better grasp on a bag, or a knife, or a pair of shoes, or some garlic.

Colouredy little stalls—like gnome houses for gnome pedlars. Imagine doing it every day? Climbing into yur hutch and shouting offers at people as dey plod by? What de hell could I possibly be arsed selling? But den, what choice is left? I can't build anything. Can't grow anything. Can't fix anything. Can't teach anything. Can't heal anyone. *Hate* working with people. Can't sing or feckin dance...

I want to be dat fat pigeon, pecking at his fancy find. And de cat watching de bird. And de girl stroking de cat. And de father smiling at his girl. A whole moment. *I want to be de whole scene again*, and not some wobbly, queasy bit of flesh furniture in it. To hell with me. To hell with halos even! I want my brother's Crown. No dodging it, Yogi, you are a bloody genius, boi. Dissolve all ego, and as de London lads say, Bob's yur uncle: *pure flux*. No self, no centre, no worries. Never get bored, sad, lost, lonely, or, if you do, it's only part of de game—background to make de foreground more vivid... or is de self de foreground? Whadevvor. Dere's a background and a foreground, and dey just play together. "You" don't get in de way to screw it all up. It all just plays and plays and plays—never get stuck in a puny self again. Genius. Game-changing genius.

I finally heard a yawp about cheap feedbags and wandered towards it. A young Chinese kid was poking his head out through a half-door, bored as sin. I gatched up to him.

"Ni hao ma, boi?" I said.

"Wo hun hao," he replied, even more bored now. Well, dat was all my Chinese spent, so I just tapped at a picture menu, said "Feedbags," and flashed twenty with my fingers. The kid said nottin, just scanned my index finger with his licker and disappeared into de stall. I paced in a circle.

Sickness was creeping back in sneaky waves so I hunkered down again. Hoped to gawd he'd hurry up so I could just get home, away from de appalling smell of food everywhere, and spend de rest of de day lit up, working on my skyscraper dives. A tramp of a flower-seller caught my eye. I glanced down but she was already traipsing over, bucket in hand, one half-dead yellow weed held out to me.

"You buy it," she said in her pathetic flower-seller voice.

"Naw, I'm grand, thanks."

"Last one. You buy it. Very good luck."

"It is? In dat case so, you should hold onto it."

"No! Luck is only for you."

"Lookit, love… Can't you see I'm dog sick here? Wouldja goan to fuck?"

She didn't like when I said dat. Her face fell, which is to say all de pinched hope, or whadevvor was holding her features so tight, fizzled out of her like a pricked balloon, and she just pulled her last useless ugly weed out of her black bucket. She took my hand, with a pitying look on her mug like I'd just lost my family or something, and put her weed right in my palm, closed my fingers around it.

"You take."

"Naw, sher… what am I going to do with…?" But she'd headed off into de noise and bodies, done for de day I spose. Now I had dis thing in my hand, and I felt like fecking it away, but for some reason I couldn't.

De Chinese kid popped out with a cardboard box. He whistled at me like I was a dog, and like a good dog I wagged my tail and came running.

"Woah, what's dis?" I said after rummaging round de merchandise. "Dese are just glucose solutions."

"Yeah. Glucose. Good for energy," he says.

"Naw boi, sorry 'bout dis now. I should've been clearer—I need multi-nutrient. *Mul-tee-noo-tree-ent.* And maybe some fiber caps while I'm at it." The boy furrowed his brow, disappeared again with his cardboard box. I sniffed my flower. Didn't smell of much. Something slight, hard to make out in de stink of de market. He popped his head out de half-door again, like a little pony. He had two *small* multi-nutrient bags and a few measly packs of fibrogel.

"Ah, what de feck is this, sher?"

"Price for multi-feed is up," he shrugged. "This all you good for."

"But my cred is good. Just put it on a tab."

"No, sorry. You lose job this week. No more credit."

"Listen, c'mere to me. Yur takin' de piss. Lemme speak to yur da, or whoever's—"

"Take or leave!" de little pony suddenly snaps. "Fucking busy!"

I got home still clutching de yellow weed in one hand, and a small cardboard box in de other. It held de three small multi-nutrient bags I'd managed to talk de kid up to if I forgot about de fiber caps—dis measly store was de last of my dosh. Unless I signed on, in which case hello dole office retina scans, goodbye halo. Scanty bastards. Still, what I had was good for about two or three days—enough time to light up and have a good think. About Zeke, and whether or not I should help him find my old folks' house, and see what's to see down dere.

I looked in my cupboard for de first time ever. What did I find only a small vase? So I stuck my weedflower next to my only window, right in de light, den sat down and lit myself up.

You lie alone on an infinite strand. Surf rumbles. Butler burrows out of the sand, shakes a crab from his long ear.

"Beautiful," he inhales dramatically. "Much nicer than that last place."

He shivers. Ignore him. The sun grows in pulses.

"You know," Butler says, standing over your face, blocking the light, "some real sunlight would help your body produce Vitamin D." He nods sagely. "That's essential for preventing rickets. And helpful for avoiding certain forms of cancer, depression, even—some experts believe—schizophrenia."

Waves crash.

"You're right," you say. Butler nods, and then does a double-take.

"I beg your pardon, sir?"

"Maybe it's time I took some sun."

Butler perks, rocks on his feet, fiddles with his tie.

I hauled my arse up like an old man, and padded bout my ugly room in my uglier jocks. Outside, big black clouds said "Don't even *think* about it." No mucking about with de weather dese days. I'd gatched out under black clouds a few weeks ago and ten minutes later I was nearly brained by hailstones de size of bull balls.

Two feedbags left. Plenty of time, so. Could hit de road tomorrow... next day, even.

I squeezed into de upright coffin of my shower unit, tried to scrub for de first time in a good few days. Chose scaldy water for a change—just couldn't face another icy shower. De body raw pink after, like a half-boiled ham. Leaving de awful heat made de cold feel worse too. Couldn't remember what it felt to be just comfortable.

Dumped my Gerries uniform down de rubbish shoot in de hall—not as satisfying as expected—and pulled on my only other clothes. An antique t-shirt I got in a jumble sale, with a faded picture of some aardvark—letters spelled "Alf says *YO!*" An itchy wool jumper I'd had forever, with holes galore and a knitted design of a squirrel holding a nut. It swam on me as a kid, but now it was tight and de sleeves were too short. A pair of tracksuit pants, and scummy used-to-be-white runners with loose, flappy soles. No socks. Erra, fairly dapper. Like James Bond on his day off.

I slumped against de wall, bored but pure determined to give de auld halo a rest for once. Butler was doing my head in. One more fucken health titbit from him and I swear I'd...

I stared at de flowergirl's weed dangling in de vase. Where was she from? I'm no good at accents. She was pretty under de muck, I'd say. Why do people come here? I've never left Ireland. Don't see de point. Sher it's all de same shite, isn't it? Wherever you go, dere you are, and dere's de Wayke, demanding yur lunch money and stamping on yur foot for good measure. Laughing when you cough up yur coin.

Dat was when I noticed a train of ants trooping round my runners.

Down on all fours, de world's worst-paid detective, I followed de beady little feckers' line to my box of feedbags. Pulled out de last two. Weren't dey both leaking, black with ants who thought it was Christmas in picnic land. My heart sank, but de tiny workers were in a party mood. Could hear dem chatting away bout getting a DJ and some margarita mix. Yur man next door must've heard, cos he chose dat moment to *belt* out de choons, louder and crazier dan ever before. Oh yeah! Oh yeah! *Oh yeah!*

Chapter 4:
Cats and Crows

Shag dis, sher. High time for de road! I fecked my halo into a cloth sack, all dramatic like in fillums when people are on de run, like it was de first of a rake of things I'd throw in. It'd been so long since I'd packed a bag I forgot I didn't need one. I scansed about for whadevvor else I could bring along to make my leaving feel official. You need to put something in a bag before you march out of a place. Otherwise yur only admitting to yurself you've got nottin. So I lobbed in a toothbrush and some bog roll for good measure. Never know, like.

I walked to de door, bag slung over my shoulder like a cool wanderer, and took one look back at my room. Bit of respect, I spose. Time had passed here. Tried to muster up a dose of nostalgia, or whadevvor big feeling is supposed to come with fare-ye-wells, even if it's only to a prison cell, or a lonely lunar outpost. Nottin. De music from next door was too loud, and all I felt was a bit woeful I'd spent any time here at all, listening to dat pissy racket.

But I did lay eyes on de small glass vase with my flower in it, and turned back to pick it up. Held it in my hands, getting a feel for de weight of it. Luvvly. Den I turned and flayked it at de wall I shared with my langer of a neighbour. Smithereens fired everywhere, just missing me. I recovered quick, like.

"Screw you, dickbag! I'm off out!" I bawled. "Send ya a postcard, y'langball!" De music cut out suddenly. Panic. I sprinted to de corridor—heard nottin but my tappy-tap soles slapping off each other as I legged it downstairs and outside. When I got to the footpath and saw no one after me I slowed to a happy, cocky gatch. *Stay in yur hutch, y'little bitch. Come after me and I'll fucken... I'll banjax ya. Bayte seven shades of… I'll bayte de* lugs *off ya!* And I realized, as I swaggered up de road, I was talking to de big bad Wayke itself. *C'mere to me! I'll ledder ya!* I claim *ya, boi! I fucken* claaaim *ya!*

De thing with taking a new path is, when you go a new way you can get lost. Alright now, dat mightn't be de most profoundest thing ever, but tis true nonetheless. I mightn't have liked my flat, but dis area—dis leafy, watery, reedy canal, with its happy-as-larry rats and swans and ducks—was sortuva home to me. Familiar, automatic, close to safe as it gets. De creeping feeling dat I was unsure of myself kicked in just a few minutes after I took a turn and lost view of my canal, and it got worse with every turn after.

During our little marshmallow session, Zeke planted a memory of his address so I knew it now as well as my own. Better even, I couldn't get it out of my head if I tried—twas doin loopdaloops in dere like de catchiest of fecken jingles. But when I got to his cursed little neck of de woods, I saw de numbers had worn off de buildings. Or a slim-fingered thief had stolen dem in de night. I was in de right housing estate, I knew dat much, but I'd a mighty sense it'd be a trial getting to his door.

Sun was low in de sky, grey clouds were everywhere, but I reckoned I still had a few hours yet before it got dark. All de grey towerblocks looked de same—great big rotting teeth looming, and me a lonely little bacteria in a dead man's mouth. Truth be told, I could do without running into any of my fellow microbes round here. Odds seemed low—a giant deranged dentist had scraped most of de human plaque away. Places like dis used be full of sounds: messers causing trouble, horses clopping and taking an odd dump on de road, nipper football teams kicking a can between two jumpers, stopping for ice-cream or chips from a van. So quiet now. De kind of quiet you can only find in a place dat's supposed to be noisy. Like walking into a nightclub in de wee hours to find everyone asleep, DJ snoring, all de music unplugged. A cursed nightclub, where de bouncer had pissed off de wrong evil faery.

Dis was a badly hit bit of de city. Maybe one of de worst. Gombrich blew in here and ate all round it. Den came de white vans, with de huff-n-puff patrol in scuba gear, to grab any survivors and tank dem for a few weeks of quarantine. Get de all-clear and you'd be chucked into a Joov if you'd lost yur parents, or in with de Gerries if you were old. And if you were in middle age, yur prime of life, sher off you go. You'll be more aerodynamic without de spouse and kids. Go back to yur empty flat, sit down in yur comfy chair, crack a beer and let de good times roll.

From de looks of new graffiti on boarded-up windows and cans of cider rattling round, a few folks had come back recently. Or moved in. I heard a bunch of survivors from places like dis had floated down-country, hanging deir hats in fancy deserted houses. But culchies from out in de sticks had drifted into cities, looking for spoils like food and water and meds. Like ghosts agreeing to haunt each other's houses. If I were a ghost, would I be up for a swap? What's more lonely—to haunt a place you remember, or some odd land where you're a stranger?

I smelled smoke. Over a ways was a commons all overgrown with weeds. Smack in de middle sat a small car, roaring in flames. Something bout dat little flaming wreck, out on its own in de open green, silent housing estate on all sides, frightened me. Anyone who came back here was either mad homesick, or tapped in de head. Or worse. What de hell was Zeke doing holed up here? What was *I* doing here, more to de point! Hair on my arms sprung up, de dead dark concrete cliffs closing in on me. I thought bout bolting, but to where? Back to my flat? Join another relikwery? Feck dat. Just get de skates on with finding Zeke's building. He was so close I could feel it. Or I thought I could. I jogged into de shadows, hugging de walls to stay out of sight, like a rat. In a sweater. With flapping soles on his shoes.

A loud *caw* cuts de air. I freeze.

More *caw caw caws*. A volley of dem, right behind me. I turn— four fiens pop up from a tangle of shopping trolleys. All have dese black ledder bird masks with long crooked beaks. Dey stand stock still, staring.

My weak heart clenches—a puny, shaky fist. I back up, slow… slow… Another *caw* fires off to my side. Three more crows stand just a hundred yards from me. Each one with a metal bar in his hand. My stomach cramps up, my legs nearly give out. Dis is de moment de Wayke loves best. Dat bit of shock before de shatters of pain. Before iron bars beat down, cracking bones, ribs, skull, brain… before de shark's mouth closes… dat split second when de hitchhiker sees de lock go down on de passenger door. Something relishes dat moment, whispering into yur ear, *Told you so. Didn't I say I'd get ya? You claim* me, *sunshine? I'm goan to fucken eat you alive.*

I'm goan to scrape out yur marrow with wire.

Can't run, can't stand still. Can't even swallow. I keep backing up in small doddery steps. De crows don't move a muscle. Terror twists in my gut—a fat hairy worm. Den it dawns on me: dey're looking for signs of Gombrich. *Right so, I'll give dem a few.*

"Stay back," I stammer, really feeling craw-sick, as it happens. Start itching, coughing, staggering dis way and dat. "Sick! I'm *sick!*"

Speaking out loud pops a bubble, or maybe dey don't like what I said. Anyway, next thing all de crows are swooping—full speed in my direction.

I flake up a stairwell, tripping over my stupid loose soles and cracking down on my knee. Didn't know I could move my arse dis fast. I can hear de lads belting up behind me, whacking de metal bars off walls, caw-cawing all de way. I make it to de third floor gasping for air, and spot a doorway completely burned to shite. Bolt into de flat, all charred walls and black lumps. Dive behind what was probly a couch and just lie dere in a ball, vibrating on soot floor. My ticker's beating way too hard—I don't get out much, I can't take dis kind of strain—and it's loud enough to give me away. *Wrong move, Tayto y'fucken wally!* I was grand dere in my flat! Taking to de bóthar like a stupid muppet, and now I'm worm munch for birds—

I hear an army of crows' feet lace up de stairwell to de next floor above me. Now! Time to run back down out of dis awful dead hole, and let Zeke come to *my* place, shiftless bastard.

But I couldn't move. My legs were jelly, useless as dis melted couch. Out a small window I could see de flaming car wreck, still burning out to heaven, black smoke jumping up to grey and greyer clouds, an offering to gods who just kept getting meaner. *C'mon, now or never.* I hauled myself up, de leg muscles seizing on me, mad offended I hadn't consulted dem before throwing dem into de game. In fairness, dey'd been warming de bench for years now. I was hobbling to de door when I heard a single pair of footsteps coming back downstairs.

I crouched behind another charred stump and listened to de footsteps: slow, quiet, like he was hunting something dangerous, or snakey clever. De crow stood outside de doorway of my hidey-hole and paused. Den he whacked his bar against de doorframe.

It was such a vicious, violent sound I jolted, nearly shouted out. Still he stood dere, not moving. I looked round for a yoke to maybe clock him with. Dere was a small plank of wood, barbequed like de rest of de room. Say it would turn to ash soon as you pawed it. I reached for it anyways. Felt solid enough.

He cawed up de stairs. No answer. *Please leave,* I prayed to de burning car, and whadevvor gods it had any pull with. *Please get dis crow fien out of here, and I'll sneak out of dis place where I don't belong, and back to my own little burrow, and I'll forget about crowns, and weerdoos with plans, and my brother who's a complete nutjob I admit, he's missing a few screws, just let me out of here and I'll never do something dis stupid and dangerous again, c'mon c'mon, leduswaywiditderewilla?* But de burning car didn't hear me, or didn't care, cos de crow came further into de room and belted his bar off a wall. I could hear burnt flakes crunching off.

"I can see your hoof, y'nobber."

Like a nobber, I drew my foot in out of sight. He walked over and peered round at me. I wielded my wooden plank, but my grip was frail. He just pulled it away from me real easy and lobbed it out de window. He poked me with his bar and I jolted again, which made him laugh.

"LADS!" he suddenly roared behind him. Den he pulled up his bird mask. He was tall, but he had a kid's face. Not more dan fifteen, I'd say. "You're not fucken sick, y'lying bollox." De others spilled down de stairs and into de room. "He's not sick, lads," de kid said. Dey all lifted masks, and I saw none much older. De biggest, a full-size lummox with a face covered in vicious acne, gave me an almighty funt into de ribs. Pain was blinding—couldn't breathe.

"Are ya not sick?" he said, calm like a nurse, or someone's mam. I shook my head, and he ploughed another massive spawg into my gut. "Y'trying to get yourself kilt, y'stupid cunt?" I hauled myself onto all fours and tried to puke. Some water came up, trickled out over de burned black floor between my hands, like a stoopid late fireman.

"He's sick *now,* Anto!" And de lads had a grand laugh.

"Gave us a good run for our munny!" another fien said. "Y'skinny bollox. I'm shagged out after ya!" More laughter. One of my ribs felt broken. I sat up, tried to breathe. *"WHAT'RE YA DOIN' HERE, FUCKO?!"* Anto suddenly roared, iron bar swung up high, ready to take my face off. I squirmed back into a ball. Laughter hopped off de walls as dey kicked me a while. I could tell dey weren't going full force, just bored cats mucking about with a mouse. All de same, a few stray kicks in my sore rib were rough as beaks pecking into a worm. I was only hoping dey'd let me live.

"I'm sorry! Sorry for coming!" I cried out. Anto crouched down to my eye level and de drubbing stopped again. He pushed de tip of his bar up against my teeth, tapping it with each word: "What-are-you-doin-here-fucko?" De cold metal at my mouth was de hardest thing I'd ever felt. A light tap could bust open my lip, and a daycent whack would scatter my front teeth.

"Please," I begged. "Please.."

"Puh-puh-please *wha*, y'culchie gobshite?"

"Don't hurt me. Please. I'll leave. Just... please..."

"What's inna bag, Paj?" Anto axed. One of de lads, first one to find me, snatched my cloth sack as de others craned deir gullets to see.

"Bog roll? Bleedin' bog roll anna toothbrush!" Paj flaked de bag at me.

"Sorry!" I said, like a gome.

"Jaysus, stop sayin' please an' sorry!" Anto muttered.

"Sorry," again. More laughter.

"Ah god luvum," said a short squat brown boy. "I tink he's simple, poor fuck."

"Aw, a halo!" said Paj, spotting my only real possession in all de world poking its stupid head out of its hiding place. "Giz some jollies off it. I haven't lit up in ages."

"D'fuck you will," Anto snapped, grabbing it before Paj could fondle it and snapping it in two. "State of this one. Wanna end up like him? Fucken toothpick with legs." He chucked de remains at Paj who caught dem, stared at de pieces.

"Ah for feck's sake, Anto, whatcha do tha for? Coulda been fun for a bit. You can be a right shite when you want, d'y'know?"

Anto fixed Paj with a look, towering over him, and dat was de end of dat conversation. Den he turned to me.

"What's your name, Muscles?"

"Tayto," I said, uncurling.

"Tayto? Like the crisps from long ago?"

I nodded.

"Jayz, that's gas," Paj grinned, a little boy again.

"He's the skinniest spud I've ever seen," said Anto. "Get Mr. Tayto here a sanger or something." He crouched over me, and spoke loud, like I was hard of hearing. "D'y'eat food, Mr. Tayto?" And without waiting for an answer he pulled me to my feet and dusted me off, a fussy mother. "You're fine, you're fine," he said, brushing off my broken rib with a wave of his magic metal bar.

Not knowing what to say or do, I followed de lads to deir hideaway in another building. Dey all seemed relaxed and jokey with each other now. Couldn't tell if I was a guest or a hostage. Kinduv didn't want to find out, so I just shut up.

De Crows' nest held enough sugary snacks to re-stock a looted Hypervalu. A sultan's ice box of chilled beers, vodka, pep pouches. A kinduv manic luxury, like. Dey even had original art. I couldn't take my eyes off one wall, covered top to bottom with maazing pictures. As de lads sat to wolf down all dis woeful crap, pouring vodka and pep pop into huge plastic cups, I axed could I look at de wall more close up. Paj, de artist apparent, was only mad chuffed and walked me over.

De colours were dark, lots of blacks and reds, and all types of stuff had gone into de mural: spray paint, chalk, acids. I wouldn't be sure dere wasn't some real blood, too. Action figures and small holy statues, all melted and deformed, stuck out here and dere. My head swam as Paj took me through it detail by detail, explaining de meaning of dis or dat, a whole swirling history of what had happened on de estate since Gombrich. First deaths were old wans, mostly. Den healthy adults. Den jobs dried up, and de looting and rioting followed. How a small few locals lost it altogether when de Scythe didn't stop, and lads started attacking folks in stairwells, even killing a few. How de army came in hazmat suits, and shot a load of dem without boddering to sort out who was innocent or guilty. Huffer units coming and sweeping de healthy off, families torn apart, de lads' time spent in a Joov, de heroic escape and return to find everyone gone or dead, corpses rotting in halls or out in de street.

"What's dis?" I pointed to a splodge of figures fused into each other, hands and legs and heads all nailed together to form a wonky cross in de dead centre.

"I see tha," said Paj, "most nights when I go to sleep."

I just nodded. Den I said, "Tis mad good, dis."

"Cheers." He seemed almost shy. "I did most of it. All of it, really. Took ages."

"I'll bet."

"I mean, it took *ages*," he said again, gazing over his work like he was seeing it for de first time.

"And c'mere to me. What's dis?" I pointed to a tree with roots running deeper underground dan de branches grew above. De roots formed a door, open just a crack. Behind de door was de only bright happy light in de whole damn scene. Looked like gold foil Cadburys wrapper.

"Hey Paj! Would you stop showing off to Tayto and c'mere and drink your bleedin' drink?" de brown boy said. I'd figured out his name was Looby. We sat with de others. Everything dey ate came out of packets and glowed rainbow colours. A magic rainbow dat could never get stale. Looby handed me a drink dat reeked of booze so bad my eyes teared up.

"Naw, I'm grand…" I said.

"Just drink it, y'puff," Looby shoved de cup in my mouth, spilling a good bit on my jumper. I sipped. Gasoline, boi.

"Are ye de only souls in dis estate?" I axed.

"Ah no," said Looby, already slightly pissed and pouring more drink. "Bout twenty or thirty live here."

"But live by our rules," said Anto, stern. "Live here by *our* rules." He took a swig straight from de bottle, den got up and strode out of de room, every bit de bored emperor.

Paj pointed to de mural. "See the crows in the four corners," he said. "We're those crows. We watch over all corners of our home. And we keep everybody who lives here safe."

"How?"

Paj flipped a crowbar in his right hand twice, like it explained something. He picked up his crow mask. "And we make these. Here. Keeps plague away."

I put it on. It smelled of VapoRub.

Drinking was a proper session, boi. My cup was never empty, dey were pure insistent about it. Dey must have thought I'd wandered in as a travelling bard—someone to fix a place in history for dem—who'd sing deir praises or bash dem high and low to all and sundry depending on how good dey got me plastered. De more well-oiled we got, de more I saw dem as children. Twas like a legend where a band of warriors warps into a gang of little boys playing soldier. I couldn't believe how much dese little shits could put away, and didn't know what to make of dem in general. Dey cawed something awful bout rules and rituals, proud of de role dey'd claimed as government and gardaí all rolled into one. De pecking order changed depending on who was most excitable in de moment, but dey seemed happy together, and after a while I gave up trying to judge dem. To be honest, dey seemed less screwed up dan I was myself. Calmer, laughing a lot. Maybe it was all fakery, scared babies pretending dey were fine. Or maybe dey were birds to de core, just hopping from moment to moment, nibbling whadevvor dey found. My cup got topped up again. A fine warm feeling was spreading up from my gut into my ears and hands. As long as I didn't move my ribcage, I was grand.

"You a saint or wha?" slurred Paj, nudging me.

"I am, yeah."

"Sorry about breakin'... your ting-a-majig. I'd have loved a go on it," he continued, leaning in all conspirator-like, "if Anto weren't a right bollox about haloes."

"Says dey started de plague!" Looby cut in before draining his cup and wincing.

"Lads, dat's nuts," I said.

"It's *not* fucken nuts!" said Looby, suddenly bolshy. "Watch your mouth, son! Didn't they come out at the same time? What are the odds of tha?"

"Well," I said, "haloes were on de market well before de first cases of Gombrich." A clamour of voices as dey all tried to win de argument for Anto's viewpoint. Again Looby got in first and loudest.

"Yeah! And then the government started to give 'em out free to everyone! Why was tha, eh? Tell me tha now."

I couldn't believe dese kids had it so arseways. "Dat was to *slow* de spread! When you sit in a room, you don't wander round spreading disease. De Health Board was trying to—"

"Ah, don't give me tha!" Looby was swaying now. I thought he might slump over altogether. "Just don't you gimme *tha*. Why were the places... like here... the worst places hit? We got the most... most free haloes... of anyone."

"Ah Loobs, I luv ya but you're being a dick now," Paj said. "Look at this fella here. He's on the halo morning, noon and night.

Bollox is right as rain. Aren't ya?" I flexed my tiny biceps to weak cheers and some claps. "I mean," Paj continued, "I luv yous lot, and Anto is the *man*—"

"Th'*man* is what he is," Looby raised his drink and spilled it again.

"Amn't I saying?" Paj pressed on, dragging his point like a limp body, "but the whole plague-halo thing is just... it's just *balls* is what it is."

An explosion roared from de green outside. No one else budged, but I scrambled to de window. Sun was totally gone now, and de flaming car was a massive fireball lighting up de night. I could just make out Anto, on his own in de dark, standing fierce close to de great orange tongues, bird mask on, arms out to his sides like some high priest, watching it burn higher.

"What's he at?" I axed.

"Just lobbed another can of petrol into our car," said a skinny quiet kid.

"Why?"

Dey looked at each other and burst out laughing, like I'd asked why things get wet when it rains.

Maybe it was a stupid question. Or maybe I was getting drunk. Whadevvor, I found myself laughing too. Laughing my ass off with dis murder of crows.

I woke face down on a grimy mattress. I blinked—sandpaper eyes. For a second I hadn't a bog where I was. *Who* I was. But my eyes focused, Paj's nightmare mural came into view, and it all slunk back: burning car, confused crows, broken rib, art history lesson, and devil's cocktail after cocktail all fucken night long. Solid food! I was surrounded by chunks of de day-glo crap we'd munched into de wee hours. Sher, I hadn't eaten solid food in weeks. Dis was going to hurt.

Panic broke across me: I didn't even know if I was trapped with dese mad kids or not, but I could be sure de worst hangover dis side of Buttevant was flaking its way in my direction. When I clocked no one else was in de room, I sat up. Too quickly. My head reeled, and just like dat de gawks had me. I hobbled to de window to spew, my sore legs screaming, and found de window jammed. I yanked like a frantic monkey. At de last second de frame slid up and I stuck my head out over a sheer drop. Must've been fifteen floors up: a floor for every year dose little shits had been growing feathers. De shock and vertigo helped me hold it in for a few more seconds, and I thought bout letting it spill all over de floor of deir little club house, or whadevvor dey called it. Deir fucken *Dáil*. Serve dem right.

But Paj's dark mural was looking down on me. After all it had seen through his and de other lads' eyes, all de terror, and cruelty, and fear, and loss... de idea of being such a mean part of dat history, de small scrawny figure puking in front it, just didn't sit right. So I put my head back out de window, closed my eyes, and opened my gob.

How it all just tumbled out of me, all evil and sickness, my head full of black and red images of demented crowds, spilling down and down and down. Felt my stomach and lungs and organs sliding out of my gawking mouth, racing for de exit at last, happy just to fall into a soundless, bottomless pit. But dere was a bottom—I heard de faint splat of a concrete landing below me. De smell, mercifully, couldn't travel back along with de echo. I opened my eyes and slammed de window shut. Mad view of de domain— dis place was a watchtower. You could see for miles. Outside, a smouldering black husk on de green—what used to be a car. Like de Wayke itself sending de survivors here a personal message: *yur goan nowhere, lads.*

How does anything work? Somehow my hangover cracked into another level of Zeke's dodgy memory implant and I shuffled over to his gaff like a spell had been broken, sure as a salmon swimming upstream to my own birthplace. Would y'believe he lived just a few floors over de lads' hangout: Cosmic sign? Dumb fucken coincidence? I was too sick to give a shite.

I hunched outside his numberless door. A little plastic sign read "Z. Zohar," but no buzzer in sight. Out of de blue, I felt a fierce urge to strangle dis gome. He'd made me come here, a place not fit to wash a rat in, and why de feck was he living here anyway? I wanted to knock on his door and dawk de first face dat answered. I was goan to find de crows dis minute: *C'mere t'me, bois. You know dat Zeke fien? Level 10? Wall to wall diseased haloes. Comin' out de wazzoo. He brought plague here. Get him!*

But instead I kept hammering. "Zeke! Open up! It's Yogi's brother—ah feck it, you *know* who it is!" Maybe he was lit up. Or maybe my whole mission was some manner of prank. No reason to think banging would get me anywhere, but some fury inside wouldn't let me give up. I kicked as hard as I could till I felt my rib roar with de impact. No sound. May as well have been de last fien on Earth.

And with dat, my anger fizzled. I crouched over, dealing with another dose of de gawks. Last man on Earth.

Tears. Big fat stoopid tears falling out of my eyes—happy to drop as de vomit earlier. I put it down to de stress and ructions from yesterday. *All bollox*, I said to myself. *Go on home and just...* I wasn't sure how to finish consoling myself. Go on home and just what?

I turned, clueless, ready to shuffle out of dis gawd-forsaken place. As I did I heard a heavy bolt slide, de rumble of stuff being cleared aside. De door opened a crack and I moved into de line of sight. Two dark eyes stared out at me.

Zeke Zohar was a shortarse. Not big on eye contact either—had his back to me de minute he hauled me into his goblin-burrow. He was gnomey, but dark skin and full baldy. First all business bout bolting his door, den all fuss clearing a space for me to sit. His hovel looked like a Chinese recyc-silo, lecky bits and halo scraps piled in tangles so bad it was Twister just to move a few feet in any direction. Windows boarded up, no daylight. He pulled a sliding plank from a wall—his bed. I plonked down. It creaked.

"Nice place, boi," I muttered, scansing round for a place to gawk if I had to. He just kept fidgeting with bits of yokes. At last he just sat on de ground and muttered back: "Maid's day off."

He voice was flat, with some sorta accent I couldn't figure. After yonks he glanced up and took me in.

"You came," he said.

"Yeah, well, like." I didn't know how to finish. I'm not de most talkative, but I found dis Zeke fien extra hard to *sprechen mit*. "What's, uh, whatsa *plan*, like?"

"Plan?" he smiled, pure *wry* like. "Your brother was a clever boy. Are you a clever boy?"

Fucken smuggest, awkwardest question I ever coggled.

"Dunnaw," I sneered. "Do I look like a 'clever boy' to you?"

He just glared at de ground again.

"Hah?" I pressed.

"I wouldn't presume to say." Pure posh—grand for some. Say he went to de best gnome college money could buy.

"You wouldn't presume to say," I turned de phrase on my tongue. "Well, you've presumed a fair old bit bout Mr. Tayto so far. You presumed I'd gatch over here, without mentioning you live beyond fucken Thunderdome. And you presumed de crows wouldn't take a notion to bayte de lugs off me, which is a fair old presumption now I must say." I could feel de anger on me again, and it was good, cos it made de gawks take a backseat. He shrank down at de tone, and dat made me feel a bit bigger again so I reined it in and just hit him with a nice hard: "So now I'd just like t'know what de plan is. Alright?"

"You're hurt," he said. Spose he spotted me cradling my rib, and de face bruising and all. His big brown eyes suddenly looked watery.

"I'm grand," I winced, pure looking for pity and trying to be de hard man all in one.

He disappeared into his washroom, even smaller dan mine, and I heard him rummage in his packrat supplies. After a minute he came out holding a lozenge in his paw. "For your pain."

I eyeballed it: was he trying to slip me de mickey? But how can you tell what a thing is until you swallow it, so I chucked it in my gob and hoped for de best. Sher, it was getting hard to breathe with de pain and I had to find succour from someplace. Here was de last place on Earth: a rubbish tip in a tower block, and inside a gnome handing out magic beans. If he's going t'skin me and eat me let him choke on de bones.

Turns out gnomes have uses. Dat lozenge was de charm, boi. A few sucks in I didn't just feel better, I felt *grand.* I lay down on his bed plank, which may as well have been de Queen of Nod's mattress, and had a good stretch for myself, smilier dan a baby in a basket floating free down a river of warm milk.

"C'mere to me, where's dis stuff been all my life?"

"Don't move so much. It's analgesic, it speeds cellular repair, but your rib is probably broken. The bone needs to knit. It may take several hours."

"What a luvvly lozenge," I grinned, sucking de big strawberry taste off it, real loud and lip-smacky. "Haven't had a sucky sweet since Joov. Nurse used to hand out orange lozzies if you got the crawlies. Rank! And dey just knocked you for six."

Things were kickin in nicely now, his room was looking more

agreeable every second, but I still had to coggle how he lived like dis. I'm partial to a small box to park my bones in myself, but dis fien clearly was no friend of empty space. Junk, stuff, tangles-within-tangles from floor to ceiling. De tangles were starting to squirm. Figurines, too: up on a shelf, a dusty Jap fisherman held a rod with no string. He'd been waiting so long for his catch, wasn't he frozen solid.

"D'ya like fishing?" I nodded toward de poor expectant bollox on his perch.

"No. I've never killed anything." He said it so flat, like, couldn't tell if he was boasting or ashamed.

"Me neither."

A *fair enough* silence followed. Zeke broke it by announcing "You should rest," and wiggling into a lotus position right dere on de floor. He wrapped a foil blanket round himself. "I hope it's not gauche of me, but I'm going to light up. We'll embark tomorrow, assuming you've healed."

Before I could open my béal with an *Oh yeah? Embark where and how?* his halo popped on. Dead to de world. His back stayed bolt upright somehow. De single light in de room shut off automatically, just like bedtime in de Joov. Five minutes since we'd met, and he'd shut up shop for de day! Fine with me. I'd wayked more in de past day or two dan could be good for anyone. Only thing for it was to stretch out like a sultan on dat sleeping plank. Gawks: gone. Hangover: ancient history. Rib pain: never heard of it. Could hardly tell you what pain was at all.

Zeke's halo was de only light in de room, a moon shining over his great techie mess of a landscape. *Suck suck suck* I went on my lozzie. My tongue was going numb. Gawd, how beautiful dis shithole of a flat was starting to look. *He's not a bad auld fella, dis Zeke,* I thought to myself as my eyelids drooped. *Sure maybe he's goan to be my best friend.* Through de thick wrap of fog round my noggin I spied de promised land. We were goan down promised land way, goan to find my brother and his Crown. Soon all our troubles would be over.

Zeke's halo beamed down on his foil blanket, not a moon now but a sun, rising over a holy, snow-covered mountain.

Came to with a jolt. His main light was back on—big garish yoke. Zeke was rummaging again, burrowed away in de jacks. My rib felt fine but dis vicious fear was on me, and I knew I'd been night-maring. De auld REM sleep was creeping back up de staircase of my spine. I'd be having fierce vivid dreams soon if I didn't get under a halo quicksmart. My mind snaked, giving me de crawlies: how long had I been out, drugged by dis weerdoo? Who knows what he'd been upta. I coughed and Zeke poked his head out of de jacks.

"You've been out for a whole day," he said, like a mindreader looking up from his crystal feckin toilet bowl. I sat up, and a rumble of hunger barrelled through me. Shocken. With de feedbags flowing freely, it's easy to forget what a pure agony hunger can be.

"Any brekkie?" I axed, not expecting to be dazzled. A hand tossed me a Snazzler, carbo-nosh variety. Fecken peanut butter flavour. "Too kind," I said, yanking open de wrapper. It looked old: crumbly instead of soft. Down de hatch, y'finicky prick. *Aww* de effect was only woeful, like dustbunny and snot. And a hint of peanut butter I spose. Breakfast of champs.

His toilet mustuv doubled as a workshop, cos he kept prodding around in dere. Maybe just trying to avoid me in dis tiny box. He wasn't what you'd call a people person. Eventually he came back into de room, but still wouldn't look me in de eye.

"What's it do?" I axed, pointing at some random tangle of crap. Figured he'd be de type to warm up by blathering bout work. See it in de Gerries all de time: *Oh, y'like auld trains, do ya?… A fireman, were ya?… Collect coins, do ya. Well well well!"* Find de tattoo, de hobby, de job dey never really left, and yur away on de pig's back. You've got yur way in if you fancy getting on deir good side.

"You're pointing at five things," he said finally.

"Oh yeah? What are dey, now?"

He moved over, eyes locked on de tangle like a kitty-cat on a laser pointer, and yanked out a pink strand of halo cable.

"This," he held it like jewelry, "is called 'Echo.' It's supposed to trigger memory. Episodic memory mainly. Like living the event all over again. Childhood parties, your wedding, the birth of your first child. An especially desirable commodity to the bereaved, as you can imagine."

"Dey-jah-voo, like? Happy days."

"Not quite. It damages the speech centre, somehow. Some users never speak again." He fecked de yoke behind him and flicked his hand at de mess all round. "Once Yogi left campus, I took over as acting director. Fruits of my genius."

He yanked another model from de tangle. "*This* little beauty is a prototype for a personal training system: 'Coach.' Through biofeedback it detects where and how you hold muscle tension, and systematically teaches you to manipulate that tension. Strength and flexibility are determined to a large extent by neurological factors, so Coach taps straight into the nervous system and teaches it how to generate focused tension for strength, or how to dynamically release tension for flexibility. *Imagine yourself as liquid steel* was our tagline. One month using 'Coach' resulted in better strength gains for our test subjects than a year on anabolic steriods. Backbends, splits, explosive vertical leaps—everything tested through the roof, so to speak. We had a contract ready to go with Olympic training sites all over the world." He gave a nervous little laugh dat was also a sigh. "It causes extreme body dysmorphia for some reason. Test subjects obsessively overtrain, and we had one suicide. No," he corrected himself, "two." More untangling. "*This* one causes false memories, extreme ADHD, *and* fine motor skill loss. Now that's a bargain! This one, um... oh yes, this one does nothing at all. Absolutely nothing." He slumped on de ground by his bed plank.

Wasn't sure what to say. "Ah yeah. Tis a tough auld gig. Tough auld gig alright, I'd say."

He looked at me like I might be witless altogether—first time dis morning I'd got some direct eyeball—den stuffed his manky failures out of sight. As good a time as any to get to it.

"So, like, what's de plan?"

He laughed, quick and dead. "*Plan?*" He shrugged. "Too many unknown variables at play. I don't know if Yogi is in Cork, and I don't know if he's alive or dead. I can't know whether he solved the riddle of the Crown, and even assuming he did, it may not be locatable. So... what would you like to do?"

I knew it. Dis snobby fien, with his *lah-dee-dah* fancy foreign accent, was having cold feet bout hitting de road with me now we'd made our acquaintance in person. Prick. Who was he to judge, living in de shittiest shithole on Earth?

"Second thoughts, hah?" I held out my hands like *just say it, boi. Just tell me I'm a scobe and get it out dere. I think you're a gome too. Not like I'm relishin hitting an bóthar with you either, son.*

"It just... *ahhh!*" he let a gawp out of him, pure weird, like he was burning in slow motion. He's rubbing his shakey hands together suddenly and I start to get fierce nervous. "The prospect of walking out that door…let's just say it doesn't appear feasible."

He was mumbling and it took a second for de penny to drop: didn't he have de filleeus fogs, poor bollox. Dat's cant for heavy users who freak at de prospect of goan outside de door. Now I looked at him right, de question wasn't whether Zeke was fogging, just how bad. I'd heard some saints starved rather dan face goan out for food. On de other hand, crayture might just need one of his own lozzies to set him right as rain.

He scansed over at de door and squeezed his eyes shut, screwing his fists into his eye sockets. Looked like he had it bad. *Balls.*

He'd gone through all his anxio lozzies and I'd *say* de auld postman doesn't call round here too often to drop off more. All he had left were a handful of analgesics and sleepers. Good of him to share one with me, I thought. We threw de last of his meds in a bag, together with whadevvor god-awful morsels of munch still lurked in his cupboard, two standard halos, some odds and ends I dunnaw what, and a change of clothes. Done and dusted. I liked traveling light. He wasn't spazzing, and I was feeling fit, so de odds looked good we were off to a grand start. Until we reached de door and he ducked toward de ground, like he expected a plasma cannon to greet us.

"Lookit, we're either doing dis or we aren't."

"I know, I know." But he wasn't getting up.

"It's hard, de fogs. Sher, had dem myself once. Pressure in yur head and de gawks, yeah?"

He managed a nod—rigid, poor langer.

"And I dunnaw bout you, but on top of all de fear and sickness, dere's dat voice saying *I'm being such a chickenshit, it's just a stoopid flight of steps, or a road or whadevvor,* yeah?" He nodded again, no neuroarchitect with a skyscraper IQ but just a toddling *leanbh* afraid of monsters outside his door. If I could get him out, even for a few minutes, de fogs might ease up. Dat, or he'd have a full meltdown and I'd be shafted. Didn't relish having another run in with de crows. Lads like dat could go either way on a body, especially on a saint with de fogs. So I put my hand on his shoulder, pure manly, like a captain to a grunt before de big push.

"Zeke, boi, I don't know you from Adam, and you don't know me, but if you worked with my brother I'd say you're a fairly solid sort, right? And yur brickin it cos... well, it's *not* de safest place outside right now, call-a-spade-a-spade. Don't be embarrassed bout it. I'm brickin it too, yeah? But if you stay here yur goan to die in here, plain and simple. In dis shitty little box. D'y'parlay-voo me?"

Dat's when he broke down completely, shakes and snot—de works. For a split second I wondered: *Can I go it alone?* But dis fien was in such a bad place, I couldn't just up and leave him. Sher, in truth I was scared of goan home on my own. And I'd nowhere else to go.

I let him cry it out for a minute or two, den resumed my pep talk. "We're gatching out of here together, boi. Just take my hand, and we'll stroll over to de stairwell—easy as y'like—and we'll just hang out, yeah? We can come back in if you aren't happy."

I could tell he was mustering something.

"*Straight* back in, swear on my only shirt." I hoisted up my squirrel sweater, pointing to Alf and his fearless *Yo!*

"Damn dog," muttered Zeke, and I gave him de full gold star for effort.

"C'mon," I nodded out de door. "Let's get crowned. Let's live forever, in a better place dan dis."

"Live forever." He scrunched up his face in pure determination and grabbed my arm back. Poor twat.

Dawn hadn't broke yet. Good. Better to leave while it was still dark. At de top of de steps he was fairly calm, like *Notsobad, can deal with dis, what was all my fuss about ha ha* and I kinduv got lulled into a false sense of security, cos four flights down he started shrieking and trying to hide his head in his fly. Took all my professional carer skills to manage him, and I was so distracted with de job I didn't notice two gallants strolling up with iron bars in hand. Twas Paj and Looby, crow masks perched up on their foreheads to reveal deir faces. De pair were like dose optical illusion yokes: deadly thugs one way, harmless kids another, depending on how you squinted yur eyes or tilted yur noggin.

"Howerya Mister!" Paj nodded at me, friendly.

Looby scowled: "State of yer man." Zeke had gone quiet, curled in a wriggly ball, trying to block out light and sound. "Trying to suck himself off, wha?"

"Jayzuz I've tried that!" Paj announces, big smiley head on him. "Always an inch short."

"Ah, he's just having a bad day, d'y'knaw de way?" I patted Zeke like a good dog. "Know anywhere I could put him till he calms down, like?"

"Maybe he's got demons," Looby suggested, fairly helpful.

"Seriously, he's in a bad way, lads."

"Yous could go to Gubna!" Paj sniggered.

Looby whacked his bar off de wall above Zeke's head, making him vibrate like a dodgy bomb.

"Ah don't!" I pleaded.

"It's just funny is all," Looby explained, squinting at Zeke. "What's wrong with him altogether?"

"Ah, he's got de filleeus fogs, poor fella."

"What's tha?" Looby squinted at me. "Some kind of saintly bollox?"

"Something like. What about a Gubna?"

The two crows scansed each other, like dey'd spilled a secret.

"Well, she might take his mind off his troubles..." Paj pointed to de next tower block.

Looby started crackin up—a cackle.

"You'll have no problem finding her," said Paj.

"Grand so. Give us a hand moving my buddy downstairs?"

De lads cawed with laughter.

"Good luck with Gubna!" said Paj, wandering off on his rounds. Looby spat and didn't de scut whack near Zeke's head again. More ructions.

"Jayzuz wept," Looby tutted, shuffling to join his partner on deir leisurely morning patrol.

A crack of light on de horizon—like someone had whipped a razor across de sky, and red light was spilling through.

Paj was right: signs for Gubna weren't hard to come by. Stuck over de front entrance to Block C was a child's skull. It didn't have a jawbone, so top little baby teeth rested against de concrete wall. It was smeared with dark stuff, blood or dried shit—maybe both. Flies seemed to like it, anyways. Around it was scrawled, in de same stuff but faded, de letters G-U-B-N. No "A." Like she owned de whole tower. Zeke was hunched and huffing like a werewolf after losing his inhaler, and as I faced into Gubna's idea of a welcome mat, I didn't see my day getting sunnier.

"Know anything bout dis byor?" I whispered. No point in axing him, he might as well have been a dog gone mad with torture. If dis Gubna wan could help him even wipe his own arse again I'd be eternally grateful, because my patience with Zeke Zohar was getting sketchy. Some dossers drive de family dog to a woods, let Rover out and just step on de pedal, flayke off into de night, leaving de cur to howl at de moon, de great big silvery sadness in de sky. I didn't want to be dat snaky fien. But dere's only so much a body can take. I reckoned Gubna was our best shot.

I nodded toward de fair Gubna's door: "Shall we?" Zeke didn't even seem to notice de skull or de flies, he just pushed past me to get into de stairwell. Bad dog.

Cold as a morgue, somehow way colder dan Zeke's tower. No working lights, but with a shaft of daylight stealing in I could make out a door one floor up. It was plastered with doll bits and pieces.

"Hello?" No answer. Fear of gawd crept over me with a million hairy little legs.

"Feck dis!" I grabbed Zeke's arm. "C'mon, outside it's just de sun and grass and a bit of wind. No more of dis shite now. Let's hit de road." He stared at me, stuck like one of de doordolls. "C'mon!" I roared in his face.

He blinked. Den I heard a creak upstairs. De doll door was open a crack. A small head peeked out. I held up my hand in a kinduv frozen wave, unsure if I should scarper or say hi. De little girl scuttled down de stairs and looked us up and down. *Well?* she seemed to be saying. Her face was doll-like too. Grimy, and kinduv plastic almost. Matted hair. She didn't look well.

"Hello dere, love." I hunched over, hands on knees, big frozen smile on my face. "What's your name?" She said nottin. Couldn't blame her—say I looked a right perv. "We're looking for Gubna. Do you know her at all?"

"Who wants to know?" she says, pure cool customer. Her green eyes skewered me.

"Well, I'm Mr. Tayto. And dis here is my friend Dr. Zohar. He's got a bad case of de foggies, see?" Zeke and de girl regarded each other like two pups just met: alert, bit wary. She skipped up de steps to her flat and shut de door. I was so flummoxed someone would keep a kid in a hole like dis, I barely noticed Zeke muttering to himself.

A few seconds later de girl popped out again. "Come up so the pair of yous!" And she nipped back into de flat, leaving her door ajar. A pale glow from inside shone on de blondie plastic faces, eyes rolled back in deir skulls.

Gubna was smoking a fag and lighting rakes of candles by de time I finagled Zeke into her flat. Place stank of de whatchamacallit dey used to use in church. Incense. Between de smoke and de churchy stink I near passed out.

I'd expected an auld wan, for some reason, but she wasn't. Just haggard as hell. Bog standard tracksuit. A stack of bracelets clanked around as she lifted her arms to light de candles—so many candles.

"Gubna, yeah?"

She ashed her fag, took one last quick drag and stabbed it into a can of cola. It sizzled.

"Fogs?" She barely nodded at Zeke. "Bring him here t'me." She grabbed Zeke by his face and held him steady while she stared into his eyes. After a while he stopped pulling and stared back. Seemed calmer already. Magic.

"Where's dat little girl gone? Is she yurs?"

Gubna ignored me. "He's bad," she muttered.

"He seems better. He was freaking before, but he's calm out now."

She shook her head, all wise and tired.

"Naw," she said, still staring into Zeke. "He's gone into himself. Bad."

"Can you help?"

"Maybe," she said, looking him up and down.

I started explaining our lack of dosh, but she cut me off with a wave. Good woman yurself. We'll light a candle for ya, or something. She led Zeke by de hand behind a red curtain all bedecked with patterns and symbols: equals signs joining up snakes eating eggs and arrows pointing to tunnels and tadpoley yokes racing each other.

"Where are you taking him?"

"Will you let me be so I can work him?" she snapped. De curtain swirled behind her and fell still. Half expected it to fall like a magic act and dere'd be nottin dere. No Zeke, no Gubna, no building, nottin, just grass and blue sky forever. *Work him?* Sounded ominous. I sat on her manky couch. No sign of a magazine, but den I spose it wasn't exactly a doctor's surgery. Had a mad itch to light up, but no way was I doing it here. Where was dat creepy little girl gone off to? Dat byor was fodder for a daycent nightmare. I tried to laugh at myself. *Muppet. Afraid of a little kid.* But I couldn't laugh. Nottin in de bag of my stomach but cold air. De dead look on her face had me hoping she wouldn't come back but nervous I couldn't see where she was. I actually scansed under de couch. Horde of cola cans—sucked dry and crumpled.

I noticed a hologlyph on de wall in front of me. One corner was peeling but de effect still worked, even in candlelight. I stared at it and it started to invite me in. Felt my shoulders relaxing, getting soft and slopey. De shapes danced a happy little gentle jig. I used to love glyphs as a kid. Dis was a good one too. One minute all de lines were sharp and cool, de next all soft and fuzzy warm.

Out of nowhere, de shapes twisted and took on a cat's face, glaring right into me, into my guts. Might as well have been a mouse staring down my whiskery doom. Heart was pounding like de clappers. *Look away, look away.*

A moan from behind de curtain. It put de wind up me, but I was half-grateful for it—anything to get my mind off dat glyph. I creeped over real slow and went to slide de curtain back a hair's breadth.

Gubna had stripped Zeke to his jocks and socks. Near skinny as me, and his back so scarred it looked like he'd been dragged over glass or barbed wire. He was face down in a massage chair, corpse-still. Gubna lit more joss sticks and waved dem over his head, humming low like a cloud of bees. She took a big swig of cola, sprayed it out her mouth onto a doll. Three big spits all over de poor sticky thing. Then she breathed all dramatic and heavy, like she was getting ready to lift a huge weight. She put her hands on his shoulders and… Nottin. Didn't move. She just left her hands on him, breathing with him, for such a long spell dat I got bored and sat back on de couch. I glanced at de glyph again but it was all eyes now, and I was queer scared of it so I shut my lids. It'd given me a headache. *Just a little nap, I'd say. Forty winks. No harm to take a short…*

I woke to find de little girl in front of me, staring. I sat up slow, no sudden moves, like I'd been cornered by a cobra.

"Hello little miss," I said, also real slow, and saluted. Another moan from behind de red curtain. I wanted to get a look at de goans on, but something bout dis kid froze me to de spot. "Are dey yur dolls?" I pointed at de door slathered in heads, arms and legs. She just kept staring through me with emerald eyes.

"I hate dolls," she finally said.

"Fair enough. You have a name?"

She said nottin, and I noticed she didn't blink. It made me blink way more. Nearly had to slap myself in de face to stop my lids flapping. *Scuse me dere, love, I'm just terrified of children apparently, won't be a minute now I'm just havin a meltdown please feel free to amuse yourself.*

"People call me Tayto." De sound of my tag sort of righted me and I got a handle on de blinking situation. "Yeah, Tayto," I repeated it and felt a bit better again, like seeing a beloved auld comic book with a long-forgotten hero on a faded cover, promising things'll be fine cos he's here now, and he's de right man for de job. Or seeing your long-lost brother again. Just a little sense of belonging, even if it was only a scrap. "It's a good name," I said, more to myself dan her now, gawd only knows what was goan on in her noggin. To hell with her, I wasn't afraid of dat little byor at all. "Like de crisps. Remember dem?" She shook her head. "Bit before your time, maybe. *Cheese'n'Onion.* You could get a rake of flavours but *Cheese'n'Onion* was de classic. Tasted of neither cheese nor onion, dat was de joy of it. Nottin else tasted like it. Probly de only thing I liked eating as a kid—bout yur age actually. So de folks started calling me Tayto. I'd eat two or three bags for lunch and *sin a bhfuil.* Dey were killed trying to get me to eat anything else. Tis de only food I miss since fucken—sorry. Since de Scythe and all."

"I like Snazzlers," she said quietly, finally looking down at her fingers. I felt like I'd been released from a trap.

"Yeah, Snazzlers're pretty good," I lied. Poor little byor, liking dat awful puke. She'd never tasted a good munch like a Tayto in her life. It made me suddenly sad for all de noobs, roaming round with never a nosh like we had before Gombrich. Dat over-enthusiastic maid with her invisible broom—just swooping in and sweeping de old world away. And I thought bout all de stuff kids her age could be doing, *should* be doing. Playing on de green. Jump rope with other girls. Hopscotch. Teasing lads bout deir wally haircuts, like. Bikes and scooters. Even bitching bout school! All simple stuff, all snatched away. Was I scared of dis kid… or was I scared of how much I didn't want to coggle how much she'd lost, and neither of us even knowing de half of it. Living in dis tower, with broken dolls as neighbours, Gubna as landlord, and Crows for government and police.

Another moaning sound, and dis time it sounded like Gubna and Zeke were at it together.

"Sorry now," I whispered at de girl, "but what in *gawd's name* is goan on back dere?"

She giggled and stuffed her fingers in her mouth, all shy suddenly.

"Serious, like!" I pressed.

"Gubna's doing her cure."

"Uh huh. And what's dat?"

She rolled her eyes and giggled again. Behind her de glyph was leering at me. *What are you laughin at, cat?*

"She's silly!" said de girl, all friendly now like we were best friends at a slumber party.

"Why's dat?"

"She's always trying to make a baby, but she *can't.*"

It took a second to put feck and fuck together: "Is dat de *treatment?* Dat's what she's doing in dere with my buddy?"

De girl nodded, half laughing. Half scared. "She's *always* trying to make a baby."

I sprang up and ran to de curtain, whipping it back. Zeke was on his back on de massage chair, grey jocks dangling off one ankle. Gubna was buck naked and straddling him like an impatient cowboy, hips jiggling back and forth.

"Get off him y'gnarly hoor!" I yelled, pure Dublin as if I'd been raised in dis manky tower myself. I reached to pull her off him, and she snapped out of her trance.

"*Fuggoff ya faggot!*" A real hiss, still grinding into Zeke like nobody's business.

"Wrong!" I yelled at myself, trying to whip myself into action. "*Wrong,*" I said again, less certain, in a kinduv finger-waggy *shame-on-you* way. I was goan to push her off him, but somehow felt I wasn't allowed touch her.

"He's nearly there, y'prick! Leave us be!" she shouted and

scrawled my face—some right talons on her. Tore through my cheek, only just missing my eye. I reeled back, falling through de red curtain and yanking it down on myself. De little girl shrieked with laughter.

"My curtain, y'bollox!" shouted Gubna, still ridin poor Zeke. De more I wrestled with de red curtain de more tangled up I got. It snaked round me like a boa constrictor. So I just started screaming Zeke's name as loud as I could. He came to, stunned like a newborn.

"Get up, you foggy fecker!" I wriggled free at last and charged Gubna, rugby tackling her to de ground. Suddenly I was on top of de sweaty squirming skanger. I was close enough to smell her cigarette breath.

"I'll rip your scrawny mickey off!" she wailed. Her forehead smashed my nose. I felt a crack, and a split second later a blinding pain. "He was nearly done! You'll pay for this, y'gurrier!"

I looked behind me and—de gawds of de burning car mustuv had sympathy for me, cos wasn't Zeke near full dressed, hopping on one leg and pulling his shoe on fast as you like. My nose was throbbing and I saw my blood spilling in fast thick drops over Gubna's breasts and belly.

"Sorry," I mumbled for some reason. I clambered off her, grabbed our halo bag with one hand and Zeke with the other, and laced it to de stairwell, passing de little girl. She was pulling dolls off de door, grinding heads into pieces with her foot, like someone freed from a spell.

It all felt like an action fillum, so I went ahead and kicked open de door to de outside—BAM! Me and Zeke exploded into de cold bright air. A sharp winter sun shone low and straight in our eyes. I winced and saw Zeke struggling to do up his fly while we speed-walked, moving at a fair clip toward de road at de far end of de green. Gubna emerged from her tower entrance, naked and livid, my blood all over her chest. She grabbed her red tits—squeezing dem as if to help her shriek louder at us—and I hunched a bit, pure instinctive, like her words could shoot us down before we raced off into de great wide world: "Yous are royally *fucked!* Hear me, y'sorry *pricks*! The Gubna *hexes* you!" And then she was sobbing, de great heaving wail of a person who'd been wronged and wronged and wronged thrice again, seen de death of all good things—weeping in pain: "A *hex!* A hex... on both... your heads!"

To make it more dramatic, like, an explosion went off behind us. De crows had blown up a fresh new car. A massive smoke tower twisted skyward, leaning in our direction. Black wind at our backs. All de young fiens stood round de burning offering, beak visors down. With de lads' faces hidden I couldn't tell if dey were cursing us too, or protecting us with some sortuv counter-blessing. Maybe dey were just burning another car of a Wednesday morning. Whadevvor de case may be, Zeke had his fly up fully now, and he was striding through de long grass with a straight back, so I straightened up too. *Caw caw, y'cunts.* We were finally on our way.

Chapter 5:
Go N-éirí An Bóthar Libh
(May the Road Rise Up to Meet You)

We were finally on our way, but after such a wham-bam escape from Zeke's auld stomping grounds, turned out "our way" wasn't operating express, like. First speed ramp in our way was de bus stop at de end of de green. I hadn't boarded a bus in yonks, and I wasn't sure Zeke had ever had de pleasure. Twas me spotted de shelter—he didn't seem to know about it. And den he seemed surprised to find de bus was tardy.

"Quarter past the hour," he murmured, tappin de printed schedule. "I love these things," he said, not even nearly smiling. "So aspirational." Twas cold, and I started to shiver. Do buses still run to dese parts? Who would use dem? I thought of a bus schedule dat was nottin but question marks. Destinations? Arrivals? Price? Bus?

Zeke must've seen me shiver, cos he opened his bag and took out a little spray, some new gadget I'd never seen before—like a small metal orange. Without a word, he took my hands and fired a short burst onto them. In a few seconds a warm second skin settled on top of my own, dead comfy. I felt how I reckon an elephant or a cow feels, or any crayture with a hide: numb, no hassles. He sprayed de tip of my nose too, and de lobes of my ears, and den his own. I was suddenly delighted with myself. A new thing! Screw hats, jackets and scarves, and all de other stuff I didn't have. Just a squirt of second skin on de cold bits and sher yur *grand*, boi. I kept staring at my hands, flexing my fingers, looking for a sign of dis strangeness. But I could barely see anything. Just sometimes, if you caught de light just right, a slight shine.

"C'mere to me, dat's *mad* stuff," I said.

"Better than gloves. It's called Skynne. S-k-y-n-n-e. It's Scandinavian."

"Peels off easy enough, ha?"

"It denudes over time. Then you just reapply," he said, putting de magic citrus back in his bag. *Luvvly. Good man yurself.* Zeke, boi. Nottin like having a minor magician as a travelling companion.

We waited. Not a soul joined us—no sign of anyone out and about. Zeke seemed fine, pure calm now like a lordly squire on a Sunday stroll, not a trace of de fogs. I wasn't sure how to talk about what had just happened with Gubna, de whole thing feeling more and more like a dream de longer we waited at de shelter.

Something bout a bus stop, tis like a pure node of de Wayke. Bus stops stop everything to make an announcement: whadevvor you've been through, good or bad, weird or mad, dis is a bus stop. Nottin dat came before matters, or even really happened. Bus stops are like de spent toilet roll holders at work: Naw, boi. Nottin can ever happen. Tis all just empty cardboard. De more I thought bout dese Wayky nodes, de vexier I got. Like how you feel yur whole stupid life has just been building up to dis: a deserted bus stop by de side of a green. Any sacrifices people have made so you could exist, all de shite you had to go through to learn to walk and eat solid food and take a dump, and learn sums, and Irish, and geo-ga, and biz org, on and on, and it's all just leading to one big bus stop and no idea if a bus is coming or what. I got so angry I felt like pulling my Skynne off so I could feel de cold on my fingers again, just so I could have something a bit more definite to hate. Couldn't even hate on de bus stop properly because nodes like dis are just a big shrug de universe does. Dere's not enough stuff, not enough knotty details and drama, like, to really get into a good hating state with it. De whole thing is so neutral, it's like trying to hate a rock, or a dead thing. I wondered if ancient lads ever felt dis way. Dere'd be some good bits to life as a caveman: munching into a bloody steak, or gettin yur bit off a fine cut of a lash come midnight down de back of her cave, all naked on some furs, but in general it'd just be walking somewhere again, hitting rocks off rocks. Not goan anywhere. Just getting older, de steak tasting mankier with each munch, teeth getting looser in yur head, and de byor in de back of de cave getting stroppier and stroppier. Fucken bus stops.

It chugged over de horizon, a big red ladybird of a thing: de R-20 bus. We submitted to de huffers and boarded. I could never get used to dese driverless buses, just passenger seats where dere used to be a man in a cap holding a big wheel. I've nottin against robots in general, and I don't know what buses are like in other places, but Irish robot drivers aren't de best. Our bus kept slowing down and speeding up again, and veering bout de road like our ghost driver had had a few jars before starting his shift. We sat up front like kids, partially cos it was de first spot available, and partially to be as far as possible from de odd auld bird sitting all de way down de back. She had her bag clutched like a shield, right up to her throat, and into her mask she rambled: *What's this his name was? Donald! Donald it was. Holy jayziz where did he get his money from, that's what I want to know! Rotten with cash, and he pig ignorant, like he was raised by bleedin' donkeys!... I ask you, what's the world coming to at all at all? Donald and all his money. Gawd bless us and save us. Donald.*

I stared out at de beautiful vista: grey towers after grey towers. Truly, a jewel of de east. We swerved on down de road.

De R-20 lurched to a halt—more or less—outside Heuston Station. Within walking distance of de footpath, as dey say. More huffers and we were inside, amid de magnificence. Heuston had been reopened for months. Politicos had made a Big Deal about de ribbon cutting, with TV crews and speeches and everything, TDs lined up (six feet apart) like a bunch of pudgy little grooms at de world's worst wedding. I remember seeing it on a screen at de geronotoplex. Some fogey with a hawk's nose and a pinched voice held his ceremonial scissors over de ribbon draped from de huffer station: *...This classic landmark of locomotion that will once again sweep our citizenry up and down the length of the country in safety and style, but more than that, it marks a substantial symbolic step forward in once again embracing a cosmopolitan Ireland, one that is beginning to put the fear and pain of the great pestilence behind us. Ours is a nation that is increasingly ready to move into the coming future, a future which, like Iarnród Eireann's trains, tracks forward with steadfast determination and resolve...* I've a great memory for cod-ology, you'd have to agree. Always have. Mirror opposite of Yogi, who could come across soft in de head he talked so little, but turn your back for a blink and he'd be rewiring de toaster into a movie projector. Me, I forget left from right, no head for figures, don't know a screwdriver from a cortico-stimulant, but fire me a line of pullaver, a signed original from a certified bullshit artist, and tis in de noggin for ever. *Grand stuff.* A perfectly useless head I have, even if it is devilish handsome.

I loved dat fogey's little speech. A gem it was. "Cosmopolitan Ireland" if you don't mind. De Good Old Times, brought to you by cosmos politicians who understand de ways of our universe. I spose Mr. Big Scissors meant scobes from Limerick could get up to Dublin on de train now, if ever dey ran into trouble hitching a lift. How cosmopolitan! But de bit dat really stuck with me was de notion we'd put our pain behind us by re-opening de *train station.* World cut to ribbons, and we stick another *ribbon* on it—wasn't it only de fecken huffer de ribbon was tied to, I might add—and call it a party. Gather up de lost dead souls! Sweep all dat spectral gunk out of de gutters! Everything's grand again. Train station's open. S'alright love, you can stop yur whinging bout de dead babbies and de ravaged bodies and de whole dancing vicious bastard Wayke dat shook us like a drunken dad—snack bar's operational and all!

Why did it make me so angry? It's just that after all de terror and screaming maybe, and den de riots, you'd think we might wake up, I mean *really* wake up. And we'd see we're alive, more or less, for better or worse. And since our mean-spirited hovel of a world has been shaken to pieces we could build... I dunnaw... we could build anything now! When you've lost everything, sher, aren't you free, sortuv? We could build a whole new world, and do *different* things with our time. Maybe we could be like Venice, with canals and gondolas floating lazy with lovers where dere was streets and honking before, and we could speak to each other in opera instead of talk—I could see it now, two Cork gondola pilots passing each other on a canal used to be North Main Street, ripping de piss out of each other's gomey-in-lurve passengers in song before parting ways and roaring an agreement to meet up at de Goldy Gondelier dat evening—and we could grow a jungle to play in and throw out all dat strip lighting and monstro-marts and tax offices and dark alleys dat smell of piss and puke and turpentine. We can live any way we want. De cosmos says it's okay, see, cos dere's really no other way to live but de way you want to. Our drunken dad of a cosmos shook us and maybe it was an act of mercy too, cos he said *C'mere to me! Wake up, dickheads! It's always closing time at de bar. Wake up and shift yurselves.* And we can just leave de old house and build any kinduv life for ourselves, and even if tis worse dan before... at least it'll be *ours.*

But naw. Dis is what we do instead. We rub our eyes, and put de little broken pieces back in de same boring, stupid, dead grey pattern we had dem in before—a puzzle yur not meant to fix—with our little grey suits to match, and cut a ribbon. Shopping! Up to de capital and back to Charleville before beddy-byes, no bodder! Just like de old days. Y'know, *cosmopolitan.*

Ah, don't know what I get so hot and flustered for. Trains are running again. Hallelujah, sher. Pricks like me can never be grateful for small mercies. I wouldn't know how to build a better life if you gave me a blank cheque, a blueprint, and roadside assistance.

Now for all de big talk bout embracing a steadfast future and all, dere was only one train a day. I remembered from someone at de Gerries it left Dublin at 9am, so me and Z-boi had a few minutes to wait. Perfect timing, really. We sat outside Hypermacs. De joint was closed but somehow still mucking de air up with de stink of stale oil. A few bossy pigeons eyed us to see if we'd cough up anything. We waited some more. Place was fierce quiet, but sher, what did I know? Just cos de trains were running again didn't mean anybody was on dem.

I heard a whirrrr behind us and turned to see a chubby gobshite in an electric cart. He made a snazzy turn at de last second and banked to a halt beside us, just missing me.

"Can I help ye, lads?" he axed. He was in a security uniform but his shirt was out of his pants, and a suspicious cyclops of a belly button gave us de hairy guzz eye from his greasy flaps. His hat was to de back of his head, so I assumed he was after dropping his cart out of warp. Or maybe he'd been walking round de place naked a few seconds earlier, panicked when he saw us, and threw on his gear in a mad hurry, arseways and inside out. Big red culchie face on him. I hoped he wasn't from Cork. Not like I'm *mad* proud of de place—being *cosmopolitan,* don't y'knaw—but can't help a painful cringe when a fanny turns out to be my countryman. Jayz, what's county pride bullshit doing in dis day and age? Bad auld habits die hard. And judging by how red-faced and wheezy dis prick was, dying hard was in his future, and soon enough.

"What are ye doing here at dis hour?" he pressed.

"Train, like!" I said, bit narky. Think I was stressed, what with not lighting up for an age, and thoughts of goan back home. Dat hairy cyclops eye peered at me from his shirt flaps.

"Lads, dere's no train till two. Ye'll be ages waiting."

"What happened to de 9am?"

"Ah de *9am!* Get a *clue,* willa!" He backed up his little veh-hickle, wheeled round, and whirred back to his hutch in de far corner to fiddle himself over fancy pictures of cake.

Zeke bought our tickets and we strolled de station. De odd tech guy and some droids were doing bits and pieces on de track, but otherwise twas quiet as a transport museum. All it needed was a woman with a posh accent, leading a fannypack of shuffling tourists while pointing at de trains: *Irish peasants used to cart themselves up and down the length of the land in these quaint carriages, and were served things called "snacks" by trolley merchants.* And one of de tourists wearing a tasteful sweater tied jauntily round his neck would raise his hand and say: *Uhhh, excuse-ah moi, whud iz deez "snacks from ze trolley?"* De posh guide would nod her head: *Excellent question, Franswazz. "Snacks" would refer to a wide range of colouredy crap, such as The Fruit Roll-up, The Chomp Bar, maybe a packet of Rancheros, or Screaming Meanies, and of course the classic: The Cinna-swirl.* And Franswazz, being a discerning man and not so easily put off from getting his complete answer, would push her just a bit more: *Ah wee! Le Cinna-swirl! I 'ave 'erd tell of it. Please, what is zis snack? It is a species of "bun," no?*

Dat's right, Franswazz, it's when you find yurself on a train, hungover, locomoting from one failure to de next, perhaps looking for a job or a home, or coming back from failing to get one, and you guzzle a whole bun washed down with a can of Tanora. And den you crap a burning ring of hell in a teeny tiny toilet cubicle with a talking door dat doesn't lock. Ah me... such halcyon days.

After a few circuits of de place we got dizzy, so we plonked ourselves down on a bench and stared at de big board with just one entry to be seen: HEUSTON—KENT 14:00. ON TIME. *On time. Are dey takin de piss or what? Five yawning hours late is more like.* De light fell in dusty golden shafts. You could see motes floating in it, like tiny thoughtful fish. Monkfish? Places like dis station had a way of slowing time enough dat even light fell slow—treacle-thick. Hard to breathe de stuff. Like in de big morgue in de gerontoplex basement. A tomb, a whole city of corpses tucked out of sight, each one an iceberg so cold it slows down time, makes it hard for de living to move on. De clock's second hand struggled through de molasses: t-i-c-k (*pant pant pant*) t—i—c—k (*pant pant pant*) T. I. C. K.

Dis is de grand drag of de Wayke. I don't mean "grand" like *okay so*, I mean *grawwnd*. Like a long velvety cloak. Whatchamacallit? Ermine. A way of making lads look and stop and know who's de high king. Dis is de Wayke dragging its ashes down de long aisle, in whatever form it fancies: dusty light, lazy pigeon-wing flaps, glowing seconds on a big departures board. Dis low sound of droids tapping away on de track is really de *draaaaag* of its sweeping cloak. You will *wait,* it whispers. I am passing, it says. Look, it announces: I am de aisle. I am de plebs gawping, watching it all go by, jaws slack. Who are you? You're nottin. Just jolly well sit here now and *wait,* sonny boy jim. Get dis through yur skull.

No boredom in my halo. Dat's *my* kingdom. No drag dere. Even de flowers sprint in my world. Ideas fire off each other—colouredy darts through a crackling sky. Dere's no cloak in my haloscape. Everything's naked and fast and twitchy and doesn't stop for nottin, boi! No pomp, like. No pomp at all. Never any worry bout things passing. Nottin's passing, only arriving. Everything's new, and even on de dark cycles, when yur scared, or suffering, or whadevvor you need to do to feel quick and alive and here-and-now-ish, yur never bored. Dere's no aisle, no bystanding, no watching something *else* happen, someone else's grand train sweep by. No *know-yur-place!* Sher, you have to find out what yur place is, and den change it, and change it again. A million edgy moths eat all de fancy cloaks in my world.

Solve, explore, invent. Why wait?

T-i-c-k.   T. I. C. K.   Teh. Ih. Ceh. Keh.

I resigned myself: two o'clock would never come. We'd die here in dis station from sheer boredom, and de pigeons would coo our last rites before rifling through our pockets to see what's what. Dey wouldn't get much from me anyways. Like he'd stolen my itch, Zeke pulled a halo from his bag and be-noggined himself.

"Woah!" I said. "Cool yur jets dere, tiger."

"What?" he looks at me, pure innocent, like.

"Yur lighting up here?"

"Why not?"

"What about me?"

"What about you?" He looks genuinely confused.

"You light up and I can go twiddle me thumbs, dat it?"

"Well... you could..."

"We can't both light up, boi! Too dodgy."

"Hmm".

"Yeah, *hmm*. How's it fair you go scaping while I hang round here?"

"A fair point. I'll just half-dome it and play puzzle cube".

I'll just half-dome it and play some puzzle cube. Now, to de uninitiated, dat might sound like fair beans. Thing is, *technically* yur still waykin, but dose basic games you can play in half-dome are fan-feckin-tastic. Dey swallow you up, not a word of zaggeration. You finish a round, yur high as a kite from de connections and you just need more. People who say *Just stop playing* don't know what it's like to score. Tis sweet as *fuuuuudge*. Plus, with Puzzle Cube games like *Molekewl* de solutions you come up with are recorded and some of de high scores are used by brainiacs in labs to invent medicines or new materials, so you say to yurself *How can I stop playing now, sher think of de poor sick bolloxes, who am I to deprive dem of a luvly new protein molecule, dat'd be pure snakey wouldn't it?* And so, if you've got game—and gawd knows I am *good*, boi—you keep playing. I've had to wait for things before (food card, medi-tab, at least three queues to sign up for game tests, of all things) and missed everything cos I said to myself *Just a few rounds of puzzle cube, I'd say,* and got shaken out of it by de janitor trying to close up de building. So when Zeke says he'll sit here playing de puzzle cube while I go swivel, I don't think so. Cos if we both play we run more dan a fair risk of missing de train. And I'm not spending another night in Dublin's fair city. Can't do it. I've de Gettin On Down T'Cork vibe now. *One* of us can cube, and de other can make sure we get de train. And I don't see why muggins here is automatically de wakey watchout. D'y'knaw? I explain dis to Zeke, pure diplomatic like, and he nods for a second, chewing it over. Dat's right, fella, you give it a think, cos Tayto's no slouch. No one puts Tayto on de wakey watch without a second thought. Suddenly he says dead serious: "A duel."

I like it. A duel. Yur stylin, Zeke boi. Stylin! Dis'll kill bout an hour, and even if I lose I'm no worse off dan I am now. Right you be!

We set de ground rules like a pair of dukes with pistols at dawn. He gave me choice of halo—not like dere was any difference, sher. Level four RNA twist jigsaw (can't beat de classics), speed round only (or it'll just go on forever), first to find a valid structure wins de title of Grand High Emperor For De Day and playing rights till midnight. Den it's another speed round and a whole new deal for de next twenty four hours. Love it. Fair. Quick. Final. *And poor Zeke won't know what hit him.* I'm a dab hand at RNA folding. Like Brer Rabbit in de briar patch! Been playing it on de auld handhelds since I was a nipper and when de halo came out sher didn't I only get faster. I remember playing for hours and my Ma forcing me to bed to get some kip and after her kissing me g'night and me snuggling into my blanket all de beautiful patterns rotating and reeling demselves behind my eyelids for yonks until dey spun me to sleep. Gorgeous things. Hard to put down. Remember thinking to myself dat if dere were angels dey'd look like protein molecules spiralling in a dark sky, with invisible hands wrapping you in a warm blanket, invisible lips kissing you goodnight…

Fair duce to Zeke, he was a solid folder, like. But gawd love him he was in no way ready for a Tasmanian devil like myself. Been a while since I'd folded, but absence made me even twitchier-stitchier, and wasn't I only flayking out de solutions left and right. I was like yer man whatsisface… de Hindu lad with a flock of arms flailing this way and dat, or a cognoctopus: a billion tentacles bending one chain after another, zipping up de microcosmos into a thousand neat little validities dat might or might not work out in real life. One minute I'm a nobody sitting on a bench, de next I'm a solution factory, everything I do is just right right right, it's a flow of yesses hoppin one into de next, you can feel de victories building up in cycles making you faster and sharper which only makes more victories, on and on into a great big cyclone and yur surfing up de inside of it in great looping spirals as yur little ape brain fuses with de cloud and you can feel yurself becoming more like just energy, like you *are* de solutions saluting each other: *ah tis yurself! Where've you been? Oh y'know, just hangin out pretending to be dis langer called Tayto.* Underneath it all is de voice: *Who gives a toss if dis could be a real protein or not, tis an elegant suggestion, and if de Wayke doesn't want it den it can go shaft itself cos my strand here is a thing of beauty and no doubt* and d'y'knaw, I find myself in full agreement with dat voice—a good solution is its own reward, sorry to say it now but sod de poor lads in de labs trying to churn out cures or potions or whadevvor it is dey do with dis stuff we fire off to dem at de end of such tournaments, or clacking away in de privacy of a kwery somewhere, unpaid, unloved, unrecognized gaming soldiers, martrys... *saints.*

We're saints, sher! We don't do things for any reason but sheer love of de Scape, to be in de Scape and play in it, our sun shining in our hearts every day cos we have a place to belong. We walk taller dan giants cos we know what play is: tis getting *sharper* and *keener* and *wiser* and *slippier*, being a saint is playing a game with no end, and no pay day, sher money's just an embarrassment left over from when we had to live in bodies and haul shit around all day and swap one thing for another to get grains and meat and threads and roofs and sod all dat bogger crap now, a saint is pure play without end, living in a million stitched solutions to puzzles, and I'm in such flow I can even remark to myself while some other part of me does de work, I can just step outside myself and remember learning as a kiddie dat uracil was formed extraterrestrially—imagine it!— but I still don't know what uracil is cos you don't need to know what it is to *play with de form*—knowledge of what is and isn't is for de professors—saints don't deal in knowledge, we deal in form, we deal in instinct, we're like de natural world, de natural world doesn't know names it just folds and twists and plays itself into new forms, just for de sheer fun of it, and speaking of fun, isn't it a cute hoor who thought to use de halo to hook up de pleasure center to puzzle-solving, wasn't dat just de brightest idea ever? Dat's up dere with sticking your buggy to a horse or using steam to chug a choo-choo, jayz I near forgot I was in a train station how long have we been playing? And as de timer runs out I can see Mr. Zeke Zohar, my worthy opponent, struggling behind my performance by a clear country mile, poor pet, I almost feel sorry for him, but it's time, HIGH TIME, for me to cast off my pleb disguise, and take my place as Grand High Emperor for de day.

"Tayto abú!" I shouted in his face, pulling my half-dome off and snapping back into my small little head so quickly I nearly fell off de bench I'd been slumping on. Zeke's half halo lit down, but he stayed staring straight ahead, not turning to face me at all. Not a word of manly congratulations, like. No smile and firm handshake or *Dowtcha boi,* or *Fair duce, Mr. Tayto, you played a blinder dere,* he just kind of sighed to himself. Den he stood and said: "I'm going to the toilet." It threw me. I'd no chance to be gracious in victory as he stuffed our halos in his bag, pure huffy like, and ponced off to de jacks. *Tsk tsk, such un-Dukelike behaviour, old boy.* Couldn't enjoy my cloak of valor at all now, so I just sat dere, being fucken Tayto.

"C'mere—was dat unsporting now, or is it just me?" I axed a pigeon, but de chubby fecker didn't even look up from pecking at his manky spawg of a claw. After sitting dere like a gom for a while I said *shag dis* and got up to go look for His Nibs. Maybe he was in de stall sobbing to himself. No shame in losing to de best, sher. Isn't it an honour to have even got to play against a class act like me?

Turnstile was broken so I snaked into de jacks for free. It didn't half hum, boi. Smelled like a tramp's posing pouch. My eyes watered straight off, and I waved my hand in front of my face like dere were cartoon clouds of pong I could somehow flap a path through. *De stink of defeat,* I thought to myself. *He's gone to console himself by hiding out somewhere dat smells worse dan de stench of his defeat.* Dark green walls sweated. Heating cranked to 90. Place was a swamp, sound of dripping water plopping from everywhere. If the station outside was de dusty desert de Earth might die as, I reckoned de bog here was how it all started out. Methane jungle. I scansed under de stalls, half-expecting to spot an early amphibian, cautious flippers on tile, feeling out life on solid ground.

His feet were planted right dere in de middle stall. I knocked on his door—no answer—so I stepped onto de bog stool next door to have a chat with my neighbour. And wasn't de blaggard only sitting dere on de throne, halo half-lit, playing again on his own! After our gentlemen's agreement. At first I was fuming, but as I stood dere, peering over de stall into his private game, de pissiness went away, which I spose is a fitting thing to happen in a jacks. It's such a rush to play de game, but to watch someone else play is a different matter. His limp body twitched like a palsy victim, his eyes staring blankly at de cubicle door as his mind saw visions no one else could see. Every so often his fingers'd wiggle, de poor dopey things thinking dey were still needed as his brain spun a scenario around to check all de angles on it. He seemed like a small helpless crayture, like a fetus, not ready to be born yet, slumped and shaking in its box, twitchy and raw and careless of any contracts or deals or anything with anyone. A thing alone.

Who was dis strange fien I was traipsing round with? Who was dis sore loser leaning on me, and I leaning right back on in return, crawling with him—two newborns now—back to de source of my stream? Someone was stomping into de jacks so I hopped off my perch and shot out de door just in time to see it was our buddy of de snazzy cart manuvers, Cyclops de Belly Button.

"Should wash yur hands!" he barked as I brushed past, back out into de great big wide open dry dusty crawling slowness of de station, dat slowness not like a soft baby crawling, but a stiff old old man lost his cane, down on his hands and knees, crawling, rigid, reluctant, down into de cold cold ground.

Got de quietest carriage on a quiet train. Zeke was sulking—sulking! And *he* de welcher! Some species of darkness had infected me too. I get pure down. Sometimes tis just a bit blue, other times black. No pattern, I don't think, just luck of de draw. Everything could be goan banjaxed, all de spinning plates falling round me, fires left right and center and I'll be grand out, no bodder on me. And den something great'll happen (win a folding speed trial, say) and I'll find myself deep in de pit for no reason at all.

Zeke sat across from me, half-doming like he was making a point. *Our bet's nothing to me. I haven't lost to a scumbag like you.* Congrats. More power to you. Scumbags like me don't beat doctors of neurotech at folding. Anybody who's anybody knows dat. I wonder what it's like to be a man of such education, skill, and personal fucken maturity. Every day must feel like an awards ceremony, hah? *I'd like to thank my ma and da, if dey're watching, and of course... Jeebus Himself.*

Train chugged out slow, feeling a bit down itself perhaps, in no mood for another long haul down de length of our great green sod. Iron Duke's stonking jack passed by on our right. Biggest in Europe, 'parently. I couldn't remember de last time I'd got a hard-on myself, but Wellington's massive member never flags. He must be buried under dat mound staring at de instructions on de bottle: *In case of erection lasting more dan four decades, consult a physician pronto.* Heard a tale once, no idea if it's bull, but it's a good scéal. De lads who got together de cash to put up Welly's stone langer (biggest in de WORLD, boi!) had a fund raiser (for adding a few inches to de top?) down in de vault under de pillar. Fancy Dans to a man, dey had a table set up, and chairs, and dined like lords one evening.

Maybe dey were actual lords, I dunnaw. Anyway, everyone had a good knees-up, and when day was done, and all de veeno drained, our Fancy Dans sealed up de place like a pharaoh's tomb, dining table and all. So what? says you. Well, a day or two goes by, and someone notices one of de butlers is missing. Slowly, it dawns maybe... *maybe* de poor bollox got a bit plastered himself, and when everyone stumbled out blind drunk dat night after such a lordly seisiún, de butler got left behind, sealed up to die inside de base of Welly's massive todger.

First saint I met in Dublin told me dat story. I'd just got out of Joov, made my way up to Dublin to try for a job as a scaper. Magine it? No qualifications, no contacts, nottin. Just came up on spec. Like dey were handing out scaping jobs at de station or something. Well, bless my boyish heart. I'd spent my childhood on dat shitty farm, and den my teens in Our Lady's Juvenoplex looking down on de luvvly Lee babbling along like a green fishy maniac, and all de while tapping away on my scaping skills. I was an L7. Remember halo levels? At seventeen years of age, Mr. Tayto was nottin less dan L-fecken-7! Conjure a world from a void. Put layers to it. Eddys to suck you in. Characters, if you wanted dem. I'd do a rake of scenes every week for de lads in my bunk section. Mostly porn, as you might expect, but you'd get a good few who wanted adventure too, and a few needed a laugh. I could do anything. Cartoon universes, nightmare matrices, name it. *You should be a scaper, Tayto boi. No foolin', yur dead good!* Yes, I said. I *am*, amn't I? So dat was dat. From a scrawny kid to an even scrawnier teenager: *What do you do, young fella? I Scape, sir.* Tisn't de best answer to give a guidance counsellor, I grant you, but it's *an* answer—something more dan most of my fellows had to offer.

I Scape. Give a young man a role and he'll fill it. More important dan bread. Sher, what's a young fien without a vision? I mean, maybe it's just me, but a fien without a role is just a scobe waiting to happen, d'y'knaw? Saw it with one fella after another up in Our Lady's. *I'm no good at dis, no good at dat,* and de light in de eyes whittles down into a little pinpoint of angry black, as dense and cold as I reckon dat anti-matter is, out in de far reaches. And den de scobe swagger swells up, arms out to de sides all pure aggro gatch like some mad angry penguin: *C'mere to me! Whatchu lookin at, faaag? Hah?* But not for me, in my little cocoon of skill, like a buddha boy, every day getting a bit craftier, bit savvier, working with de psych-art teacher, Big Macca, every Thursday afternoon, developing "nuance" and "shading." Every week a new discovery. May as well have been a prince waiting for coronation.

I Scape, derefore I am. Not like you… I'm special. You can glug on my back, launch spit balls at me all day every day, gentlemen. But I'm goan to be somebody. Watch. I can feel it in my bones. Dere's a light shines on me even while I'm getting lost in maths class, with Bozo shrieking at me bout some Arab called Al-kwarizmi dat I've never met and should have by now. While ye shiver at night, alone in de dark, I'm warmed in my cot by a certainty beyond all reason. Watch dis space. Even as ye bustle about, all noise and swagger and *Whatchu lookin at, haaah?* I can see ye dwindling away, fizzing out into de reaches of blackest space. But not me. I Scape. I am filled with colour and form. I wield worlds. Watch me in de ages to come, out dere beyond de lesson plans and de endless fucken indoor five-a-side soccer games we have to play for some reason known only to Razor de gym coach with his fag in his mouth and his *you and you: captains,* and me de last team pick so bloody often even *I* start to find de humour in it. Watch. Illuminated saint dat I am, some day de warden, ancient Dr. Finch, with his facial tick, will have me visit and introduce me to de freshers: *Lads, we've a very special guest with us today. Mr. Tayto is de winner of a rake of scaping awards—Edge, Visigoth, OpenSource-VR, Lanier—such honours. I always knew he'd amount to something great. Even when I told him he was barely a smear of excrement, sher he knew it was all in good fun!* And den de fateful day, when you come of age, and dey hand you a cred card with a little score on it, and I didn't party or anything, didn't say bye to anyone (except Macca, who barely looked up at me, just said "work on your proprioception, it's woeful"), I just grabbed my ticket and bucklepped up to Dublin. Like a child, like a stupid daydreaming child, just figured I'd float into some fabulist's office, unannounced, and chuck out a folio of my best scenarios, and let de kudos rain.

And den some langer in Finland develops integrated AI metacircuits and everyone's suddenly a scaping genius. *I Scape.* Yeah, and d'y'go to de jacks by yurself and all? Integrated fucken AI. Everyone's Michelangelo now. Anyone can merge worlds. And halo levels? What are dey? A gammy ladder cobbled together from rods and weeds. Some culchie kid used a ladder once to peer over a wall, get a quick scanse at de world.

What was I bangin on bout? Oh yeah. Dead butler. Buried alive in de Conqueror's cock. Magine it. Waking up in de dark, pure hungover, dry mouth like sand, and just… a wall of black in every direction! Air already thick with must! Scrambling round, walloping yur knee into de fancy dining table, heavy expensive wood, glasses and plates falling—shattering darkness—yur nails scraping a wall once you find one. Scraping and scraping, digging till nails come off, an animal…

My first night in a Dublin kwery I met Qwerty, old know-it-all Qwerty, and de man took one look at me and just knew, and took me under his wing and told me de world was full of things like integrated AI metacircuits coming out at de wrong time. Sher, wasn't de world *mostly* things like integrated AI coming along, new hardware replacing old skillsets, and upending it for some chump who'd put all his chips down? *So be it!* was Qwerty's mantra. *No one's taken your halo, young fella. They just don't give a monkey's what you do with it now, is all.* And with his gravelly voice like a stubborn old mumbly engine grumbling away, he shared de story of de dead butler on my first night. *So be it. Least you're not trapped in the base of some prick monument. You must have passed Wellington's coming into town, well, I say 'monument' but its more correct appellation would be 'testimonial' as Arthur Wellesley was alive when it was made, which is more than can be said for a certain butler I could tell you about, now sit and listen to this…* A hairy, grumbly, mouldy, tweed-wearing encyclopedia. I'd spend de day lighting up with a motley corona of saints, and in de evening Qwerty'd show me where to score food. De city was like a ball of storytwine to him. We'd turn a corner and he'd reach out and yank a legend clean out of de air. Everywhere we looked, *now see that lamppost/ tree/ gargoyle, there's an improbable tale behind how that came to be…* It wasn't a show-off thing for him. More like a deep, constant need, real as de need to light up. Like de sponge of his brain was filling all de time and he needed to wring it out. Like Gertie's udders, our cow when I was a kid, and how if dad was drunk and forgot to milk her she'd get swollen and it looked mad painful and I'd kind of whinge but I was afraid to go near her to milk her cos she was *big* and I was small, and she tended to ignore me anyway and walk off from me, so ma would have to come with de pail and squirt-squirt-squirt. Old Man Querty had story udders, and my job was to milk dem. Ugh. Not de best image, dere. Hairy, tweedy… but den again, it's a fair account, like. *Now there's a story behind that…* Yeah, Qwerty, we know. A story behind everything. Stories behind stories, all de way back to de Big Grunt and de Pointy Finger at de stars.

I thought of my own butler, de jackrabbit. Never thought I'd say it but I missed him. If I died out on an bóthar, he'd go to de crystal forest. Sealed up forever. Cold as deepest space.

And dis is how it is when I'm down—my brain stitches two thoughts together dat have nottin to do with each other, just out of spite or something. How close greatness had felt… even if it was nottin of de sort, coming up here dat bright summer day to Dublin, portfolio burning a hole in my halo, ready to blow de world away. *Almost in my grasp!* And den I woke up. De Wayke let me daydream, led me on day by day, hour by hour, whispering *you can do it, boi, I know you can. You've got de stuff, and by gob you'll go up dere and DO it* and, at de last minute, like a master prankster, it just yanked de carrot away and opened wide with silent laughter and did a little psycho jig with de trash in de breeze at getting me to buy what had never been, and was never to be. And tears suddenly came stinging in my little carriage, sealed off from any trace of disease and death dat might be flying by outside our window, and it didn't feel hard to breathe because de air purifier was on full blast and it was a good unit too. It didn't feel hard to breathe, but it felt hard to want to.

Woke with a start, my cheek smushed into de window. Gorse zipped by outside, yellow blur and a billion green prickles clawing at de glass. Loud cackles spewed and spurted from a teenage couple sitting cross de aisle. I scansed up and down de carriage and saw we were alone with dem. Well, if dey wanted money or something dey were barking up de wrong dog's hole. I was strapped, and Zeke was twitchin away to himself still in his half-dome, paying no mind. For a second I fancied him replaying my solutions, trying to figure how he got his Trinners arse so royally handed to him. Maybe he was just worming, or spinning a chrysalis. Who gives a toss? I did a shrug. De move felt weird. I hadn't done a shrug in yonks. What is it? Shoulders come up to ears and back, big pantomime move all to say just *I dunnknnnaaaaaw*. Shrugs. Stoopid things.

Another blast of gorse lashed at me through de glass. I spied thin scars scrawled across de pane. Jagged streaks of lightning. Someone needs to hack dat gorse back, I'd say. Can see de Iarnród Eireann operative who's given the mission, big shruggy shoulders on him. *I will* yeah, *boi. Hand me some clippers!*

Hate gorse. Hate de word. Big hefty byor with meaty, callusy hands. Huge teeth. Thick flat nose. *C'mere to me! Give GORSE a kiss!* Can't move in dis country but you plod knee deep into a big pile of gorse. One step away from de concrete—wallop! Mouthful of gorse! Teeny tiny pretty little yellow petals and a shitload of vicious green behind. Mean-spirited, dis Gorse. Must work for her too, cos she gets around.

When de couple weren't cackling dey were chewing de faces off each other. Didn't seem dey wanted anything from us, just an audience. Some langers are always *Whassa point of scoring if no one's round to cheer?* She was perched on his lap, slip of a thing, a pretty little ventriloquist dummy—two red dollops of something on her pale cheeks. Red hair worked into manky dreads. Splodges of flaking red on her nails. But from de looks of it she was controlling him, not de other way round. She had her hand on de throttle, opening things up and slowing dem down. He was a long, lanky buck culchie, his legs stretched on and vanished under de opposite seats. Big open face on him. Buzzcut bazzer. Despite de length of him you could tell he was thick as two short planks. Gawd, such a moron laugh—de dumbest husky in de pack, down de back of de sled team where he can't hear de joke but laughs along anyways. *I luv you guys! Hur-hur-hur wag-wag-wag.* Dey didn't fit together, him and her. Glowing lines curled round de jet black of her bodysuit like I seen de young wans wearing up in Dublin. Pure Waker Aktivist paraphernalia, full of its cant about light in de dark, or some such shite. But he looked like something from before de Scythe. Wore a Gaelic Athletics Association jersey. I don't know de county colours. Shame on me. Made me wonder: are dey playing GAA down de country again? Seems risky, like. But if GAA is back, must be a good sign. Dat, or de hardcore Gaa-heads are goan to fire off de next wave of Gombrich swift as a nifty own goal. Gaah.

Dey were ridiculous, dis pair. Children showing off. But something in de light round dem was softer now, like a snatch of spring: two young nobbers dry humping each other. Not beautiful, like, but... Hopeful, maybe. Winter ends, d'y'knaw?

He was relentless with trying to drop de hand and she was brushing him off pure playful, egging him on, like *Keep up yur effort and you never know where you'll get.* She was shrieking and rolling her head when he'd go for a big points zone, and goan *Oh my gawwwd yur such a cheeky monkey! Can't believe you—AHH!—I don't think so, not in yuuuur lifetime—HAAHAHAHA!*

I could feel a pressure building in my head. Her laugh was country cute as a vixen's—I'd say she could run rings round him— but at de higher pitches it was nails on de proverbial board. I screwed my eyes shut and wondered if I had de sack to say: Hey! Keep it down! No, was de short answer. No way was I asking dis huge gom and his bint to shut up. Move seats myself? Dat's de diplomatic route, but naw. Wasn't I here first? Am I not a human being? If you prick me, are you not a prick? Romeo must've put a long digit in de wrong place because I heard a loud slap and glanced to see her looking dead serious now. Stern, like her playacting pup had nipped a bit too hard.

"No!" Index finger right up in his snout. "I mean it now, Mossy." Poor Mossy. His eyes dropped, a humbled mutt. She hopped off him, fired herself cross de aisle and plopped into de seat next to me. *Ah Christ no.* I'd brought dis on myself by looking in deir direction. Never look at anyone, sher.

"Alright Mossy. For that now I'm going to shack up with this sexy karoo."

She bent over double at dis. What's so hilarious, hah? I may be no Mossy, but a body's got feelings. She grabbed my arm, green eyes flaring. Made me flash back to fluorescent flames I'd put in a hellscape once. Dat was a fine hell. A masterwork.

"You don't mind me being your new muffin now, do you, pork chop?" She was panting like she'd run a mile, and she smelled of some kinduv candy."Call me Gus."

"Sorry about her, old fella!" Mossy called from his seat. *Old fella. I'm twenty feckin two, Mossy boi.*

"Don't you be apologizing for me at all!" she said, still boring into me with her hellgreen eyes. "I'm not yours to be speaking for." She leaned in and twirled a finger around my ear. "I'm with a serious older man now."

"Yeah, good on ya. Hope he buys you a diamond ring. Ride him raw and send me a postcard." He whips a handheld from his pocket—poor child! A handheld!—and starts playing de most noxious game imaginable. Beeps and jingles to beat de band. In fact, a brass band would have been more welcome. Goms like him eat dat shite up with a spoon: revving engines, exploding pots of gold, a hedgehog rapping in Japanese. Dis, to Wakers, is a "game." So pathetic I can't even dwell on it. A small screen for small minds, tinny sounds banging away relentless, and grainy visuals dat'd hurt yur eyes: same stretch of road, or battlefield, or coliseum again and again. Kill kill kill. Drive drive drive. Using *thumbs*, for gawd's sake… stumpy little monkey digits for holding sticks and stones and breaking bones. Jabbing away trying to win fucken *points*. How dense is dis shower of Wakers? To turn away from de great pulsing waves of our haloscape—de great, loving Halo, which accepts everyone, and lets dem melt and flow right into de spirals of demselves until dey aren't demselves anymore, but, like, just… *more*. Way more. How can you play a"game" as yurself after you've touched de cloud? Stay in yur long lanky culchie GAA jersey staring cross-eyed at a puny screen? It's pure blasphemy, isn't it? I don't say it much, cos I don't like waxing sanctimonious now to be fair, I *don't*, but a mouth's got a moral duty to call a spade a spade: tis *sacrilege*, dis little screen stuff. Pure and simple. Game is our highest calling. Game is what we were born to play, to drag ourselves up out of our bog, rise up out of our bones, and join de great always-unfolding-and-refolding waves of Game. Forget yur mammy and daddy, and yur brothers and sisters down on de farm: dis is de call. Game. Now and forever. And de more I coggled it, de more I found myself hoping, in a fierce strong way dat bordered on prayer, dat whadevvor de state of Yogi when—*if*—we found him down in Cork, dat de Crown would be glowing away, and Zeke and me'd have a chance to build ourselves one each, and kiss our own meatbag jerseys away for good.

Mossy hit another pot of gold and *yesss*-ed to himself. I considered what blunt trauma my body might suffer diving from a moving train. Would clumps of gorse break a fall?

"Now," she leaned her head on my shoulder, easy as if we were newlyweds, "what are we up to tonight, chicken?"

"You talk a lot bout food," I said, leaning back from her. "You hungry or something?"

"Always." Her candy breath curled round me. "Why do you ask? Got any meat on you?" She squeezed my thigh. 'Terror' is too strong a word, like, but I felt something in roughly dat flavour. De auld pump got fluttery. Sweats. I'm 'sposed to put word after word in real time to natter away with her? Twas all a bit *much*, d'y'knaw? I'd no stomach for getting on de wrong end of a tool like Mossy, himself growing darker by de second across de narrow aisle from us, sliding down deeper into de big slumpy head on him to de choon of his manic looping soundtrack, one eye roving out over his cheating queen. Another rake of gorse lashed de window.

Zeke shivered. I'd nearly forgotten he was with me. When I'm worried my vision tunnels up. Always struck me as a curious bad adaptation for survival. Suddenly I was grateful for Zeke, de soppy nob. He was kinduv moral support, if only in de abstract, like. I kicked his shin, but he just shifted a bit in his seat.

"We've company, y'lout", I said.

"Friend of yours?" Gus nodded at Zeke. *Erra naw, girl. On empty carriages I like to sit with strangers. Much like yurself, you crazy gant.*

Almost as soon as I realized de loony choons cross de aisle had gone dead, Mossy was upon us. He lurched into de final free seat, next to Zeke.

"This is fierce cozy," he said, rubbing his hands together. *Aw yeah, dis is de bit where you lace into me for yur auld doll pawing me, and she puts up a lame "Ah Mossy no!"but really she's soppin herself at de sight of her fella leddering a beta and reminding her little chimp brain why she picked Big Mossy in de first place. Slaps, boi. Here come de slaps!*

But no. Almost instantly he flashed me dat slack-mouthed smile of his, and I relaxed. He had slow eyes. Like a cow. Not to be funny or mean or nottin, comparing him to a cow. Just he had big brown marbles floating around dere next to his nose whereas his byor had quick small darting cursors. His were kinduv sad. And den didn't he pull out cans for everyone and lob one at me. I grabbed it automatically.

"Hey! Giving away my tinnies?" she snapped. He seemed shocked, and dat satisfied her. "Ah go on so!" she grinned. "If de Hulk here's going to be my new karoo I'll have to limber him up a notch."

"Is yur name really Gus?" I axed.

"Aisling," she muttered, suddenly shy. "I prefer Gus."

I slugged de beer. Pisswater.

"What's his story?" Mossy nodded at Zeke. He didn't mean it like a loaded question, but it felt dat way when I realised I didn't have an answer. *Fire me de question again in a few days and I'd let you know.*

"Lookitim!" he snorted again. "Spazzin away to himself. Are you bringing him back to his ward or what?!" His girl approved his effort at a zinger. She stretched out her leg and planted her spawgeen right into his crotch, wiggling it happily, like feeding her parrot a bit of cracker when it said something right.

Mossy hur-hur-ing at Zeke as he slogged his way through a dense puzzlemine was a bit like de village idiot sneering at a math whiz for cracking code when, sher, he could be getting shitfaced down de local! With all de lads! *Hur-hur-hur... nurd.* Twas pig ignorant, no mistake. And yet, de mean spirits in me wanted to sneer at Zeke too with everything I had. For getting a position in de world, even if only for a while. For being listened to by smart fiens who made things happen. For speaking like he knew he'd be listened to, expected to be listened to, with de big poncey head on him. For knowing my brother probly better dan I did. For his clothes, made from fancy bio-fibers. For having seen a bit of de globe, and for his kinduv cool accent. For my needing him to help me go home, like a kiddie clutching a blankie, a proxy brother to help me find my real one, who in truth scared de life out of me more dan anything cos he was such a deep dark unknown like dose spots in ocean chasms where impossible weird fish live impossible lives in impossible caves. Worst of all, I hated de fact I admired Zeke Zohar because it was his mission we were on. I'd a sneaking suspicion I was his sidekick, and not de other way around.

I was so tangled up about dis Zeke Zohar fien, and goan home, and what might be waiting for me dere, I didn't know what to do with myself. I just wanted to do something simple. And dere's nottin simpler in dis life dan de *sneeeer,* so sneer away I did. Maybe he'd hear me, maybe not. Sher, I'd be happy either way.

"Yeah, he's my cousin," I said. "Fraid of de train, like. De rocking makes him pure nervous." Dey sniggered more. "Not to mention de sheep out de window. Give him de heebie-jeebies."

"Sheep!" Aisling-Gus shrieked, spilling beer on my leg and wiping it off. "Go away!"

"Gospel. Too woolly, he says. I've to haul him down from

Dublin to Cork to marry someone. He's bricken it. A huge virgin. So I had to let him hide in his halo for de trip."

"Someone marrying him?" Gus axed. *"Lucky girl!"*

"Who said it was a girl?"

"Only half that yoke is lit up," Mossy observed, fierce astute.

"Yes sir. Right you be. He's afraid of droppin fully into a Scape. Everything scares him. I can't underscore dis enough." Dey laughed again.

"Shite, does he have any nuts at all?" Mossy supped on his can, pure mystified.

"Nope. Just plays his little games, bless him. But I think we'll be okay once we get him back home and tuck him up in his auld bed. With his toys and his teddies and whathaveyou. Like de good old days." And as I said it I envied Zeke his privacy, his long clean line of unbroken concentration.

"No label on dis beer," I said. "What's it calling itself?"

"Carpay Deeyum." Mossy held up his can. "S'good, izzn't it?!"

Carpay Deeyum. Dat was some Waker glyph doing de rounds. I'd seen it on walls all over. Wakers, boi. What a toxic dose. You don't want to be a saint? *Fine.* More power to you. But why you feel de need to impose—no, *inflict*—yur values on others is beyond me. So now dere's official Waker slopwater. Woop-dee-doo. It tastes like yur ideas: shite.

"It's Waker," Gus said.

"Is it now?"

"No waste on bullshit logos or marketing. It's all grassroots. Word of mouth." She nodded, no hint of de giggling now. *Important stuff.*

"Yeah, all profits go to the cause." Mossy. Bless.

"De cause?" Me letting on I was clueless.

"Been living under a rock?!" she rapped my head with her knuckles, none too gentle. That's more of it now! No respect for boundaries. I leaned away from her.

Mossy was only wriggling to explain: "See, Carpay Deeum is Greek... or is it Latin? Anyway, means, y'know, get up out of it now and stop hiding!"

"Yah, stop playing with yourself! We've got a future to build!" she chimed back to her luvvah, one unified head case echoing to itself. Mossy threw up his arms and whooped: *yeh-hup-yeh-HOO!* It was all I could not spew my manky beer all over him.

Even de girl seemed put off by his display. Mossy wagged a long sanctimonious finger at Zeke, a man I envied more by de second.

"Wake up! Throw your old headcages away!" He looked back at me. "Y'know? What have you got to lose?!"

What have I got to lose? Mmm. Good question, Mossy. I spose, off de top of my head, a body might be afraid of another Great Scythe sweeping through our fields, cutting down wave after wave of family, friends, lovers, neighbours, and all our random butchers, bakers, and candlestick makers. A body might already be stained up inside with memories dat never fully wash out, of a mother hawking up blood in de middle of de night, screaming her kids be taken away quick before dey see de vicious, rigid smile dat comes at de end, and how she'll tear at de skin on her face and hands because it itches and burns so bad she'd rather flay de skin off dan leave it be. A body might be scared of what way our country's turning, with gangsters and gombeen men clearly running de show, raping our frightened, frozen, invalid of a nation day after day wearing de same big terrifying grin again, but more frightening now cos on dese monsters de grin is actually a sign of fucken glee. What have we got to lose? Sher, what haven't we lost already? Our sense of home, our hope, de feeling we belong on dis ball, our trust de soil won't try to eat us tomorrow, or our wells won't turn to dust. Or, more personal, like—and I can only speak for myself here now—I might just be scared of ending up a delirious lobotomy patient like yur good Waker self, with yur everything's-grand-now-jersey and I-dodged-a-bullet-so-I-guess-I'll-live-forever hard-on, and yur thick-as-pigshit fucken driving game. As for what I have to lose when I throw away my "headcage," let me see: our most mind-expanding technology ever invented? De greatest artform man has ever experienced? A path out of my puny head? Near unlimited doorways to senses and insight you'll never know and are either too chickenshit or too brainwashed or too criminally incurious to even try, you unbearable lanky Scape-virgin twatpocalypse?

"We've got a future to build, babe!" Mossy fired her slogan back at her. She smiled back, another little cracker held out to de birdbrain.

"How long have ye two been goan out?" I cared so little it made me sick to ask, I just needed dem to stop talk about building de fucken future together.

"Oh," Mossy smirked, "we just met! At Heuston."

"What, today?"

"We just…" Mossy dug for de poetry: "clicked." I could feel de watery swill rising up my gullet again. Steady. *Steady.*

"You have to take risks," he continued. "Carpay…"

"Deeyum!" says she.

"Seriously, he's got to wake up." Mossy was pointing at Zeke again.

"Oh yeah? Why's dat now?"

"Cos if he doesn't…" Mossy hitched up his jersey. A small scar ran up his ribs. "…he'll never live. Never get a scar. Girls love a scar."

Like dey were acting out a scene, she leaned toward him and—out with de tongue—licked slow, deliberate up de length of his scar. Wonder what she'd make of de warzone I'd seen on Zeke's back.

"Getting hungry again, sweetheart?" Mossy leered. "C'mere, I've something to feed you in de jacks." Dey grabbed all de stuff and upped demselves.

"Good luck with your friend there," Aisling-Gus winked back at me. Maybe it was my magination, but I could swear she rolled her eyes, like *sorry bout dis tool I'm with.* As soon as dey left de car, Zeke lit down.

"He's feeding her something in de jacks," I explained. "Doesn't sound too clean, does it?"

"Insufferable people," Zeke sighed, like he was de one had to deal with dem.

"Well, dey're young." Don't know why I was defending dem.

"Yes, *well,* carpe diem is Latin. And it's from Horace. And the full quote is *carpe diem, quam minimum credula postero.*" He waited for me to beg him to translate, professorial prick dat he was, dangling his nugget o'knowledge over me. I kept schtum and he ploughed ahead anyway: "Pluck off the day, placing as little trust as possible in the future."

Huh. I pictured plucking all de yellow flowers off de gorse, leaving only de vicious green spikes. *Place as little trust as possible in de future.* I loved it! Like, de latter part of dat saying is exactly what a saint would fire back at one of dese optimistic Waker wankers. *Fuck yur future, langers!* Good man Horace, whoever you are when yur at home!

"I'll say dis for you, Zeke boi: You know yur Greek."

"Latin."

Christ, whadevvor.

All dis choo-chooing and nattering to randomers had me flaahed. An adventure in de Scape has you rearing for more by de end, but traipsing in de Wayke is pure stressful. I conked out again and got shaken awake by Zeke. Twas dark outside. De train was stopped, but we weren't in Kent station.

"Where are we?"

"I don't know," Zeke said, scansing round, agitated. "Not Kent." A cleaning woman was coming down de car, dragging her trash bag with her, hair cinched back all severe. She stopped to collect de cans de Love Connection had left behind.

"Scuse me, love. Where are we?"

"Just past Mallow," she rolled her eyes at me, pure thick accent on her. From Eastern Europe, you'd know by her face. Almost too good-looking, but harsh. What is it about these wans and de hump? What goes on on dat side of Europe dat has deir pantaloons in a perma-twist? "Typical! Train always…" She blew a loud razza and stuffed de cans away.

"Dey're not ours," I felt de need to say. She looked at me like *pull de other one,* and took my nearly full can from my hand without a word. I'd been clutching it like a knob and was glad to be rid of it.

"Uh, be stuck here long, y'think?"

"Let me check magic rubbish bag!" She stared into de brúscar like a gypsy fortune teller: "I see *looonnnng* delay… followed by no refunds… and I have to call my boyfriend for lift back to Cork to put my baby to bed." She offered me a look in too, and like a wally I craned my head toward de bag. She shut it fast, and dragged it away down de car. Sorry I didn't have any silver to cross her palm, or whadevver fortune tellers are charging dese days.

A mumbled message spluttered out over de speaker system. Think it was in de new official language of Irish Rail: Swahili. Whadevvor it was bangin on bout, a minute later de doors opened and passengers gatched along de tracks past us, suitcases in hand.

Me and Zeke made our way down a slippy embankment to de road. Nottin against glamorous Mallow, like, but we hadn't reckoned on staying a night dere. Our "plan," if you could call it such, was to get a room in Cork somewhere near de station, get good and lit up, and next morning rent scooters or de like and flayke out to de sticks to see what we could see in Lord Tayto's ancestral home. But naw, sher dat'd be too simple. Instead here we were, by de side of a road at nightfall, not a clue between us. I heard a rumble in de black sky. Praise be—a storm looked on de cards too. And den I saw her in de distance: Aisling-Gus, her Waker get-up curling dazzling lines in de dark. Dunnaw why, but I started drifting toward her like she was a beacon, and den I noticed she was moving toward me too. Mossy was trailing her.

"Alright dere, Aisling-Gus."

"It's just Gus", she said. "You never gave us your name."

"Tayto. Dis is Zeke."

"Welcome back to the land of the living!" Mossy made a big deal of shaking Zeke's hand. De sky rumbled again, more bolshy now, and Mossy tried to wrap his gangly frame round Aisling-Gus like a rickety old scaffolding.

"What? Tis cold!" he snapped when she tried to squirm away.

"I told you, I'm fine!"

"Trains, eh?" I muttered.

"Nothing works anymore," she said, looking me in de eye again. "I've people coming to collect us. Need a lift?"

I was giving dis a good coggle when Zeke just put his arm around me and frogmarched me down de road a few feet. For some reason I felt mortified, like here was my stepdad embarrassing me in front of an auld doll.

"Let's order a cab. It won't cost too much," he said. Dere was fear in his eyes, but a bossy old tone in his voice all de same.

"Lookit boi, it's goan lash down in a few minutes, and d'you see any taxis doin de rounds?"

He granted a car hadn't passed, not to mind a taxi, but I could see him crestfallen (see his crest, it was *fallen* like) at de prospect of staying with dis couple another minute. I sympathized. He'd only just got over his fogs; I don't wanna *know* what dat Gubna thing was about, and he wasn't falling over himself trying to fill me in; he'd had his arse handed to him in our little duel (and I mean on a *platter*, boi); and now dese two Waker pups to contend with, who'd in fairness been ripping de piss out of him half de way from Dublin. And worse dan piss-taking, way worse, dey were shifting into preach mode. Waker preaching is something despicable. All dese gnats who didn't get splattered on de windshield of history, getting to live a gnatty little life a split second longer because dey were two inches to de left at de moment of truth, and dey get all joyous bout deir *calling*, as if missing dat windshield means dey were chosen by a higher power! How big a wanker do you need to be to buy into such a back-slapping crock of crap? And why should a "calling" mean chucking yur halo? *Put away childish things*, dey say. Fuck you and yur *childish things*, boi. Who's to say de Scape isn't why we're here in de first place? Maybe de little gnat body dey're so proud of prancing round in and celebrating is some kinduv bad dream we're supposed to be waking up from! *Dey're just so goddamn certain bout everything it drives me...* But enough. Aren't we big boys? So we put up with some woeful sermons on de ride into town. Get over yurself! Bit of Waker propaganda and we've a free ride out of it. No bodders!

I glanced back at de love connection. Trouble in paradise, I'd *say*: Mossy was hunched down to hear her, and she wagging her finger like de clappers. *Ooohhh Mossy boi, you've a handful dere and no mistake.* More ructions up in de clouds. Over yonder I saw a forked tongue dart out, lick de sleepy hills and light dem up.

We all fell dead quiet waiting for de lift. Mossy seemed well put out, slumping on de side of de road with his head in his hands like he'd been told his dog was dead. Zeke lay down and lit up—for a change, like. I stayed on my feet and kept watch. Wouldn't trust a pair of Wakers not to get up to mischief round a pair of lit-up saints. Plus, for some reason, dunnaw why so don't ask, I didn't want Aisling-Gus to know about my saintly ways. So me and her stood around together, but no talk. Like we were floating in a bubble in space, and de quiet was de only thing holding our atmosphere in. If anyone popped it we'd all suffocate in a vacuum.

Aisling-Gus started to dance, lazy and slow at first, but getting fierce involved as de lightning got bigger, brighter, closer. Her glowsuit flashed too, pure impressive whenever she broke into a one-arm handstand or threw de auld spin kick. At first she was a flicky bit of ribbon, but soon she was liquid light. She flipped into backbends easy as you please, like she was moving underwater. So free, just playing with gravity. *She's not from round here*, I thought. *Dis wan's visiting from a better place. She's just pretending to be one of us.*

And den I caught myself. *Careful, Tayto. Tell de dancer from de dance. She moves well, but she's still a muppet. Don't get confused now.* Fair duce to her, all de same. Never saw someone dancing to speed up time before. It worked! I stared at her de whole wait, and just as de rains started to feck down on us, around de corner came headlights. Twas one of dem yokes you cobble from a kit—a velopod. An egg with wheels. Popular enough up in Dublin, but strange to see in de sticks. It slowed to a stop, bangin choons from inside. I yanked Zeke's halo and we all piled in as de rain spat down, hissing with frustration it had just missed drowning us.

I wasn't half inside dat bloody egg before I regretted it. One look at de driver had me ready to wail with remorse. Wasn't it only Foxy Mulligan, and hadn't he only expanded since I'd seen him last. *Burly*, he used to call himself. Go way with yur "burly" boi, de big bullfrog bolg on ya. J'ever meet a pie you didn't get on with? Typical, like. Dare to set yur foot in fecken Mallow, Mitchelstown or Macroom, and one way or another you run into a gobshite like Foxy Mulligan—curse of de Corkiverse. Perched next to Roly Sir Poly was some manner of sidekick, a wiry, weasel-faced scobe with nervy hands. Kept flipping a razor blade round his fingers scary fast.

"Alright Guzza, gizza kiss!" Mulligan bellowed over de choons. Mossy was all bent out of shape as Aisling-Gus shoved past him to greet Mulligan, a squeal of delight out of her, like kissing de blobby bollix was just candy Christmas come early.

"Foxy, you're a grade-A *legend*!"

"No bodder, girl. Anything for Guzza, like. Who're dese nobbers you've caught in yur net!"

I had my hand half over my face, on de off chance Mulligan wouldn't recognise me. Helpful, Aisling-Gus fecked herself into my lap and hurled her arm around my neck.

"This hunk of muscle here is my new karoo!" she said, pure wired suddenly. "And this is... what is it your name was again?"

"It really doesn't matter," said Zeke, staring past her at me in a *I told you dis was a bad idea* way. De fear had him tight now. Didn't know what to say to him. How was it my fault? Sher, you never know what sort of surprise you'll find in an egg. I just shrugged at him again. Gettin handy with de auld shrugs. Maybe dey weren't so stoopid after all.

"I'm Mossy, by the way, and there's plenty more room on my lap than his."

His big slow cow eyes strained at her. She was a waif, but I wasn't used to any weight on me. My legs hurt something awful, and I wished she'd throw Mossy a bone and plonk her arse down on him for a while.

"Well Guzza girl," Mulligan said, "Let me introduce Blades. From de Togher chapter."

"S'up?" says Blades, twitching a kinduv greeting from behind his razor.

Den Mulligan turns off de choons, pure dramatic: "I know yur face!" He's fixed straight at me. "You Lofty's cousin?" Silence roars all over de egg.

"Naw, boi," I say, trying to manuver Aisling-Gus to block my face even more. "Don't know any Loftys now."

"*Sure?*" Mulligan squinted at me. "I'm good with faces." Way he said it, twas like a threat. Thought he'd drop it, but he kept squinting at me, and now Blades was at it too, like he'd be able to remember for his buddy.

"What's dis yur name is?" Mulligan pressed.

"Tayto!" Aisling-Gus blurts out. "Are ye friends? That's gas!"

"Tayto…" Mulligan's doughy face melted—if you could say it wasn't melted already—into a big leering grin, and he slapped his hands like he'd cracked a code. "Dat's it! Tayto boi! Foxy! Foxy Mulligan! From Our Lady's Joov!"

I'm no actor, like, but I put on de show of my life for dat pudgy bollox. *Awww yyyeaah Foxy boi, aww I knew yur face too but wasn't sure blah blah blah* and all de while I was nearly drowning in de flood of memories—Mulligan pinning my face to my pillow and farting down onto it for all he was worth (de man was a human alpine horn, like, long deep honks dat filled de room), and swanning over to us in de canteen to swipe whadevvor we were trying to eat—yeah, twas manky enough slop, but hunger is hunger—and just grabbing it, taking nearly de whole thing off in one big gaping *NYOM* and saying, pure polite like, "Munch of dat dere." *Munch of dat dere.* I wouldn't be surprised if he had de phrase tattooed over his gut in Celtic lettering. He's de kind of beast de Wayke *loves*, a tube more dan anything else, a tube with a butthole at one end and a mouth at de other—a mouth dat just takes and takes and keeps getting bigger and smugger, snatching what it wants, left right and center. A great powerful appetite dat never gets sick, not at its own gluttony nor at anything else, just keeps gorging and ripping into de flesh of de world, filling de tube, working its way up de food chain till it's sitting at de very top, pinning everyone to de pillow and farting away to its heart's content. *Munch off dat dere*. I defy you to find a swine dat cries out more to be spit-roasted and fed to de poor, with a shiny red apple stuffed in its gob. But naw: everything has to be backwards and upside down in de Wayke, so instead dis is de lad who gets to host de feast, and it's de scrawny prawns who get cooked. *Nyom nyom nyom... luvvly*. Never any kind of a teacher or monitor around to put a halt to his gallop. Cos in de Wayke, monsters somehow get to be invisible, or at least everyone gives dem de blind eye. To be fair, Foxy Mulligan taught me a valuable lesson at Joov (more dan can be said for most of de teachers or psych-techs): big fish eat de little ones, so if yur smart get out of de water quick as you can grow legs.

He held my eye till I said it: "Foxy, boi... great to see you again." Dat was de tap out. Still pinning my head to de pillow, I spose. He heard it, smiled, and took de wheel again, choons back on full tilt. No surprise he'd be driving a top-of-de-line velopod with a girl in de back squealing happily at de sight of him. I pictured jealous Mossy mashing him to spud or turnip or jelly—or whadevvor Foxy Mulligans are made of—and pasting him all round de inside of his own smug eggmobile. Now dat's a sight would be worth de price of a rail ticket.

"Whatcha think of de ride, lads?" Mulligan blared back at us. "Smooth little number, la?"

I hated to say it, but de langer was right. Even compared to de train, which barely rolled in its tracks, dis velopod—even with Mulligan's shite choons rattling away—just flew on a cloud, humming low over de gentle globe of de earth as it curved toward Cork, and whadevver waited for us dere. Maazing shocks on her, I'd say. De shell was probly lighter dan Mulligan himself, fashioned from some kinduv see-through carbon. No clue how it operated (what else is new?) but you could see out easier dan see in, and soon my home city lights and de goldy fish atop Shandon steeple glowed like in a dream, or an old storybook. Lightning tore ribbons out of de sky, but de thunder we barely heard through de pod's shell. It was like being in a see-through womb, warm and round regardless of who you might be unlucky enough to share it with. Funny dat de smoothest ride I'd had would be driven by de brashest prat I knew. But again, dat's de Wayke's idea of a nifty joke. Mulligan is yur ferryman back up de Lee. Ha ha. *Classic*.

We floated alongside de river, right into our city's heart. Twas quiet enough, but we slowed to a crawl for some reason. Coming up to Pa'na, we passed De Vic.

De Vic, where all us Joov scobes used to mope once huffers were installed and we were old enough to get out for an afternoon. I'd go even when I didn't want to, proving to myself I could hang with other lads. De Vic's downstairs was all laser park and vids and noise and knacker byors gossiping and de odd wan trying to flirt, but upstairs was like something from granddad days. Just de flat felt of billiard tables, long cool lights shining down on each green plane, darkness between dem. Quiet like a field at dusk. A weird room: a blister pack of rectangular Irelands, all floating in space. No people, no buildings or junk, just field after flat green field.

I never played—don't like games with my hands—but I watched others dusting off cues, stooped like hunters, heads low to de spear, planning de next angle. Everything in life depending on just a few ounces of pressure to de left or right. A whole world of winning and losing, glory or wankerdom, played out on whether yur arm was twitchy or cool dat split second, on whether. you took de extra breath or not before tapping de white ball into action—*pock*—and once it was off, sher, dere was nottin to do but watch it all roll out, too late to change anything.

No teachers up in de billiards room. No cops. Nottin but de Game, and a bunch of skinny hunters chasing it. And me, of course, watching from de sidelines.

"Ready lads?" Mulligan yelled suddenly, yanking me out of my *reelin-in-de-years* showreel. I was suddenly back in his eggmobile, floating down de quays. "Let's raise de dead!" He poked his tainment system and pointed cross de river. Suddenly images of de departed, all claimed by de Scythe, went trotting along de buildings facing us from de other side. Twas all a projection spewing out of our own pod: De Taoiseach-before-last, and her Tánaiste (both daycent Munster women), and many great Cork hurlers, and Súgradh and Rí Rá (de class-act glyphers, not de shitehawk rappers), and even old Roycroft, de storyteller, all out of de soil and back to rude health, gatching fast down de quay, twenty feet tall, a parade of good folks, reminding us of, well, not *good* times, but times before dese times. I stared out through de shell at de glowing parade, watching as familiar faces mutated into cartoon ghosts, monsters, ancient heroes of de Fianna, on and on, dead arisen. Twas funny, cos floating down the streets of Cork, bunched in between de living in Mully's egg, I felt more like a ghost dan ever before.

Zeke didn't seem much impressed—well, it'd pack no nostalgia for him, I spose, big immigrant head on him—but Mossy de culchie pushed past me to gawk at it better.

"That's fucken *mmmental!*" was his verdict. "Did you make those glyphs, Mr. Mulligan?"

De notion Mully was any good at art made me want to whoop with laughter.

"Naww boi, dat's my man Blades here." He pucked Blades in de shoulder and Blades winced and twitched at us again—his idea of a stage bow, I'd say.

"Blades," said Aisling-Gus gently, leaning over and stroking his sore shoulder, "that is some talent. Truly beautiful." Blades didn't shift, but his hard features just... how would you say it? Just for a second he looked like he'd been told he was *definitely* goan to heaven when de final trumpet sounded. And Mossy looked like he'd just been told de opposite. I sat between both parties, de Saved and de Damned, with de angel perched on my lap, boring a warm crater down into my crotch.

"Guzza, dat's *nottin* girl!" Mulligan bawled. "Wait till you see what we have planned for de silo!" He held up a black bag. "Glyph show is just a warm up. *Dis* is de real deal, girl." Something bout dat black bag, clutched in Mulligan's mála hand, made me feel craw sick.

Mulligan killed de choons and projector. Our pod floated to a stop on Pope's Quay, just before St. Mary's. De church was a halo silo, one of de oldest in Cork. It'd been supplying citizens with tech since before I'd moved to de Juvenoplex up de river, before I'd made best buds with pure *legends* like Foxy Mulligan.

"This is good here, Mr. Mulligan," said Zeke, stiff as a cat in a crate full of dogs. "Thank you for the lift. I think Mr. Tayto and I will be fine on our own from this point on." He tried de hatch by his side. Nottin doing. He tried again, more agitated. Still no budge. Our driver turned round to him, huge face dead set, blank.

"Where d'you think yur goan, saint?"

Zeke started to answer but Mulligan just said, "Shut yur hole!" De way he said it, sure enough, Zeke puckered his hole up right tight. Both holes, probly. Blades took de black bag and unzipped it, hauling out three metal cannisters. He handed one each to de girl and Mulligan and kept one for himself.

"Are they… what I think they are?" Aisling-Gus said softly, getting a heft of de container in her hand. It had a bio-haz warning smacked on it. "Is it finally ready?" Something like a smile was breaking out on Blades's face, but twas strangled—his face wasn't used to it, didn't like it, and didn't know what to do with a good feeling.

"Once word gets out bout this," grinned Mulligan, "we really will be legends." He stroked his cannister and gave it a loving peck.

"What's going on?" axed Mossy. I felt like shaking de culchie nobber. Aisling-Gus just cradled his long face in her hands and kissed him full on his lips.

"Do you trust me, karoo?" His big brown eyes drifted from me to Zeke in search of some kind of guidance. Finally he nodded, flummoxed. "And do you trust our cause?" she pressed, holding his cheeks and boring her green lightning eyes into his poor bovine brain. He nodded again. "I knew I could trust you," she whispered, and kissed him again. Then she grinned at me and Zeke. "Lads… enjoy the show!" With dat, Blades, Foxy and herself launched outside, shut de hatch behind dem, sprinted up to de silo, and disappeared inside.

"What was *that* about?" said Mossy, mystified when he should have been fucken bricken it. He squinted out at de grey walls of St. Mary's, like he'd forgotten how to use X-ray vision. Poor gom couldn't see de light if it was shining off Lex Luther's baldy dome. Zeke didn't bodder speaking, just lay back and started slamming his little stick legs at de reinforced carbon shell, a yoke dat could handle a few tonnes of impact.

"Ah hey hey! What are you doing? You'll mark the shell," cried Mossy.

"I'll mark the shell?" said Zeke, so stunned he actually stopped kicking. He sat up, trying to get a handle on dis lummox of a child. "I'll mark the *shell?*"

"Look, I'm not *stupid*," began Mossy, trying to sound grown up, but before he could continue Zeke grabbed his face like Aisling-Gus had done a few seconds before.

"No, you look! Mossy, is it? Mossy, if you are not in a full panic right now, I'm going to have to dispute the last assertion you made." He went back to kickin de shell from a fresh angle.

"It's not about being smart or dumb," was Mossy's next pearl.

"I think you'll find it frequently is," said Zeke between kicks.

"It's a matter of *faith*." Mossy raised his pompous voice over Zeke's stamping. "Gus is... someone really special. She *stands* for something, something good. She wants to help. Her friends are on a mission. She explained already. She's asked me to trust her." He finally knocked Zeke's legs to de floor and pinned dem. "And I do!"

De weight of Mossy only made Zeke more frantic. "That silo is a state-owned facility! Whatever they have planned in there— *whatever their benevolent intent*—is a terrorist act. Those bio-haz cannisters could contain anything. They might be poisoning public halos. My god..." he froze, thinking it through for himself. "We could be looking at the deaths of thousands of people."

"But Gus wouldn't do that," said Mossy, starting to sound uncertain.

I tapped him on de shoulder: "You mean de byor you just met in Heuston station and don't know from Eve? You mean de little scut who just wound you round her pinky in ten minutes, and den spent a velopod jaunt driving you nuts by sitting on mine? Who just left you trussed up in a shell with two other turkeys like us? We're all to trust her?"

Mossy's brows knitted. I could almost *hear* him trying to sift all dese awkward bits and bobs we'd dumped into de mossy drinking trough of his brain. *Pretty girl... got a handshandy off her in de jacks... shared some beer with me... but I am locked up in a see-through egg right now, outside a crime scene, so dere's daaat...*

"Bit of perspective, Mossy boi!" I snapped. "We're in it up to our gullets—we get caught here, with dose three bell-ends... Like, messing with public halo silos is twenty years, isn't it Zeke?"

"At LEAST!" squawked Zeke, getting shriller by de second. And den he dove into Mulligan's driving seat and started hotwiring de pod. Mossy let him off, slumping back, pure consternated. He stared out at de silo. Even now you could see he was hoping she'd return and reward him for his trust. For his blind faith. More likely we'd get a visit from gardaí, a few hours' interrogation in a windowless room, and den blamed anyway for whadevvor dat fat bastard cooked up to amuse himself dis evening.

Wow. Not a half hour back in Corcaigh, and Mulligan was

unloading on me all over again. I could almost smell it.

"Can you spark it?" I axed Zeke.

"It's a weird homemade effort. Might take a few minutes." He'd barely finished his breath when we heard a loud snap. Zeke screamed and reeled in pain. A calm synth voice over de speakers: *Please don't try to steal me, bitch*. Posh English voice and all, pure proper, like it was trained to address de royal family: "It is a purebred Springer Spaniel *bitch*, your Majesty, thank you for asking."

"You okay?" I axed Zeke, careful not to touch him.

"I've been in tech my whole life, and that was the most vicious shock I've ever had."

"Yeah, well, I've known Foxy Mulligan for too much of my life, and he's nottin if not vicious."

De three of us stared at each other, levelled, all dumb animals now. Between de three heads on us, we hadn't a bog what to do next.

My mind was on my halo in Zeke's bag. He must have been thinking de same, cos we were both staring at his bag so hard we jumped when de three musketeers piled into de pod again, huffin and puffin and looking generally off deir tits with triumph.

"What's going on?!" Mossy demanded. Good man, Mossy. Get to de bottom of dis! Aisling-Gus grabbed him again, about to plant another smooch, but he stopped her. Gold star. he didn't miss a beat. "Just watch, *mo peata leana*," she said, and pointed out at de silo. We all fell silent and stared out. Nottin….

"Waaaait for it!" said Mulligan, rubbing his hands, probly thinking of a big plate of spagbol he was gonna demolish after dis. Still nottin…

Zeke was panting away and I thought he might pass out. What de hell was goan to happen? Who were dese loonies, crouched and salivating, gawking at a grey ex-church at night?

An auld wan limped past our pod, pulling a tiny Pom pup along with her. Her back was stooped nearly to a right angle and her demented pup was like a brand new star spinning round a dying one, all fizzy fur hopping and bouncing and yapping. De codger kept getting tangled up in de leash and we could hear her mutter: "Ah Jayz, Cha, will you take it handy." Cha and his pogo legs weren't having a bar of it. De auld wan stopped, bent even further down, and said real firm: "Cha! Ye little divil! If you don't calm down I swear I'll—"

She didn't get any further before a fucken waterfall of light exploded from de roof down all sides of St. Mary's. Glittering waves of light sparkled and rippled, a trillion flashing points jigging together, babbling to each other in blinks. A riot of light. A mob. A rebellion! Light fell over itself, tumbling like names off Adam's tongue, sploshing grey walls with every shiny smear of genesis.

Even with de tinting of de pod's shell I needed to squint. And when de auld wan turned and saw it, she shrieked. Blessed herself right off de bat, like she'd been training for dis moment her whole life. She crumpled to her knees, a scarecrow come loose from its stick, hands floating up in prayer to de blazing colours. Cha de Pom couldn't hurl his yappy barks hard enough at de spectacle. Just as loud, Aisling-Gus, Blades and Mulligan all burst into cheers, belting de shell and whooping. Mulligan grabbed Blades in a headlock.

"DOWTCHA *BOIIII*!" he roared, fecken Blades's baldy head around like a great white shark ripping through a baby seal.

"What is it? How did you...?" axed Mossy, pressing his face up against de shell.

"It's bacterial. Some kind of bioluminescent culture," said Zeke, weirdly calm, backing away just as Mossy clambered to get closer. I didn't budge either way.

"Tis indeed!" Mulligan waved at de auld wan, who was scansing round to see if anyone else could see dis. "We did it!" he shouted at her, pointing at himself. "Dat's all us now, dat is!"

Aisling-Gus stared dead ahead, her fingers buried in her dreads. "It's so much more glorious than I ever..."

"It's moving fast. Can it reach us?" Zeke wanted to know. De glowing waterfall stopped tumbling right as he fired off his question. It was almost down to de ground. De church walls were lighting de whole quay now, shimmering—a Mexican wave.

"It's living light..." said Blades, first thing I'd heard him say yet. "It's living fucken light." His voice was wobbly, breath coming in jerky little fits, soft as a small kid in de dark of his first night in Joov, wishing dere was some glimmer of a nightlight near his bunk to keep him company, give him de auld wink dat everything'd be okay.

We just sat together, mesmerized, watching waves breaking into different forms left and right, spirals mostly. Only time I'd seen light like dis was in my own scapework. It felt weird being in de auld corpse but still getting ringside seats to a universe being born. Had to give credit to dis Blades fien: if dis was his creation, he was a dab hand.

"It's a masterpiece," Aisling declared finally, breaking de spell. She put her hand on Blades's shoulder again and dis time he clasped her back, like he'd earned a touch.

"Takin nottin from Blades, y'knaw, but *muggins* here paid for it," Mully snapped, looking for his own pat on de head. "Dis shite isn't free. Producer credit, like!" He gawked back out at de spectacle with a dramatic kind of a sigh. "Folk'll be talkin bout dis till doomsday, lads. Let de wankers over in de Douglas chapter try to top *dis*!"

"Douglas!" said Aisling-Gus, and blew a razza.

"Or Knocka," said Blades, allowing himself a shakey laugh.

"Or dat Bandon shower!" said Mulligan. All three musketeers chuckled hardy-har-har.

"Seriously," said Aisling-Gus, "Blades has blown the whole thing wide open. *This* is the new Waker glyph, the only glyph from now on. Our cause is the living light. Now and forever."

As she said it, de light began to fade in spots. Like de bubbles in a fizzy drink after pouring, de mad glow just fizzled off till it was a grey wall near a streetlamp, no trace of anything different. Like nottin had happened. Dead stone. De three musketeers slapped their hands together in a great round of bualadh bos. Mossy was still pressed up to de shell, staring in awe. Zeke was still with his back slammed as far as he could from de scene. I stayed right in de middle, frozen.

Outside, de auld wan, slowly, awkward as all hell, ratcheted herself back to her right-angled stoop of a stand. Cha de Pom still growled away at dark walls. Yur wan dusted off her knees, and we could just about hear her, muffled, through de shell.

"Well shaft me sideways," she said.

Mulligan turned to us, already kinduv bored.

"Chalk dat up to a daycent test run." He nodded to Mossy, Zeke and myself. "You'll be coming up de Manor with us now, I'd say."

"Serious?" Blades fired de guzz eye at Mulligan. "Taking *dem* up de Manor?"

"What's this now?" axed Mossy.

"Oh, dis maaad free gaff." *Free gaff.* Like someone's folks were out of town and Mully'd de keys to de drinks cabinet. I could see it already. Him and his ghouls had taken over some victim's big house and were eating it hollow, maggots in a corpse.

"You have to come! You'll love the Manor!" Aisling-Gus was full of de joys.

Zeke had his own ideas. "Let me out!" he shouted and bolted for de hatch again, clawing at de shell."Let me out right now!"

"Naw. Can't be having any of dat now." I didn't like Foxy's cool tone. With a sinking feeling I watched him lift his phone to Zeke's face. "C'mere to me, have lick of *tooba*."

Display lit up, and a loud, ugly horn sound sprawled out at Zeke. I felt my eyes being sucked into de display but I managed to suck dem back into my head. Even with my fingers rammed tight into my ears I could hear great yawning note after note, de tones piling up and filling our pod like hundreds of bullfrog mouths. I opened one eye to see Zeke, jaw dropped scary wide open, eyes stretched even scarier. He looked like a fish from de darkest waters, de fellas with de lightbulbs growing off deir foreheads. Mulligan de hypnotist was grinning wide. Everyone else seemed grand, so I unplugged my ears and watched as Zeke melted into himself, locked onto de display with de face of a nightmare baby, or an ape, or someone watching de end of de world. I don't know where it came from, but a laugh bubbled up out of me and I had to catch it with my hand. Nottin funny, like—I was just so shitted out to see a man melted into a mask of awe so fast, with just a little hand-held yoke. De tooba sprawled out thicker and wobblier, some kind of backwards beat playing under it. Hard to describe: I'd say de beat was upside down, if you can follow dat at all. Fucksake, how could anyone *talk* about what it sounded like? Twas de sound of madness itself, all narrowed down into a tiny screen and fired straight at Zeke's face. And den, sudden as he'd done it, Mulligan turned it off, and Zeke sat quiet as stone.

I poked him, holding my breath.

"He'll be right as rain. Sher, isn't he happier already?" Mulligan started up de pod. "To de Manor, eh what old chaps?"

"Indubitably!" chimed Aisling-Gus, putting on her best upper crust English accent. Mossy poked Zeke too. Nobody home. *He'd better be okay, Mulligan*, I thought. *Or I'll figure out some way to stick dat tooba app up yur hole and make it play a polka.* Surprised myself how angry I was on Zeke's behalf. I barely knew him. But tis something about power... control. Savages like Mully using any force dey want on a body. He'd been a bully as a kid, fine, but now he knew what was *best* for people—Mully de Do-gooder!—he was so much worse.

We pulled off, and I thought I'd sidle up to Mulligan, figure out how shafted we were. "So, Foxy. Whatcha been up to?"

"Oh, not much Tayto boi. Just making a *legend* of myself, like."

"Aw yeah, how's dat now?"

"*Wellll,*" chuckled Mulligan, taking us smooth as silk up Sunday's Well, "don't like to blow my own horn, d'y'knaw?"

Is dat so, Foxy? You don't seem to mind firing a tooba at someone else.

"Foxy Mulligan is one of the great promoters of the Waker cause!" Aisling hopped aboard our little catch-up session. Always *hoppin onto* things, dis wan. Like a fucken flea. "Foxy is the life blood of the Cork chapter!"

I heard a crafty *nyutch* tongue click from Blades. Dunnaw if it was Aisling's performance, or de notion a septic like Mulligan might be de "life blood" of anything, but our artist-in-residence was coming down from his high. *Dat's de thing about Art, Bladesy boi,* I felt like whispering to him. *It's grand for de few seconds you nail it, den it's all just farters standing round scratching de dandruff out and wonderin what's for dinner, like? Yur still in de Wayke, yur back still hurts, yur belly's still too empty or too full or too sick, and you've ages to kill till bed. Don't fall for big flashy exit signs. Art's just another cul-de-sac you have to back yur van out of. Let us find de Crown, lads. If it works we'll share it with ye. No more cul-de-sacs for any of us.*

"Guzzy girl, you'll give me a big head," Mulligan crowed. We were heading along de Lee valley now, and de city suddenly fell away, all de streetlights, steel, bricks and business warping into trees and nettles, a soft dark giving way to our humming little pod of light.

"Nuff about me. What about *you*, Mr. Tayto? Last I heard you were goan up to Dublin to join de enemy, be de next big thing in scaping". He could barely get de next few words out, dey were so hot with humour for him. "Howdat work out for ya?"

"Ah well, Foxy, y'knaw how it is. A.I. revolution and all dat."

"Bad business for people like yourself."

"Less dan ideal, tis true, Foxy. But, sher, when Gawd closes a door he kicks you out a window, so I got into de mental health field."

"Didja now? Good man yourself."

"Oh!" Aisling hopped herself back into my lap. "What sort of populations are you working with?"

"Hah? Oh, sher, de elderly."

"That's wonderful. Isn't that great?" Like a nobber, poor Mossy nods along with her.

"Well, it's not de easiest gig in de world," I said, warming to my own line o'bullshit. "But it's *rewarding*, d'y'knaw?"

"I knew there was something special about you."

"I used to look after my nan!" No one said anything to Mossy's little nugget, so I gave him de thumbs up.

"Aisling, girl," I finally had to say, "It's not dat yur heavy, love, but you've a bony arse on you. Could you maybe...?"

Mossy saw his chance: "Loads of room on this lap for you, Gus!"

"How about this?" said Aisling, and she pushed me out of my seat, took it herself, den pulled me onto her lap. "That's better now, isn't it?"

And sure enough it was. She held me like a big baby, and I curled up in her arms like it was something I did every night, like her pet bloody cat. She might be annoying, but she was damn comfy, it must be said. It was all I could do not to purr, or suck my thumb.

Down in de valley below ran de luvly Lee, moon-shiny, glittering all de way longside us. Like he knew de scene was special, Mulligan threw on some classical choons. Out of de opening organ sound of "Where The Streets Have No Name," de silver stream sang to me. I wondered if maybe dat tooba had got under my skin after all, cos I felt way too comfy for a man being shanghai-ed out to de sticks. More like we were on a family drive. I leaned further into Aisling's snug little bosom and thought of my ma. Her beautiful skin—pale like mine but without de bulgy veins. When I was sick as a kid she'd just hold me like dis and it was nearly worth being sick for all de stillness and comfort of being held.

De city seemed far off now, falling away like a planet we'd never return to, our pod floating on and on into dark. No more streets, no more names... I felt more flaahed out dan I'd ever been before—could barely keep my eyes open. Aisling stroked my hair, my bag of bones getting lighter in her lap, smaller and smaller, drifting up de Lee on nottin but de light of de moon. *I mightn't be goan home directly*, I purred to myself, *but I'm headed in de right direction*. Zeke was mumbling something now, and drool was glinting on his lips. I caught a few words here and dere: *bubbles, bubbles, all just bubbles in a bubble…*

"We'll be okay, Zekey," I murmured, tapping his leg with my foot. At dis stage I didn't care if it was true. Dey could bury me upside down and get no quarrel from me, long as I had a place to rest a while. Fingers running through my hair, fish swimming through de river weed… *Ma, I can see all de night-time colours.*

"And he tells me *I've* got a bony ass," whispered Aisling, scooching out from under me and sliding over to Mossy suddenly. De seat felt hard without her. She figured I was asleep so I let on I was. Aw, how I missed her warm lap. Could hear Mossy's voice, whispering: "Poor guy." Moss, pitying me! In a flash vision I saw her leading him out into a meadow and letting him off, den vanishing on him. And him lowing out over de crystal field… *Where has she gone? Why has she left me?* She'll disappear, Mossy. Everything vanishes, de warm lap and bosom, fingers through hair. Pity yurself, boi. Yur de one getting lost. I'm riding a silver stream back to de source.

Chapter 6:
Carnival of Peacocks

Mulligan must've been in a golden oldies mood, cos I was woken to Sultans of Ping FC, in deir usual state of agitation 'bout a missing jumper and groovy guys in anarchist parties. My little bit of kip had somehow made me uptight again. De seat hurt my arse. Aisling was curled up on Mossy's lap. Zeke's eyes were open, but didn't look like anyone was home.

Same couldn't be said for Mully's place. Our Egg slid down de gullet of a serpentine driveway, and at de bottom was a house big enough to give you a nose bleed. Floodlights. Columns. A skull-grey mansion dat had eaten all de other houses nearby, towering all alone now, wondering what else to gobble.

Dis yoke was *problematic*, as a sagging professor in de gerontoplex was fond of saying. Not one but two fountains in de front lawn. And peacocks! Never seen a real one before—half-fancied such lads weren't real, like dragons. But look! Poncing about on de grass... whadevvor you call a full set of dem. A *vogue* of peacocks, say.

"Welcome to party headquarters," Mulligan announced. De Egg hatched and we spilled out. Blades clutched Zeke's arm, but my travelling chum was calm as a peacock. De birds scansed at us but were none too interested. Couldn't blame dem—I felt fierce bland beside such dapper fellas. Pure bored aristocrats. One shook out his tail-feathers—a hundred bright eyes shimmered at me: red, blue, green, gold. *I seeeee you.* De Wayke, with eyes on its tail.

Alright boi, I saluted back. *Like yur style, birdman.*

A young lad opened de door and I'd swear he bowed. I'd never been bowed to before, but maybe it wasn't for me, like, cos he greeted

Foxy as "Lord Mulligan" and handed him a whole tray of cocktail sausages. Auld Foxy wasted no time but got chomping. Guess he took over de right coop for himself. I had to admit de Lordly title suited him. No body could lounge more comfy in his skin dan Mulligan, de Stately Sausage himself. I spose de very things dat made him despicable in a right-side-up world made him superior in de eyes of craytures who'd been beaten down by de Scythe. De way he fucken loved his own fat, arrogant hide. Nottin like a bit of torment to drive all de chickens in de coop mad, kissing de ring of a sionnach cos he seems to know de score: Buck-buck-buck… he's not a chancer, he's *glic*… buck-buck… he's not cruel, he's *tough*… buck-buck… he's not a tool, he's a *weapon*. Our weapon, to keep us safe forever buck-buck-buck….

Foxy Mulligan. Lord of De Chickens. A cute hoor sucking down sausages, draped in fleshy finery. It sortuv made sense.

No word of a lie, Foxy's free gaff was bigger inside dan de Laser Coliseum down de Mardyke, but, y'knaw, classier. Chandeliers, marble staircase, wall rugs with pictures—de works. Place was packed to de gills with Wakers. No huffers, no masks, just sweaty red-faced gombeen men, swilling booze and chatting up girls and boys too young for dem. Some hardcore members had de lumen pigments injected into deir skin, highlighting an earlobe, or an eyebrow. Flashy lures. Everyone trying to hook de eye, trying to fish each other back to dry land. But dese fishers of men were only pulling demselves further down into de depths.

Mossy was propping up Zeke, waiting for Aisling's instructions. She put her hand on my shoulder.

"Don't worry about your friend. He's going for a lie-down. You'll both stay here tonight and he'll be his normal self in the morning."

"Normal my arse."

She led Mossy-plus-Zeke up de huge curve of stairs, and de three of dem disappeared into de shadows like mites into a conch.

Mulligan had been surveying de scene, pompous lower lip jutting out. Now he swallowed some porkies whole and cast off de tray to a toady. He coiled his arm around me, warm and heavy—de slow certain weight of a python. I noticed blue and pink pigments glowing behind his ear.

"Yur a dark horse, arncha?" he breathed in my ear. "Made quite de impression on Gus."

"Have I now?"

"Could be she's acting de maggot—she can be pure demented when de spirit takes her. But she wants you and yur buddy to stay here for a while. All our cards on de table now: does dat rank in de bastion of all-time great ideas?"

"I don't think so, Foxy."

"Thing is, what Guzza wants, Guzza gets. So…" He trailed off.

"De offer's generous, Foxy. Class gaff here, too. But I need to make tracks. Kinduv family reunion thing to get to, soon as Zeke recovers from dat dose of tooba…"

"Naw."

"Naw what, like?"

"Naw is naw, Tayto boi. You and yur friend aren't goan fucken no place till Guzza says so." He tightened his coil round my neck. "Now, just relax and make yurself at home, why don't you? Enjoy de craic, ya little wisp." And without even looking at me, he let go his grip and floated off to join de other zeppelin-sized nobs.

Maybe I'd been living in de wrong hole for too long, but I kinduv understood an angry young crow beating me, an outsider, with a metal bar. Watching Foxy Mulligan, my auld buddy from Joov, swan calmly around a mansion, guzzling sausages and informing me I wasn't free to leave his peacock prison, just smacked of nightmare sweats.

Who de fuck were dese people? I scansed about, but I couldn't get a handle at all. A few fops and dapper dandys who'd gone overboard with de lumens, but de rest of dem looked so plain. Joking and chatting—nottin odd. Or not at first glance. But maybe… could've been my brain squirming, trying to find puzzle pieces, I dunnaw, but when I looked closer I thought I could see on dese mugs de hard lines of fiens who'd cracked. Minds dat woke sideways in bed one day and said: *I can't take isolation no more. I've got a plan, and yur onboard—or yur overboard.* Wakers are sanctimonious nobs, no mistake, bangin' on bout "headcages" as de source of all evil. But I couldn't coggle what dey'd want with a couple of bog standard saints like me or Zeke. And why did dis Aisling-Gus loon enjoy such *meas* from Mulligan? Who was she?

I tried to reel in de nightmare sweats and just think straight for a second. I was kicking myself for conking out on de ride up here— now I'd no idea where I was. I could be minutes' walk from familiar territory, for all I knew, but my memory for de auld geoga was pure corroded after years of lighting up and rewiring myself for de halo multiverse. Get de heartrate down now, Tayto boi. No one seemed to notice me in de crowd, twas all just laughter and music, scoffing and swilling, some culchie kids eating de faces off each other and dropping de hand in darker corners. Make a break for it? But where? Out onto a dark country road? Into a darker woods? And what about Zeke? Well, what *about* Zeke? Maybe he was more trouble dan he was worth. He'd only put me through crows and Gubna, welshed on a bet, and got himself floored by Foxy'stooba since I'd met him. But I needed him—someone—*anyone*—to chew de situation over with, just help me digest dis big nervy ball of worms de Wayke had handed me like a tray of party bites.

De glut of worms were twisting faster in my stomach when Mulligan smacked his fork off a crystal goblet full to de brim with what I'd bet my halo was manky diet cola.

"LADIES AND GENTLEMEN! Can I get some whisht now? As you know, tonight's de Spring Rites festival, and it fills my heart to see so many of you joining us at de Manor. Nice wan, lads!"

De only thing filling yur heart is dose sossies, Foxy boi!

"I'd like to introduce a special guest of honour. A dear old buddy of mine from my humble Joov days: de one and only Mr. Tayto. Put yur hands together and give a big bualadh bos for him please!"

Whoops and yehoos, farmers slapping together de great meat paddles at de ends of deir arms.

"Our Lady's Joov!" someone shrieked. A lackey handed me a flute of shampers, and like a gome I took it.

"Mr. Tayto here," Mully pointed at me, "wanted to join de enemy. Be a scape *designer*." Boos and barnyard sounds went off at dis. "Tis true! But it didn't work out for him, did it?" Laughs right on cue from his adoring acolytes. "Nope, de fake world he was planning on trapping us with just left him homeless and wandering round Mallow! *Pathetic*. No bodder. He's with us now. As far as I'm concerned, he's home!" He raised his glass: "Stay as long as you need!"

I felt something snap and tighten round my neck. A metal collar—I gasped as it dug into my throat.

"Sorry!" a young butler fien blurted, backing away from me. I fingered de collar and found a little metal clasp near de back. I tried to pry it open. *ZZZAP!* An unholy shock for my troubles.

I growled. A sharp-toothy part of me was rising over de fear. It said *naw* to dis shite. I raised my shampers flute and just *flaaaayked* it onto de fancy floor. It shattered mostly over myself—don't know why I didn't hurl it at Mulligan—but at least it stopped de clapping and whistling. I stood my ground right in de smiddereens. Some shocked "ohs" and "ahhs" from de auld dolls, and threatening calls of "Careful now" from de bigger boggers.

I wanted to bellow at Mully and his guests to go shaft demselves. But dere was something bout Mulligan... with his airs... and his size... and now his mansion, and servants, and fans... My mouth was dry (*should've drunk de drink first*) and I couldn't feel my legs. Shaky hands. *Can never think on de spot.*

I was searching for de ugliest way to curse dem all when Aisling appeared, standing by Mulligan. Her manner was completely changed again. Ditzy flirt on de train, motherly in de egg. Now she held herself pure regal, like. Gait of a queen. Hard to believe twas de same girl, and for all I knew it wasn't. Maybe dere were as many Aislings round here as strutting peacocks.

"A chairde!" she held up her hands, all dramatic, soaking up de atmos like a sponge, and she gestured at me."What you see here before you—shaking, pale, and famished—is the face of our world. It's been frightened to near-madness. It's been hiding in a synthetic hole for so long it's forgotten the light, the warmth of life."

I yanked at de fashion statement round my neck. "I might be feelin de warmth a bit more without de shock collar, d'y'knaw?!"

"You are lost, wandering saint."

But I'm not lost, I thought. *I'm on a mission to find paradise.*

"You and your friend upstairs are both very sick young men. And I think you know that." De auld fellas round de room leered at me.

"My husband, Lord Mulligan, and I are here to nurse the sick back to health." An audible gasp from Mossy standing near her, as his jaw crashed to his chest. Oblivious, she beamed at her audience: "Through the only way Wakers know: love! It won't be easy at first. But with time and effort, we can win you back to health, to life. Your eyes will be opened and you will pass it on, reaching out to other poor saints in ways we can't predict. And with our combined efforts, friends, we can save Ireland. Take back our world!" More baying and lowing and culchie bualadh bos from de farmyard. She lapped it up.

"To the light!" came a shout.

"To the warmth!" came another.

Through the cheering and whistles, Mulligan held up a sausage in Aisling's honour. He regarded it, skewered on its little stick, den chomped it in half with his sharp front teeth. I wanted to hurt dat smarmy bastard, any way I could. Someday, somehow. Hold him down on a pillow and just let it rip.

I almost wanted to cry but I was too freaked out.

I felt a slap on my shoulder. I didn't turn to answer. Whoever it was dey'd be no help so fuck 'em—dey could just come round to de front of me, and sure enough like a nob he did, some prick with freckles and a center parting like he was trying to look as dooshy as possible. He had a beer in one hand and a glass of wine in de other.

"Tayto! Howzitgoan?! Gawwd, dis is a blast from de past!" he said. I just stared, no clue who he was.

"D'y'not remember me?" de nobber said. "*Nnnnoooooelly Baaa*!!" He threw a shape where he held out his hands wide and bent his legs in an athletic stance, like him and me went *waaaaay* back and had *grrrrreat* memories together. I looked at his shoes; fierce shiny.

"You used to do make porn scapes for me back in Joov, remember? Jeezuz, dey got me through de worst of it I tell you—oh here comes de missus, listen, not a word bout de porn alright?— how are ya girl?! Lemme introduce you to Mully's guest of honour." Noelly's lady friend sidled up and took her wine back from him, barely looking at either of us. She was caked in make-up, high arching eyebrows drawn on with pencil. A massive diamond ring sat on her finger—a real knuckleduster.

"Line for de jacks is out de door," she hissed. "And de sluts dis year are just…" she pinched her nose.

"Aw, sorry to hear it," said Noelly Ba. "But listen, dis is—"

"Mingin'!" she said, finishing her thought good and proper.

"Yeah, so anyway, dis is…" said Noelly Ba, still struggling to introduce me to de light of his life. I couldn't stop staring at his shiny shoes. He shifted around in dem, always sortuv dancing a little bit. De lady friend stood stock still in high heels, in a stance, one leg out straight to de side, like she fully expected fashion paps to spring from behind de couch and start snapping shots.

"Tayto, dis is de auld ball'n'chain: *Aurora*." She finally turned to gawk at him.

"How many times…" she hissed, "do I have to tell you to drop dat 'ball'n'chain' shite?"

"Sorry love."

"It's not funny, like!"

He nodded, mortified.

"I mean, is it just me?" Aurora axed me directly. Noelly Ba kept dancing right along beside her. He shot me a smile, pure awkward, and for a second he looked like a kid. It clicked: Noel Prendergast. We all had shaved bazzers in de Joov—no center partings, like, and no shiny shoes to dance around in. Where'd he get de "Noelly Ba" shit from? Nobody called him dat. He was just "Prendergast."

A whole sled of memories huskied through me. De Joov would hold rallies in de gym, practicing stupid chants in honour of Our Lady's for saving us and keeping us. *Whaay, sheyadayada, upp-upp-upp, whayyyy Our Lay-deeeees!* Along with de chants was fiddly choreography, which Prendergast always ballsed up. He'd pivot left when it should have been right, or whadevvor, and den some wag would slap Prendergast up de back of de head. You'd hear a good loud *SLAAAP* every few seconds as Prendergast got nervous and made yet another fuck up with his hands or his hips or his lips, setting off a ripple of suppressed sniggers all round: *Whaaay sheyada-SLAAAP-ada, upp-upp-SLAAAP-upp, whaayyyyy Our Lay-SLAAP-deeeees!* Poor Prendergast. Some cruel bastards became cheerleading experts within minutes, knowing every mistake spotted could be punished. I wouldn't be flabbergasted to learn Mulligan was one of Prendergast's super-attentive tutors back den. And now he'd tutored him into Rora's spray-tan arms. Dat big loony grin, de nervous shiny-shoed dance. Noelly Ba. Ladies' man. Still, what harm in making up a new profile for yurself? Ditch de porn—hopefully—get a wife and just… live yur life. But I felt a heave of sadness roll in my stomach all de same. De sight of Prendergast "living his life" was almost too much to bear.

I suddenly missed my halo severely. Shouldn't have left my humble hovel near de canal. Things weren't perfect, but I probly could've weaselled into another job. Dere's always janitor work up for grabs… maybe even another physio gig out in de gerontoplex near Tallaght. Sher, de staff at a Gerries never check a man's references. But no, I had to follow de pied piper of chaos down to Cork.

Well, to be fair, Zeke had begged me not to get into de

eggmobile with Aisling and Mossy. Dis peacock manor situation was my fault. Poor Zeke, hidden away somewhere in dis mansion, toobaad out of his gourd, all because I couldn't ignore a glowing catsuit. Some saint was I.

For all my sneering at Zeke's fogs, and panic attacks, I was starting to coggle dat maybe he'd a better grasp of de Wayke dan me. Trust *no one*, boi. Everyone's got an agenda.

"It's tough at first," said Noel, pointing to my shock collar.

"But collars are kinda sexy," said Aurora.

"Are dey now?" I said. "Care to try mine on?" They both laughed.

"Been there!" said Noel. He lowered his shirt collar: a glowglyph, all intricate Celtic stuff. "Symbolizes casting off my chains," he said, tapping de colours. Aurora suddenly kissed his neck. Noelly blushed.

"Loads of converts here tonight!" said Rora, pointing round de room.

"Dey nab people regularly, like?" I axed.

"Not as many as before," said Noel. "Wakerism is really taking off now. Most are volunteers. But every few weeks dey nab a hard case, like yur good self. Sucks at first. I mean, you wriggle like a fish in a net," he said, "but, once you stop struggling and wake up... great things can happen." He stroked his wife's arm. She smiled a tight smile, like it was hard to stretch her face past its usual sneer of disgust or boredom.

"Look at *her*, Noelly," Rora pointed at a young girl wearing a pencil skirt. "Muffin top from hell. Wouldn't you think someone would say something to her?"

"Woeful," said Noel, loyal as a lapdog.

"A dhaoine uaisle," a waiter called above all de nattering and glass clinking. "If you would make your way to the lawn, the Spring Rite is about to begin." De crowd drifted in clumps toward de back garden, and Noel and Rora each took one of my arms and led me along. I couldn't stop touching my collar.

"Tell ya, boi, last time I saw de Spring Rite I was new to my collar too! Squirming around in it, fierce uncomfortable." Noelly laughed. *Ha ha, shock collar. Sher tis all in good fun!*

Garden was like a circus. Everyone showing off how *alive* and *in deir bodies* dey were, I spose. Girls spinning flaming poy; a juggler with wine bottles for clubs. I saw a shaky unicyclist serving drinks, with guests deliberately taking ages to choose a tipple from his tray, cos dat's what Cork people do to unicyclist waiters: *Ehhhh, I'll just have... ehhh, what's in dis wan again?* Everywhere people were gabbing excitedly, like de mothership or whadevvor was finally coming.

Something tickled my leg and I looked down to see a pure white peacock fanning his feathers. Didn't know dey came in white, like. I'm no stranger to not knowing stuff, but dis fella was cogglesome. Why white? Isn't it de one thing peacocks have goan for dem—colours? I don't think dey're smart or fast or tough, like. Just look de bee's knees. But not dis poor albino gom. He struck up a stance by some peahens and gave it one of *these*, but de birds just looked right past him. He lowered de tailfeathers again and went back to his gatch, pure casual, like it hadn't happened. Tragedy.

Rora steered us to de buffet table. "Do ya eat shrimp?" she axed me. "What am I saying?! Dat'd be cannibalism!" She guffawed, and chucked some of de curly pink lads into her gob.

"Ah now..." Noel tried to caution her. "Dat was me just a few months ago, chickpea."

"What's de ska with de white peacock?" I nodded toward Casanova de Pale making his casual rounds.

"What about him?" said Rora, chewing.

"*State* of him, like," I said. "It's not right, breeding birds like dat. He'll never pull. Lookit, he's making a move on dis wan..." Casanova did his thing and de hen pretended someone had called her name and wandered off.

"That's *hilarious!*" Rora cracked up. I half expected Noel to say *Ah now don't laugh, dat was me just a few months ago...* Instead he offered me a plate of salad: "You should eat. Start small."

"Any fibrogel to be had? Or a feedbag—"

"No!" snapped Noel, dead serious. "None of dat here."

"Poison!" spat his byor.

"Did someone say 'poison'?" It appeared one of de peacocks had transformed into a man. He stood beside us, floppy hat just about balancing on his head, exquisite peacock feather arching from it. Crushed velvet jacket, long white socks up past his knees, black shoes with brass buckles. Best of all, a cane in his hand with a duck's head for a handrest. "So someone besides my good self has tried Marguerite's margaritas. Turpentine with a salt rim, eh whatwhat?"

De stranger took Noel's hand and kissed it, den did de same to his missus. "Aurora, radiant as the Northern Lights."

"Dis is Tayto."

"Tay-to," said de stranger, carefully.

"Like de crisps!" said Noel with a little dance.

"And who are you?" I said.

"Dis is de Fop," said Noel.

"Enchanted," said de Fop with a bow.

"You look like a resourceful fien," I said, checkin out his style.

"*Indeed,*" said de Fop, stroking his feather.

"You wouldn't have a key to dis yoke, would ya?" I pointed to my collar. Dey all laughed again, like it was a delightful ice-breaker.

"I'll wager you had no idea Kubla Khan's Xanadu would be found just west of Cork city, eh whatwhat?" said de Fop, waving his cane toward de lawn.

"Eat some shrimp, serious now," said Rora, forcing a small plate into my hand.

"Gilbey!" shouted Noel. Gilbey from Joov wandered over and joined us. He was tucking into a stonking great plate of shrimp himself.

"Howsa form, lads?" said Gilbey, deadpan as always. "It's like a school reunion up de Manor dese days." He was wearing a shock collar too.

"Gilbey," I whispered, pointing to his collar. "Story, like? Dey got you too?"

"Oh yeah sher. I've been here a good while now."

"Yur a prisoner?!" I cried.

Gilbey shrugged, like what-can-you-do? "Well, dunnaw bout *prisoner*, like... I was hitching on de Ballincollig bypass, trying to reach a kwery out Ovens way, and doesn't Mulligan pull up alongside me *Aw Gilbey boy, long time no see, hop in de pod, check out de new gaff* and I needed a place so it's all *Yeah, sound Mully...* next thing I know I'm collared up de Manor." He told his scéal like he was explaining how he got a jacket half price. Kept munching his shrimp and all!

I looked around. About half de guests had collars, each with a blinking red light at de fastening. De whole garden was blinking, like a bunch of fairy lights had escaped from deir cable—gone free range.

Have you tried dese shrimp?" Gilbey axed. "I've been gobbling all evening and dey just keep coming. I thought de poor little lads were extinct!"

"Dey're not *real* shrimp," Rora said, rolling her eyes.

"Oh," said Gilbey, peering at a specimen. "*Class* imitation, mind."

"Gilbey!" I clicked my fingers in his mellow face. "Focus! Mully's kidnapping saints and locking dem up here?!"

"Ah no. It's a… a whachamacallit? A *process*," said Gilbey.

"Dat's de word for it now: a *prohh-cess*," said Noel.

"Dey get you off de halo, and you can, y'know… you can…" Gilbey trailed off, picking around his salad in case a shrimp might be hiding in de green clumps.

"You can what, Gilbey?"

"Dunnaw. You can stop being a twat with a magic head band."

"You can start living!" said Noel, wiggling my arm. "Get a wife, maybe have kids. Find a real job. Y'know! Be a winner at de game of life!" I glanced at Mrs. Prendergast giggling and flirting with de Fop. Noel was holding her up as de Big Carrot. She was orange enough, I granted.

"I'm in household wares," announced Noel, standing up straight for de first time dis evening. "I supplied all de plates and cutlery for dis party, as it happens." Gilbey raised his snack as if to say, *You give good plate, Noelly Ba.*

"So, what are we up to this evening?" axed de Fop, sticking his long nose into our chat.

"Who *is* dis langer?!" I said, appealing to someone—anyone— to help me make sense of dis place.

"Sher, dat's de Fop," said Noel. "First European to win de Solar Regatta."

"You have heard of the Solar Regatta, I assume," said de Fop with a raised eyebrow.

"Don't follow sports," I muttered. "Specially not rich twats racing round like tools in space."

"Yes, people *doing things* must be such a bore to chaps slumping in pools of their own urine, daydreaming their lives away!" He chortled and ran a finger along his hat feather as if testing a blade.

"Ah lads!" said Noel.

"Ah lads," echoed Gilbey, scansing round to see if any more shrimp were up for grabs.

"Calm down, willa?" said Rora. "It's a party!"

"It's a prison!" I said.

"Naw, it's a *process*," said Noel.

"It's a pretty sweet deal, must be said," nodded Gilbey.

"Oh yeah?" I replied. "Why are you still wearing a collar if it's so great here?"

"Just part of de process," shrugged Gilbey. "I need to do a few more tests of faith before I'm ready to walk free into de Great Wayking."

De Great Wayking. You had to hand it to Wakers. Dey'd a way with de big labels.

"When's yur last trial, Gilbey?" axed Noel.

"Ahh, I missed tonight—still gotta find a flesh partner—so I'll have to wait for de summer solstice." He saw me gawking and cupped his crotch. "You need to find someone to...y'knaw?"

"You need to reconnect with bodily pleasures," said Noel, all Mr. Expert."It's losing touch with our body pleasure caused us to stray into de halo in de first place." He glanced adoringly at Rora, who was still whispering to de Fop, who had his hand on his mouth, a big pantomime of being scandalized by whadevvor she was saying.

Noel's lecture galled me. To take a vast mystery like de halo, a million-roomed mansion dat'd put Mulligan's manor to shame, and just say it sucked us in cos we couldn't get a partner, like sainthood was just a loser's substitute for sex, was plain stoopid. Like saying de ancient lads painted gorgeous horses and lions on cave walls cos dey couldn't hunt for shit, or yanks rocketed to de moon cos dey forgot how to jerk off or something. I couldn't believe what I was hearing, but Gilbey and Noel were nodding like it was gospel. I knew dey used toobas here. What other brainwashing yokes did Mulligan and his cronies have up deir sleeves? Or were dese lads just thick?

"What's de final test?" I axed.

"Varies," said Gilbey. "Tonight it's Spring Rite, so de theme is resurrection." He pointed over at a fresh-dug garden plot with some long tubes sticking up from it. "Dose yokes coming out of de ground are breathing tubes."

"Dose... are *people*... buried under de soil?"

"Imagine!" cried Noel, delighted. "Coming out of de grave, being able to breathe free again. How rich de lights will be, and how good de food will taste. Risen again, to join de living. It'll be de greatest night of deir lives!"

"Preach, brother!" said Gilbey.

"Don't worry, Tayto," said Noel to me with a wink. "You'll see it our way soon enough." *Righty-o,* I thought. I've gotta scarper *now.*

I raised up on my tiptoes and scansed at de perimeter to judge de distance. Could I make it to de trees before anyone would notice? My hammy was still pulled after sprinting from de crows. Always been a snail, too. De lads seemed distracted, giddy as geese, gabbing on about Spring Rite, so I took a few steps back, nonchalant as de white peacock, like, and den let loose and bolted for de trees. I accidentally shoved a few fiens as I ran—most of dem were well-polluted and tumbled like skittles. De peacocks were more savvy and shifted to make way for me. I could feel my loose sole flapping away under me, a huge airbrake, but I just pumped my spawgs for all dey were worth. I figured whadevvor kind of electric perimeter dey had set up was de kind for dogs. It'd hurt for a few seconds, and you just wince and grimace through it and den yur home free. Spend a night in de woods trying to avoid capture... how bad? Couldn't be worse dan a fecken school reunion. Or being buried alive. My heart pounded as de treeline got closer. *Maybe it's a bluff,* I thought. *Dere's no shock perimeter at all.*

Just as I reached de daffodils I felt a lightning bolt skewer my spine to de grass. I struggled to catch my breath when another punched through me—I felt my heart pop. De next shock made my entire skin snap off me and den slap itself back on again. I tried to crawl backwards but four more shocks lit up my ghoulies before I managed to slither back to a safe distance. I lay on de cool grass, panting. *Never, never do dat again...* Right you be.

Sat on de ground for a while, watching de wind blow free through de trees. I'd never envied de fucken wind before. And dat was dat. I got up and walked back to de lawn party. All de guests I'd shoved just ignored me. I wasn't sure where to go so I slunk up to Noel, Rora, Gilbey and de Fop. Noel didn't say a word, just handed me a small plate of shrimp salad and a fork.

Maybe dey were synthetic, maybe dey were real. But as I poked dem about on my plate, I found dese shrimp to be pure sad lads altogether. Curly little pink corpses. Dinky fetuses, hunched over, like I should place a tiny teddy bear in each one's grasp and let dem sleep forever in a row of matchbox kiddy cots, with little fishy mobiles over dem playing gentle underwater music. Mermaid pajamas. I think de perimeter shocks had scrambled me. Stress, boi. Can bend de mind into a pretzel. I was standing, staring at my plate, and trying to work out if I was looking down at death or not… death in curly pink form… and I hoped it wasn't death after all. So small, dese craytures. Hoped dey were fake. It'd be too sad if dey had lived once. I ate, rolling de question around in my mouth. Something about de taste was off. I decided it was just a good imitation of flesh. Funny thing was, as soon as I made up my mind it wasn't real flesh, just a clever trick, pure sleight of hand, dat's when I felt a few tears well up. Didn't make sense, like. Crying once you've realized a thing never really lived in de first place.

A horn sounded. Foxy Mulligan stood on a giant turtle shell; thing was bigger dan himself, like two black currachs, one chucked on top of de other and glued with molasses.

Mully struck a more dramatic stance on de shell and honked again into a long smooth animal horn he'd stolen from de house. And sher why wouldn't he swipe it? Everything's stolen. In Joov you own nottin. Uniform, halo, bunk: all state issued. Den, scuttling from kwery to kwery up in Dublin, you learn all you need is about six feet free from de langers on either side, to just think and light up. Sin é. But dere's always fellas want de Big House. Need de clutter. Need de ab rollers and Nordic trainers and didgeridoos and chandeliers and original paintings from some poor damaged bollox who blew his brains out and tripled de value of his dollops on a canvas, and on and on, just cramming yur great big colon of a house, and as it mounts and mounts you need more new stuff to hide from how numbing it all is, till yur just stuffing stuff in just to stuff it in, like de way people used to watch telly and flick through channels just to avoid watching anything too long cos dey knew it was all shite, but stopping watching de telly would only force dem to be alone with demselves and who wants dat, like? But den again… I'm a saint. What do I know about de world of men? What do I grasp of craytures de likes of Gilbey or Noel, cupping deir junk and trying to get deir hole? Maybe you need de Big House. And all de stuff. Otherwise yur just a white peacock, invisible to hens like Rora. Maybe not being able to get a Rora is like death to a Noel. Maybe de Noels of de world will work all de livelong day to sell plastic forks so dey can have a *giant house* made from all sorts of stuff dat had to be hauled all over to get here, full of shite dragged out of de ground or ripped from animals or forests? Maybe dat's a glorious thing, to have tailfeathers plucked from all over de shop—horns and shells stolen from extinct beasts' graves—and be able to say: *I stole dis. Mine now, la!* Maybe's it's even better dan having yur own tailfeathers: to build yur own collection, to manage it. Dat's right up a Noelly Ba's alley, I'd say: Managing. I know it's up Mulligan's alley. To take. From de living or de dead, sher what's de difference? Anything to lord it over others. Maybe dat's what it is to be a man in de Wayke. Either we do dat or we just turn out de light.

Extinct. Is it me, or did de old manor owners have weird taste? All dese shells and horns and whadevvor. Why remind yurself of things dat were gone and wouldn't come back? Funny how all de palaver about resurrecting mammoths and dinosaurs and whadevvor went de way of de dodo after de Great Scythe. *Let de dead stay dead, and let de living make it to de morn.* Fair nuff. But for some reason, Wakers couldn't leave saints—de un-dead, like—alone. I spose cos you can't fuck a saint, you can't eat one, you can't use dem to decorate your mantelpiece, you can't sell anything to dem, buy anything from dem, can't win deir vote, or set dem to work. Saints are too busy being still, de snaky bolloxes. So now here we are, hangin round in de Big House garden, getting ready to yank de un-dead back into de big party, so dere'll be more mouths to kiss, and arms to get hugged by, and nobbers to sell plastic forks to. It's all so moving.

Mulligan was in his ceremonial kimono. He blew de horn a third and final time. De first two tries were spitty muffled efforts, but de third blast was sound as a bell, soaring over de night. Folks spilled from de manor like vomit, mixing with de pools of prats already outside. All de gabbing got louder and den fell away to a few whispers and den silence. Mully, ever de showman, let de silence hold, making everyone suck up de atmos, de fierce expectaaytion, like.

Dat was some giant black shell he stood atop. Solid. Empty. Like a deserted house, or a vacated tomb. A reptile mind used to live in dat shell, used to float through a deep green sea, scarfing jellyfish into its beak. Fuck knows how far it floated, all de crazy things it'd survived, like crabs trying to eat it as an egg, or birds swooping for a munch when it hatched and tried to waddle down to de waves. What killed it. Shark? Hunters? Choked on a plastic bag thinking it was lunch? Now dat shell, dat little boat, sat in another green world: an Irish garden of all places... Now it was a shark's hollow soapbox to bellow about how great life could be. Another classic specimen of de Wayke's sense of humour.

"Bit of whisht, lads!" someone shouted, but de garden was fairly hushed already. Every nobber dere gaped de jaw, just waiting for de Great Leader to open his craw. I mean, he was de one in de fancy dressing gown, straddling a giant turtle shell. Holy mother of gawd, dey were well ready for dis fien to lay down de Word.

"Life," said Mulligan, "is nottin... without ritual. You can have yur sausage rolls, and yur auld doll in de bed with ya, and yur maad set of wheels, but enda de day, what you want most is a bit of meaning. Even if tis only a scrap... you want some sense of purpose. Direction." Some scattered clapping, but Mully held up his hand to smother it. "Dis is our Spring Rite," he pointed over to where de ex-saints were buried, breathing through big straws stretching up from de dark, out of de narrow grave into de wide night, blinking away with stars and satellites. "Over in dat plot lie our new brothers and sisters. Earlier today we buried dem. And why did we bury dem? Cos dey let deir old lives go. De were saints—leeches—sucking our world dry. Dey hated demselves—and rightly so. But dey came here to de Manor, boys and girls, and dey got de heads down and did de work. And now dey're ready to be reborn. Tonight dey'll burst from de soil, sprout up from de cold clay itself. No more flying high in a cloud. Naw. Dey've chosen to live and die as real human beings. Dey're joining us in de great hooley of life. So let's welcome dem. Let's get dis party pumpin' so we can rattle deir bones, wake de dead! And when dey rise, let's give dem something to dance about!"

Whoops, cheers, stomping, screaming, clapping and carrying on. Mully gave a signal, and waiters wheeled out a giant tooba set—two big flat tablets with spirals on deir faces—and set dem standing upright on de grass.

"SPRING RITE!" Mully howled, and de toobas burst into tones. De blast hit me from de side, and de garden warped under my shoes as de tooba beat sprawled through my skull. Such a *dose*, boi... I dropped to my knees to hold onto de grass. De lawn shimmered and waved, all fluid now, every blade a separate rhythm. I cursed Mulligan and his bloody toobas—*stop dosing people you langer! Dese yokes can cause psychosis!* All round me de guests went mental. Some fiens peeled off deir tops and stalked on all fours, demented hounds and gorillas. Byors gyrated, slithering and licking each other... I felt another lectric jolt, but it wasn't my collar. Rora had coiled round me and now she was staring into me with her great tooba eyes spiralling. I squirmed up to see de pulsing tooba moon in de sky, big as de First Predator's eye, trying to figure if I was food or fun or what was I at all. And what *was* I at all? A little tube covered in skin, with nostrils and limbs sprouting out all over. Rora was getting ready to dislocate her jaw and swallow me whole. Where was Noelly Ba? Why didn't he shimmy over here in his shiny shoes and save me from her? I managed a burp—all prawny, my stomach still wasn't up to solid food—and I watched it ripple across de lawn, ruffling de hair on de dancing animals' bodies, and shaking de feathers of peacocks, poor flappy gatchy septic bastards. Why were dey not in deir leabas at dis hour? Special breed, no doubt. Some Waker monster breed, bred to be awake as long as de floodlights are on, gawd it never ends for dem, like genetic beauty queens on parade, wishing for dark but doomed to endless pageant. And dat *sad* white peacock, what monster allowed dat to happen, hah?!

My heart was goan into parallel beats, I was nottin but hearts now, all goan like de clappers, wind-up toy teeth. *I just want a quiet kwery to call my own and dive into de cloud and leave de bonebox to sit still. I don't want all dese hearts clapping away under de Predator Moon.*

Amid de hooley on de lawn de Fop, cool eye of de storm, twisted slowly into himself, holding his duck cane gently, like a beloved, as he spiralled away alone, Lord of de Beasts, all style and pose and apparel, his skin so pale twas almost green. I realized with horror he was waltzing toward me. Rora let me go to sidle up to him, but he just put his hand right up in her face and pushed her down to her knees and she stayed dere. I was afraid anything he'd say might shatter me.

"You must give me the name of your tailor," he purred, waving de duck head at my jumper and tatty pants. "He's taken your look in a daring direction." And with dat he moved off, swaying slowly again with his only beloved partner: himself.

Septic bollox. *We can't all be pilots at de Solar Fucken Regatta, yur lordship.* And den it happened. Earth on de fresh-dug plots began to rumble, and filthy hands and legs burst out of de soil. I just screamed my lungs out den, but what's a scream amid a hurricane of tooba? No more dan a fart in an anti-matter bomb blast.

How dey rose den, shaking into de night air, wobbly on legs like newborn foals. Once upon a time dey'd been saints like me and Zeke—now dey gasped blinking into light, wiping brown crap out of eyes and ears and noses, spitting and hocking into life. Dey were naked, soil falling off in clumps and pale skin pulsing up at de Guzz Eye in space, and de party wound round dem and everyone was kissing and stroking dem, and like madmen, who once were saints and now were not—unhaloed, unsainted—dey brayed like idiots laughing up to de sky, like dey'd come home, like life was a friend, and dey weren't already rotting like meat left out. I puked up a bit of my salad, and started to wish I was de one under de ground now, just to get free from dis party spilling all over de place.

And like an angel, she came to me, Aisling-Gus, and she held me close, not in a grabby way, but like a gentle huggy way, and whispered: "You're safe, Tayto. I'm here to help bring you home to us. I won't let anything bad happen. I promise." And I dunnaw if I was just scared out of my wits, or de tooba was bending de night so everything was slanted in de Manor's favour, or what, but in dat instant I believed her, and clutched her like a baby grabs its mother right after it's been slapped into dat first stark scream.

Aisling-Gus led me back indoors, up stairs, stairs and more stairs until we reached a library. Quietest place in de house, she said. I was a bit shakey on my feet but I made it by leaning on her de whole way. Nuther huge room. Were dere no pokey corners in dis manor, like? Twas dark, dusty and mouldy like de inside of an old trunk, or a judge's wig. Fierce soothing. I slumped into a cool ledder chair, grand plush yoke, and instantly felt less craw sick.

After a while I wandered over to a window. Below I could see all de ruaille buaille: cheering circles of fanatics jigged round newly-risen ex-saints, poring booze down deir gullets.

I screwed my eyes tight shut for a few seconds and sat in de cool dark of my head, just pure baby, curling away from the world's orgies. A tooba echo rang in my ears, spiralling fractals in a million directions. It was fading… I'd be okay soon. I slumped deeper. *Luuuvly.*

Finally I opened my eyes. De room was less murky now: rakes of books, shelf after shelf—a little wheely ladder yoke to get at de hard-to-reach ones.

"Feel better?" Aisling axed after a while.

"Yeah. Thanks for saving me." I looked down at de Spring Rite again, huffing and puffing away on de grass like a tangle of manic caterpillars. Mother of gawd, dere'd be none of dem able to walk tomorrow after de congratulations dey were givin and gettin. Aisling stood behind my chair, stared where I was staring.

"Do you like watching that?" she axed, real quiet and gentle. "From this safe distance?"

Her tone reminded me of our psych tech at Joov. She'd always get fierce quiet and gentle before axing something bizarre about whether we liked taking a dump, or ever dreamed about tickling our mothers, or whadevvor. Never liked dat psych tech. And now here was Aisling-Gus, breathing in my ear and talking bout "safe distances." Nope. I got up from my chair and strolled over to de shelves. Some titles were in goldy letters. Dey glinted. I slid one out, felt de heft of it in my hands. *Homer.* Huh. Who's he when he's at home? *Poe.* I opened dat one at random and saw a frozen line drawing: a hot-air balloon sailing its dreamy way to de moon. Another glinted up at me: *Kepler—Somnium.* I didn't know what "somnium" meant but I liked de sound of it. Kinduv rounded, soft. Probly meant something like a cool smooth stone. I could almost feel de weight of it in my hand, de weight of a small book. You could skip it over a moonlit lake, send it flying like a UFO till it disappeared into de muckwater, invading de frogs and little fishies. A sinking somnium.

I heard muffled shrieks from de lawn. For a second I wished I could float off up to de moon myself, but den it struck me: lurking in dis weird auld library I wasn't in my own world, anyways. Books. So many. Lumps of wood pulp. I don't think bout de weight of words, like. Dey're always floating out of my mouth like fleets of hot air balloons, rising and vanishing, never catch hide nor hair of dem again. But written down, printed, dey sit heavy on shelves. Trees. Stones. 'Magine sitting down and poring through all dis lot. Yur back and neck killing ya. Squinting at de little letters just sitting on de page, a little sitting figure squinting at little sitting figures. Some pages were glossy, others were rough. Maybe it was de tooba talking, but de smell when you opened one of dese books would hit you vivid like a… like suddenly remembering childhood… dose funerals for yur dead fish, and gerbil, and toad. Buried in de finest matchboxes, under ice-lollystick crosses. Almost too much to take.

Well, no one'd be reading dese dusty yokes now. Saints have a halo and live in a cloud, a bodyless body where you never have any neck pain, and everything is dancing with senses: colour and sound and speed. And de Waker nobs are too busy congratulatin de pants off each other down in de garden. Between de lot of us, who'd be arsed sitting up here alone on de moon, poring over dese old trees, pale as death with black marks on dem?

Aisling-Gus threw on a desklight. Glare caught me off-guard. Tis funny how quick you get used to dark. A scream sheared up from de lawn. Pleasure or pain? Did it matter? I strolled round de library, putting a bit more distance between myself and de window. I wasn't really looking at or for anything when my eyes clocked a stain on de ground. A person lying curled up, like a shadow forgot to get up and follow its owner. Death stain—hop enough kweries and you'll see your share. When de Scythe came, many died at home. No one came to clear out bodies for months, and de stain left by a corpse could soak deep. Shadow people. Can't wash dem out. Some lie on deir backs, others on a side. Most died near a toilet or bed. Never saw one in a library before. 'Magine dying in here. In de last few seconds, and de eyes glance around like an animal's, hunting for some scrap of comfort or recognition of de auld human world, of home, of sense and sanity, what you took for granted would always be dere, and you see dese tomes, staring down, stacked, neat, solid... closed shut. I dunnaw. Maybe it doesn't make a difference. Maybe it's no worse dan huffin yur last in a field surrounded by clueless cows or sheep, or cradling yur dead baby, or watching yur partner flee out de back door. Maybe dere's nowhere right to die, and it's always kinduv, dunnaw... ridiculous.

Aisling-Gus clocked me staring at de stain and crept over, all soft and gentle and psych-techy.

"Don't look at that," she said.

"See how clear de outline is. Dat's a perfect specimen right dere, girl."

"I said stop looking at that." Her Ladyship was getting stroppy.

"I might be wearing a dog collar, but I'm not your mongrel," I snapped.

"I just don't understand," she ran her bitten-down nails through her hair. "Why would you turn away from what's outside in the garden right now—life at its most beautiful!—and focus on this... this..."

"Stain," I said.

"Yes. A stain. I mean, what's..."

"Wrong with me?"

"That's not what I was going to say. I was going to say what's wrong with *now*? Why does everything have to be about the Scythe, the past, the lost, the dead?"

"Cos it's real. It happened. It's true."

"And the party isn't? Why does the ugly get to be the only truth?" She was getting worked up but trying not to. Well, to hell with her. Let her get worked up. Her and her hooray-for-everything party morons outside.

"Why don't we go back to the garden?" She touched my arm. For some reason I felt fierce angry at how gentle she was being, creeping around me, and trying to get me to look at dis, and not dat, like some kinduv feckin nanny. I slapped her hand off me.

"Why don't *you* go back to yur garden? Hah? Why're you with me in de first place?"

"I wanted to make sure you were okay—"

"You just don't want me looking at dis stain. Well Aisling girl, I love dis stain. D'y'hear me now? *Love* it. Dis stain has de common daycency to just lie here and not put on jigs and reels bout how great life is. It doesn't pretend to be anything except what it is: de truth of de matter. What happens to all of us. Dis stain is going to be here forever to remind us of de big picture, and I salute it!" I tapped my finger to my forehead and winked at de stain. "Dowtcha, boi! Good on ya."

"Forever? Is that what you think?" she said, seething. I'd really got de wind up her. Nice wan! Den she stormed over to a writing desk and rustled round in de drawer till she put her hand on something. She marched back to me, and I saw in her hand a big heavy crystal decanter yoke. Next thing she emptied its contents onto de stain.

"Are you tapped? What're you doing?"

"There's no such thing as forever, asshole," she muttered. "Just the here and now."

Before I could piece it together, she had struck a match. We watched de tiny flame jump about, dancing down to her fingertips. Finally it bit her, and she flicked it at de whiskey lake and de dark figure lying at de bottom of it. It went up fast—I had to hop back. Flames shot up de spines of de auld books, and Aisling's look of triumph turned to panic. She flayked out de room and I turned to watch de tongues dance higher on de bookcase, licking all de words up in a black sizzling sweep. Outside, de shrieks were getting louder. It was like dey were cheering for de flames as dey gobbled up history. Soon all de little black marks would be gone, swallowed into one big black hole. De wall of heat got so strong I backed all de way to de door and collided with Aisling sprinting back in with a fire extinguisher. She was reading de label and trying to figure out what to do with de safety pin.

"Give it here," I said. Twas a fierce old model but I'd used its like at work once. I yanked de pin out and de stoopid thing went off in my hands for a few seconds.

"Tayto!"

"Cool yur jets, I've got it." I moved toward de fire. It was spreading so fast I had my doubts I'd be able to stop it with dis piddly little canister. How bad. Let de whole of Brainwash Manor come roaring down while dey hump each other on de croquet lawn. A good fire might be a sweet chance to pull a swift legger. While everyone's all flappin and shrieking trying to put out de west wing, I snake round, find Zeke, and maybe... But dere was something sad in de crackle of de paper as it got eaten. Dese books were old, boi. Dey'd managed to find a final resting place in dis cemetery of a library, and it was more dan a lot of folks had managed for demselves. To just lie together, bunched into families—histories, tragedies, comedies...

"TAYTO!"

I started, like a cur kicked awake. Maybe I was her mongrel after all. De canister just jumped to life in my hand, and I unloaded all over de roaring shelves. Dese canisters, la! Scrawny yokes, you'd think nothin of dem, but dere's a good bit inside. I just blasted de white stuff all over dat crackling animal till it was nottin but a black whimper. Felt good, like cutting a urinal cake in half with yur wee as a kid, times a thousand. Fire: man's oldest friend and enemy. Gets out of hand and you let it know who's boss.

We gathered round de smoking shelves. Kepler, Poe and some other lads were curled into crispy black roses. *Sorry, lads. Sher, ye had a good run.* Not de loftiest eulogy, but I'd de canister in my hand and felt more of de fireman dan de priest about myself. Better to be de fireman, I thought. Whether Kepler and his buddies were floating off to de moon in invisible balloons I couldn't say, but I'd just slapped de shit out of dat fire, and dat, as dey say, was a fact.

Aisling was still panting when I lobbed de spent canister back to her. "Yur a bit mental, aren't ya?"

She stared at me, den burst out laughing—high whoops. I found myself busting my hole too. For a second we sounded like a donkey slumber party. Probly stress. Den we stopped laughing and just stood dere. Thick smoke curled round us. It stank.

"C'mon," she said and grabbed my hand.

I followed Ais fast down winding stairs to a cellar sort of place, a pantry. Where toffs keep food. Bare brick walls, cobwebs in de corners. But not a fancy animal shell or a marble pillar in sight. It wasn't cosy, like, but it was de first human-sized place I'd seen in de manor yet. I could imagine servants hangin out here long long ago, taking a load off on one of dese stools and having a crafty bitching session about His Nibs.

"I don't care how saintly you are, you must be hungry." She poked round in a huge fridge-freezer, no bodder on her, and pulled out some ice-cream and fresh fruit. Fresh fruit, if you don't mind. Too good for fruit-flute tasti-paste up de Manor, boi. *Excuse me, Farquhar, won't you pahhss the frrrresh frrruit?* We pulled up chairs to a small counter and plonked down. Aisling sniffed herself and winced. She touched a panel on her belt and a small pellet popped into her hand. She swallowed it.

"Whazzat?" I axed.

"Just give it a minute," she said, popping it in her mouth and pushing de ice-cream at me. Den she sprang up and rummaged round in a hamper, pulling out a wrinkly dress. She sniffed it. "Avert your sensitive eyes." Suddenly she was peeling off her bodysuit. I looked straight at de strawberries. Red. Her suit flopped to de ground and my eyes sortuv... strayed over to her again. De line of her back, arching. Waist tapering in and den curving out to her hips—she glanced back to clock me. I stared at de strazzas, pure innocent, like. She whipped on de dress and sat next to me again.

"Why don't you eat?" she axed.

"No spoon."

"Ah now. Who says you need cutlery to touch what you want?" She picked up a strawberry, dunked it in mint ice-cream. I was hungry, but I just wanted to hook up a feedbag; I didn't want to get into dat whole thing with food and yur mouth. She didn't care, just shoved it into my gob. I hadn't tasted fresh fruit since, I dunnaw, de Garden of Eden. Dat tang hits you like a slap. De cold chisels into yur teeth, and den de sweetness, and de sides of yur mouth clench up, reeling... Real fruit, boi. Almost too much to bear.

"How's that?"

I didn't know what to say, so I just nodded.

"The correct answer," she said, smiling. She sniffed her arm: "Aw yeah, it's kicking in now!"

"What is?"

"My pheromone pop. Smell my skin." Stuck out her hand.

Pheromone Pop: never heard tell of it. But den dat's de way with me. You could reinvent de wheel anywhere: bionics, medicine, energy, politics, space travel, bloody pop music, a whoop-dee-doo new fizzy drink... doesn't matter. If it doesn't interface with yur noggin through a halo—if it's not Game—it may as well be de wind whistling through a field of thistles far as I'm concerned.

"It doesn't matter what goes on in de world, does it? Dey're always coming up with things to make byors smell nicer. Most reliable industry dere is, I'd say. After undertakers."

"Do you want one?"

"No! Thanks."

"Sure? You won't smell like smoke anymore. Might have to get out of those old clothes, though." She stroked my arm. "Go on. Sniff. Don't be scared."

Green fire blazed in her eyes. She held her hand out, still as a surgeon's. I brought it to my snozz and sniffed once, quick and shallow.

"Alright, it's very nice. Thanks." I only meant to have a fake sniff and den get some more ice-cream—just to get her off my back, like—but as I reached out to pick up another strazza I realized de little whiff *was* very nice indeed. Couldn't put my finger on it. Reminded me of something, maybe.

"Want a little more?" she axed, raising an eyebrow.

"Well, maybe..."

"What makes you think I'll let you?"

"Okay. Fair nuff..."

"Just kidding! Gawd, Tayto." She offered her hand again. I got a careful hold of it, like it was a dangerous weapon dat could go off in my face without warning. Breathed deep dis time. *Mother of...*

"You like?" she axed, but I could tell she wasn't curious. It was pure... what's de word? Coy. Dat smile said she knew bloody well. My heart started pounding hard, and for a sec my eyes went fuzzy. All my attention just—*shhhhhhyupp*—narrowed down to her hand, which seemed perfectly formed. Even de flaky horrible nail varnish was art now. My mouth started watering.

"It's nice," I managed to mumble. She nudged de fruit and ice-cream at me again, but all I wanted now was to smell her more and more. Her neck, her earlobe. Dip her fingers in ice-cream and suck dem clean one by one. Gawd, suck more dan just her fingers. Slide her dress up over her head and den dip—

Coming down de stairs I heard a tumbling and rumbling and walls being belted, and in a second a shower of tossers from de back yard spewed into de pantry. I sprung from my seat, like I'd been caught cracking into de safe or something. Lads didn't even look at us, just stopped jostling each other and started sniffing and groping bout in cabinets and presses. Most were wearing next to nottin, and covered in muck.

"C'mere to me, where're de chocolate biscuits?!" one of dem blared to no one in particular. When nobody answered he just said: "Ah feck it anyway! I could murder a chocolate bikkie right now."

As de savages rummaged everywhere for nibbles, and started loading de dumb waiter with bits of munch and de odd bottle, my shock wore off. I felt dis heavy disappointment weigh down on me instead. Dere'd been a bubble round us two, and it'd gone "pop," and you can't get a bubble back. People, like. Dere's always a ruction of nobtards bursting in somewhere, isn't dere? With de *hur-hur-hur* gorilla laughs and de pushing and shoving, and de *You will yeaaahh boi!* shouts and de big stompy feet crashing through de world *hur-hur-hur...* can never fucken knock, d'y'knaw?

I gazed at Ais. She was sucking ice-cream off her fingers—no bodder on her. Maybe dere was no bubble. I just wasn't used to perfume. Jeez, if dat was true it was worrying. What kinduv beasty nob am I when I'm out of my box and away from my halo? Tis a sad state of affairs: years building up yur sparkling palace with a billion rooms, a prince of a multiverse, like, almost no shitty little carbon bone-bag left of yurself, and what happens? You take a few days down from de cloud, fall outta practice, and BAM! You're a huffy-puffy mammal again, all nostrils and hair and hormones and opposable thumbs trying to grope another smelly fleshpuppet.

I couldn't even be mad at myself. It all felt so strong, dis narrow monkey sensory array. *Sniff sniff. Ah-ah-ah! Monkey wanna hug.* So automatic, like something falling down when you let it go.

And den, at a low ebb in a bad evening, sher who gatches in only de Fop himself, fucken maculate, like he's fresh in from Fashion Week.

"Where are these famous biscuits I simply must try?" he said, spinning his cane like a majorette. He clocked me and Ais near each other, and put on another of his scandalized faces. "Well hello you two. Oh dear. I hope we didn't… interrupt anything."

"You're grand," said Aisling, licking ice-cream straight out of de tub now. Dere was a blaze of pleasure, proper fucken glee, on de Fop's face. He just kept staring at me, grinning, spinning his cane and catching it. For some reason I didn't know what to do. Look away? Stare him down? Dance a fecken jig? He glided toward me.

"Tayto with ice-cream," he murmured to himself. "Unusual combination."

"I wasn't eating," I said, cool as I could manage.

"I see. You don't mind if I have a taste, do you?" He leans in past Aisling, whiffs her neck, and raises his eyebrows in appreciation. Den he dips a strawberry in ice-cream, sucks it clean right in front of my face. Something bout de way he did it, twas pure filthy. Had to hand it to dis Fop character, he had a great gift for charging up de air around him. I could imagine him playing some old game in a parlor room. *Charades, Farqhuar!* After he does de symbol for "fillum," or whadevvor, he just sticks his finger in yur gob and leaves it dere, staring into yur eyes, daring you to pull away.

"How's de ice-cream?" I axed at last, just to shatter dis silence.

"Decadent. Puts me in mind for biscotti. Gentlemen—" He broke away. "How are we doing on this biscuit situation, eh whatwhat?"

I felt released. He'd had his fun. But dere was still a little anxious lump in my gullet. He could go to Mulligan, say gawd knows what about Aisling and me, doesn't matter de facts of de case. I don't remember Mully being de best at sharing.

"Ah *balls!*" said de topless fien searching in vain for de biscuits. I found myself agreeing.

De yawn came out of nowhere. It roared out of me, on and on and on, like a team of engineers'd been building it down in de deepest part of me since before I had a mouth. Dis yawn was epic, boi. It rooted out de insides of my fingers and hoovered up de marrow of my shins; it popped my ears; it clicked my jaw; it even twinged a muscle in my back. I had to bow down to it, dis tornado of a yawn—let it wipe de pantry clear, spiral out of dis low room and rise like yeast through de whole manor, getting thicker and hardier as it spilled from my bottomless pit, clutching up all de culchie squatters and hauling dem over de woods and fields, spitting dirty intruders out one by one onto banks of nettles and thorns, fecking fake-tanned dollybirds facedown in dirty streams and dumping fat-faced farmers, deir willies flapping free in De Great Howl, into piles of cooling cowpat.

But no. For all de welly I gave it, de yawn only buckled me and no one else. Hungry hordes still crawled over de pantry like locusts, *nyom-nyom-nyom-ing* like dere was no tomorrow. Dey'd bleed de place good and dry. Ais wasn't looking me in de eye anymore, so just like dat a switch was thrown and I could feel de legs and eyelids goan on me. Never been so flahed, I'd say.

"Poor thing. You're only fit for bed," she said. De prospect of a bit of kip was so sweet dat her words felt like a blanket. She led me out past de buzzing swarm in de pantry, chucking flour over each other and giggling like sprogs or newlyweds.

"Sweet dreams, *mes petits enfants*," whispered de Fop as we passed him. "I'll see you on the course tomorrow, Mr. Tayto."

"Whazzat?"

"Never mind him, karoo," said Ais, tugging me onward. "Tomorrow can wait. Get a good night's rest now." She glanced back at me and tutted. "You've had such a big day, poor poppet." She was treating me like a babbee, but truth be told, I was so tired I wished she'd pick me up in her arms and carry me to my leaba, wherever it was, and tuck me in.

But no. She had to see some underling bout fixing a place for me, so I was left in another plush ledder chair in de middle of de main hooley. When yur knackered, de stomp of hooves is full-on hellish. Yur eyes keep trying to close, two marbles floating back up into de dark of yur skull on weak bungee-cords, but De Party keeps prodding you: *T'bed?! Don't be a langer, boi, stay up! We're hilarious! Don't you see dat byor over in de corner shrieking with laughter? Poke. Stay up! You'll get yur hole. Poke. Stay up! A few cold sausage rolls still*

knockin about. Poke. Stay up! Singalong comin up next. How can you
sleep at a time like dis? Don't you know dere's only dis and den nottin?
Poke poke poke. Stay up…stay up… stay…

Aisling-Gus woke me in my chair. My bed was ready. I hauled
my bones. De party was even louder and drunker now. Shirtless
lads wrestled, de mob shouting things like *C'mon ye good thing!* and
Stick it to dat dirty tinker, Kev. Round de murkier edges of de room
fiens were dropping de hand like escaped prisoners, fumbling
with bra straps, mashing faces, pure exhibition, like: *lockdown's*
over. Zoo's back open.

Tired as I was, I had to stop and stare. What was worse: de sex
or violence? I pointed to de display, and said straight out to Ais: "I
think it's is just woeful. *Woeful.*" And she laughed. Something bout
de way she did it, I laughed too. *And now,* I thought, *to bed.*

I trotted after her, head down, a tired little horsey. Wasn't my
bed in de manor stables. Dey'd been converted into a bunk room
for saints being "de-haloed." Nottin fancy, but I'd stayed in many a
kwery dat was worse. No sign of rat droppings, neither baking nor
frigid. A body'd kip here no bodder.

Most of de Wakers-to-be were still out partying like it was 1999.
Good. Bit of whisht. I just flopped on de mattress Ais pointed out
to me. *Hello, Bed.* She yanked off my shoes and folded de blanket
over me so I looked like a Tayto taco.

"You're going to like it here," she whispered.

"Ais, girl. I need to see Zeke tomorrow. Need to know he's
sound."

"I promise. Now get some sleep. We rise early here."

"Course you do. I'll just have de continental breakfast so."

She moved in for a kiss, and as she got closer I got a mild whiff
of her pheromone pop. It was fading but still luvvvly. My heart
picked up: what to do, what to do? But she just pecked me on de
cheek, like a ma. I touched de spot where her lips had been. In
de shadows she could have been any age: mother, girlfriend, little
sister. Just enough light to make out a kind face.

"Gus," I whispered, tapping my shock collar. "Get dis off me,
willa?" I could make out her shoulders hopping up and down with
quiet laughter.

"You're too cute," she said at last. "Sleep tight now." She up and
left me, goan back to her party, back to de barechested wrestlers, and

bra un-doers, and tongue swordfighters, and pantry locusts, and all de general brablach dat might want to smell her skin and swing her round for a dance. Even at dis distance I could hear music thumping into de night. My eyes burned, but de little blinky red light on my collar made it hard to keep my lids shut. Couldn't believe it. I finally had a bed in a dark, quiet room and I couldn't sleep. Not used to beds, like, just lie in my recliner. And I don't sleep usually. Sher, an hour's low-halo is better dan a whole night's worth of natural REM. Wakers aren't too quick talking bout dat at all, like. Fact of de matter is: sleep's a shite way to relax. Yur brain's bouncing round with no idea what's up, waking here and dere, pillow's too hot, feet are too cold, need a piss, back's sore from lying on it wrong... and of course dere's nightmares. Fucken nightmares. Saints don't have nightmares, unless dey want to. And den dey have proper ones where you get to *be* de monster, or kill it with yur own teeth. Rise de next morning feeling like de champ: Lord of de Manor!

Bloody blinking red light. I twisted de collar round—fierce careful not to set it off—so de clasp light was buried into my pillow. Still a bit of glow leaked out. No forgetting a tight leash.

I don't remember falling asleep—sher, who ever does?—but I well remember being woken up. Bunch of pavees with scary bazzers booted in de door and fecked on de main lights. Blinding! I was livid before I even knew what was goan on.

De pavees were shirtless, glyphed to de nines with lumen ink, whipping blankets off de few of us saints in bed, and whooping like Clare supporters. I found myself wishing violence on dem. If only I could get at my monster avatar, I'd rip dem all new ones. But we were saints after all, so we lay still in our bunks while de riot squad bayte a noisy path down de aisle, shrieking and yanking blankets to de ground.

I saw Mossy staring out of de bunk above mine as de riot squad moved further down de barn.

"Psst! Mossy. 'Story, boi?"

"Aw, alright Tayto," Mossy murmured, bleary. He'd no collar on. What was dat about? Why was he in with us?

"Who are dese fiens?" I hissed.

"Don't worry," mumbled Mossy. "Gus told me to expect them tonight. They're ex-saints. Graduates. Y'know, from the program. Shakin the new lads up."

One blaggard reached our bunks and grabbed my blanket.

"C'mere, I was using dat!" I snapped.

"Ask me *ghee*, boi!" *Ask me ghee.* Could dey really have been saints once? Were dese loud mouths once sealed shut? Dese roving eyes closed for days at a time? It was hard to credit such scuts, who couldn't stand still, who were so intent on whipping light onto everyone else, once reclined in a fertile dark, all light glowing on de inside except for a thin arc round de skull. If dese were "graduates" of Mulligan's hedge school, de master had a lot to answer for. I'd rather end up in a bed of gorse.

Ciunas! Ciunas le do thoil! One huge fien shouted above de others. I figured he was de capo, but as soon as everyone shut up he curled into a ball on de ground, offering his back as a platform for a small lad with a wispy mustache to step up. Little Caesar hopped onto de big lad and wobbled a bit, getting his balance. He cleared his throat and spoke in a high nasally voice: "I've your attention now, I'd *saaay*." Heads nodded. "And you all know me, I'd *saaay*." Heads nodded again. I couldn't tear my eyes from his little 'tache. It was like a baby Hairy Mollie had crawled onto his face without him noticing, and might sneak off again at any minute. I waited to see if it would.

"Big night tonight, *lllaaa*? Impressive stuff no doubt. What did we see... hah?"

"Sir, we saw, uh..." a lad in a bunk near Little Caesar held up his hand to speak, like we were back in Joov. "Uh, we saw a graduation. Sir."

"Mm. Nnyah. 'S one way of putting it," said Caesar. Den he shouted as loud and harsh as his little trembly voice could take it: "*WE SAW DE DEAD RISE!* Is another way to put it, like." He let dat version settle in. "Now, what did we see tonight?"

"Saw dead rise," muttered about five or six heads.

"Nnyah, didn't hear dat now at all," whinged Caesar, hand held pure theatrical to his ear.

"*WE SAW DEAD RISE!*"

"We did, lads. We saw de dead rise. And a good thing too. Not a minute too soon. Too many dead lads round here. Not enough living ones. De country needs living lads and lassies. It needs to get its life back. Yur all dead, like. But yur trying, aren't ye? Trying to live again. To wake up. Like dese real men!" He gestured, and de yobs started to flex biceps and pecs. I felt a stress headache coming on.

"We are Neo-Wakers!" Caesar announced, stomping a spawg on de big fien under him. "We've swum with mermaids, and flown with angels. And we have de strength, de steel will, to leave all dat shite behind. To come down from de cloud and live as men, with our two spawgs on solid ground." A few lads clapped for dis, including Mossy, gowl dat he was.

"Tomorrow ye face... de Course," said Caesar. "It won't be easy—de Wayke isn't for namby-pambies. But—" He scansed round, his wispy tache twitching. "Dere are rewards to dwelling... in de flesh." He clapped his hands, and two goons led in a young byor. She had on a sparkly bikini top and black ledder pants, de queen of clubs. But de way she catwalked, twas like she was moved with strings, and her face, caked in make-up, looked dead blank—a mask.

Some whoops shot up from de bunks: "Aw de *talent!*"

"She's a fine half, I'd *saaaay*," leered Caesar. De leer spread through de stable like a virus. I could see an evil glint creep into de eyes of de yobs. *I'd saaaay* snaked from deir mouths, curling round de ears of all dese lost, lonely, confused saints. *I'd sssssssaaaay...* faint but hard to ignore, like a wispy mustache. Pure malevolent.

"First three to finish de course tomorrow..." said Caesar, and he gestured at de byor. "Well, to de victors go de spoils. Stella and her sisters will be waiting for you in de caravan off de west wing."

Caesar pointed at Gilbey. "You!" Gilbey pointed at himself, confused. "A little birdie tells me you should've graduated tonight, but you didn't have a flesh friend."

"Ah yeah," chuckled Gilbey. "What can you do, like?"

"*Scuse me?!*" thundered Caesar.

"I mean, *Sir yes sir.*"

"Reluctant to leave, are ya? Like de food here too much, I'd *saaay.*"

"Grub's not bad," admitted Gilbey. A few lads laughed.

"Or maybe," suggested de little fella, adjusting his stance on de big fella's back, "you've nowhere to go?"

Gilbey said nottin to dis, but he stopped smiling.

"COS IT'S NOT A FUCKEN *HOLIDAY RESORT!*" Caesar roared. "TISN'T ALL-YOU-CAN-EAT SHRIMP AT ALL, BOI!" He was so worked up he slipped off de big fien altogether. "Fucken stay still, willa?!" he hissed at de lump, and carefully re-mounted. "Where was I?"

"Not all-you-can-eat shrimp," muttered de lump.

"Ah sher, I'm only *messin* with you," said Caesar, holding out his hands like Christ—if Christ was a bollox with a wispy tache whose sermon on de mount was a peptalk on a bloated gobshite. "Yur sound as a pound, Gilbey boi. A model Neo-Waker. You cast off yur halo like it was no bodder."

He clicked his fingers and de girl stood by him. In her heels she was de same height as Caesar on yur man's back. "Stella heard you've been a good boy: done all yur exercise, eaten all yur veggies. Yur *jacked*, boi!" He clicked his fingers and de girl clambered up halfway to Gilbey's top bunk, grabbed his arm and squeezed.

"Ha ha! Ah no..." Gilbey chuckled.

"Because you've been so good—and because we can't be feeding you anymore, y'langer!—we're going to cut yur collar tonight. How's dat for you now?"

Gilbey nodded, confused. A few lads clapped.

"But c'mere—dat's not all!" announced Caesar. For some of ye, dat halo is de only comfort ye've ever known. Tis tough, lads. No denying it. So Stella here, bless her cotton socks, wants to give ye all a luvvly gift. A *beautiful* gift! She'd like you, Gilbey, to take her right here in front of everyone. Would ye like an eye-load, lads?!"

Stella's eyes sank in deir make-up mask.

De yobs started cheering and whooping, trying to work up de crowd. Most of dose godforsaken saints looked scared, or just blank, but some started cheering along like deir lives depended on it.

"How 'bout it, Gilbey boi?" Caesar eyeballed him. "Up to it?" Gilbey scansed round, and I'd swear he threw me an S.O.S. glance.

"Listen, I dunnaw bout dis like..."

"Don't tell me yur turning down a fine half like Stella here!"

"Sir, sir!" Some other hands were raising. "Pick me, sir!"

"Naw. It's Gilbey's show. Whatsit to be?" He glared at Gilbey.

"*Goan* Gilbey!" someone yelled. *Gil-bey, Gil-bey!* De chant swelled, and soon de communion of saints, and de devil yobs standing at deir shoulders, only missing deir pitchforks, were bawling his name.

Gilbey tried to smile but he looked like a man being backed into a cage corner. Caesar glared at Stella now, baring his teeth. De girl tugged at Gilbey's shorts. He clutched dem, still trying to chuckle like twas all in good fun.

"Playing hard to get!" Caesar shouted to de crowd.

And den something in me broke. Dunnaw why. Could've been dat rictus of a smile on Gilbey's mug as he struggled to keep his shorts on. I saw him as a kid again, back in Joov, with de big daydreamy head on him. Always cheered me up. *No bodders on Gilbey—maybe we'll be okay.* He never wanted anything from anyone, never *took* anything. I'd never seen him tense, like he was now. Or maybe it was de sadness on Stella's young face, breaking through her mask. Or de smugness of Little Caesar as he fanned de cheers and chants of de crowd. Maybe it was just dat one prat in de corner, de nobber who kept doing biceps flexes and push-ups. I can't say. But whadevvor de cause, something snapped in de auld soft machine, and a voice went in my head: *Erra feck dis. Need to get some kip!*

As soon as I thought it, my stress headache vanished. I sprang out of bed and walked over to Gilbey's bunk, shaky but resolute, like. De big fien Caesar had been standing on was up on his hind legs now, and he pushed into my chest.

"Where you think yur goan, *amadán*?"

"Listen love," I said, speaking straight to Stella over de big mong's shoulder. "You seem like a luvvly girl and all, but dat's my bud Gilbey. I'll say dis for him: he doesn't force anything on anyone. So, like, if dis isn't his *cupán tae*, let's be leaving his shorts alone, yeah?" De cheering and clapping died down. I was spoiling de *mood*, like.

"Who are you?" axed de big fella of me.

"Who am I?" I said, holding out my skinny arms like I've seen scobes do before a fight. Like peacock feathers. "I'm Mr. Tayto. Who're you?" And I tapped him right back in de center of his barrelly chest. He drew himself up to full height.

"I am Otis!"

"Otis, is it? Well I don't blame you being angry. Dat's got to be some burden of a name to haul through life."

And den he dawked me with a stone fist and finally—*finally*—de lights were out.

Otis gave first class tickets to de Land Of Nod. I dreamed my first dream in ages. Unlike a haloscape—which is just about de most vivid experience you can have—dreams are hard to remember. But

I recall sailing, or surfing sortuv. I stood astride a currach made of turtle shell. Dere was a feeling of no turning back. I was headed to a new world, but as it grew from a speck on de horizon to a huge roaring shore, I clocked it was also, somehow, my first home, my origin. Dere, past de shore and through de trees, was my parents' old farmhouse, with de tire swing and all. It was only den I looked down to see I was surfing on a real turtle—his flippers were paddling away, fighting de sea. Pure effort. De poor crayture's head poked out of his shell and rotated to look up at me. At first it looks sad, big eyes straining like blackberries, about to burst... but then a change comes over de eyes and now tis pure fear. I lifted his shell like de lid of a sea trunk: curled inside with a rake of prawns, like a fetus waiting to get born, was Zeke. He kept trying on all dese different tiny hats, frantic. Aisling-Gus was breastfeeding all de prawns, real gentle and loving. But when she was done with each one she'd put it down and Mully would gobble it up. He was working his way over to Zeke. I shouted at Zeke to wake up and run, but he just kept trying on more hats. In a panic, I scansed over de shore, looking for someone to help us. All I could see were dese preening white peacocks, strutting around de water's edge...

Dreams. Stoopid yokes. Hate dem.

I felt de cool muck under my cheek first. Slowly, a smeeer of pain wrapped round my head. I blinked into ... morning. I was lying facedown in a field. Otis's royal dawk had re-banjaxed my nose dat was banjaxed since Gubna's headbutt. As soon as I sat up I wished I hadn't. A dose of gawks hit me worse dan de headache, and I missed de cool muck. It was like a dirty great acres-long icepack. But de cold ground dat felt good for my noggin wasn't de best for my chest: my lungs were wheezy and I kept coughing. I looked down at my squirrel jumper, de one I'd had since I was a smallee. Destroyed.

I stood up, groggy. Right beside me were de stables. So dey hadn't dumped me in de middle of nowhere after all. Tayto was still part of de "process." Hallelujah.

I went for a slash into de hedge, drowning nettles outside some poor crayture's hidey hole. A shout went off behind me: "Hey tough guy!" It was Otis, squeezed into a skintight black bodysuit, hands on hips, belly slumping out over a pair of surprisingly spindly legs. He looked like a massive frog. I nodded to him and went back to my slash, but he bawled again about *getting-with-de-program* like some manner of Yank. He pointed a meaty digit to de field's end. All my stablemates were stretching and hopping about in de muck, squeezed into snazzy unitards, dodgy superheroes in training. Beyond was a big water slide, and an obstacle course rigmarole. Dorky triumphant choons squawked from a speaker. *Twill be a long morning,* I coggled to myself, wishing I could wiggle deep into de hidey hole below, and snuggle up to whadevvor crayture was curled up in dere, listening pure casual to de leaves dripping outside.

We gathered round de bottom of de water slide. Otis lobbed a bodysuit my way. I stripped to my jocks. De only fien in normal clothes was Gilbey, sitting back in a rickety deckchair. He gave me a thumbs-up.

Scrawny as I was, dis suit was tight like skin on a sausage. Otis lit a little bonfire I'm pretty sure he'd made just for my stuff and chucked my antique clothes onto it, no ceremony or nottin. Alf disappeared in flames—poor hairy bollox. De last thing to get swallowed up was his *YO!* De tongues licked-licked-licked it up, lickety-split, just like last night in de library with Kepler and de lads. Hungry flames out dese parts. And now more cold black muck where once dere was stuff—friendly *YO!*s and de like. So here we were, mincing round in black tights like a bunch of shadows lost deir owners.

"S'story with dese black rubber johnnies for tracksuits?" I said. Someone muttered something bout *microfibers* and *neurotransmitter modulamification* and, long story short, I figured I was in a full-body fucken nicotine patch. Every few minutes we'd be getting a dose of get-up-and-go to see us through whatever joyous Waker circus they'd rigged up. I got my first taste of it as some fien helped velcro me up at de back. Nottin drastic, just a kinduv *right-so-let's-go* hoppity-jumpity buzz. Whazza word? Pep! *I had pep in my step!* You'd want it too, knockin about with a rake of nobbers in a damp field.

De Damp. Even with a catsuit and booties on, you feel it. You can't get out of it. It's wet, yeah, but not like de sticky closeness of a jungle. No blazing orange tigers here, lurking in a hedge, flashing switchblade eyes. None of dat sweaty, sexy kind of wet. And it's cold, but not de proper icey death-grip of de tundra. No big silvery Siberian cats either. Tis damp. De opposite of sunshine. Opposite of comfort. It settles on a place and den radiates out of everything, a chill, watery ptttthhh. A drain of air from your tyres. De Damp. Hard to be a hero in it. Or a hunter, or a jumper, or a climber, or a lover. No weather for cats.

We all looked a sight. De thing about mucky Irish fields and pale skin, you can dress up like Tron all you like, but you'll still end up looking like a knobbly-kneed GAA player in a leotard. How bad? Seriously, have you ever met a sexy person you could stand to be around? Sod de sexies! Langers de lot of 'em! Jeez, it was some pep I was getting. Even while I was bashing de sexies I felt a tingle in my Dingle dolphin, d'y'knaw? Getting antsy to just get *goan!* Dat's when Otis blew a whistle and two sheepdogs came belting out of nowhere to his side, proud, official, tongues hanging manic.

"You're being timed," was all Otis said, and fired his whistle again. Sharp as tacks, de two dogs herded one poor bollox to de foot of de slide, nipping at him. Dey barked and he launched himself up de steps. And I'm not being mean or smart, like, but it wasn't poetry in motion. Dis guy was no cat. Sher how could he be? De Damp was seeping from everywhere, like a gawd of mediocrity, and his sister—De Grayness—draped herself over us all.

Otis tutted at such a display. De slide bounced as Chariots-Of-Fire launched himself down it, and de dogs met him at de end to yap him up a rope climb over a high wall.

"Each obstacle is a *symbol,*" some twat whispered in my ear. Dey are yeaaah, boi. Looked like a metaphor for a pain in de arse. Yur man made it down de other side of de high wall and into a manky puddle. De dogs were waiting again, ready to herd him on through a rake of other doodads: slippy balance beam, some kinduv monkey bar yoke, and—would you believe it?—an actual hoop.

Tell you, boi: dose sheepdogs had all de moves: de crouch, de spring-loaded pounce, keeping it all moving and never getting in de way. Pure enthusiasm—perfect Wakers: *Hey! Ho! I've got a job! Purpose! I'm lovin' life, never pausing long enough to think bout it. I launch from my basket every morning with my tail wagging!*

Yur man made it to de tent and disappeared inside. De dogs fired demselves back over to bully another sheep: muggins. Dey barked at my ankles and I wandered over to de slide tower's steps. Cold. Metal. Bit damp.

"Jesus whatcha waaaitin for?!! A gilded invitaaaation?!!" Drill Sergeant Otis bawled.

"Looks a bit slippy is all. Might take a tumble."

"I'm *timing* you!" Otis shrieked. To be honest, I think his bodysuit was a few notches too high on de pep.

Started to climb. Slippy metal, cold fingers, head still woozy. Recipe for an injury, la. At de top I peered down de chute. Red and dark. At de bottom was a glimmer of light: two thick lips you needed to squeeze through. More re-birthing craic. Did you ever hear of anything so stoopid before breakfast? Someone in de organization had read one too many self-help books.

I looked down at Otis. From dis height he looked small at last.

"Just taking a moment!" I called down. "Bit emotional, like. Fierce symbolic process dis, d'y'knaw?" Another blast of pep hit me and I wriggled onto my belly, feet dangling toward de waiting lips. I fell a few inches until I was holding onto de ledge with just my fingertips. I had de collywobbles bad: my hands were cramping holding on so tight. Fear had me by de ghoulies good and proper. De more I said *Sher dis is silly* de more de fear said *Oh gawd ya, tis fierce silly* and dug my fingers into spasms. Panic comes like a sunrise. A faint hint off in de distance, and den suddenly a crack of brilliant terror, and all de birds shriek together up and down de tree of yur spine. No pause, no reverse, and no changing channel. You are where you are and you can't get out. Nottin for it but to go *through*.

My fingers couldn't hold forever, and I let go. Twas a fast ride down. I hit de lips with a *whummp!* and stayed still for a second, curled up, my palms stinging from friction burn. I tried to kick my way through de lips, but dey were tighter dan I expected. Should've built up more speed to break through. Next thing a moon-faced kid bombed down and cracked headfirst into me like a canonball. We plowed into daylight, bleeding twins.

As we sat in de muck, moaning, de sheepdogs scampered over—furry stormtroopers.

"Still timing you!" screamed Otis.

With de help of de dogs and de pep in my fancy pants, I managed up de gnarly rope to de top of de high wall.

In de haloscape my speciality is heights. I basejump from cliffs, somersault off skyscrapers dat'd shame Everest. But it only shows up my normal meatbag cowardice all de more. At de top of de big wall I froze again. I knew I'd only be a second or two falling into de puddle below. But de resolve it takes to push off... dat awful instant as you leave yur perch... I couldn't do it. I was fixed well and good, like a fridge magnet holding up a failing report card.

After a while de other lads were sent over de wall and I just scooched aside to let dem pass. Some tried to encourage me: *Don't worry boi... in yur own time...* De kindness made me feel worse. Just shut up and huff and puff along yur way. I watched dem clamber and scuttle. *Hey! Ho!* Sheepdogs in training, little waggy tails starting to sprout in de seat of deir tracksuits.

Eventually even de sheepdogs gave up on me, barking after de final stragglers and leaving me to my frozen kingdom.

"Yur a disgrace!" Otis shouted up. "Not even worth timing!"

So dere I sat, De Untimed, up on my wall like Humpty Dumpty. I thought bout climbing back down de rope but somehow dat was scarier now dan jumping, so I just stayed put. Aw, de symbols de symbols. Wakers and deir snazzy symbols. *Yur paralysed, brother. Stuck in one place. Leap of faith and you'll get yur life back.* Wankers. Being stuck on a wall above a big dirty puddle is nottin like being a saint. To a Waker, life is an obstacle course, maybe. Sometimes you get stuck, but with a bit of gumption you can work yur way out of it and get back to de party. Saints see it different. Or at least I do: Life is *de wall*. You cling to it, not goan anywhere, till it gets too boring or yur shoved off. And den it's down into de Big Puddle. Enda story. Dere's not much worth doing up on de wall—fairly flat place, like—so yur better off donning an auld halo and goan to de infinite obstacle course of yur lit-up mind. And once yur gaming, dere's no need for fecken *symbols.* De Scape itself is enough. You don't need one thing pointing to another, like. Doing one thing but trying to do something else entirely. Just be. Just play. Symbols are for de Wayke, dat flat high narrow place surrounded on all sides by a fall. All dese symbols and self-help activities... makes me think dese Waker lads have too much time on deir hands. Maybe dey don't fully trust what dey're selling, so dey need to dress it up a bit, like. I reckon if something is good—really and truly essential—dere's no call for symbols to sell it to you at all at all. Or drill sergeants. Or sheepdogs.

I figured someone would come and get me, or throw something at me to knock me off, but naw. No one came. Abandoned. My fancy-pants pep supply had run out, and I felt hollow. I think de pep was what had me wound so tight I couldn't go down de slide or jump off de wall, cos now I felt fairly normal and dropped off de edge easy enough. Splash—cold puddle, bit manky but no big deal. I waded to dry land and, since no one else was watching me, wandered past de rest of de obstacle course rigmarole. I was passing de tent at de end when an auld wan popped her head out. She clocked me and rolled her eyes: "Lordblessusandsavevuss I thought ye were all long done by now!"

"I've a note from my doctor, love. Zempt from P.E. today." I winked at her, pure awkward. Never know how to be cutesey or folksy—or even just normal—with older citizens, even with all my time in de Gerries. Or because of it.

"Ah no sher," she cried. "C'mere to me and we'll get you kitted out in no time!"

Kitted out?

Dripping with puddle water, I gatched into her pokey tent. She sealed de flap behind me. Twas fairly dark inside. Dat smell: musk and age, de smell of attics, basements, garages, trunks. A lot of kweries smell like dis. It's de musk of someone else's memories, another person's nostalgia. All small pokey places draw it out of me, like I'm creeping round an old person's head—no clue about de details, but massive mothball emotions clinging to everything. All de puddle-mucked bodysuits lay in a heap.

"What are you now so? A small, I'd say." She was sizing me up and rooting through a pile of clothes at her feet. She wore sandals. Her grey toes curled over each other in crooked lines, wonky treeroots. "Sorry now, I'd say de trendiest stuff is long gone... and getting yur fit might be a divil... but if yur going to be a johnnie-come-lately... you've to make do, don't ya?"

"No bodder. Not too up on de fashions anyway."

She smiled at me. "Arra, don't all saints say dat? Be up on yeer tombstones: *Here so-and-so lies—wasn't too up on de fashions.*" She rooted some more. I liked de odd bird. Reminded me of my own granny: not too fussed. Doubt she'd take Otis and his timer too serious. In fact, why had she truck with dese Waker knob-ends at all?

"Now so!" she cried, triumphant, hauling a pea-green shirt and jacket from her tangled mound. "Try dis for size, my darling."

"What's dis get-up for?"

"For de dance hall. Everyone has to go to de dance!" she chirped like some demented fairy godmammy. She stood staring at me, and after a while I clicked she was waiting for me to strip. *Second time today I've been down to my jocks in front of an audience.* With her help I peeled out of my black skin like a rotten 'nana. She rubbed her hands slowly over my back.

"Aw yeah," she cooed. "Dry as a bone. Dose jumpskins are de job, aren't dey?" I finally pulled free of de skin and stood in my unmentionables. She stared at my stomach, my ribs jutting out, black fluff in my belly button.

"Always a luvvly view on you young fellas," she sighed, almost sad looking. "De slim abs, like."

I said nottin, just took de shirt and flayked it on. Bit short on de arms and loose round de belly. Typical. She began to button me up, her swollen fingers working slow and careful.

"Dey do call me Biddy Hen," she said in a low voice. "I've a fine cut of a rooster at home, but he's seen better days, gawd love him."

"Oh yeah? Well if dere's a dance, come along, sher. Maybe you'll pull a peacock."

"Arra go way outta dat! My dancing days are long over!" For a second I caught a glimpse of a young byor peeking out through her wrinkle mask. Even in de low light, her eyes were green fire, so like Aisling-Gus I got a shock and stepped back.

"Y'alright dere, love? Look like you've seen a ghost."

"Bit too much pep in dese jumpskins, d'y'knaw?" I froze where I was in de dim light, in de heavy musk.

"Now try dese pants on, karoo." She was pointing to rancid green trousers. I got a paranoid chill at de sound of *karoo*. Biddy Hen, or whoever she was, stared at me, and not knowing what else to do I pulled on my new green pants. Too short on de leg and loose at de gut. Typical. Biddy gave me a green tweedy jacket, and smoothed my shirt's wide collar out over de shoulders.

"Now so," she said. "Handsome man, off to de dance." And as she said it, something broke in her. I saw de greenfire eyes fill with tears. I saw an aging animal caught in a trap, knowing no way out. My paranoia melted away, and wished I could haul her out of her sadness, whadevvor its cause. She must have sensed it, for she fell into me, pushed her lips soft onto mine. Dunnaw why, but I was surprised at de warmth of her mouth. Spose she looked so grey and ashen, I figured she'd be cold too. But even a dying fire burns hot to de touch. She clung to me, and I just stood dere, frozen, as she lobbed de gob like an awkward young wan behind de bike sheds.

Her skin reminded me of de old survivors back in de Gerries, tucked away safe and silent in a maze of rooms. Twitchers who didn't sit still like young wans when dey lit up. All de times I crept into rooms and emptied a bin, or gave dem a quick wipe down, trying not to touch deir rubbery-papery skin with my own. Maybe I felt I owed one of dem a moment of real—dunnaw. Would kissing a scobe like me be *comfort* to anyone? Dis awful pea-green suit probly reminded her of some fien she was loopy over once upon a time. Her rooster back in de day. Or someone else—de fancy fowl dat got away? Twas a long kiss, boi. Her final kiss, felt like. And it practically my first. Maybe I *was* her old rooster, at de end of a long life, magining he was young, on a mission, searching for a Crown dat couldn't be. I'd never coggled what it'd be like to be old, not figuring my body would last long enough. De image of myself, wrinkled, hunched—a cough spluttered up out of me. I pulled away just in time not to cough in her mouth. And why wouldn't I go consumptive, lying in a damp field for a night? Wondered did Otis time how long I was facedown in muck.

"Nasty cough," she said, stiffening.

"Rough night. Slept outdoors."

"A body has to be careful round here. You'll catch yur death."

"A lot of it goan round dese days."

"You've no idea," she said, cold suddenly. "On yur way now, young fella," she held open de tent flap. "Yur already late for de dance."

"Feck de dance, girl!"

"Everyone must go to de dance. C'mon—shift!" She was all commonsense again, no bodder on her. I walked to de flap and she began stuffing de dirty skins into great big bags—Biddy Hen, pure industry.

Dunnaw why, but I felt bad leaving her, like once I was gone she'd turn into a pillar of salt or an auld tree or something. Cop on. She was probly eager to wrap up her wares and head off home to her rooster, get a bit of cheese on toast or whadevvor auld wans eat for lunch.

I could hear a bassline and drums pounding from a pre-fab shed across de way. A dance.

"I can't go dressed like dis. I look like a trainee leprechaun."

"De apparel oft proclaims de man," she said. Hadn't a bog what dat meant, so I raised de eyebrows and gave her a nod. *So long Biddy Hen, scratching and pecking about in de dirt. I've to fly to de Royal Ball now... Elegance and glory await. Ta-ta. Flap flap.*

I strode into de ballroom, bedecked in my leprechaun finery. First thing I clocked was four female saints, hunched in a huddle. More like a life raft of survivors, trying to steer clear of small gomey sharks cruising nearby—sniffin at dem from de edge of de dancefloor.

Otis and Little Caesar were doing rounds, both wearing shiny shirts, blasting a whistle or remote-shocking any poor bollox not dancing, or not dancing *enough*. Shock collars glinted like tiny disco lights, or SOS signals.

A stage was set up, and who was spinning de choons and giving it all *dis*, but Gilbey. He was pointing to randomers and blowing on his fingers like smoking guns as he spun decks on de old-fashioned choonalizer. Haunches shaking on him, la!

Honest now, not being smart, I've seen more erotic energy at de social evenings we forced on de auld wans back in de Gerries. Tell ya, some could still shake it. But dis saintly scene in de shed was woeful squared. Not dat I was judging. Not keen on tripping de light fantastic myself. Dere's two kinds of people in dis life: shady gatchers and shiny dancers, and I know which way my shoes shuffle. Otis fired his whistle in my ear.

"Let's see some shaaaapes, Darby O'Gill!"

"Dey're *yur* clothes, boi," I replied, dead cool, like. He'd flattened me once already, but I just couldn't take him seriously. Big glinty gold necklace...

"Had enough out of you now, runt. Dance, or by gawd I'll put de hop on ya." He levelled his remote in my direction. Herr Kommandant sailed off on his rounds again, and I stood still. My feet grew roots: down through floorboards, through topsoil, past all de little worms, deeper until I was hitting cold rock. I was rooted, boi—deeper dan gawd's own aching tooth. Haven't been dat still while wayking in all my life. Pure *anti*-dancing. Luvvly. From my stillness I watched de jiggling all round me. Free-floating saints formed little inward-facing circles, bobbing and twitching shoulder to shoulder, with much staring at shoes, and nervous glances at DJ Gilbey.

Considering how my saintly brethren had been plucked from haloscapes—wings yanked off and genitals stuck back on—I'd say dey were making a brave stab at it, clopping hooves on de Wayke's hard floor. But twas nervous kiddies trying to warm up by a make-believe fire, afraid of de long night ahead. No jigging for joy. Caesar chewed his loudspeaker: *Loosen up, fuckssake!*

Neither hot nor cold, wild or barren, just embarrassed. A petty hell.

A leg whipped into mine and I tumbled—so much for my deep roots. It was de moon-faced kid who'd cracked into me down de water slide. He'd been spinning in a headstand, but now he was on his back. "Balls," he said, rubbing his noggin. "I'm a cyber-breaker. Level four. Lot harder doing it in the Wayke." Something bout his earnest mug told me he was ready to cough up a pure culty nugget—no stopping it: "But once I learn how to do it in real life it'll be all the more rewarding!"

"Uh huh," I said. "C'mere, any way of getting off dance duty, kid?"

"You can spin choons," he pointed at Gilbey, who was flailing a pair of nunchuks while he mixed tracks. It sounded like a car crash and a New Year's Eve party trying to have a baby.

"No other options like?"

De kid nodded weakly at de four ladies clumped together. "Dere's a shifting room out back," he muttered.

"My gawd," I said. "De bastards have us any way we turn."

Otis was eying me so I cha-cha-ed over to de Four Lashes of D'apocalypse.

"Just when you think it can't get any worse," says de tall blondy in a ballgown, looking me up and down.

"Howerya ladies? Had a less dan stellar performance at de obstacle course today. Last in to Biddy's tent so..." I gestured at de green duds. Blondy stared at me horrified, like I'd just clambered dripping out of a well and ribbited my love to her.

De Life Raft Ladies were fine halves. Deir apparel was proclaiming dem, like. Contrariwise, de lads—gomey craytures with gaping fish mouths, or hopping like seagulls—were kitted out in raver gear from last century, scruffy blue tuxes, assorted GAA jerseys, top hats and de like.

"So," I said, whirling my hands in case de Lord of de Dance was watching. "Anyone fancy a shift?"

De words were hardly out of my gob when everything hushed. Gilbey stepped back from de choonalizer, head low. De lanky figure of de Fop loped over to take his place on stage. He was wearing some kinduv raspberry kimono and walked pure deliberate, like he was balancing an egg on his noggin. A man walking to his death, or floating, state executioner-style, to drop de axe on someone else. He reached de choonalizer and slipped off his sandals, like every little move was some big zen deal. From a pouch on his belt he took out some rings, and slowly stuck one on each of his fingers and his big toes. Den he strapped a white e-mask over his mouth and nose. His scarecrow eyes glared. Everyone was still now, even Otis and Little Caesar, gawking at dis unworldly crayture.

De Fop lifted his long hands wide above his altar. Den he moaned into his mask. A voice slithered out, mutated, multiplying, swelling and wet: *Aaaaah'm an aaaamphhhhhibian.* Dat voice, tell ya, it scuttled right under yur skin. He said it again and I clocked a bunch of fiens crouch, coiled, waiting for de release. *Aaaaah'm an aaaamphhhhhibian.* Alright boi, yur an amphibian. Dowtcha, like. Den he fecks his head up to de sky and roars it—*AMPHIBIAN!*—and explodes into a mad lanky dance. De music goes off like fireworks, and suddenly all round me lads are on de floor goan mental. Fiens are hoppin off de walls and off each other, grabbin each other in headlocks, swinging demselves round like ragdolls. *AMPHIBIAN!* Every movement of de Fop's fingers and feet warps de sounds; it's like he's bayting de shite right out of de song he's singing, and I'm not sure who's winning, but everyone is getting deir digs in. Man versus Music, like. De Fop is punching in a blur, but I can make out some fancy fingerwork too, some subtle kung-fu goan on inside his boxing.

I threw a glance at de four-byor life raft, and Blondy looked well impressed: "His bodybreak is so technical!"

"Self-indulgent tripe," said de small goth with a roll of her eyes.

Ah'm an amphibian! screamed de whole zoo again, all de beasts of trees and caves and rivers howling from de Fop's crackling snout, a tangle of tongues. He was trancing now, weaving sound pictures with his digits, a sonic spider. Into his web left and right, arms flapping like manic wings, saints buzzed in deir new chains, needless shock collars blinking—here was de new pied piper come to swoop up all de holy little boys and girls. His long hand filled de floor, was de floor. It gripped dem. No more confusing dis with de Gerries—de dancefloor was squirming. It suddenly looked to me like one great clear pane, sticky but see-through, onto another world. And no one was scared now, cos dey could see through de little fires dey were trying to kindle, feel right through to de heat at de heart of deir brave new world. Fair duce to de lanky bollox: He was mesmerizing.

De small gothy byor grabbed my hand.

"C'mon," she said. "I can't stand any more of this *septic*." Her grip felt warm as she hauled me through de twitchy zoo, and I took comfort in it, which surprised me. Don't normally like to be touched. Probly a sign I should light up soon as possible. Don't want to find myself selling plastic cutlery, making payments on a pokey semi-detached near a shop and a daycent school. Naw, boi. Not for me. But for now—to navigate my situation, like—I held dis little byor's hand and let her pull me like a tiny Goth tractor. She took me to de door by de stage, with a single red light bulb shining above. I'd no love of dis ballroom, or de looderamawns in it, or de Fop's wriggling rhythms spreading with a thousand tails, but something bout dat little plain red bulb made me wish I was still stuck on de obstacle course wall. Or back in my kip of a flat in Dublin. Or anywhere else, really.

De door shut behind us and de zoo outside vanished. Everywhere was lazy with low red light. I heard hissing at first—a rake of couples were lolling like serpents on de biggest inflatable mattress I'd ever seen, and dey hissed at me for letting de door slam.

For a shifting room, dere wasn't much shifting goan on, like. I saw two lads snoggin de faces off each other, but mostly it was girls laying round, holding each other, whispering. Who could blame byors for wanting off de dance floor, with a load of dancing fools moving in on dem? Why hadn't more lads flayked in here to admire de scenery? Who was I to talk? Heavy halo use is a bucket of Odd, and it pushes you out of de Wayke in lots of unexpected ways. Forgetting stuff, mainly. It starts with subtle little things like street names. If yur unlucky it goes on de rampage, till yur hard put to swallow, or go to sleep. You forget to want things with yur body. Nearly every saint I knew had lost interest in meeting men or women, and de few who might still be into it had lost de bottle to actually do it. Ended up just clambering on sex drones with stoopid knockers. Whadevvor de reason, dis "shifting room" looked more like a harem at rest.

My own little goth was standing next to me now, hunched, frozen. I'd a dose of bravado out on de floor axing for a shift. Think it was me throwing two fingers up at Otis, Caesar, and Blondy. But now I was in de low red light, big mattress dere, la, and I hadn't a bog what to do. At last, more for shelter dan anything, she pulled into my side and squeezed me. I felt my usual panic in de grip of a hug, but it passed. Her eyes were closed. She was so small, and lonely looking. I felt so sad suddenly dat I nearly hugged her back.

And den who do I see, lying on his belly in a pool of white light, getting a massage from a lady in hotpants? None other dan de bold Zeke—not a bodder on him. I was struck by de race of feelings. *Thank gawd he's okay!* was out of de gate first, but overtaken on de inside track by *Why de fuck is he so chilled out?*, and driving up fast from de rear was *Puck him in de head.* I was so off balance I was glad of de gentle little goth holding me upright. You get used to sitting in yur chair, numb to life. A few days on de road and suddenly yur having Big Emotions like de all-singing,-all-dancing star of *Knobber, De Musical.* But dere was no music here, just whispers and sighing, ghost sounds low as de red light, skin sliding on pumped-up rubber.

I took a deep breath and told de weird anger to back off for a second, as I looked down at my goth buddy. She was still clinging to my ribs, eyes closed.

"Scuse me dere, love," I said, gentle as possible. She opened her eyes but held on. "I've to go over here a minute. I see someone I know."

"Oh," she said, like I'd told her her breath stank.

"Naw, seriously. Not trying to offload you, like."

She didn't make a move, so I just started inching dat way and she crawled after me across de wobbly mattress, a lost pup. I tapped Zeke.

"Mr. Tayto!" he said with a smile, like he'd been roused from a nice dream. He reached out an arm: "You're one of the good ones."

"You alright, boi?" I squinted to see his pupils.

"Sher I'm only luvvly," he said, trying to do my voice. "Candice here was just giving me a massage. She's a nice lady."

"Zeke, what'd dey give you?"

"Just some nice chocolates. They were *very* nice." He smacked his lips, slightly drooling.

I heard de door open and shut behind me and didn't a byor in full black burqa float through de red room. When I say floated, I mean it—head didn't bob up and down or nottin. She drifted, slow, like she had all de time in de world, like she was only half in de world, a jet-black ghost. When she knelt next to us, Zeke was so surprised by dis apparition he let out a laugh.

She didn't laugh. Her peepers stared out from her headdress slit: green disks, perfect and still. De little goth next to me crawled over and lay her head onto de burqa byor's lap, just curled right into her like a loving moggy. I think I heard her purring.

"Are you a shadow?" axed Zeke, reaching out to touch. Dat was pure acting de maggot now, so I held his hand down. *Don't touch her. Don't touch anything.* I was well shaken by dis arrival. Queenly, too dignified to be looked at. Dose eyes, boi. Emeralds. Didn't like how she'd zeroed in on me and Zeke. She stroked de goth's hair. Maybe de little thing was already her pet. I tried to tell Zeke with my eyes we had to be careful here, but he kept smacking his lips and looking so carefree. Candice was back to rubbing his shoulders. I nearly preferred him when he was losing de plot.

As I wondered how I might maneuver him back to de noisy dancefloor, so we could plan our escape, her majesty started talking.

"Hello Mr. Tayto." Knew my name. Well, dat couldn't be good now, could it?

"And yur name is?"

"That's not important." Her voice was too calm. My spine was bending, a chimney stack falling in slow motion. "Do you like it here, Mr. Tayto?"

"Um, let me think," I scratched under my shock collar, "who's dis you are again?"

"We are your friends. If you want to leave this place, then trust me, Mr. Tayto: We can get you out of here. Tonight."

"Ha," said Zeke, "ha"—too relaxed from his luvvly massage and whadevvor was in de chocs to cough a full laugh out.

"Pull de other one, sher," I told her. "It has bells on."

"I understand. You have no reason to trust me. You can always stay here until your captors let you go. But their standards get steeper by the day."

"C'mere to me," I whispered. "I've no love of dese Waker langers, but what's it dey say bout de devil you know?"

"How well do you know these devils?"

"Didn't I go to Joov with at least one of dem?"

"Francis Mulligan?"

"Foxy, yeah. De Big Cheese."

Her majesty stopped stroking de goth's hair.

"Mulligan and his cronies plan to forget you," she said, an edge to her voice.

"Forget me? So what?" But de little goth was looking at me, scared.

"It's a euphemism. They're going to forget you in the woods." Dere was dis little space between de queen saying dis and sheer panic stabbing my chest. It was a nice little space. I liked it while it lasted. Den I had trouble breathing.

"Goan t'fuck!" I squeaked.

"Keep your voice down," said yer wan. I wanted to grab onto her, a drowning man clutching at a buoy. Her green eyes broke away from me. I wanted to jump up, plead to de whispering couples curling in de red light: *Fucken help me.* But I couldn't move. Weight on my chest. I'm not cut out for danger. Dat's for square-jawed lads with moustaches, necks as thick as my thigh. Zeke, you *laaanger*, get up.

De queen was laser-focused on me: "I take it you're interested in our help." And den de goth left her mistress to hug me again, and her hug said everything I wanted to hear: *I know you. You stay in yur room and don't hurt a soul. You used to fish with yur brother down near de stream, and watch bees get drunk on sunflowers in de back yard. And when it rained you'd watch de droplets flayke down de window like mad fellas in a race, and find de whole world funny. You've done nottin wrong.*

My thoughts circled round to my murder. I wondered if Otis himself was going to do me in with a shovel out behind de stables, or would it be dat little gurrier Caesar with something mean and common like a Stanley blade. Just jab me when I went for a wazz in de bushes. Probly scuttle out from a hole in de hedge, den scurry back underground to hump a ferret, or whadevvor creeps like him are riding dese days. I glanced round, paranoia getting its claws in good.

"Focus, Mr. Tayto," interrupted de queen of de dim red harem, cool and calm in her pool of white light. "We have conditions to discuss."

Come sunset, all de saints were given a platter of sangers. Thick white bread streaked with great gobs of butter, squelched onto beef and cow tongue and whadevvor. I couldn't look at dem, but my fellow obstacle-hoppers horked right in, mouths mashing up soggy balls of cow mess, eyes rolling with relief. After de dirty sangers everyone was hustled back to de stables for bed. Dey'd really got into de leppin about; what with de shape-throwing and obstacle-coursing of de day, most fiens hit deir bunks with moans and chewinggum yawns that stretched on forever. I was flahed too, despite being de laziest bollox dere, having spent most of de day slouching on a wall, and de rest of it slouching on a crashmat. Well, second laziest after Zeke, de massage-seeking missile. He'd sobered since our little chat with our burqa byor. Now he lay stiff as a plank in de bunk under me, staring straight up at my mattress, brow knitted—a man possessed with fear.

Everyone was soaked. It'd pissed down on our way back from de shed, a real Munster monsoon. No towels. We dried ourselves as best we could with our blankets and lay shivering in our draughty stable. Every drop bounced loud off de corrugated roof. How far had dey fallen to batter us? I thought of dark wet woods. My body decomposing in rain, circled by trees—bunch of mute witnesses waving in de wind.

Fien in de top bunk across from me squeezed a teddy bear. Wasn't a bear, like. Twas a penguin. Big eyes, friendly beak. Kid was young but his penguin looked older dan any of us. I heard de kid whisper-sing to his penguin: *You are my sunshiiine, my only sunshiiine, you make me haaaappy, when skies are grey...* He was hugging it for all de world like a lover, one of dem about to be exiled and dis deir last night together. I sure as shite hoped it was *my* last night here anyways.

I stared up at de roof, clattering away to beat de band, and went over what little bit I remembered her majesty telling me. An agent would come fetch me and Zeke, she said. We didn't need to know details. We just had to be ready. So I lay dere, being ready.

Agent. De word was all adventure and bad-ass-ery. Didn't seem real. In fact, de more I coggled it, de more it felt like a collosal leg-pull, or worse, a trap. But sher, when yur already strangling on a leash, what's de threat of another trap, like? Unless it's a hungry fox coaxing you out of yur cage. *Don't worry, bud. I'll free you.* Tell ya, if Otis or Caesar or some lapdog came at me tonight I'd jab dat langer right in de eye. *Whhhish!* Just like dat! Whip de eyeball out of him with my nail. *Pock—squelch! Picked de wrong scrawny to mess with tonight, boi.* Zeke and me lay on our bunks, stiff as corpses but ready to rise.

Some skinhead yob clapped his hands and off went de lights: beddie-byes. Nerves hardened to knots in my gut. I imagined a rope dropping from a hole cut in de ceiling, and me and Zeke having to climb up, neither able to haul ourselves more dan a few inches. Just trying and failing, failing till our hands were raw and our arms were jelly, and den our rope and hope would just calmly haul itself up de hole and out again into de rainy sky and disappear, de pain of not getting out all de worse cos we'd been offered an exit and weren't up to taking it.

Climbing, hopping, fighting. Sher who'd be up for any of it? Awful, exhausting stuff. Weren't we de cute hoors to get far enough away from our ape family to know better? And here were dese Waker bullies, forcing us into doing it all again—de pulling and stroking and punching and dancing. Ugh. How de mighty have fallen. Dat kid dere, half-riding a fluffy penguin, should be streamlining a flight program or hacking a cloud to ruin some nob celebrity's credit. What's he doing in a fecken stable? What are any of us doing here? De more I thought about it, de more humpy I got. Why did no one rise up, like? Don't we outnumber de goons! *If we could just get it together to form a gang…* After a while I was so hoppin mad I nearly forgot about de imaginary rope I couldn't climb. I was praying to de God of Rage. Just when I was a mess of clenched fists and couldn't take another second, de lights sputtered on—long flickery strips lashing out at me. A searing horn of light.

Mulligan. Conjured by de strobes: De Big Bad Wolf himself. He crouched by my bed, a snatch of feverdream. I sucked in air sharp, like I'd been dawked in de gut. A meaty hand pinned my arm. Den he was up in my ear—his stubble bristles slicing my skin, face twisted into a vicious grin, panting, all landfill breath.

—*How'r'ya Tayto boi?* Same harsh whisper from Joov, same brute power nailing you in place—a pin through a bug. I flapped weakly. *Didn't knaw you were in de stables at all. Old cara of mine!*

Won't do, boi. Got a much better place for you and yur delicate friend dere. Private room. You'll both sleep sound. Get dressed dere, willa?

  —*Ah no bodder, Foxy. I'm grand here, honest.*

  —*Don't fuck around.* Breath harsher, faster, eager, like he was about to gobble his dinner. *Can't have a fellow Joov alum kipping here like a stranger. I've de very place for ye both. Get up.*

  He clicked his fingers and de skinhead guard appeared at his heel. Lads moaned and bitched, squirming under damp blankets.

  —*Sorry, gang. Ye'll be kipping again in no time. Quick bit of business to take care of. I've an escort waiting to see dese lads out.*

  Mulligan pointed to de door. Dere, waiting, a catwalk model from a nightmare—De Fop. Duck cane by his side, thigh-high boots up his legs, raincoat like a cape down to his heels, and neoprene all around—tux, gloves, goggles, swim cap, all black. He bowed at us, den stepped back out into de rain. Vise grip back on my arm, de breath flooding my nostrils, sucking all air out of de bunkroom, big as it was.

  —*Tayto I'll dash. No rest for de wicked, d'y'knaw? Fop'll sort ye out.* He turned to go, almost running now, like he could hear de chow bell. He stopped dead, his back to us, and said in a flat voice, whisper gone: "Aisling says hello."

And den de great glaring light shut off and de stables were plunged back into dark except for de guard's beady torch beam firing at us as we hauled on a pair of jumpsuits. Guard was pure chuffed. *Slaps, lads. Seeeeerious slaps,* he kept saying. Didn't he know Mully and me were best buds? Fucken *chums,* boi. Weren't we getting de royal treatment? A private place for me and Zeke, away from plebs in deir damp blankets. Some people are just destined for de finer things in life. My heart was pounding so hard now I was sure it would wake every saint living or dead. But as we walked up de aisle past de sleeping bodies, I heard nottin only snoring. One wanker in de last bunk joined in with de guard: *Slaps. Slaaaaaps.* De more I heard it, de more it sounded like de baaa-ing of sheep. Or stuffed penguins. I dunnaw. Some kinduv crayture dat's easily shafted.

  De stable door shut hard behind us, and we stood in a realm of rain. Nottin but rain, cold but clean. You could barely open yur eyes with de torrents. Soil was breaking up, sods were floating past us. Trees were dissolving, I'd say. All de badgers and foxes were drowned, snouts facedown in pools—shrews clung to twigs, hoping for a better life downstream. All de owls had emigrated. *Good,* I thought. *End it all. Wipe de whole rotten slate clean and start over. Best thing for it.* Standing in de floods, like he'd been born to it, was De Fop. He leaned against a tree, easy as a man taking de sun on a May day. *Moment of truth,* I thought. He was either de "agent" leading us to freedom, or an angel of death—Foxy's blade in de night. Neither would surprise me. Dis guy didn't belong in de Wayke. I'd met avatars like him a million times before: cool, dead-eyed, unreal. Beings like De Fop weren't supposed to be trotting neat and fancy over de great green earth. I must be gaming. I wasn't Tayto, like. I was Gamer again, de hero who never dies.

He advanced. We backed against de stable door.

De Fop's eyes were hid behind dead black goggles. Quick as a ferret he went for my throat. I shrieked and tried to push him off, but he slapped my hands away. I heard a solid *click* and my shock collar came off. Cold wet air whipped at my neck, and I gripped it, panting, my jugular pounding under my fingers.

"You're welcome, Mr. Tayto," said De Fop, fecking de collar into a ditch. I glanced at Zeke. He'd hedgehogged himself into a deep crouch, head under his hands, quivering.

"Your collar has activated an alarm," announced De Fop next, bending to pick up his cane. "We'll be set upon in a matter of seconds."

Zeke shrieked, unballing himself. "What do we do?"

"Simple plans work best," said De Fop. "Run."

And just like dat he was off and sprinting, lanky legs kicking up sprays of water as he flayked to de woods. A spotlight fired from de manor roof, sweeping toward de stable. Panicky prey, we bolted after De Fop's flappy raincoat. He was fast, boi. Only a few seconds head start and already he was fading into de downpour. I saw glints of light where his duck's head cane rose over his shoulder. I lurched after dose glints—a Will'o'de'wisp on speed. Dey say never follow Will'o'de'wisps. Kiddie tales, I know, but when yur mind is flaring with fear… tis funny de notions can pop in yur head. Even with bright lights sweeping behind us, dogs howling and baying like dey were drowning, de image of dis auld fella up de road from us when I was a smallee just welled up out of de flood. *Don't follow de Wisp, Tayto me little spud.* Don't remember why. Something to do with de snaky bollox leading you out of de world. Turn your coat inside out and you break de spell—but I'd no coat. De Fop's cane flashed weaker as he pulled farther ahead. Jesus dat langer could run. I got de head down and pumped a bit harder, lungs and legs on fire.

I tried to be my avatar, leaping over space in giant bounds, pure loving de speed and power, but it only made my spindly pins feel worse, so I concentrated on breathing. Counting breaths made de gawks ease off a bit, but den Zeke pushed past me. I was managing in second place, but last place was a pure different kettle of shit. It could be only a few dark yards between me and some dog's teeth, coming to slice meat off my sparse arse. I pumped like a Kenyan. No mutt getting a free meal off me, boi. I focused on catching Zeke, but de gnomey little fecker was mad belting it. Must be all his massages. Well-rested and ready for action, de prick.

Soon enough I couldn't make out a thing ahead of me. Not a duck cane in sight. No sign of Zeke's runner soles flailing left and right. All light things had been swallowed up into de great mouth of rain. Panic. Were we meant to split up? Does it help or hurt yur chances? I looked back, pure certain I felt a breath on my neck, but—nottin. Zeke shouted *Tayto, this way!* He was way off to my left—I just managed to catch a glimpse of him launching through a wall of nettles. I pelted after him and stumbled into a fast stream. De slick mud sucked off my shoe (cheap plimsol yoke) as I fired through de nettle curtain. I squinted my eyes and held my hands out to protect my face, and tumbled into de dark woods. Finally: out of sight. But relief didn't last. My hands and face burned with nettle sting. Zeke just kept running, and I followed hot on his heels. De itching was brutal, but truth be told it distracted me from my fear, and de burning in my legs and lungs, and my pukey gut, and my missing shoe, with my foot finding every sharp stick and stone on de forest floor. Pain distracting from pain. *You've gotta love de Wayke, don't ya?* Slower, I pounded on through de trees—stinging, hobbled, and free.

Chapter 7: Woods

Soaked to de bone, and it was starting to freeze. Rain eased off just as de ache in my shoeless spawg kicked into high gear. I limped to a halt and listened. No nostril-flaring dogs. No lights through de trees. I was alone, and my neck was free from its shock collar. I made big circles with my noggin, and looked to de sky. Rain fell light but steady on my face: Irish heaven. I was too worried about finding de lads and getting a safe place to sleep, like, to say I was happy. But for de first time since I could remember, I felt free. I took a breath. Free. *Free to what?* says you.

Dunnaw, boi. Maybe free is too big a word. But no one knew where I was. No prick expected me to show up for work, or run a stoopid obstacle course, or dance a monkey dance. I was unstuck. Sher, how bad? And de more I coggled it, de gladder I was to cut loose from everyone. Not just de scumbags back at de Dublin kweries, or Copperknob in his Gerontoplex, or Mulligan and his Waker gowls slapping collars on people till dey fell in line, but everyone. Even my grand liberator, His Lordship De Right Honourable Fop. And even Zeke. *Especially* Zeke, now I thought about it. I was fed up to my eye teeth with him—twitchy oddball. Why'd I even need dat gowl? *If* we find Yogi's crown back at my folk's gaff, *maybe* Zeke can get it working. If, if, if. I was happy as larry to gatch on alone. Find a halo, turn de folks' house into a personal kwery. Raise some chickens. De good life. To hell with crowns and Zekes and Fops, and Waker nutjobs with shockcollars and sheepdogs.

So, despite my foot, and de shakes, and de rain, I was feeling fairly champy as I tromped deeper into woods. Fairly fucken champy.

Will'o'de'wisp was back. I saw a glint through de tree trunks. *Go on, Will. Lead me out of de Wayke. I'm ready, boi.* I laughed as I thought it. Me and de Wisp, hand in hand, tiptoeing out of de world while it slept, sneaking away from dat whole slimy mess dat eats itself. I laughed again, louder. Must've been de hunger, and tiredness, and pain, and shock—big night, like. Den I realised dis light wasn't dancing. It stayed still, rooted like de forest itself.

A house. A shambles of a place, but dere was light in a window. A home. De opposite of de Wisp—a cosy hearth, where people ate breakfast and made plans for de day, and hoped to get through it all without too much bodder. I'd say nice, quiet culchies lived here. Not fussed about deir clothes or haircuts. An auld fella with dirty nails and no clue what mad craic goes on in L.A. or Tokyo. Maybe he's got a chubby wife who's good at banging out de soda bread. Cuddle into each other at night. I could curl up at de foot of de bed and wouldn't let out a peep.

But a light was on, so dey couldn't be sleeping. Maybe he's dead, and she's banging out de soda bread all night long with no one to eat it. As I got closer, dat light didn't seem so warm. Who'd live here, in de middle of nowhere, keeping watch at de darkest hour? Some scared bollox, dat's who. A guy with an arsenal. Sleeps sitting upright, clenching a 12 gauge with his knees and a knife between his teeth. A twig cracked under my remaining shoe—I froze.

No movement from indoors. Couldn't decide. Keep going? Now I'd got used to light from de house, de woods looked fierce dark. It was a solid dark, and gave off a solid cold. No pushing through it anymore.

I stalked to de window, pure hobgoblin, all crouched and snaky. I even held my hands to my chest like de Mantis back in de Gerries. Creeping up like dis I wouldn't blame anyone for letting me have it with both barrels. Step. *Shush*. Step. *Shusssh*. Chrissake dere were a lot of twigs on de ground. Twas like trying to pick a man's pocket while a gang of urchins surrounded you, pointing and shouting *Hey! Yur doin it wrong, y'langer! He's goana spot ya!*

By de time I reached de poky little window my nads had shrunk good and tight, frigid sultanas. But my shoeless spawg was shredded fairly bad. I just wanted to take weight off it, snatch some kip in a dry place for an hour or two. So I snaked one eye up to de pane and took in de scene.

Barren. Gaff was deserted, but right in de middle of de floor was some kinduv flare. It puked out sick greeny light. Chemical. Made de stone walls harsh, corpse grey, pure horror sim.

Big woods, boi. Dey stretched on and on like a coma. It was drawing de superstition out. One tree after another, de same tree again and again, till you haven't a bog where or who you are. Just a few days out of Dublin and I was good as a smallee again, all taken with fairy tales and legends. *Pooka*, I thought. *Dis is pooka light*. I could fucken *see* it was a chem flare and nottin more, but all dat spooky stuff no one believes when dey live near a streetlight snaps back like a branch of thorns when yur in de dark and far from home. Well, sorry now, but pooka haunt or no, I needed to sit on a chair and be a human again. Door was open. Right so.

I was so exhausted twas as good as dutch courage on me now. If three bears lived here I'd just pat their furry chests and mutter "no fuss, lads" before taking a seat. Dere was no gear to plunder, looked like. Anyone here was probly a squatter with no more claim on de deed dan my good self. Might even be a kwery. How bad. Maybe I could bum a halo off a fien. Air was dry—praise be to walls and doors and windows! I listened. Still no sign of life. No point in putting it off—I called out: *Hello!*

Nottin. I was just about to relax my shoulders when I caught a rustle of movement in de back room. De cardiobox spazzed out, ready for warp, but I wasn't sure de legs would follow. I heard de steps come closer.

Den who comes round de corner?

Feckin Zeke. So relieved I nearly toppled right on de doorstep.

"Y'bollox," I said, clutching my heart. He stood, staring. Usual weirdo self. It started to feel awkward.

"Any munch?" I axed. "I've a hunger on me." He kept staring, but off to my left. Wouldn't look me in de eyes. *Okay*, I thought, and pushed past him to snoop round. Didn't expect to find shite, but I couldn't play gawping goldfish with him one more second.

"Don't go back there," he said, pure quiet.

"Why?" I axed. No response. Too tired for dis, boi. "You're being an oddball. More dan usual. Are we alone?"

He paused, den nodded yes.

"Where'd you get de flare? De Fop?" He stared at de ground, nodded yes again. "And where's Mr. Fancy Pants now?"

"Just stay in this room," he said.

I wasn't having dat. I wouldn't be taking any orders dis fine night. So I gatched into de back. A mattress, a couch, any soft surface would be de job. But de only thing back dere was De Fop's body, lying face down in a corona of blood.

I didn't feel nottin. But my mouth just spluttered like I was rolling helpless down a steep hill: "Fuck me! Oh *fuuuck* me!"

No response from de other room. Images from de Gerries fell on me like black drizzle. Ruth's body. Home-sweet-home Ruth. I knew I should check his vitals, but I didn't want to touch him. Sher, what would I do if he was still breathing? I hunched over. Lanky jet-black limbs, shiny black coat—all I could think of was a swatted insect. No movement at all. I reached for a pulse, but at de last second I prodded him with my one shoe instead. *Lot* of blood, boi.

Zeke sat in de front room, staring into de green flare. He was so still I half thought he'd died as well. Maybe we all had. Why else would I feel nottin at all? My bare foot didn't even hurt now. No cold, no fear. I took a notion we'd been killed trying to leg it from de Manor, and dis whole forest, dis empty house was... Well, y'knaw.

"I'm leaving," I said. "Don't follow me." His eyes were glued to de flare. I opened de front door. Bucketing. And beyond: woods. Would dey go on forever? Just a blink ago I was only too happy to leave de world behind. Now I missed it.

"Goodbye, Tayto," said Zeke. He inhaled sharpish, like he was finding it hard to breathe. Den he started shaking hard. Only three places existed now: de room with de giant smashed insect, Zeke's green hell, and de woods. Only three places in de universe, and I didn't want to be in any of dem. I closed de front door and sat where de welcome mat should be. It was de farthest I could be from Zeke and de dead thing without being outside.

Rain fell, same droplets on a treadmill, closed loop. Zeke did de shiver and shake, same twitches and sighs replaying, loop-loop-loop. I saw patterns, glitches, beats. Screensaver, I thought. A cheap one. Some noob programmer's homework ekka, fecked off at de last minute for a daft new temp teacher. Everything outside on repeat. Same raindrop, copied a billion times.

I sat and watched, cool as a Butler, just spooling it into memory flakes. But den de green flare flickered, dazzled, and went dead. Dark popped de screensaver effect. I could hear all de drops outside, and each one was real, as real as every poor bollox that tried to huff and puff deir last when de Scythe swept through. And now Zeke's sobs were real too. Dat shaking thing in de dark, not ten feet from me, was a flesh thing, trying to snort air through a clogged sewer of a nose.

De thing about pain, real pain: tis slippy—won't sit still in de room with you. It keeps twisting from second to second, so you can't get to grips with it. Always new, fresh. Like dose infinite-sided shapes in de puzzle cube—turn dem as many times as you like and get a new face every time. Unsolvable. Only option is to keep playing until *you* change. Den you don't solve de problem so much as... dissolve it.

In de dark left by de gone-out flare, thinking de word *dissolve*, I was pure certain I could smell rotting. Twas all roaring silence from de back room. Nottin on loop, boi. We weren't goan round and round: We were falling.

A vague dawn broke, and smeared de walls. No comfort in it—what good would de sun bring to dis state of affairs? But it reached Zeke. He'd been slumpy for hours. Now he straightened and looked up. *A new day*, he reckoned. *We're still in de Wayke.* Or maybe he just needed to stretch his back.

I hadn't slept either. No rest to be had in dis hovel. No rest for us two, anyways. I hauled myself up. Every joint creaked, knees especially. Not used to de pounding I'd given dem last night. Fecken knees, boi. I'd sooner lop dem off and strap on kangablades. What do I need feet and shitty shins and knees for? My modelling career, is it? A few seconds of standing and I had de gawks. Good. I could do with a dose of gawks. Muster up a bit of escape velocity, den fire out into space.

Rain had stopped, so I hobbled outside. It was so thick with trees I couldn't see de hovel behind me after only a minute. Like it never was. Walking made me feel better—de joint pain was easing off and de gawks were too. It was a good half hour before I scansed Zeke tracking along behind me. I ignored him for a while, and he kept his distance. I was taking a breather on a fallen trunk and noticed he was using a duck's head cane to whack plant life out of his way.

"Shouldn't have taken that, boi."

"Useful for getting through obstructions."

"Show us it a minute."

De way he gripped de cane changed, like a toddler told to give over his toy. But I held my hand out, and he passed it. A blood mark on de metal head—a little stain. Hardly notice if you weren't looking for it. I screamed like a maniac and made to swing at him. He cowered as I held de cane above my head, bellowing. I bayte de cane over my knee to snap it in two, but may as well have been trying to snap an iron rod. It only hurt me.

I whacked it a few times off a tree trunk and reverb wailed through my arms. Dere was no breaking dis thing. It'd outlast de woods. So I fecked it into de trees. Can't throw for shit so it didn't go far. I bellowed again, den fetched de cane and used it to hack open a long narrow hole, like a grave for a snake. I just hacked and hacked deeper into hard soil, and I could feel my blood pounding and my throat throbbing, but it was good to feel. It was good to bury something. I finally had a long shallow furrow, so I laid down de duck cane and kicked loose soil over it. Fucken duck's bill sticking out. More hacking, and now it was deep enough to hide de bird's head. Gone.

"Good riddance!" I shouted, hoarse, and not sure if I was bawling at de cane or what. I started walking again, but Zeke stopped me, grabbing my shoulders. His eyes were crazed, and now it was my turn to be freaked out. I scansed about for a rock.

"I had to do it," he whispered. I didn't like de whispering. "I did it for us," he kept whispering—wouldn't let me get past him. "They'd never let us keep the Crown... it had to be done. You understand that, don't you?" He squinted, like he was trying to see under my face. So dat's when I nodded. Cos at dat moment, I'd no mind to learn what would happen if I didn't.

My brother used to have a poster in his room. His only poster—small, but set dead center of a blank white wall, so you noticed it, like. An old rover shot of Mars. Dunnaw why he liked it. Looked like Earth to me, only colder. Lonelier. Sun was just a pale moon over a desert. Some mountains in de distance.

I remember sneaking into his room sometimes to knick dis or dat yoke, and staring at de scene. Made me think I was gawking at a photo from de future, not de past. I was staring at de last photo taken by de last person on Earth, or taken by a machine as our dying planet spun away into space, leaving warmth and hope behind.

Hadn't thought of Yogi's poster in donkeys. But dat same pale

Martian sun was lighting our way now. I was traipsing cross a strange planet, an alien trudging behind me.

Leaves ripple, thousands of tongues. De Wayke saying it knows. I know it knows. We shuffled on, no talk now, not even whispering. Cos how do you talk to an alien?

We were getting close—things were starting to ring bells, like. Just a few more miles till home. If I was ditching Zeke, I needed to do it soon. Either dat or lead him right to my folks' house. No way I wanted to show up with Zeke Zohar in tow—tek skills or not. Whadevvor was waiting for me back at my house, wouldn't it be better to face it alone? But den again...

Whether I was ready for it or not, de notion "home" started turning into solid stuff all round me. De way a stream over dere twisted. De familiar look of hedges out beyond de trees. We were sticking to de woods for now, case anyone was searching for us along de road. Woods *where we sporrrrted and plaaaayed, 'neath de green leeeeafy shade*, hunting each other with stick guns.

How do you go home? Can you just gatch up to a place you haven't seen since de huff'n'puff patrol whisked you off to Joov? Stroll back again, like it was nottin. No bodder on ya. Strange to say, maybe, but I started half-hoping it just... wouldn't be dere anymore. We'd walk up de drive—a bit overgrown, maybe, but nottin drastic like—and den we'd reach where de house should be, and it'd be gone. Eaten by mice. Washed away in a flood. Blown down bit by bit by every March gale since I'd left. No house, no crown, and no Yogi. And dat would be dat. End of quest. De boss level was missing. We'd run out of program, like some ancient arcade game where you go too far and everything just shuts down—out of RAM. I got to having mad dehjah voo, figuring *Ah hah! De Wayke's run out of RAM cos it's old-fashioned. I'm free and easy. Reboot. Start again.*

And so we plodded on, but I wasn't too worried now, cos part of me was sensing a big loop was coming up. Soon I'd be back somewhere else, no memory of my trip, teleported back to Dublin, maybe, working in de Gerries, tending to Ruth, late for my shift, Copperknob scowling. Or further back, holed up in Joov, dreaming of Big Things. Or tucked up in my bed in my folks' house as a smallee, long before de Scythe... Or whadevvor. Just not here and now, like, trudging through woods with dis alien beside me, and de Fop lying facedown... Nope. Here comes de loop. Any minute now. Must be; whole world is loopy. Only fall so far before yur back to de start again. And I was thinking dis to myself, getting giddy despite de fog drifting in, when we came across it.

A mountain.

Now dat was new. Don't remember dat before.

And dat was when my dehjah voo bubble got popped. We hadn't run out of RAM. No ancient arcade game, dis. And I felt real fear, because I knew, really knew, dat dis fucken thing was not goan to loop. Dere was more stuff to come. Too much.

Maybe *mountain* suggests something bigger dan de pile ahead. But given what it was made of, it couldn't have seemed any bigger. We stopped at a distance, squinting to make it out. Somebody with a dumptruck, or maybe a tractor-trailer, had left dem here—at de edge of de woods, spitting distance from de fields and main road. Dey slumped over each other, blackened. Tough to tell if dey'd been burned, or if twas just rank decay. Was it flesh or old clothes hanging in strips from de limbs and torsos? Some were holding each other, even melting into each other. Didn't want to think of dem as neighbours, like. So dey were just figures. Not even figures, really, cos dey were all dissolving into one black mass. A great tangle, like a tree root. Fog rolled in heavier now, but through de veil I could catch details: eyeholes, shoes, de odd glint of jewellery on a wrist, a neck.

Zeke crouched with his back to de pile to retch. Nottin to get up, of course. But he kept heaving, searching around in his tank for something to spit out. Anything. Dat's when I tiptoed off, skirting round de pile and off into de fog. *So long, Zeke. Happy gawks.*

As I sprinted fast and crafty as I could into de gray, a chill rolled up me. Was it guilt for deserting him? Or was it de pile? Was I deserting dem? Naw, not getting into it. As I put distance between me and de tangle, I hoped my old house would be waiting for me after all. I wanted nottin more now dan for de mice to put back all de pebbledash, de gales to replace de roof, de floods to cough up my old bed. It had to still be standing. It had to be. It just had to.

Woods got too rough and I chanced traipsing de road for a bit. I kept an ear out for cars, but it'd always been quiet here. I remember strolling dis road from de woods back to our house when Yogi and me were kids, and one time in particular when it started to snow. It was de last snow I remember. A few flakes at first, and den heavier.

Big fluffy flakes cupped de air so it was even quieter dan silence: anti-sound. We didn't utter a word—it would've been wrong. And den we got to our backdoor, and into our kitchen, and de light and human bustle inside was almost too much, and we got de feeling back in our fingers and toes, and de tingles were mad strong, and I, being me, ate two packs of Taytos. Cheese'n'onion, boi. Ma bought six-packs, and Yogi would let me eat his, so I'd eat two at a time. Not too shabby for Mr. Tayto, His Spudulence.

Passing Spillane's house. Mr. Spillane—never understood a word he was saying. He only lived down de road, sher, but he was as foreign to me as someone speaking Lower Boglish. I'd be sent down to borrow a drop of milk, or doss with his kids or whadevvor, and he'd engage me in chat, and I'd have to just nod my head and say vague things like *mmhmm*, cos I'd no clue what he was banging on about. A culchie squared. Purple nose. Might make out a word here or dere, but it was no help. *I'll tell y'now, hurump-say-didderamawn-but sher tis cutting up de back field, and didn't I say to him yerra hupp! Goan now and don't be fedderen didden dawww. Hah?* And den he'd press me for a reply. *Hah?!*

And when I took a shot and said *yyeaahhh*, he'd look at me like I was simple. Better to knock on de door and wait outside till his sons came out. Never cross de threshold. Another family's homestead is a foreign country.

Spillane's sovereign nation looked long dead. All de houses near de crossroads—derelict. Who knew where dey'd gone, or if any were melting into each other in a black tangle in de woods...

Wish I'd put in a bit more effort to understand Spillane when he culchied at me. It wouldn't have killed me to try.

Sun was setting as I turned off de main road and onto our boreen. De twin petrol pumps still stood guard at de crossroad— last two teeth in an auld fella's head. Dey were rusted and rotting even when I was a toddler. Now dey hunched like relics from an ancient past. Ogham stones. Yokes planted for long-forgotten reasons by druids, or some lads like dat. Whispering away to each other in an Irish so old even Spillane's decrepit father couldn't make head nor tails of it. De same language nettles and gorse speak.

Chapter 8:
Gentleman's Entrance

And suddenly it was right before me—home. Or at least, de farmhouse I grew up in. In dusk it looked smaller and plainer dan I remembered, but it was still mad to be gawking at it again from our rusty gate. I'd seen it a lot in my head de first few months in Joov—not so much de house from outside, but my room, and odd random things like foxgloves sprouting in hedges, poking a paw in one of deir purple pouches. But den I started scaping, and our old place just sortuv fell away. De raw here-and-nowness of my folks' place gawked right back at me. *I know yur face*, it mumbled. *Where've you been?* I was stunned. Hadn't really visualized it de whole time I was making my way here. To be fair, I'd run into a few distractions, like.

Twas a bit overgrown but it didn't look broken up or nottin. I wondered if de spare key would still be behind de gnome, or was dere still a gnome, and was about to gatch over and investigate when a light came on inside. Shit. Could be Yogi… maybe. Dat's de best case scenario and it was awkward enough: *Alright boi. Been a while. So, are you gone de full March Hare or what?* Way more likely, twas squatters. And if squatters? Well, dere was de teeniest chance dey were friendly. But given my luck lately, I needed to be glic as a fox here. Between de dusk and fog I had a bit of cover, so I crept along de hedge leading to de main door, which was actually round de back, away from de drive. De Gentlemen's Entrance, we called it. Always felt our place was backwards.

I slunk up by de edge of our kitchen window, and as I did I got something worse dan day-jah-voo. When I'd crept up like dis on de cabin in de woods, I'd seen something pure unreal to me. But dis place was real, maybe de realest place in all Waykdom. What if something was waiting in here dat made de cabin in de woods like a happy daydream? Maybe I should break into Spillane's place, spend de night, and den, in de morning, come back… But de thought of spending a night in Spillane's didn't sit right either. Entering any house in our deserted neighbourhood would be like breaking into a grave. How bad. It's de living you should fear.

I glanced round, trying to soak up any force of goodness dat might be dwelling in de hedges, de small trees, anyplace at all. My eye was caught first by tiny blue flowers trying to creep from cold ground. Don't know how I even spotted dem: puny sprouts straining in slow motion, clawing demselves back to life. And den de whole garden came into focus, and it wasn't just a garden at all. It was a thousand little histories everywhere an eye could scanse: de dirt path where you learned to peddle a bike with a slippy chain. Sheds where you fiddled with bits of junk electronics and imagined spacecraft wreckage—proof you were from somewhere better. Proof dat something whole was possible. It had been one long line of wreckage leading me here, de whole sorry traipse of my days. Dis had to be leading me somewhere, didn't it?

But it was de living things spoke up loudest. *Hey. Over here.* Hedges you hid in as a useless young Jedi, practicing mind-control on jackdaws. Burrows and tree trunks looming over injured birds, paralyzed voles, mice: you nursed dem all in yur vet's shoebox. De weird yellow day you and Yogi heard de sudden tongue of de hunt, and over de halloooing hedge he hopped: Reynard. Furry fien nodded to us, I think: red, beautiful as a bushy Christ, den leapt on into de misty meadow, hedges all hurdles, de whole world howling after him in a pack of sloppy brown hounds. I hid my snivelling dat day—at de vision of canines shredding him. Hid in de foxgloves. Didn't want to explain in case de folks thought I'd gone round de bend, blubbering over a fox. De unfairness of it…

I could see everything.

Alright lads, I said to all living things, tis now or never. Heroes go into de cave. And my allies, my posse, all de tiny flowers, and de holes in hedges, and de hidden nests in trees, dey … well, dey didn't say shit, to be fair. But all de same… I dunnaw. Can't explain it right. Sounds crazy but I felt dey were with me. Not exactly a cavalry, like. I was on my own, of course. But some glimmer of goodness was dere too, something I'd left behind as a kid, a hidden treasure, and it said: *I'm behind you, Tayto. Always have been, always will be. Dowtcha boi!* I peeled my back off de wall and faced de window.

Inside was a little boy, about six. He was sitting on de floor with a grey rabbit, trying to feed it a carrot. Rabbit wasn't fussed, just sniffing. I was so flummoxed to see a kid and a bunny I kinduv forgot I was staring through a window at things alive. Fell into thinking twas a nostalgia scape. De kid looked up and saw me, face right up to de pane. He didn't do anything. For a second. Den he shrieked like a steam kettle. Shook me awake, and couldn't I hear feet thumping down de stairs. *Fuck!* I scansed round for a weapon. Sweet F.A. Started to jolt but I'd been walking too long on no fuel, and de legs felt bandy. A woman shot out de kitchen door. She was nearly short as de kid, and so pregnant she looked like a space hopper with legs.

"Hey!" she shouted. "Who are you?!" She had a fierce strong foreign accent.

I dropped to me knees, hands in de air like she'd a gun trained on me: "I'm Tayto!" I cried. "I... I lived here! Dis was my home."

Bogdana, she was. From Poland. She'd given her little fella an Irish name: Eoin. He gawked at me from de safety of de stairs, still clutching his bunny. I wasn't scared anymore, but I was trying so hard to come off as normal I didn't know what to do with my hands. Bogdana was awkward too. She kept edging round de kitchen table. We were like two strangers spotting some stray cash afloat on de street. *Lucre! Is it mine? You goan to...? Might dis end in a scrap?* I'd no intention of telling dem to shift, and I didn't fancy my chances of kicking a family out anyways. But I needed to stake out my right to be here. She was suspicious, and who could blame her? As I stood in de old kitchen I felt lightheaded. Twas all too much. All de years away had never happened, I'd never left. But somehow yesterday I was a kid, and today I was a grown man, not recognizing de people in my kitchen. Dis is what it's like to go round de bend, I thought. To not be able to tell where yur life ends and someone else's starts. Not a bog what're real memories and what's just wishing something to be real so much you end up on a stranger's doorstep yelling: *Dat's my life yur inside! Get out!*

"Look," I said, turning to de first random thing: notches on de door frame. Yogi and me, having our heights checked with colouredy marks on white wood: him blue, me red.

Bogdana hadn't noticed it before. De lines were faded, but you could see dem if you got close. Not many blue marks—Yogi wasn't too into being measured. But at one level de frame was a red barcode. I'd be always pestering Ma to mark it up. Such a hunger to be further along, like de future was above me, some sortuv beautiful glorious ceiling, if I could just reach it. And den de Scythe swept long and easy through our fields, and de hopping marks on de frame cut short.

It all just caught me off guard, like. A weird laugh snorted out of me. It was a goblin of a laugh. I bottled it up sharp. Last thing I needed right now was to shit yur wan out.

"Sorry," I said, like a knobber. Next thing I knew I was wiping off tears. Ridiculous waterworks. She'll be reaching for a butcher's knife any second, I reckoned. Quit acting de maggot now and cop yurself on. "Ah, sorry bout dis." I focused on my feet.

But when I checked her again all I saw was pity. I was pitiful to her. Not ideal, sher, but better dan her fumbling for a pointy yoke to jab me with.

"Tea!" she said.

Hate tea. Dunnaw why it's so hard for my countrymen to believe me. *How do you like yur tea? WHAT? Never at ALL, like?! Some kinduv pervert, are ya?* Dis byor wasn't even Irish, but dey say if you lick de grass here long enough, and sure enough she'd a kettle on and de Barry's out before I could protest. So I just let her make de fecken tea. Dey trust you more once dey've handed you a cuppa. It's magic, la, like having a puff on a peace pipe in a teepee. And I'd admit, during our Recovery Era, tea was more important dan ever. I'd spent time in kweries dark as dungeons, holed up with some hardcore saints. Dese were fiens who couldn't give a toss bout de Wayke, lads who curled into a tight sneer de minute dey lit down. And I tell you now, even in de blackest pits, you'd find a kettle. Forget yur crucifixes, yur rosary beads, calm little Buddhas and Fancy Dan elephant gods. Tea said de world was working again. Tea meant normal. Lads out in de bogs and boreens of India, shrugging off de tigers and monkey pests, picking leaves from dawn till dusk—just like before. Boats chugging again over de deep-bowelled sea, hauling leaves round de blue ball. Do I fancy a cuppa? I'm alive, aren't I? Pots a-brew all day every day—liquid hope. From de boat's horn all de way down to de stove whistle, nottin more snug, safe, sane and plain. Homeyness held in a cup. Twas tea time. I got it, like. Sortuv.

"We've no milk," she said.

"No bodder," says I.

"Sugar?"

"Yeah. Wouldn't have it any other way," I added for no reason. Like I was mad for de tea. Like if she'd handed me a cupán tae with no sugar I'd take one sip and flayke it against a wall, screaming: *Takin' de piss, are ya?!* A fine how-do-you-do: pretending to love tea so I can seem normal as possible to strangers who've set up a squatters' nest in my own parents' house.

She pulled out what looked like two saucers but curved dem (like dey could read her thoughts) into a pair of neat cups. Dat's novel. Who were dese people? Where'd dey get such able stuff?

I supped my tea. Sup, sup. Not used to hot drinks. Barely used to drinking, really. My I.V. looks after hydration fairly well. Otherwise I mostly stick to uisce. But now I had it in my paw, de auld tea wasn't too bad. Maybe I hadn't given it a fair enough lash all dese years.

"It is okay?" she axed.

"Hits de spot," I said. Dat relaxed her.

"You look famished," she said. An offer of food—always dodgy. Truth be told I was starving, but you never know what a stranger will serve, and I'm a Finicky Fergus. No chance of feedbags here I reckoned.

"Any Carbo-nosh bars?" I chanced my arm.

"Oh no, we make everything on our own," she said, pure proud. Balls. Homemade munch. I had notions of stinky homemade cheese... goats milk... big lumps of brown bread dat taste of turf. But instead she opened a drawer and pulled out something like peanut brittle.

"Try, please," she said. I bit in. Kinduv crunchy, but marzipan-y too. Hard to place de taste. Like a veggie burger but more crumbly. Bland but nice. Some relief, boi!

"Dat's blásta now! What is it?"

"Glad you like it!" she was beaming. "Mostly animal protein."

"Oh yeah? What kinduv animal, like?"

"Insect," she said. I stopped chewing, feeling de stuff sit on my tongue. Before I even knew it I had spat de lot in my hand. Couldn't help it—pure instinct. Dese insect banquets weren't my notion of cuisine at all. I checked de tiny carnage of mush for little legs, bits of wing, shell. And no messing, but de pile of black bodies tangled

up in de woods flashed into my pan for a second. No faces. No
clothes to speak of. Nottin left of status, wealth, or wit. No keeners,
kin, or stones to mark de site. Never knew a funeral. Just a knotted
twist of limbs, melting into one all-you-can-eat buffet for bugs.
Even in de cold, de air was pure buzzing.

"Oh dear," she sighed. "It upsets you."

"Insect?" I said. "Like, flies?" I kept staring at de lump in my
hand. Twas probly exhaustion, and de ructions from escaping
Peacock Manor, and De Fop facedown in a bare cabin, all reaping
deir claim on me now, but I'd swear I saw de Crows' mural hidden
in my chewed pulp. Could dis meat be de Scythe itself? Or maybe
our revenge on it all? Our way of saying: our time to feed, maggots.
But, sher, no one would offer me dis in my own Ma's kitchen, after
such a long walk. "Yur acting de scut now, right?"

"Scut?" She winced, grappling with my alien vocab. "I'm
sorry, my English is not so perfect. Our biscuit is made from mix
of plant and caterpillar protein." She sniffed. "It's good for you."
Fair enough, I thought. Biiiig sup of Barry's to sluice de taste off.

"I show you. See?" She pointed out de window to de backyard.
Light was almost gone now, but I could make out a tower—a looming
beanstalk—several meters high. Whole thing was covered in some
kinduv dirty see-through film. Inside it I spied with my little eye a
mini-jungle. A figure moved about, inspecting de plant life.

"My partner, Bram. We grow it all."

"Yur business partner?"

"No, my… how do you say?" She rubbed her swollen belly and
laughed. "My partner?"

"Oh yeah. Got it."

"Man of the house," she laughed.

Didn't like dat title. I knew de last man of de house here, and
me and him didn't see eye to eye.

"Much work, is it? Raising teensy flying cattle?" I was thanking
my stars dere wasn't milk in my tea Where might dat be from? A
lobster milking parlour out in de shed?

"Not so hard. No need to feed them or clean up, you know?
Bram just likes to relax in his tower. It is alive, you see? Whole thing
is alive. The high stalks are alive, and around is smartskin. That's
living organism too—Bram engineers it. It breathes, but keeps the
inside warm, like tropical place. The insects like it very much there."

"Bram's no daw," I said. "I had a brother like dat, when I lived here." She said nottin, and it hit me only den dat Yogi was gone. His trail was dead.

"No... daw?"

"A brainybox. Smart, like."

"Ah, smart—I must introduce you."

"No rush boddering him if he's busy..."

"I'll get him," she said, and flayked out de door. As she got closer to de tower a floodlight filled de yard.

Starving! I flung open de cupboards where Ma used to keep bread and crisps and jam. All I found were stacked boxes full of creepy-crawly delights. Maggots, mealworms. Tubs o'crispy millipedes. Treats for Halloween, I spose. Dese people had to be sick. What are de acres of fields out back for? Cows! Goats! Sheep! Get a fucken chicken coop, la. No need to be eatin fecken nits like a pack of chimps at all! 'Tis not like dere's any shortage of space anymore. I'd got wind of insect farming when I was a kid. Wave of de future it was, back when de world was getting heavy with hordes, spawning like, well, insects. But plenty of space now. Mostly space. Great fields gone fallow. You could have cows everywhere if you wanted. No fear of de methane, sher. Fart away, girls. A world full of gentle swaying mothers, all chewing. At night de drone of lowing, and one lazy bull off in de distance, making his rounds, setting off de moocow moans. A green world running with rivers of milk. I suddenly had a craving for a bar of Cadbury's. Nottin fancy. Simpler de better, in fact.

I stopped my snooping in cupboards and watched from de kitchen window. Bogdana had reached de tower. Her hands pressed against de skin, talking at yur man inside. He listened without a word, den forced his fingers through de skin. It tore away into a hole and he stepped through. De skin just knitted back together behind him—a nimble answer to fencing. I wondered if maybe dis guy was Yogi's real brother, and me just some confused bollox wandering in from de empty fields.

My belly rumbled. I picked up my "biscuit" with de bite taken out of it and gave it a sniff. No smell. I nibbled a crumb off it. Crunch, crunch. You'd have no idea what it was, really. But it was no Dairy Milk. Dat was for sure.

Bram Brakkenhof stooped into de kitchen—my kitchen. My Ma's kitchen. He stood before me while Bogdana brewed another big pot of peacepipe tea. He had a young fella's body, slim and strong, like a hurler, but an auld fella's face. Besides de age lines and jutting cheekbones, I saw de pock marks. Gombrich. Dis guy was one of de genetic freaks who'd been caught but didn't fall. I'd heard tell of beasts like him but never met one before. De man must've got a glimpse of hell. Whadevvor he'd seen, he wasn't too keen at looking me in de eye.

"How'r'ya Bram. I'm Tayto. I used to live—"

"Yes, Bogdana explains everything to me outside."

"Alright so. Well, anyway—"

"Now you're back. What does this mean for us?" He didn't sound scared, or even angry. More jaded. Like a guy who'd had a hard day at de office and now he had to put up with a Waker pamphleteer at de door.

"Bram!" snapped Bogdana.

"What?" he said to her. "This boy is here. He has a claim to the house. I want to know what now." He turned to me. "Well?"

"Uh, listen, I'm not here to cause you or your kin trouble, alright?" Pure diplomatic. "Dere's no problem, like. Just came down to see if my brother was here. And it looks like he's not, so I'll be pushing off." But as soon as I'd said it I wasn't too sure. What was de rush, d'y'knaw?

Bram said nottin. Tell ya, it was hard to tell what he was coggling. Fien was stone.

"If there is any way we can thank you…" said Bogdana, looking like she'd won de lotto.

Dis was my opening. "Well, tell de truth, I'm between living arrangements," I said, giving myself a good stretch, arms out to de sides. Lot of space here, but fierce cosy. Plenty of room for a Tayto to hang about for a while—get his cheese'n'onion tang back. "So could I stay here with ye for a bit?" I phrased it as a question, to ease it to dem, but dere was no question, like. I was down for a few nights at least. Nottin a body could do about it.

De Brakkenhofs swapped blank looks. "I'd be much obliged," I said. Fierce cosy.

"Of course," said Bogdana. She wasn't smiling as wide, but she seemed untroubled. Bram gave a short little bow and said: "I must get this dirt off." He vanished upstairs, taking Eoin and his rabbit with him.

"Thank you again for letting us stay here," said Bogdana,

draining her cup and flattening it back into a saucer shape.

"Sher, ye probly have squatters' rights by now or something," I said. Squatters' rights. Would you listen to Judge Tayto. Dis is my house! Would I ever just shut up?

"Please excuse Bram. He can be... direct."

"Yeah, he's a survivor. I noticed." We both fell silent. I added,"Ye don't have de same accent."

"He is Dutch," she said. "I am Polish. Our children are Irish. And you, Tayto," she smiled, "are welcome home."

Dinner time. I sat at de table while Bogdana stirred a pot of mysterious paste. Didn't make any inquiries, like. What I didn't know wouldn't hurt me.

I never in my life sat at a proper family dinner. Yogi liked to eat alone in his room; Dad ate on de go throughout de day and gatched down de pub come evening. So I used eat with Ma. How bad, sher. Most lads'd roll deir eyes at spending time with de Auld Lade, boi. But I know dis: I'd burn de last feedbag on Earth to have one more stoopid banter session with her at dis table. Tried it in de halo—miserable fail. No smell in de Scape, for starters. And it can't capture plainness, all de odd moments between two sad simple little mammals. A halo is great for adventure, fantasy, everything except re-building de world you came from. Probly just as well.

Spose part of de problem too was I couldn't remember exactly what Ma and me used be nattering about, other dan whadevvor puzzle or riddle or clue she was fizzy about on a given evening. But dose were de last times I'd eaten like a human being is supposed to. Den dere was a big chunk of time in de Joov (snakk-box, mess hall), and a string of Dublin kweries (feedbags and whadevvor we could scrounge), de staff room at de Gerries (microwave crap, nosh-bars). More feedbags back in de flat, de odd fibrogel chaser... Now, magically, I was back in our kitchen. Bram was still upstairs with Eoin, so it was just me waiting for Bogdana to get stuff ready. Ma and me, just like old times.

Bogdana looked pure delighted working away on her paste. She was humming. Confections made of love. Dat's what Ma used to call de little cakes and whadevvor she'd make for us. I spose bug paste could be a confection of love, right? Airborne love—all de weightless souls flittin from flower to flower, spreading de love, and whoosh! Swipe de little bolloxes up in a net, mash it all down... luvvly job. A part of me kinduv warmed to de notion of airy love, winged and pretty, getting ground into paste for family dinner.

Funny, it was de familiarity of de room made it so fucken strange. Everything in its place, yet totally changed. Home. I was saying it so much, it was starting to feel like a made-up word. Cant from some dodgy cult.

I must've been mad into my coggling cos when I looked up Eoin was sat across de table from me. Hadn't heard him at all. A careful kid, you could tell. He was watching me, not quite giving it de guzz eye, like, but suspicious all de same.

"Hi Eoin," I said. "Where's yur rabbit? Is he gone to bed?"

"What's for dinner?" he axed his mother. Aw you little shit, you just had to know, didn't ya! Eoin wanted details. Some kinduv mashed larvae and honey, it was. Cheers for dat. Little fella was pure chuffed. He called it his slurry. Well, nottin says good munch like slurry.

Bram came downstairs in a long robe. It was thin and crinkly, and changed colour depending on what angle you gawked at it.

"Mad duds," I said. "What's de get-up made of?"

"Synthetic bacterial waste. We grow it in tubs out back."

"So... you grow yur own clothes?"

"We grow many things."

"Mad. I mean good, like," I spazzed.

"Do you cultivate anything, Tayto?" axed Bogdana, spooning out de slurry. She gave me a big fucken helping too, and molded the plate into more of a bowl shape to hold de sticky mess.

"Hand on heart, I don't think I've grown a single living thing in my life." Eoin laughed—must've been de way I said it.

Bram looked me in de eye for de first time. "If that's true, I pity you."

Sign yur pity on me hole, y'poxy prick. Yur man thinking he's all dat and a bag of feckin chips, with his manky germy farting jacket, and his stoopid Dutch accent, and his skeleton face... I've got some skills myself y'lanky prick. How's yur protein folding, hah? What's yur scaping index? Over a 7 is it? Y'fucken green-fingered bug gobbler.

"Yeah," I said. "Tis a sad story, Bram. I'm a victim of institutionalization." He watched me, figuring if I was taking de piss maybe. Didn't seem too fussed either way.

"Let's have grace," said Bogdana, cutting de tension short.

I expected everyone to bow heads—de usual stuff. But instead dey lifted deir arms up, looking to de ceiling like dere was a mothership hovering over us only dey could see. I wasn't sure if I should join in, so I kinduv half did, arms up—a nobber caught in a stick-up. All three started humming.

"We offer our humble thanksgiving," chanted Bram to de ceiling, "for the mysteries of pheromones... the bounty of pollen... and the glory of sunlight. The world is unbounded wealth. For this we raise up our hearts."

And dat was dat. Wazzie humming stopped dead, and all three faces were into de bowls, scooping up golden slurry with deir hands and sucking it greedily off fingers. I wanted a spoon, but no one was paying me any heed: Chow time. Fair enough. I dipped my pinky into de bowl and tasted de tip. Sweet.

De door clacked and a girl gatched in. She was somewhere in de neighbourhood of my age, but healthy, so she may as well have been a different species. She looked so bored. Or sad, maybe. Something bout her sent a circuit shorting in my head. Snap-crackle-pop. With all de bad wiring crammed in, spose it was bound to blow one day. Twas de way she stood up on her hindlegs, cool and straight and... regal. She was so sad she was regal, boi.

I'll be de first to admit I'm no poet. Don't talk well about beautiful things. I don't see much of dem anyways, so I don't get much practice. Tis a shame, cos de less you see beauty, de bigger a wallop it packs, and so when it gatches into a kitchen, all bored or sad, you've no defence at all. Yur so used to de sewer dat it's shocking to see something dat's not a rat.

A luvvly thing is scary. Doesn't belong here. Or doesn't belong near you. And so my heart was pounding now, but not with de usual fear of danger. Fear of being too close to... dunnaw. Glory. Say it straight out: she was de biggest flahh I'd ever seen floating bout in de Wayke. Course, up till de past week I wasn't too into byors, so maybe my judgment is off—maybe a sudden halofast after many saintly years was turning me into a humpy dog. Who's to say? Whadevvor it was, Aisling had snuck under my skin, and now dis girl in my old kitchen nearly had my jaw drop clean into de slurry. Twas all I could do not to stretch my arms to de sky and start humming.

I know what Noelly Ba and his shiny shoes would have me do: slap a wedding ring on her, open a plastic cutlery warehouse, and start shopping around for a daycent baby stroller. But when I peeled my eyes off her I caught Bram scowling: *Touch her—and I'll make a robe out of you.*

"Sol, where have you been?" asked Bogdana.

"Out. Who is this?"

Her eyes met mine, and I nearly jumped out of my skin. Don't look straight at de sun! I stared at my pile of dinner and clamped up, like when yur teacher fires a question at you in Irish, and you forget how to use yur mouth, cos you only barely speak Bearla, so let us away with de *Gaeilge*, willa?

"This is Tayto. He is our guest," said Bogdana. I stole another sneaky glance at de girl. Jeez, boi, talk bout glower power. She'd her dad's withering stare and no mistake. Dis was one apple didn't fall far from de stern Dutch apple tree.

"I'm going to bed," she announced, and vanished. I dipped my pinky back in de squelchy, sticky, sweet golden mess.

Our family munch got tense. Bogdana was all *Yur daughter's pure rude, Bram* and I reckoned she was de girl's step-mom. Didn't look anything like her anyways. Sher, for all I knew Sol had no mam, she just burst straight out of one of her stern dad's deeper pock marks—invincible. But naw, a fine half like herself needed a better origin story. Maybe I'd learn it.

We ate, pure quiet. But den Eoin told us five things bout his rabbit, and dat got us nattering.

Maggot slurry. Dere was no way round it, so I just got de head down and guzzled. Funny enough, de bigger de mouthfuls de easier it was. Twas fierce sweet after all, so I ended up hoovering de lot. I thanked my hosts, who were really my guests, like, and dey said yur welcome but really meant thank you, Mr. Tayto, for being such a cool customer.

And dat was dat.

I was knackered. Bogdana showed me upstairs to where I was kipping: Yogi's old room. Perfect, cos I couldn't handle de ghosts of my own quarters. Dat was Sol's place now, Bogdana told me. Of all de places in de wide Wayke, a being like Sol was in my old room. I thought of her adult body filling my little boy's bed, her golden hair fanned out over my pillow. If I listened maybe I could hear her fresh dreams spreading wings in de dark, rising over my dried-up nightmares, swept under de bed like so many shriveled husks.

No one was boddered using Yogi's old room, and who could blame dem? For starters, it was poky as fuck. Tiny little garret window, set at a wonky angle so de place got no sunlight, even in summer. It just had dat oddball vibe: de guy at de bus stop with something off bout him, you can't quite say.

No bed; just a mattress and plain sheet. No posters; even de one mouldy photo of Mars, with its tiny cold distant sun, had gone missing. No toys. Nottin with any colour to it. Who'd lived here? A small Martian child. Or a drone replica of a human kid, operated by a Martian scut back in his plush cave, laughing with his cronies, ripping de piss out of de Earth family fooled into housing deir cuckoo robot.

Yeah, twas always a right little hole, and it had only got worse, till now it had me thinking of a hokey haunted house, manky cobwebs everywhere. I spent a good minute just spluttering and waving de dust and webbage away so I could breathe. Me and de spiders—enjoying bugs for dinner and now sharing a room.

I sat down at Yogi's too-small desk and wiped it clean, and as I did I realised this was no haunted house but a shipwreck. I was a nosey tourist diver probing de underwater murk. Half expected an eel to swirl out of a drawer soon as it was opened. But naw. Just a tangle of electronics, some rusty memory sticks. Nottin I'd a bog how to open. Too ancient. He may as well have kept all his stuff in Egyptian hieroglyphs. Den I spied a little notebook at de very bottom, under bundles of cable. I fished it out. Couldn't make head nor tail of his notes. Backwards handwriting, a stoopid precaution: even using de cracked mirror on his wall I couldn't understand a word.

On de opening page was an Irish Times clipping from after he won his first big competition. Dat Turing yoke. At 12 years old de snaky fecker had coggled a way of getting a computer to write poems, poems odd enough to fool a rake of A.I. experts into thinking a human had penned dem. I didn't understand all de fuss at de time. Sher, Yogi was always figuring stuff out. But he was different after winning dis Turing thingamagig. A turning point, he called it. Got him thinking about how he might "contribute."

…Munster IT community celebrates arrival of budding savant… panel of 15 artificial intelligence experts (including UCC's own Prof. Rani Sarma) happily admitted being confounded by a 12 year old boy from a small rural community in Cork, whose autonomous poetry-writing

program BERTIE managed to fool the judges into assuming a human author… the Lit-tech test stands as an alternative to the traditional Turing test, where typed dialogues with a judge are evaluated as being human or machine in origin… BERTIE's poem was produced extemporaneously in response to a title selected by the judging panel… non-binding criteria included the presence of wit or irony, scansion, effective metaphor, and abstract themes…

Dere was a photo along with de story. It could've been nostalgic to see young Yogi staring back at me, only his hair was combed so neat for it he didn't look like himself. It was a shot of de Martian drone who stayed in dis room, alone. Below de photo was Bertie's poem:

The Ticket

A god tried his hand at yoga one day,
but his mansion was filled with guests come to stay
so he bid them begone, and stop cramping the place,
and cleared out his furniture to free up more space,
but still he could not unfold in his house,
so he put out his parents, his child, and his spouse,
(Just for a second, just for a minute.
For only an hour, the day that's in it.)
Still he couldn't release, and fuse with the waving,
come-and-go playing, destroying-and-saving,
so he gouged through his chest to cast out all belief,
every hope and despair, any strain and relief.
But still he felt cramped as a crouching caged pet,
unable to melt into frequencies yet,
so he shed all his limbs, his trunk, and his head,
until there was nothing, which graciously said:
Ah. That's the ticket—not alive and not dead.

Twelve years of age. Funny thing was, like, Yogi barely read. Doubt he'd written a poem in his life. But he could build a poet. Poet-maker beats poem-maker hands down, boi. Sher, any knob could flayke out a poem—even dad had scribbled a few half-daycent limericks in his time. And pure coincidence Bertie's poem was about yoga, like, cos Yogi got his nickname after Yogi Bear (smarter dan yur average bear...). No interest in yoga himself, far as I knew. But he'd forged a yoga-mad poet in dis horrible little hole with no view. My job was to leave his food tray outside de door, and inside I'd hear him jabbering away quietly to himself in his own made-up language, like a toddler playing with blocks. *Yogi! Grub's up!* And he'd just go silent. So we were all in de dark till he won dat lit-tech prize. C'mere, de first we heard of it was from a neighbour! And den wave after wave of online interviews with bigwigs from Japan, China, India, Russia, Sweden, de States. I remember some guy with a knighthood calling over in person from England, and I was so stoopid I expected him to have a horse and a suit of armour. He was just a skinny guy in a cardigan. Fucken knight.

De penny dropped for de whole neighbourhood den. Never had much in common with my brother, but now we all looked at him different: a changeling. De Scythe tore down from de north soon after. I got swept off to Joov, with Mully and Gilbey and Noelly Ba, and all de other survivor dregs, and Yogi got himself installed in some kinduv accelerated learning program in Dublin. Never saw him again, but he posted me de last packet of Taytos I ever ate—last pack dere ever was, for all I know. Just when I thought I'd never see His Spudulence again, one day, a box from Dublin. And inside a six pack, long after the crisp factory had shut doors, like so many other factories. Where'd he get his hands on it? Sotheby's? I ate five of de six packs—faster dan I meant to—but I kept de last. Just stashed it away, trying to hold onto it as long as I could, not only de final taste of a world before de Scythe, but a reminder of my bro, till some vermin sniffed it out and stole it on me one day. All I had left of Yogi now was a notebook stuffed with gobbledegook.

Bolshy voices echoed up de pipes: Bram and Bogdana having a go at each other. Put my ear to de wall, but sher I didn't even know what language it was goan off in. Reckoned Bram would be all *why is he staying? How could you let him?* And she'd be firing back *whaddya mean? What am I to do? Tis his house, y'daft Dutch gowl!* But she seemed to be doing most of de nattering, so den I thought maybe it wasn't about me at all. *Yur daughter's knocking around de crossroads awful late dese nights, Bram. Wanna lock dat down!* And he's sliding on his self-made pjs and fussing over his butterfly schemes: *I'm too busy to deal with dat pup right now! Dese bugs don't grow demselves y'know!* Dead right, Bram. Give a young byor her space.

I curled into Yogi's stone-cold bed. It'd be warm in a minute, like it'd never been empty. Sleep drew over me fast, and I got lilted off to Nod by de clinky-clanky lullaby of partners yelling up through my old rusty pipes.

A slimy shore. I feel like a kid again, exploring. I'm looking for wreckage from space, a hunk of rocket or something cool like that. *Dere, la!* Washed up on de stones, half in, half out of de lappy water: a dirty wooden chest. Yank off de seaweed, kick open de rusted padlock. Inside: a packet of crisps. Mr. Tayto smiling up at me in his cheery 1950s jacket, all bright colours. I take him out: still crispy crunchy. But once outside de trunk de packet suddenly looks old, faded, like it's been floating in de flotsam or de jetsam, or whichevvor gets more direct sunlight, for years. De words and images are all backwards, so how am I to know where to post if I'm unhappy with my purchase, like? At first I'm all gob and gung-ho to scarf de tasty feckers, but den I suddenly wonder: could I sell it for cash? Antiques can be worth a few bob.

What if it's too valuable to eat? Or sell? I can't even dump it now. Does dat make it worthless? Or priceless?

Woke up like a bolt in de dark. Fucken dreams. Stoopid pieces of shite.

I nodded off again, but not for long. Was woken by light tonguing through Yogi's runt of a window. Flickering orange flames in de yard. Fire. I blinked off my sleep. Should I be alarmed?

Fatigue, in de haloscape, is just another name for fun. It drags you down only when you call on it to up your difficulty level. Dere are saints (call demselves Dequinceys) who work with exhaustion same way Waker fiens use weights to build up biceps. Dequinceys haul a new body through long swamps of Tired, fantastic limbs, mile-long fins or wings, say, all kept moving through sheer will, yearning to cross an ocean, a desert, sailing on and on long after most people'd get bored, switch to a game, or a pornscape, or a war, y'knaw—ape stuff. But high saints know how to ride out all impulses—sher, fecken with impulses is de best part of de Scape!— and sleep is one of de deepest urges. Ancient as hunger. Thirst. Dunnaw if anyone messes with thirst—I don't. Anyhow, cos of regular fighting through an infinite edge of sleep, when Dequinceys Wake, everything is pure buzzing. Having a neat, simple human body dat's not dragging, weighed down with hyper-gravity,

straining against de pull of event horizons... life's a blast again.
I'm no Dequincey, but I've known de remove from yurself you can
get in de Scape. Pure strange—like yur de sadist pressing a button
to torture someone else, and also de pervy masochist on de other
end saying Yup, same again please sir! Why scaping's so popular,
spose.

Fatigue in de Wayke is watered-down death. Burning eyes,
shakes from shot nerves, de cold jarring into every cranny. And de
worst of it, de self-pity. *Will I ever get a night's sleep again?* But dere's
no snuggling to be had with a fire raging downstairs. Mr. Tayto
would have to investigate.

From de kitchen I saw Bogdana and Bram standing round a
bonfire with an auld fella I didn't recognize. Everyone nursed a
cuppa. Codger looked familiar but I couldn't place him. Suddenly
he clocks me, freezes a second, and waves like a wally.

"Tayto! Is it yurself? C'mere and let me get a look at you!"

Ah feck dis now.

"Story, folks?" I said, gatching out.

"Bram was telling me you were back but I..."

He was getting pure emotional and I hadn't a bog who he was.

"How'r'ya?" says I, awkward.

"Home sweet home, hah?" Squeezing my arm and leering. I
inched away, took my arm back.

"What are ye doing out here?" I axed.

"We break the night into blocks," said Bram. Course you do.
A witching hour hokey pokey and a fecken prayer to de moon.
Bogdana blathered something bout circadean sorcery—I wasn't
paying her much heed. Too weirded out by dis codger I couldn't
place. No sign of Sol either, which gutted me.

"Where's Yogi dese days, hah?" de codger kept grinning. Put it
down to knackered paranoia, but I was starting to fear dis old man
"Any word from de brother?" he persisted.

He went to squeeze my arm again and I shook his hand off
sharpish. "Sorry now, but keep yur hands to yourself!"

De smarmy smile fell for just a flash, and a death mask caught
me in its sights. Den de grin was back, bigger. "Amn't I Yogi's
godfather, hah?"

"You're telling me..." I said, real slow and careful, "you are
Martin Spillane?"

"Who else?"

"Are you okay, Tayto?" axed Bogdana.

"Martin Spillane," I said,is dead. Long dead." De codger cackled, and sipped his cup.

"Dead? B'jaysus, someone needs to inform my wife, hah? It'd get me out of all manner of work." He eased down his laugh. "Ah lookit, you've had a big day. You're upset. I'll leave you to get yur bearings." He emptied his mug and handed it back to Bogdana. "You know where I'll be," he added, looking me dead in de eye. Den he turned and waved, all cheerfulness and light. "Morning all!" Off he went through de yard, darkness swallowing him.

Could barely stand I was so shitted out. Bram and Boggy stared at me, faces flickering in and out of flame light. Any safety I felt around dem, de little patch of solid ground in de middle of de flood, was suddenly melting under me. How fast I'd put trust in dem. Who were dese creatures?

Bogdana could see I was shaking and went to give me her jacket.

"Don't want yur jacket!" I cried. "Who de fuck was dat?!"

"Calm down," said Bram. "We thought you knew him. He said he'd heard you were back. Wanted to say hi."

"I wouldn't wake you," added Bogdana. "I told him to come back in the morning. He said he'd wait up."

My hands couldn't stop shaking, even with de fire crackling beside me. Could it be him? So many folks dying so quickly, so long ago… Might I be wrong? But he looks nottin like… How could he hear I was back? I hadn't met a soul on de road.

Didn't know which way to turn. Fatigue and fear had me twitching at every snap of de flames. Felt like crying I was so wrecked. One long tunnel of problems, de Wayke, getting tighter and tighter till you can't breathe, till earth gobbles you up entirely. I buried my face in my hands. It felt good. Maybe I should find myself a nice grave—get a bit of kip for once.

"Come," said Bogdana, putting her hand on my shoulder. "See our livestock. It might calm you." Paranoia was rampant now—was dat a real baby bump? What's she goan to do to me if I follow her into de bug tower? But she seemed so short and motherly. Daycent, like. What choice is dere? Flee? Roam de night? She took my arm and I followed her to de tower, sheepish, too sad to think dis luvvly woman might be anything but goodness. She told me to dig my fingers into de tower's skin. It ripped apart like tissue. We stepped into a dark sleeping garden. Air was warmer in here, and thicker. Sultry. She jiggled some plants. Dey lit up!

"Bioluminesence," she said, like dat explained it nice and neat. De glowy plants were dim, but we'd enough light to see de floor covered in tiny shiny lads, marching in every direction, pure businesslike.

"Careful where you step," says she, while a commuter train of a millipede bustled over my foot. I could feel de weight of de bastard! Dere were giant roaches, and a motley crew of ants, and crickets whirring all around.

"Dunnaw, Bogdana. Not too into creepy crawlies."

"Just close your eyes for a second." I did. At first all I could think of was spindly spawgs marching straight up my own legs and into my jocks, all pretending to be my old dead neighbours, working deir way to my hole—hoping to gain an entrance, eat me from de inside out.

But slowly I changed focus. Everything was alive. De air was gently buzzing and shifting. Such rich air. Clicks and whirs and pitter-patters. Jungle air. Eden air. I opened my eyes and now de glowing plants seemed brighter. I could make out more details.

De hole I'd torn in de tower skin was already sealed up, like it'd never been. Like we'd been born in here—sprouted right up from de dirt. Outside I could make out my old house, and de flickering bonfire, but de view was foggy, like a mirage. Den Boggy pointed to some giant leaves above us on one of de tall vines. I squinted hard. Gawd almighty... Dey weren't giant leaves, but black butterflies de size of bats. Still as roof tiles.

"Ye... eat dem?" I was whispering now, like I'd broken into a secret place, afraid to set off some kinduv alarm.

She smiled and nodded. "We get medicines from their eggs too."

"Handy," I whispered.

"Why do you whisper?"

"I dunnaw," I laughed. "Who am I to bother dem?" And I felt foolish saying it, but didn't know what else to say: "Dey're living life."

Woke alone on my brother's mattress, a cold light scalpeling into his room. All de bodder from last night, dat stranger at de fire saying he was Spillane, and de garden with glowing plants, all fresh life in it, didn't seem any realer to me now dan my dream about my Tayto packet and de treasure chest.

Twas nippy. I could see my breath, and rushed to chuck on some clothes. And den I heard it... a long note on de air. Hard to describe: like a cry, or a horn, sad and cold and piercing. What was it? Downstairs de gaff was deserted, but out beyond de yard I could see Sol standing stock still inside de beanstalk. She held a box in her hands. All round her a blizzard of tiny wings, a kinduv butterfly whirlwind. De box was beckoning all life, dis weird note just winding out through de bald grey day, and everything was flocking to her, trying to be as close to her as could be. It was so gorgeous I couldn't move at first. I wanted to join her too, but it didn't seem possible to just gatch over. Rip through de skin tower and be all *Story, girl?* More I coggled it de harder it seemed. Can a mortal puncture de moment? Bodder de death goddess right in de middle of her harvest? Seems de height of arrogance.

Ah well. Nowhere else to go dis nippy morning. A blizzard of bugs usually wouldn't appeal, but Sol seems so in control. She'll keep me safe from all dose tiny feckers, deir ugly alien faces. Sher, for all I know tis deir planet. Maybe our huge holey skulls horrify dem. Horrify me anyway. Bags for our stomachs. Breathing with de face instead of de whole long body. Born helpless. No armour. All memory and longing and hope. And de lanky levers of our limbs—only four—swaying and swinging through space. We must seem like old sad songs to dem, giant flags of dying countries flapping slowly on de winds.

Everything tarmacked over. No more Tara. Newgrange is a megamart is a deserted housing estate. And de tiny new lads are here in de billions: buzzing start-ups. De world is dere to be eaten. We're past tense, and dey're de flappy, fidgety future. Dey fly—all vivid colours. We lope like legends, boi. Fading. I hope Sol lets me in. Could do with being in dat flurry right now. I've nottin to say to insects, but I'd like company today. A million sparks must add up to a fire somehow. Not feeling de best...

Woke up on de kitchen floor. A surprise. I spose you never expect to faint, like. Sol was crouched over me, brow furrowed. Couldn't tell if she was worried or pissed off.

"Are you having a stroke?" she axed. I was struggling to find my bearings, and her question made it worse. Was I?

"Dunnaw. Why…?"

"I thought saints were always having strokes," she said. Cheeky byor, dis wan.

"Never felt better," I said. "Just taking a power nap." Mortified. Who faints, like? Ladies in de days of hoop skirts who get bad news in a letter. Cartoon fiens sniffing de wavy green stinklines of a skunk! And now de bould Tayto, felled to de lino. Naw, girl. No stroke. I'm just a bloke who fucken swoons when he sees pretty things. Sound.

"Have you eaten?" she asked. She got up and chucked me some bug bickies from a tub. "These are good for getting the blood sugar up," she said, scarfing into one herself. It tasted of apples. I wolfed it right dere on de floor.

"You should lie down on a proper bed. C'mon. Let's go to my room." Something bout de way she said it: so sure, so kind.

"Help us up," I said.

"Dis used to be my room," I blathered, but I didn't believe it. Dis room never belonged to anyone but Sol. It was hers, one hundred percent. Wasn't girly, just neater dan I'd ever seen it. Place smelled of rightness and goodness. De Solarium, she called it.

She shook morning rain off her brolly, and I thought I saw it breathing. Yoke looked like one big stretch of butterfly wing wrapped round in a cone. I squinted: twas inhaling and exhaling. No mistake.

"C'mere, is yur brolly alive?"

She shrugged: "My para-sol? It's a grey area. It blossoms in extremes: sun and rain."

Of course it does. I'd say everything bout you blossoms out to meet extremes. Yur brolly and me have nottin in common, girl. Aside from us both being skinny specimens, like.

I scansed round. From de blues and greens of her umbrella to de glyphs bedecking her walls, I didn't see a single grey area. Twas wall-to-wall colour. De glyphs warped and spiralled, lines of glowing reds and yellows coiling and corkscrewing. Feckin beautiful.

"I like dese," I said, pointing at some busy glyphs. "What are dey?"

"Just a thing I'm into," she said, head down.

"Ah, give us a clue, willa?"

"They're maps." She held up her black box, de same yoke she used to harvest insects, and as she touched de box off a glyph de image updated, exploded in new colours and lines. "Flight patterns of various species over twenty-four hours."

Millions of strands, but no tangles. No mess. Like everything knew how to fit together already. Like de Scape, my true home. Scape-tacular.

"Dat is fucken tasty," I said, feeling a bit woozy again and slumping onto my bed—her bed. She smiled, all awkward suddenly. "Is it art or science or what is it?"

"What a question!" she cried, covering her face with her hands like I was axing her something pure nosey and bold. "You can track growth over time from the more to the less successful species, and pollination rates, so there's a pragmatic aspect. But unfiltered searches like these produce billions of strands, so… It's a tapestry. A mandala."

"Whazzamandala?"

"It'll sound crazy to you, but when I look into these patterns… I just…" She broke off, and I knew she was getting pure meaningful, which made me craw-sick again. Whenever anyone gets dat meaningful look in deir eye you just know some bullshit is coming yur way and you have to be polite as you duck, like. Can't mess around with dat septic tank of big reasons and bigger hopes people slosh round with dem like a tub of fizzy jizz somewhere between deir gullets and groins. Dey go ape if you do.

"I look into these patterns and I think there's a message hidden there. An order. Like, if we could understand what this means, we'd be ready for the next phase of evolution. You know?"

I nodded. Dat was some bullshit alright, fairly steamy too. I liked de colours and shapes, but why stick a higher meaning on it? Why couldn't it just be what it was: a loony-choons random record of flappy fiens flayking round dat happened to look cool? Sher, what's wrong with random? Random's got no baggage. Doesn't need to pack a toothbrush. Dere's no quiz at de end. No measuring stick. No stopwatch, no rulebook, no ref. No center or edge. You just bob and weave and keep moving. Or better yet, stop moving and light up. Could murder a body for a halo now. Do dey have halos on farms? Be a fierce distraction from chores.

Tis a funny farm, I thought to myself, and like a magic spell de words funny farm made de room reel. Suddenly I felt as far from home as I could be—further dan I'd ever been in de Gerries, or de peacock manor, or even de woods at night. I mean, you think yur getting to know someone, start thinking dey're cool, all de instruments say nice wan, boi, and den, right when dis so-called daycent skin has you lulled into thinking *Sher, maybe I can maintain dis orbit*, dey tell you dey can see a mystical order to stuff. And it just breaks yur heart, cos you know you can't land here after all—dis alien's world isn't huffable to you, so keep drifting alone through space.

But what can you do? De Wayke's a bollox. He'll take yur "order" and shove it right up yur mandala, boi. You can have a moment when you feel good things egging you on, but tis all in yur head I reckon. You hear dem cos you need to hear dem, get some shit done of a Monday. Maybe dere *is* good stuff out dere, but tis small spuds next to de Wayke's knife teeth and lawnmower eyes. Dis wan, with her black box and her flashy pictures of bugs flapping round de place, and she telling me tis proof of a fucken order... I leaned over my knees.

"Gonna spew," I said.

"What? Seriously?"

I nodded. Keep it together, keep it together, don't gawk yur ring out in dis poor byor's bedroom. She chucked a towel on my lap.

"Use this!" she cried. "Don't get puke on my carpet!"

"I'm okay... Tis passed."

"What's wrong with you?"

"Nottin. I'm grand," I moaned, lying down on her pillow.

"Don't vomit in my bed," she said, pure stern now.

I stared at her brolly. It was taking little even breaths: in... out... in... out. Calming. In... out... in... out. Nottin to it. Just keep it together. If a brolly can do it, Mr. Tayto can.

Eoin stuck his snout in de door.

"Out," said Sol, lazy like someone used to being ignored. De scut pushed right in, clutching his rabbit tight in his arms.

"What's wrong with him?"

"Tayto's just... under the weather."

"He's sick?!" de lad shouted. It bolted me up in bed.

"Alright kid, easy! Just having a lie-down—"

"He's sick!" Eoin shouted again. "I'm telling mama!" and de little fien hustled out of de Solarium. I could hear his feet thumping downstairs.

"What's wrong with him?"

"We don't get sick often. Eoin thinks all illness is serious."

"I better shift."

"No, just stay put," said Sol, certain and kind again. A minute later Bogdana was fussing into de room. She moved so smooth—her huge belly sortuv glided toward me.

"Not well, Tayto?"

"I'm grand. Got a bit light-headed for a while, tis nottin." She checked my eyes and pulse and whadevvor. She had a bunch of questions and I started to wish Sol wasn't in de room, cos twas all a bit embarrassing.

"When did you last see a doctor?" Joov.

"When was the last time you ate any fresh fruit or veg?" Not sure. Good while ago.

"How often do you drink water in a day?" Dunnaw.

"Exercise?" Naw.

"Close friends?" Nnnnaw.

"Bowel movements?"

"Lookit, I'm grand. Had a spell, took a little lie-down, and now I'm right as—"

"You're not well, Tayto," Bogdana held my hand and I shut up. "You are malnourished, dehydrated. This is not small deal. Big deal. I think you are having a panic attack."

Tis de weirdest thing: she's dere half-scolding me, but it felt so warm—twas all I could do not to wrap my arms tight round her and bury my face in her boobs. Instead I just nodded.

"I'm right as rain," I muttered, but it was pure scheming for attention now.

"I feed you properly tonight!" she announced. De words made me shake dey felt so good. She could feed me bugs. She could feed me muck for all I cared.

"Eoin, fetch a big glass of water!" And his little paws thumped down de stairs again.

"Panic attack is normal in weird times," Bogdana said. "Strange to come home. To find strangers!" She laughed, but it didn't sound happy.

"Serious, Bogdana. You and yours belong here. More dan I do."

Eoin came back with a fuck-off jug so full of water it was sloshing everywhere. "Is this enough Mommy?"

"Yes, Eoin, very helpful," said Bogdana, rolling her eyes at me.

He'd forgotten to bring a glass so I winked at him and guzzled de stuff down straight. Started as a joke, but de more I glugged de better it felt. Luvvly water, boi. Don't remember it dis good. Bogdana smeared some type of oil under my nose. It was cool and tingled and smelled of pine forest. Like Christmas, and springtime too.

"That will help you relax."

"You a nurse or something?"

"I was pharmacist in Warsaw. Once upon a time."

"Do y'miss it? De medicine?"

She was having a think when Bram gatched it. Well, de Brams of dis world don't gatch. Soon as he came in I felt giggly, like a kid in mild trouble. Must be de oil tingling under my srón.

"I see you're in my daughter's bed."

"Ah, y'know. Feeling a bit worse for wear." And den, dunnaw where it came from, but I just bust my hole laughing. Twas bad timing.

"He is hysterical?" Bram axed Bogdana.

"Nervous patch. He'll be good again soon."

"C'mere, I've been meaning to ax ye since I got here..." I figured I'd go for it. "Have ye a halo anywhere bout de place?"

"Halos are banned in this house," said Bram.

Well, dis made me crack up completely. I tried to apologize, but it only made me worse.

"Banned!" I was wiping away tears. "Why?"

And den Bram went right up in my face, and he spoke slow and careful so I caught each of his serious words: "Because life is short. Pare it down to essentials: growing, healing, and making meaning. I grow things. My wife can heal. My daughter seems to be the meaning-maker."

Maybe it was his breath, or de hard glint in his eye, but I stopped laughing.

"Right," I said. "I don't see any place for me on yur list."

"Maybe you should look into that." Yes, Bram, yur a dab hand at firing a low blow from a high horse. So good yur almost a hard man to hate. Almost.

Den he was gone. I never have de comeback cocked and loaded, and soon as he left I could feel de bad things bottlenecking. Grow stuff. Or heal... Or make meaning. Sher, what does dat even mean? And who de fudge is dis Dutch squatter to decide de Big Three?

Nuts to him and his little list. Just because he has a big butterfly net, growing bugs is de beez kneez. His auld doll can rub some oil under yur nose—Medicine, you've made De List! His daughter talks balls about an order in de tangles. Philosopher, you made de grade. I can't wait for de little boy to say he likes blowing shit up. Dynamiter—de fourth column of de republic. "Making dust," spose he'll call it. Septic wanker. Admire me and my family unit—we've got it all figured out, you scobe runt scumbag. With our dipshit rituals and bug slurry and praying to de ceiling…

Bogdana must've sensed me goan into a mad rant inside, cos she suddenly confessed: "I used halo."

Even in my huffy humpy mood, I shook it off at de chance to natter some halo: "What kinduv tek? Were you rated, like?"

"No. No rating, casual user. But one summer I experienced orgasms of over seventy species of animals," she said proudly.

"Animal orgasms? Why?"

"Why does anyone do anything in the Scape? Because they were free. And I was curious."

"Which was the best?" Now it was Sol's turn to be curious. Bogdana chewed it over, and I couldn't work out if she was trying to answer de question, or wondering if she should answer at all.

"Tortoise," she said at last. "Male tortoise. Best orgasm imaginable. I screamed like a bird." And with dat she upped and led Eoin out of de room. Sol and me looked at each other. I'd say we were impressed.

Grace time again. Same every night, certain as sunset. I felt a right wally doing it, but I couldn't be stand-offish after de soundness I'd been shown. Besides, I'd a hunger on me, and if all I had to do for food was bang on a bit about pheromones and pollen, sure dat alone was enough to make me grateful. Ahh, grub. Probly grubs, like. Screw it, I was starving. Bring on de wriggly rascals—I'd have a go at anything dis evening.

Earlier I'd helped make a new hutch for Eoin's rabbit, Bongo. Spose I was trying to prove Bram wrong bout my being totally useless. Bram didn't let on he had any opinion on de matter, just handed me a rusty saw. Didn't do much, like, just cut some wood and snipped a stretch of mesh with pliers—Bram did de assembly. But mucking about with tools and planks and spraying a mess of sawdust all over my sleeve made me feel pure manly, and now my belly was playacting de lumberjack. Cleaning rooms in de Gerries, washing de auld fellas and making up dodgy physio exercises—all dat was hard, but not in de same way. Shifts in de Gerries, dealing with Copperknob, made me want to get out of de Wayke even more dan living in a kwery with dissolving saints and de twitching tails of rodents round every shadowy corner. Soon as I got back to my box of a flat—light up time. No exceptions, no deviation. Religious. Same as dese lads here and deir grace. But making Bongo's hutch felt different. Twas a project, like. With a goal. Start and a finish. Dere, la! Hutch off dat dere!

Twas weird having a real appetite again. Mad nostalgic or something. And so strong! Full-on ravenous, boi, stomach growls and all. Half-wanted to take a chomp out of Bongo's furry haunch even as I was helping build him a flat to live in and show some sexy doe a good time. May as well have raised a barn, or even a great ark to keep two of every animal, predators and prey, all agreeing to get along so dey can stay in out of de damp, keep dry in a flooding world. Even had a blister on my sawing hand! Sounds septic, like, but I kept admiring it during grace—couldn't stop pressing it. Tap, tap. Manly pain, right on tap. Manual labour, boi. Hungry work.

As we built de hutch together, I fired off some questions bout dis bug farming lark. Bram told Eoin to gimme de ska: "It's not like an old farm, where everything takes up the whole ground. Our farm starts way down there"—he wiggled a finger at de dirt—"where the worms get fat. And our farm is mostly air above the ground. So it's mostly air, not ground."

"I see. Clever."

"Yeah. And our livestock, that's our bugs, they don't make us sick, cos... cos. Why is it again, Dad?"

"Remember the word?" Bram prompted him. Eoin screwed up his nose. "Alien," said Bram.

"Oh yeah! Insects are too different from us, so we don't make them sick and they don't make us sick. Cos otherwise we'd have... viruses."

"Uh huh," I said, hacking away into a plank with a rusty saw. "And c'mere to me. Are you goan to be a bug farmer like yur old man?" I winked at Bram.

"No. I'm gonna be a spaceman."

"An astronaut?"

"No, an alien!" Eoin hopped at dis like he'd just won something, or at least made de shortlist.

"Cool. Think I want to be an alien too. Sign me up." I looked over at Bram. He was staring over at his beanstalk. De skin shimmered rainbow. What was he thinking? Maybe just remembering a chore he had to do. Or he was thinking bout de future his son might really have. Or maybe he was axing himself if we weren't all aliens in dis place.

It was a fine hutch, if I say so myself. Bongo was one lucky coinín. During grace I noticed de smooth look of de dining table. Daycent material, wood. If you know what you're doing it can be cool and sober, or warm and welcoming, or whadevvor you want. A rake of personalities, has wood. De lads who made dis table knew what dey were doing—twas one big circle of warm, like de sun we were thanking with our hokey pokey dance. And once de dance was finished, a platter of butterflies was passed round, fresh netted today, straight from butterflight. Craytures came of deir own will, flocking to Sol's black box—a million martyrs seeking glory. We picked de wings off, careful, stripping de pretty off to get at de flesh.

Second platter was dumplings: snails fried in batter. Pretty hearty fare.

"So many species," crowed Bram, waving a dumpling in de air. "We get to eat something new nearly every day."

We all nattered away, me boasting bout how evenly I cut de planks, and Eoin conflicted bout how snug Bongo would be now he had his own place (bit worried dey both might be lonely at night), and Sol ignoring hutch talk altogether and waxing lyrical bout her latest mandala, and Bram banging on bout circular farming (plants help insects help plants or something like dat) and Bogdana... Bogdana just smiling. Had she sprinkled super-spices in our little treats? Dunnaw why I was enjoying my munch so much. I mean, I was pure horsing into it all. Maybe it's not the ingredients, but how you serve dem.

Joov flashed into my head, dug up from some long-buried old warren of images. Twas understaffed, so dere was a lottery every week selecting older fiens to help feed de babas. I "won" it once. Remember a bored slag of a nurse called Sumpta supervising me and a few other dirty scobes as we slung dollops of paste, spoon by spoon, into all de tiny opening mouths. De nursery smelled of powder, which was kinduv nice, but dese little wans… I remember dem all sat in a row inside a long frame, held in place like little bottles in Bogdana's spice rack. Every one of dem rocking. No crying, like. Just rocking back and forth like tiny monks who got lost in an endless prayer. De strange quiet of a room full of babies not crying. Wrong quiet. De saddest quiet. And as soon as I was done with my week of spooning out de babyfood, I got de feck out of dere and never fed de babas again. Haven't thought about dose sprogs till tonight.

I ripped another pair of wings off my next morsel. How did Bogdana get dese yokes to taste just a wee bit fruity? De butterfly was as quiet as de babas in Joov as I pulled him apart and chewed him up. I reminded myself to thank everyone for de meal. And de banter. My eyes traced de circle of our dining table, a curve like a smile without end.

Chapter 9: Spectres

Roar of an angry swarm swelling round me in de dark. Panic. Half dreaming, I sprang out to de corridor. Bogdana was huddling with Eoin and Sol. De bugs have rebelled, boi! My first thought. De sound was like a whole hive raging.

But naw, twas an alarm, and a mad scary one at dat. Proper order: Dere was call for achtung alright. No coppers out here in de sticks—need yur own way of dealing with any showers of shites chancing deir arm, raiding houses. You hear some stories dat might incline a wiser body to stay in de city, nice and lit up of an evening.

Bram appeared in his jocks, clutching a shockstick. He paused at de top of de stairs.

"Be careful, Dad!" shouted Sol.

Eoin said nottin, but his face was frozen—pure bricken it. De kid's terror sharpened my own. Bram took a breath and charged down de steps. Bogdana turned to me, begging: "Please stay with him, Tayto. Help him. Help us! Please!"

Help? How was I to help matters? Captain Tayto doesn't swoop in and save de day, d'y'knaw? Tis one thing playing at manly chores like building a rabbit hutch. Dis was de Wayke calling my bluff. Think yur home and off de hook, worm? I'm goan to rip ya in two and guzzle yur entrails raw. How much are you willing to pay to act de hard chaw?

Sol could see me inching back from de stairs. "Please!" she echoed Bogdana. "Don't leave Dad alone down there."

Alright girl. Why don't we all go down together so? No one'll expect a preggers woman and a child. I'll be right behind ye for *moral support.*

But I was too chicken to bear looking like a chicken in de eyes of Sol, or de others really. So I found myself creeping after Big Papa, wielding a hefty metal candlestick like a sword up by my shoulder. Dug my bunny-shelter blister into de metal: made me feel sharp. Right so. Just brain de next noggin you see, boi. Whip de scalp off it.

Bram killed de alarm. Silence was solid. Nottin but dark outside—and whadevvor was waiting in it. We waited too, hunched, me behind himself who pointed his snap-crackling shockstick at de door. I was ready to explode apart and leg it in every cardinal direction at once if something burst through into our world. My breath was so sharp, I was tearing at de seams. Still neither skitter nor scratch from beyond.

"Any chance it's just a fox snouting for scraps?" I whispered. Bram hissed. I held my candlestick higher and practiced downward swings. I tried both sides (left leg leading, den right), and different grips (left hand over right, vice-versa) but every way felt backward. A life spent in a recliner looking at light. How do ya swing a fecking stick?! Jesus wept!

A rap of knuckles on de door. A weird sound escaped from me, a loud and raspy Haaaaah. Haaaaah! before I could hold it back. Den a voice from outside pierced through: "Taaayto?" I stuck my eye to de spyhole. De release was so mighty I dropped de candlestick, arms pure jelly.

"Yeah, coming," I cried out. "Hold yur horses."

"Who is it?" snapped Bram, still wielding his shocker.

"Tis no bodder," I said.

I unbolted de door and pulled it open. Zeke slouched in de rain, a drowned rat.

All my relief vanished when I saw his soggy spectre, standing before me, laughing quietly. I suddenly wished it was a stranger, a robber, a villain—someone I could just clobber and be done with.

Well, dere was no shortage of guzz eye from Bram Brakkenhof as Zeke stepped over de threshold. I felt like a cur cringing under de glare of his ticked-off master. But Bram was not my master. And what could I do? I was only in dis house cos it was Yogi's last known halo location. I'd promised to escort Zeke here and… well, I'd more or less done it, like. Wasn't my letting de good doctor indoors kinduv Mission Completed? But I'd a notion it would really be de start of Level 2, and Level 2 would, y'knaw, suck balls.

"Introductions are in order," I sighed, going all formal without even meaning to. "Mr. Brakkenhof, dis is Dr. Zohar, my brother's colleague." Using de honorific landed on Bram—I saw him chewing on it. Still, de auld shockstick ticked away to itself, snapping and popping, only aching to bayte de lugs off some poor bollox. Or fry skin, or shatter bone. Wasn't sure if it was me or Zeke it was crackling for.

Zeke was nearly as blank as Bram, except for de odd chuckle here and dere. What was he laughing at? Some knock-knock joke he'd heard haunting de hedgerows? I wished to God he'd rein it in and pretend to be normal for half a minute. If only I could shut down and reboot de whole situation. All I could coggle was de strong pull of bed, de flahed eyelids melting into each other.

"Dr. Zohar's my travelling companion. We lost each other in de fog."

"You never mentioned him before," Bram said.

"Well, I didn't expect ye all to be here," I replied, snark edging into my voice. "I got distracted, like." It was pissing even harder outside now, a billion watery knuckles rapping away, begging for a bed.

"He sleeps down here," Bram said, calm but gaze locked on Zeke like a mongoose on a viper. "If he comes upstairs..." Bram slapped de stick off de banister—a crack like a bullwhip rang out clear and sharp round us, searing a vicious scar into de wood. I was bolt awake again.

"Ah now. Is dat necessary?" I protested half-hearted, cos part of me was bloody glad of Bram's weaponry and strength. Dat sizzling scar on de banister told madness it could move so far but no further. All de important stuff would stay safe, at least for tonight.

Bram flashed his glare through me now, as if to say *Necessary? Dunnaw, boi. You tell me. You brought dis psycho on us. How scared should we be?* Den he turned and tromped upstairs, leaving me alone with our new house guest and his low, scattered laughter.

I gave Zeke a towel to dry off, and lobbed a blanket over de couch for his bed. But Zeke sat at de dining table instead. I joined him, pure reluctant to hear whadevvor he had to say.

"Have you found it?" he whispered. His breath stank.

"Would I be sitting here if I'd half a notion?" I said, squirming in my chair. Didn't like his eyes, boi. Dey were empty, piercing. Tis a starved look I've only seen on a few hardcore saints despite all my years of kwery dwelling. A look comes over de saint who can't find what he's searching for, in any realm. He gets restless, desperate... before he unravels altogether.

"Have you found any traces? Yogi's files?" he pressed.

"I've been to his room and all over, la! Got nottin, boi. No sign he's been knockin round here since we were kids." Dat deflated him sure enough. Wondered if I should apologise for slipping him in de woods. De unspoken wrong was driving me nuts, but I wasn't into drawing out our little chat. *Shag it. Goan to bed. He's not bringing it up so neither am I.*

"Get a daycent sleep." I rose us both to our feet.

"It wasn't easy finding your house," he said, dat hollow chuckle returning. "Most of your old neighbours are gone. No directions. I had to walk down every small road... knock on a lot of doors... ha ha." I opened my gob to say my sorries, but before I could let out a peep de spectre grabbed my arm, bony fingers ice-cold.

"Have they come here? Left any signs? Warnings, threats?"

"Hah? Who'r'ya on about?"

"Amphibians!" He leered at me. A flash of memory: de Fop on stage, yowling to saints-cum-Wakers *Ah'm an amphibian.* Hadn't given it much thought at de time. Kinduv figured it was a comment on de Fop's personal style: big flipper spawgs, greenish pallor, lizardy stare.

"They know." He squeezed me harder, gave me a rake of nods. "They know what happened by now—they'll be coming."

"Who will, boi?"

"The amphibians, YOU MORON!" he shrieked and tried to shake me but his legs gave out and he crumpled to de floor. His hands clasped me like a drowning man, and I sank down with him. *Shhhh!* I did my best to quiet him, coggling de nervous family upstairs, and Bram de Owl perched on high, one eye open at all times, talons sharp.

"Who, or what, are amphibians?"

"Amphibians are cold-blooded. They have no notion of sharing. If we find the Crown, they'll have no qualms about... well, let's just say that won't have a problem taking it from us. They'll sell it to the Pharaohs for billions."

"De *who?*"

"Some sort of cabal... obscenely wealthy... terrified of death... want to be gods."

"Like we do?"

More chuckles from his nibs, and I couldn't be in less of a mood for it.

"We *deserve* it, Tayto. They don't. Did you know the Pharaohs probably unleashed the Scythe? A plague to thin down the population, break its spirit—make it easier to control!" I eased Zeke's hands off my top. More gentle *shhh*ing.

"C'mere, are dese Amphibian lads onto us?" Something bout de way he stared at de ground... "Zeke, are we *racing* people to find Yogi's stuff?"

"Not sure exactly..." Zeke nibbled his fingers, looking as confused as I was. "But there have been *agents* trying to breach my cocoon scapes—our marshmallow conversation. I doubled my encryption, but, one never knows for certain..." He jolted. "Have you been contacted by anyone besides me?!"

My mind flashed to de fake Spillane, cheerily inviting me to his house. Naw, wasn't sharing dat particular item right now. Zeke was too on edge, needed a kip. We both did.

"Naw, boi. Place is sound as a pound."

I hadn't a bog who Fake Spillane was, but de more I coggled, de worse de sinking feeling in my gut got. To be fair, he could be any species of chancer. World's riddled with imposters dese days. Harmless enough, most fiens—just pulling on a dead man's slippers and trying to get comfy. And de old rural neighbours so lonely for any company, dey don't let on dey know a thing—*aw, glad to see yur back, we missed ya*, like. But something bout dat auld fella's rubbery face lit up by bonfire flames... Mask for an amphibious lizard. Can you ever trust a beast perfectly at home in two opposite worlds?

Twas weird to watch Zeke move his lips, making silent points to himself, nodding like de clappers, and know de poor bollox probly wasn't paranoid at all. He might be spot on.

"Forget all dat noise," I said in my calmest, fakest tone. "Get some fecken sleep, willa?" His laugh and his cough had fused into one single wheezy monster now, and he bent double with it. When he finally got it under control he grinned at me. "You alright?" I axed. I didn't know what to do only sortuv smile back at him. And as he went on wheezing and shaking, it was all so nervous I felt a ripple of de same hollow laughter shake itself out of my own mouth. Ha. Ha ha ha. Hardi-har-har.

Breakfast was woeful. De whole family acted like I'd invited a leper warthog to drag his rancid hide all over de gaff. Gawd knows

I could see it from deir point of view, but what about seeing it from mine? I'd obligations, like! You hit de bóthar—an bóthar *fada*—with a fien, and promise him a spot in your old place… can't just turf him out, la.

I'd barely slept, and what little kip I got was one long nightmare of frogs and newts and de like, ambushing de house, squirming over demselves, cramming in through every window and door, de house hive-alarm in conniptions de whole time, forcing us all up a beanstalk into another world, full of giant insects, antennae all over us, testing if we'd be any good for a munch…

Zeke wasn't helping. Sher all he had to do was pretend he was even half-sane and de lads would probly be okay with him staying a night or two. But naw, de gowl was pure twitchy as he mucked about with his bowl and spoon, and when dey ax him a plain question he acts so suspect dat I start to think myself: *He's out to burn de joint to ashes, and us with it.*

Finally I got de go-ahead from Bram to bundle Zeke up to Yogi's hole of a room.

"Some breakfast banter you have: *'I've no legal obligation to answer your questions!'* Are you a total tool or what?"

"They're squatters. It's your house, isn't it?"

Dunnaw. I looked into whether I could sell it once. Didn't have any documents and de lawyer just laughed me out of it. I can't prove much about what's mine… Lookit, just cop yourself on, alright?!"

"This is the notebook?" He was already ignoring me, flicking through pages and snorting: "Never knew him to write something down." Dis was a barrel of laughs, like, de notion of Yogi using a pen.

"Fuckssaaake, stoplaughingwilla?"

And he did.

"Code!" He tapped de book. "It's written in code."

Course tis written in code, I thought. *My brother never said anything straight out.* And boom: I'd a fierce need to leave. Zeke would fail to make heads nor tails of de notes, and who knows what ructions would come. Or worse, maybe—he'd crack it! And I'd be faced with more proof, if proof were needed, dat I was perpetually locked out of my brother's head, his trails all left for someone else, jewels to others and plain pebbles to me.

"I'll get out of yur hair," I said, but he didn't hear, too busy squinting and pinning notes against de mirror. He was already acting like he'd found de Word of Gawd, and was scrambling to coggle which end was up. I left him to it.

It started out as a stroll round de old neighbourhood—get away from all de tension back at de house. But one turn led to de next, and soon I found myself sniffing round Spillane's. Twas odd, cos I'd made a clear plan with myself to stay far, far away from dis haunt. I could see plain as my nose dat coming here alone was risky, but here I was, standing with de gate latch in my hand. I half wished Bram was with me, bodyguard style. Nottin doing dere, I'd say. Any good credit I might have had with him had slipped through my fingers like nutrigel through a slashed feedbag. Fien was well odd at me, and who could blame him? But fair duce, he was keeping his hate under wraps. Hadn't seen hide nor hair of de shockstick all morning. Should be grateful for small graces, spose.

Bram. Why was I after de thumbs-up from him anyway, like some suckup student round a teacher? Doesn't he take a dump like everyone else? Pissed me off to catch myself coggling bout him at all, trying to earn a wink or a slap on de back, when twas clear enough he didn't traffic in winks or backslaps at all. Even when I cut wood for de rabbit hutch—he just took it. *Straight as a board*, I said. Not a word from de ingrate lowlander.

Couldn't get my picture of him straight. One minute he was some species of scientist, but after last night I wondered if he wasn't an ex-copper. De episode with Zeke had me picturing Bram a few years back, stern Judge Dredd mug up on him, bayting seven shades of shite out of activists in masks acting de anarchist. Gowls convinced dey could topple de giant puppet masters stalking past crowds on deir sleek black stilts on de way to carving up our little planet between dem. Dis Brakkenhof I saw in my head wouldn't flinch as he whaled down on poor idealistic lefty goms with deir homemade signs and songs. Must have felt noble as de Right-Hand-of-Gawd to be such an enforcer, whipping impudent pups.

And den de Scythe sweeps, and everything Bram's ever known falls down, even long-legged, stone-faced Bram himself. But for some reason Bram de Guard is spared. So he has a think to himself one feverish night dat stretches on forever: *C'mere to me, need to change my ways. Dis isn't on at all. I'll go somewhere quiet and green and grow bugs. And I'll live in peace with things, and remember control is an illusion, and I'll give thanks and praise for not being a guard anymore, and defending auld rich bolloxes I should have been whipping instead of de poor dossers with deir homemade signs and little songs bout peace and sharing and all dat shite.* He's packing up his stuff, chucking most of it. *Toothbrush—check. Badge and uniform—naw.* He's ready to march out to greet his new kumbayah self, but he pauses at de door, caught by a loose thread of doubt. And he says to himself, *Erra, bring de auld shockstick. I'm all for de pacifism and enlightenment now, but... never know.*

You never do know. What would I do with a shockstick of my own? Or something brutal with a bit more range to it? Oh, I felt naked alright—bricken it really. But something bout being on my home turf, and de stolen screwdriver I had tucked in my back pocket, helped me feel champy enough to pass de gate and gatch to de door. *You trying to haunt a house in my hood? Snatch a part of my history—and haunt me? Dis is de Rebel county, y'nob. We don't take dis at all. Claim ya, boi. Claim ya!*

De door I'd knocked on so often as a kid creaked open at my touch. Lock was melted by something. *Can yur lads come out to play?* Inside everything was burned. A fire had happened long since, started in de living room where everything was blackest. Bits of tinsel glinted here and dere, and I could make out a black plastic Christmas tree in de corner. Limbs were curled and warped, and de spine had melted into a hunchback.

"Hello!" I called. Over de fireplace hung a goldy banner: *Happy New...* De rest was singed. Bad case of de willies. *Screw it, sher. Whoever he is, he's gone. Must've scared him off.* I'd turned to leave when I saw a pair of green eyes staring in de low light. *Aisling!* No—a figure in a black burqa, camouflaged, almost invisible against charred walls. De Amphibian Queen was here, patient as a toad lying in wait for its dinner. A trumpet blast of shock shook my mammal bones.

"Ah, tis yurself," I said, pure cool. *Mr. Tayto, you've balls on you de envy of de Irish squad.* But still I backed up against a wall, in case another froggie (or whadevvor cold blooded beasts dese Amphibians are) was with her and fancied hoppin me. My hand drifted to my back pocket. "You been waiting for me, girl?"

She rose, her eye slit levitating toward me. "For you," she said, and handed me a box. It was a proper present, like, wrapped up in fancy paper with a ribbon and all.

"What's dis?"

"Something you deserve." I stared at dis pretty parcel in my hand—too pretty by half. Like something a god would give a mortal to destroy dem. Something Itchy'd give to poor auld Scratchy.

"You open it," I said. Her majesty gave a little *as-you-wish* bow, and undid everything, lifting de lid slowly, a magician teasing a big ta-da. I leaned away, and when nottin happened I peered in. Nestled into some tissue paper, two halos curled round each other, sleeping babes.

"A just reward for two brave souls." She paused. "It's not easy to quit suddenly, is it?" *Yeah, tisn't so easy to track us when we're not lit up, either.* Who knew how long she'd been spying on my scapes, learning how I tick, seeing if dere was anything in my gaming might help her find Yogi, or his Crown? Nottin private anymore. No place to hide from butlers and spies.

In spite of myself, I gave her gift a good eyeballing. Such curves. Things of beauty. Candy from a stranger. I just wanted to cradle one for a bit. My meatpuppet was suddenly all wrong for me, and a good monster sprint through a jungle, or a basejump with no parachute, was all I craved. Who cared if a creep was peeking out from under a rock? Maybe privacy is overrated. Yur always innocent when you scape, no? Always free, or close enough.

I reached for de box. "Yur too kind, miss."

She held it back. "Let's get retribution out of the way first."

"Get what now?"

"One of my agents was with you when you left the Manor. Correct?" Dis was it. No way out. Deserve to be punished, I know, but I couldn't get past my confusion. Why make a pressie of halos first? Before I could think straight, didn't I hear some trip-hop wafting in from de back room. Who strolls in only De Fop, Foppy as you please.

I wanted to hug him and scarper at de same time. He wore a fancy velvet jacket and matching shorts, silk white socks. Frilly doodad round his neck.

"What? No greeting for Lazarus?" De Fop axed. He started dancing, real chilled out from de trip-hop—coolest guy at his own wake. Her majesty started to groove a bit too. She cooed along to de music. Sight of de pair dancing, real slow and relaxed, made me feel I was losing my mind.

I looked at de charred floor, guilt just one kinduv smoke winding round me. Confusion more dan anything else: turning on myself. What should I have done back in de hovel in de woods, seeing Foppy brained and lying doll still? And den anger: *Why are dey dancing?!* What have I to feel ashamed of? Always shame. Fucken knee-jerk response to everything. Sher, I've no medical training! Can't whip up an ER out of sticks. And I wasn't de one who brained him! As it grew, de anger ate up everything else. He was alive, grand. But all I wanted to do was kill. I'd burn dis place all over again, smash up deir little party. I readied myself for whadevvor he'd blather bout next—I'd be ready for it with a screwdriver up his snout.

"Don't you like my new shoes?" De Fop stopped dancing and stuck out a high-heeled bróg, buckled, with a pointy elf toe. Something meant maybe for a dainty woman of olden times, but on his monster spawg dere was a nightmare look to it. "Authentic enough for Louis 14th, *n'est-ce que pas*?" he said, pure thrilled with himself. "But there's one significant historical inaccuracy. Can you tell what it is?"

Who de fuck is Louis 14th when he's at home? I'd hardly time to ponder, when de giant elf shoe ploughed into my nads. I dropped before I even felt pain, and just lay in a ball waiting for de agony to hit.

"That's right!" he cried. "Steel toe-caps!" He clapped for his new shoes like an excited kiddie, den hawked a great glug at me. It exploded between my eye and nose. "That's for leaving me to die in a shack. I mean, really"—he appealed to his queen—"is that how you thank someone for freeing you?" He frisked me lazily while I dealt with de pain in my personals. Found de screwdriver and lobbed it away, tutting to himself.

"What do ye want?" I managed to cough out.

"My cane back," whispered De Fop. "Thief." He blew me a kiss, and started to throw shapes again.

De queen gazed down on me. "You don't understand us. If you did, you wouldn't be so scared."

"I'm not *fucken scared*." As de words growled out of me I realized I meant it. Nice daycent bit of rage. Who cares where it came from, here it was. Pure anger strength! Felt good in patches, but excruciation kept wailing up through me too. I clocked de hunching Christmas tree in de corner of my eye. Maybe it had taken a good funt in de knackers too and just couldn't recover. Hunched for de rest if its unnatural life.

"Raise him up," de queen ordered. De Fop hauled me into a carbonized lounge chair. Leaning back helped, sortuv. De chair was like de one I had back in my Dublin flat, but crispier.

"This divide between Saints and Wakers is absurd," she purred. "We need a better way."

Even with only her eyes showing, I could tell I was facing into yur wan's own private septic tank of Meaningful Ideas. De voice slips into a gawd-awful visionary tone and you just fill in de fecken blanks. *People, people, hear me now. Everything will be grand, but first we need to find a…*cosmic pogo stick. *They will know the path, but they must build a…*temple to Porky Pig. *We shall have wisdom, if we destroy all the…*leftover Creme Eggs. Whadevvor. What was on de menu today?

"Life's not about mass-producing offspring or joining the workforce," she said. "Nor can we abandon the world by hiding in private fantasies."

Finally, someone with de Big Answer.

"Goan so. What's it all about?" I axed.

"Glory," she sighed, turning to gaze into De Fop's eyes. "To achieve a state of being you might call pure style."

"Uh, glory?" I said, squirming a bit in my crispy lounger. "Howjamean?"

"Come come, Mr. Tayto, don't play coy."

"Not being smart, love—I haven't a bog what yur bangin on bout."

"You really never play with others, do you!" De Fop sniggered.

"Mr. Tayto," she peered at me, "you *must* be aware that those in-the-know have been speculating about your brother's latest work for some time now."

"Well how bout dat."

De Fop rolled his eyes and looked ready to fire out some snark, but she stroked his arm and he buttoned it.

"We know all about it," she said. "Where do you think your brother and his colleagues got the money for this research in the first place?"

Could it be true? I kept on missing pieces. Important pieces. If dey'd paid for Yogi's research… did de Crown belong to dem?

"It's so hard to get funding these days," de Fop added, all sly smirk. "People are too easily satisfied by the mediocre, the status quo. But we believed in your dear brother and his vision. And we so nearly had it, the results of all that work. But then he vanished—" he blew an air kiss "—in a puff of smoke."

"But we had you, my beautiful creature," de Queen gushed. "We kept a steady eye on you."

De green girl in my scape? She did seem to be... amphibian... in nature...

"Once Zeke found you, the game was afoot!" de Fop clapped, like we were all playing a fun parlor game, like. "All we had to do then was make sure that you got properly waylaid by Lord Mulligan's crew."

"Is Mully yur boss?" I axed. De pair exchanged a look like I'd pure insulted dem.

"Lord Mulligan," de Fop managed to spit de words out, "is good for exactly two things: throwing garden parties..." He stroked my face. "And catching lost souls."

"So he works for *ye*?"

"Let's just say he scoops up the lost souls, and we sieve for fallen angels." De Queen stroked de other side of my face.

"Sooo," I coggled to myself, "I'm supposed to thank you... for freeing me from a trap... *you guys* set for me?"

"A night at the Manor can be quite elucidating, no?" de Fop said, all mock-insulted again. "You can see clearly the appeal of overcoming this impasse between Saints and Wakers."

"Being the first to find Yogi's work and open-source it could be one of the greatest humanitarian triumphs in history," she said. "And we have all the right connections—manufacturing, marketing—to make this go global."

"What about... de Pharaohs?" De pair broke up laughing like I'd axed de dumbest question in Kerry.

"You believe in Pharaohs. That's *adorable!*"

"Pharaohs!" heaved De Fop, fanning his face. "He's just too much! Isn't he! Utterly adorable." He was in convulsions. Finally it started to ease off, and Her Majesty informed me dey were *definitely not* laughing at me. Funny, cos it fucken well felt like dey were.

"Fine so," says I, "if wankers like Mully are launching a holy war against halos, how'll dey respond to Crowns knocking round all over de gaff?"

"The future doesn't belong to men like Francis Mulligan," sneered de Queen. "You know this. It belongs to the Crown. It will be the end of emaciated saints, of reliquaries, and the hopelessness they represent. Ours will be a new amphibious age: saintlier than Sainthood, more woken than the Wakers. Our world, our shared home, will become a hub for psychonauts travelling to billions of realities, acquiring wisdom for eons. But they'll return in full health, having stepped away for only an instant. No more nations, just a globe of enlightened beings who have known ego death—become living ecologies unto themselves. We can wipe out greed, war—history and its sorry catalogue of petty squabbles. Find the Crown, spread the model, begin civilization again: Year zero."

Great. Sol with her mandalas, and dis wan with her history wipe. Clued-in fiens dodge all dis global utopia shite as you would de Scythe. I'm a scobe—call a spade a spade, like—but even I've coggled enough bout history to know tis Meaningful Ideas cause most of our hassles. Gizmos may change de world pretty sharpish, but dere's nottin—no gizmo, no notion, no magic handshake—bringing world peace to us anytime soon. And anyone gushing bout it is de last bunch you should trust.

"Right so. And what's dis bout glory, la?"

"There's a special place in heaven for the messenger," said de Queen. "Debussy. Monet."

"Coco Chanel," whispered De Fop, like he was saying a little prayer.

"People who dismantle selfish delusions and usher in a new age are angels. Don't you want to be an angel, Mr. Tayto?

"Don't amphibians creep out of de river muck?" I muttered.

"Indeed they do!" gushed De Fop, pure chuffed. "Come, dance with us." He hoisted me out of my recliner and squeezed me between himself and yer wan. De three of us swayed, me as tense as a lady cat sandwiched between two Pepé Le Pews.

"Mr. Tayto," de queen held my face in her hands. Her hands on my skin were damp, something tingly seeping under my pores. "I want you to open your mind as wide as you can. Don't you grasp what's happening?"

"Probly not, miss," I squirmed in deir hug.

You're an amphibian too, they whispered in my ear. *You just don't know it yet.*

Don't you hate this primate world?

How absurd and petty and cruel it is?
How limited the vision?

I was shrinking and de pair towered around me, swaying to hypnotic music, holding me up like a wriggly newborn, still wet, not used to cold air. *How fertile the Nile mud,* she whispered. *Life spills from the dark void…. A legion of frogs. Amphibians bridge realms: water and land, chaos and order… death and rebirth.*

"You can trust us to share Yogi's gift," De Fop reassured me.

"You must trust us," breathed de Queen, stroking my face. "Don't you trust us?"

"Who can you trust?" axed De Fop. "Can you trust yourself?"

"What if you hoard it?" de Queen sounded worried. "What if you find the Crown but fail the bodhisattva test—stay in nirvana forever—keep it all to yourself."

"Keep it all to yourself? Where's the justice in that?" De Fop wanted to know. He was a man of principle. He was concerned. About me, about *everyone*, la!

I traipsed home in a heavy mist with my pressie tucked under my arm. Meeting with de spectres in Spillane's had somehow left me more put out dan if I'd been threatened. I'd been *spooned*. Like a big dollop of cheese'n'onion ice-cream—pure *wrong*, like. Dese Amphibians had some knack for slipping under de surface and working on yur depths. I was practically saying de Crown was deirs by de end of our slow dance. But de empty-headed flowers in de hedgerows had no agenda, like, and I could feel dem deprogramming me from de green-eyed girl and her slimy-tongued cult. Her majesty's condescension! *Try to open your mind, Tayto.* Why don't you gargle my goolies, y'gant? Big presumptuous heads on de pair of dem! Fancied dey'd get deir clammy hands on Yogi's Crown, forge some copies, be de too-cool-for-school heroes dey reckon dey already are. Instant enlightenment or whadevvor. I could see de drop party now: De Fop DJ-ing for de world's biggest posers. Burqa Byor, Her Majesty, announces dey've a little goodie bag for everyone. What's in it? Aw, not much, just a doorway to being a god. Use it or give it away to a fancy friend. No big deal. We're only Amphibians, de legends who changed history. And me just some scobe gowl dey need to gladhand to get what dey're after.

Questions squirmed in me—electric eels. Why would Yogi not

opensource his tech if it worked? Once you lose yur ego, do you also lose any will to come back to de Wayke and help others? And sposing I found it, and it worked. Did de Amphibians have de right to take my bro's stuff? Did I? My only real memories were of him as a kid. Couldn't shake de notion I'd be stealing from a child.

But dat kid was long gone now. Stolen hair by hair in a long slow whirlwind. A sadness fell on me, so thick it gripped my stomach, and I near forgot de happy parcel under my arm. We didn't talk much, but we spent ages together tromping through woods, fields, along streams filled with sticklebacks, beheading flowers with weed whips. We shared a wordless world. In silence, he tolerated me. Naw, he *welcomed* me.

No joke, boi, what I wouldn't give to see him again, even just one more time. Just for an hour—two grown men, or two kids again, wouldn't matter. Wouldn't need to speak, just sit together maybe. Down near a stickleback stream, watching puny life bustle before us.

Sadness is strong, boi, even when you work to block it out. It's de basic law of de world, constant as gravity, dragging you down to itself, trying to hold onto ya, like. Even de spring flowers felt de pull, bending deir innocent heads.

I ditched de box and its wrapping in a hedge. De shock of perfect right angles in de dark twisting thicket looked wrong, but I'd no way of explaining de box to anyone back at de house—figured I'd play it close to my chest. I pushed de halos into my back pocket where de screwdriver had hidden. Hope Bram had a back-up screwdriver if he was planning DIY, cos I was never goan back to Spillane's again.

I found Eoin out de back feeding Bongo some kinduv kibbly bits through his hutch mesh. I thought you gave dem lettuce, but Eoin said it gives bunnies de collywobbles. Shows what I know. Bongo was making short work of de kibble—happy out, but a hard crayture to envy all de same. Under his long furry spawgs lay a mesh floor to stop him doing a legger. Anybody inclined to burrow out from deir comfortable life can't be too comfy after all.

Sol, Bogdana and Bram were in de beanstalk. I'd never seen all three together in dere before. Didn't like it—I took a notion dey were planning something. What to do bout Zeke, maybe. Or me. I gave a wave over but dey didn't see me, or made out like dey didn't. Fine so, langers. Of ye go, a-harvesting bugs together. Just remember ye're guests here. I've let you stay cos it pleased me, but turn on me too long and ye'll find I've turned on you too.

I'd been coggling whether or what to tell Zeke bout de Amphibians trip-hopping out of the rushes. I was coming down on the side of keeping my mouth shut. Knowing De Fop was alive might ease Zeke back from de edge, but den again it could push him over too. I spied into Yogi's room looking to see what state de twitchy bollox was in.

I found him lying on his stomach, like a kid doing a jigsaw. He'd pages of Yogi's notebook ripped out and he was assembling dem on de ground. Dunnaw why but I nearly had a conniption when I saw my bro's ramblings fecked about de floor.

"Y'taking de piss, hah?" Expected Zeke to lep like a dog caught with his snout in de fridge, but he hardly glanced at me. "Wheredya get off? Who said you could rip up his stuff?" Tears were stinging me—couldn't believe so much rage pouring out so fast. Like it was right dere on tap. But it wasn't de fresh, spring-cleany rage I'd felt back at Spillane's. It was blinding, confusing, helpless now. Sher it wasn't even my notebook. I threw a few lame pucks at Zeke's head, and it was all he could do to calm me down enough to focus: *Look!* In all four corners of each page, knacky little doodles showed how all de pages fit together. He had to lay dem out to follow Yogi's clues.

I almost didn't want to hear any explanation. No more words, no more plans or reasons or theories. I just wanted to go buck wild and hop off him. But he kept talking and talking, caught up in his own frenzy, until I started to cotton on to de image forming on de floor. Shape of a tree: roots spread down in wonky lines, a clean horizontal for de earth, and sprouting from it a trunk and branches under a big round umbrella canopy.

I should've been impressed. I mean, fair play to Zeke for figuring it out—I'd been trying to read what was on de page like a daw. He'd seen right past de words to a bigger structure. No flies on dese tech fiens, boi.

But instead I just felt empty. Naw, not empty. I felt a limp hate for myself. Yogi was my only brother, but it took a stranger to decode his notebook. Just another reminder I was nottin but a pig-ignorant scobe. Product of a first-class schooling in de Joov. A national treasure.

"What does it mean?" he said, a terrier onto a scent.

"Looks like a tree."

"And what does *that* mean?" Pure prickly.

"I just walked in, la!"

"Please, Tayto—think." Cheeky wanker. Everyone's pure comfortable ordering me to *think*. Like I'm mostly just fumbling my gonads and drooling.

I stared at de shape on de ground. A tree. Or a brolly with roots. Who knew? My mind was circling back to de Brakkenhof band out in de beanstalk, backs to me. I couldn't concentrate. Just wanted to get out of dis room, maybe leave de house altogether, when it flashed into my head like some quiz show host had cheated and showed me de answer to de prize question.

"Ah, it's never de shroom, is it?" I was speaking half to myself. When we were young scuts Yogi went through a gene-splicing phase. One Christmas he got a beginner kit. Instructions weren't even in English. Not even sure it was legal in Europe, but Dad knew a fien who knew a fien, and he'd managed to smuggle it in. Maybe de only time Dad got Yogi a pressie he actually liked. Yogi being Yogi, he was off to his room, mixing up all sorts of yokes and mostly making a mess. But he managed to splice a fungus with some manner of tree. De outcome was a few inches tall. Looked like a whachamacallit? A bonzai. Just a big warped toadstool if you asked me, but he was over de moon with it.

One day he took me aside—said it was time and he needed "a witness." He wanted to do a whole mar-yah Japanese planting ceremony off in de woods. I remember getting glammed up in an auld dressing gown meant to be a kimono. Yogi had us wandering forty fecken years in the wilderness searching for de perfect place to plant his shroomy offspring. Finally we found de spot: not too light or dark. I had to ring a little bell while Yogi spouted some gibberish (Japanese? His own rawmaish?) and chucked salt in de air.

"So you planted it. Where was this?" Zeke kept rubbing his hands over his head, like he was trying to stop de thoughts bursting out of his noggin. But I hadn't a bog where we'd planted it, and scansing for such a tiny thing would be like trying to find a leprechaun's thistle. And anyway, what did a little scut's frankenshroom have to do with de Crown, a grown man's masterpiece?

But Zeke was already on his knees, scooping up de loose leaves of paper like windfall, laughing in fast hard fits. Twas goan to be a long auld day and no mistake.

I led Zeke into de woodland near our house. Poor bollox followed like I was a prophet bound for de promised land. We squinted into de undergrowth here and dere—something bout de way Zeke visored his hand over his eyes as he scansed was pure panto. Should've been an audience of sprogs shouting *No no! De other way! It's behind you!* But nottin could make de scene more ridiculous. For my money, dere was no way Yogi's little sprout had survived to tell its tale. Not to mind after years of lighting up, my sense of direction was hopeless, boi. In de haloscape I could find my way round multi-dimensional labyrinths. You'd think it would translate to better spatial awareness in de Wayke, but naw. If you made yurself beautiful in de Scape, you'd be uglier to yurself in de Wayke. Or if yur smart in de Scape, yur stoopid hits you like a brickpile later. I practiced moving in space mostly, finding my way round jungles and spinning shapes to solve puzzles, and what happens when I wayke? Lost as a dyslexic in a library. Nottin short of a miracle I'd managed to find my own fecken house. I could feel de halos burning a hole in my back pocket. *Later,* I thought. *When I can enjoy it good and proper.*

Hours passed, sun was setting, but to Zeke I was still de man with de plan. Dat's some denial, boi. Maybe de penny'd drop when we had to turn round and head home none de wiser for spending a whole day sniffing about in a wood like two clueless pigs gone truffling.

But den we chanced upon a little culvert, and I'd a vague memory of such a stream, so to keep from walking in circles I said we'd follow it. Hunger was on me and my mind drifted to thoughts of dinner, de luvvly warmness of our round table. Would I be welcome at grace? It suddenly seemed a great and heavy question. What would it mean if dey'd started eating without me? If I wasn't part of de circle, banging on about pollen? I pushed de question away. Follow de stream, Tayto. Follow dis stoopid, random, shallow, babbling streak of nottin, with yur loony in tow. An edge of worry crept in with de fading light. Should've left a trail of insect-cookie crumbs to find de path home. A long line of oil-rainbow wings and shell fragments, winding deir way back to de kitchen door. *Always leave a trail back to home.*

De last pinky-purple fingers were sinking behind hills. We'd barely said a word to each other since leaving de house. I was reluctant enough to pop de silence, but I was working up to it when Zeke tapped me.

"What is that?" He was staring over into a dark thicket. I squinted after his pointy finger. In de distance stood a grey-ish dome big as a circus tent, but raised off de ground bout twenty feet on a giant stem. Something wrong for de scene. Zeke was off and running to it. I jogged after him, eyes struggling to focus in de gloaming. Sher what I saw was impossible, after all. A monster shroom, towering in de woods of my childhood, big as an oak, smooth as a whale, out-of-place as a dream on de way to work.

Chapter 10: Digging

Even as I stood under Yogi's childhood experiment, gawking up at de spooky canopy and poking de stem with my finger, my brain was still saying *naawww*. Something bout de evening light, maybe, made de big grey shape in de woods look fake. Not fake like a stage prop, I mean like a hallucination. It was so dim now I couldn't see my breath plume out from my face anymore. Maybe I'd stopped breathing.

Zeke was a terrier again, sniffing round demented for clues. Like what? A meaningful squiggle? A barcode cut into de... what was it even? Not bark, but like bark. More spongy. No wonder de lads in Brussels said *Down with dis sort of thing*. Sher what poor greengrocer would be up to writing a catalogue if twas all one neverending genetic pik-n-mix? Schoolboys stirring up dis with dat. A giant mushroom is distracting, like. Funny to coggle how tiny it had been when we planted it here donkeys ago. Fair duce to Yogi: he must have got dose "growing conditions" he was looking for spot on. Our Japanese ceremony worked a treat. C'mere, I should wear de auld kimono in de beanstalk. Ring my magic bell and feck some salt around. We could be munching off butterflies big as de table itself.

De dinner table conjured a hunger pang—*high time to make tracks for home.*

"Look!" Zeke cried from behind de stem. When I met him he was down on all fours. Jaayz, maybe he *was* turning into a dog. *What is it boy? Yogi's trapped down a well?* He swept his hand in an arc over de ground. "All around this xenoflore... The soil has been torn up fairly recently. Growth is minimal, see."

"Maybe it's to do with de... shroomy yoke, la. Blocks out light? Gives off poison?"

"We need to dig here!" cried Zeke, certain as a fien clutching a treasure map marked with a big X. "Something's buried under this."

Won't lie, as soon as he said it I felt a pulse of excitement—a pure kiddy thrill, like I used to feel playacting whenever I found a scrap dump in de woods and made out it was a crashed UFO. But I'd barely finished de first *Yay!* when a chill ran through me. I scansed round in every direction, squinting into de trees, hoping against hope I wouldn't spot—didn't even know what. Pair of eyes, I spose. Peepers locked on us. De whole forest felt like a nest of thieves, breaths held, hands on knives, and us two clueless tourists back in de days of ATMs, plonkers ready to punch in our PINs and fondle our cash with soft hands.

Impressive as de Eighth Wonder Of Munster was, twas too dark to dig and we'd no tools for de job. And I needed another night of wandering in a wood about as much as another funt in de knackers. Zeke had already started digging, first with his hands and den hacking into de soil with a sharp rock, but I managed to talk him into getting some kip—*de morning, boi. Fetch tools and we'll start in de morning good and proper.*

We marched home, de puny torch I'd borrowed casting more of a dribble dan a beam. Even de dribble was getting spitty, on de verge of conking out altogether, and we'd fallen back into quiet. Twasn't de peace I used to share on my strolls with Yogi. I was checking behind me every few minutes, pure paranoia licking de nape of my neck. Zeke must've sniffed it out, cos suddenly he was up in my face, demanding to know what I was at. Screw it, sher. I'd tell him.

"Here, don't get mad, alright?"

"What?"

He sounded angry already. Press on, Tayto. Press on.

"Look, tis good news really. I was just slow telling you cos you seemed a bit… delicate. But c'mere: De Fop's alive! I met him, and he's right as rain. Not sure, but I think he was disguising himself as my old neighbour, Spillane. Or someone was. Anyway—"

"The Amphibians have found us," he said blankly.

"Yur missing de point, Zeke. You didn't brain anyone! And Foppy's being a daycent skin about de rap on de noggin. He gave me one good funt up de nads and called us square. He's a gentleman, at de end of de day. Old school, like." Zeke shut up for a bit. Thinking, probly. Or shitting his pants. But den he started in with de auld nervous chuckling again.

"What did they say?" he practically whispered between laughs.

"Uh… tis simple really. If we find de Crown, dey'll open-source it—"

And dat was dat. He was off and giggling to himself, lost to me for about a minute solid.

"They're going to steal it and kill us," he finally managed to say, and his laughing stopped dead. He didn't even seem scared, just matter-of-fact. Half-relieved, almost.

"Kill us? Dunnaw Z-boi. Dese guys are whachamacallems. Idealists. World-savers, la? I mean, dey're posery tossers, but dey're do-gooder tossers, d'y'knaw?"

"You have a special talent," Zeke said, "for ignoring basic questions. What do you imagine will happen when we find the Crown? That they'll wait politely while we use it, let me study it properly first? Decode the—"

"Zeke, what does it matter if dey take it? If dey're planning to share it with everyone—"

I didn't say anything about how dey reckoned dey already owned it, having paid for de research and all. Maybe just as well.

More fucken giggles.

"Yur finding plenty to laugh at dis weather."

"Please entertain the possibility they are lying to you. They get their hands on the Crown, and we can bid it goodbye. It becomes another trophy in the pharaoh's crypt. A door to post-human consciousness—the promise of life everlasting—sealed away as a solo enjoyment for some asteroid mining magnate. Valuable precisely because it's kept from the stinking masses!" And den he started pawing me, like de looderamawns who get tired rummaging in skips for scraps and just grab randomers. *Have ya any food on ya at all, any rubber, any auld used photovoltaics, anything I can build myself a life with,* just mad desperation trying to get me to see him, hear him. I eased his paws off me, but pure gentle, like. He was brittle now as I'd ever seen him.

"Pharaohs!" he banged on. "They hate us. Fear us! Global enlightenment would be the end of their empires! What's the point of a pyramid that lets everybody in?"

"Dat… had not occurred to me."

"Oh really! *Dat had not occurred to you?*" And up he went in giggles.

His ripping on my accent made me sound like a pissed-off garden gnome, or a squinty-eyed pirate. A cartoon. Was dat all I was? Had I ever been anything more?

But truth be told, I *must* be thick as two short planks, parently, since now he mentioned it, I realized—for de first time—dat having a fortune might be no bad thing!

Kwery fiens, hardcore saints, good skins as we thought ourselves, we lived for de Scape. We grew it and tended it day after day, night after night, our sacred little community garden. No making any cash from it. Sher, in Ireland de whole service was given free of charge straight outta de gate—government trying to flatten de curve of Gombrich—and a kinduv we're-all-in-it-together vibe was de order of de day. Fair fucks to de suits who'd come up with the idea of subsidies and all, cos it looked like (knock-on-wood, don't wanna jinx it)—after so many yonks—de pendulum of de Scythe had swung to a halt. Halos are free, de Scape is free, saints wander into de sacred garden from any number of gates, and dere we play—together or on our own, happy as de larry is long. Don't screw up, don't get landed with a permanent butler, and whatdya know? Life's bearable! So who'd worry bout money, beyond what you need to mind yur bonebag?

And yet, despite all dis, Zeke's rant got me thinking something different.

"What's wrong with money?" I suddenly wondered aloud. Something had changed, like. Even Zeke stopped giggling for a bit.

"Scythe's been and gone, boi. Lads like Wakers and Amphibians and whadevvor, popping up all over de shop, all blathering bout *a new world,* and getting back to work—dat drumbeat getting louder and louder means one thing. Rat race is starting again. Kweries and free halos and all dat will be gone with de dodo. If a Crown exists..." And I didn't know what to say next, cos I was swept up in notions of pure power. Power! Something I never thought I'd have in my life. Sher, de day I left Joov and got my first solo bed on de dirt floor of a Dublin kwery, and no messing now, I'd convinced myself I was an emperor. No bunkmate above me, just de plain grey ceiling of our relikwery. Silent. No chats, no lads jerking off nearby. Just shifts of light and dark, regular as de moon and every bit as cool. Emperor of de moon.

But back on Earth, moon emperors aren't much more dan scobes. I didn't even have my own folks' house in de bag. Only whiff of inheritance was my brother's genius, and here, under de mega-shroom in de gloaming, was de possibility of his genius being unearthed. If I had wit enough to track his treasure, granted with de help of my trusty terrier Zeke (or me leading him—we seemed to take turns at master and dog), maybe I could spiff up with some new duds. De Wayke's a shifty song-n-dance number after all. Just tweak it here—new pair of shoes, a tie, firm handshake with de right bunch of lads—and BAM! Yur practically a new species altogether.

It was dis idea of warping into something else dat fired a regular conga line of adrenaline through me. A man flashing some real cash could sweep off any girl he fancied. Not like Noelly Ba with dat demented skanger he called a wife. I mean a fine half. A lash. And a proper *daycent* auld doll. Sol, say. For argument's sake. Get Bogdana and Bram's blessing. Sher, dey'd only be over de moon, dat moon I used to be emperor of, back when I'd nottin. Get our own place. *Man of de house.* Felt weird to be coggling it. But not so weird I couldn't entertain it for de time being.

"Zeke, think now for a second. Maybe de Amphibians'll pay us. If dey're as mercenary as you think, dey might be in a position to set us up for life. How bad?"

"You cannot be that naïve." He was chuckling, but something bout his tone got right under my skin. Dat *I know better dan you, poor gowl* haughtiness made me want to crush whadevvor dreams of his own were tapdancing round de wonky globe of his heart.

"C'mere to me, Zeke, you've some brain on you. De way you figured out de tree thing from Yogi's notebook doodles… dat was mad. Hat's off, serious now. But it's got to be said. If anyone has a special talent for not axing basic questions, tis you."

"Is that so?"

"Yup."

"Please enlighten me, Professor Tayto."

"Well, why would Yogi bury it?" And dat softened his cough for him. "He uses it, it works. So he takes it off, says *Great stuff,* and fucken buries it in de woods! Dat makes sense to you, hah?"

"Why would he bury it if it *didn't* work?" Zeke seemed to be axing de sky.

I stopped short den, cos I wanted Zeke to be right. At least about dis. Wanted my brother to have left something of himself, maybe de best of himself. I needed a time capsule waiting for me to dig up. Waiting patient in de cold earth to share some private trip with me. Reckoned it was de least he could do, having left me to rot in de Joov shithole with dose bastards for so long. Not to mention my empire of kweries, and such ever after. *Gimme what I have coming.*

Something bout de unnatural break in our quarrel helped de truth of de situation click into place, and I had more news to break.

"Anyway Zeke, de long and de short of it is, we're lost."

Now we were both chuckling.

"I thought you grew up here."

"Never been one for de orienteering," I shrugged, "but I've good news, too." And I whipped out de two halos from my back pocket with a magician's flourish. "Ta-da! A kick in de crotch wasn't de only thing de Amphibians gave me!"

Zeke took one off me as if it was de most natural thing in de world I'd be handing him top grade neurotech at dis exact moment. "Reckon dey're firewalled?" I axed, with no notion of not trying dem out immediately.

"Unlikely," he said in a pure level voice. "But that doesn't really even matter right now. And it doesn't mean we can't go for a quick jaunt." He gazed at de pearly band: "I love you."

"You talking to me or de halo?"

"Both."

"Ah, goan outta dat!"

We lay on cold ground.

"Bit nippy," I said. "We'll catch our deaths." Zeke said nottin. We lit up.

Oh, de drop. Terrible, evil drop. Falling back into my body de next morning was worse dan ever. Savage pins'n'needles as de nervous system came back online—woeful fierce. And worse again, de grey of de dawn. Was pure depressing after basting my brain all night in vivid supercolour and free flight. Twas like a butterfly waking to find himself as a fat grub lying on some prat's dinner plate. I dragged de dead halo off and shifted upright. Everything ached. Back especially. Fecken ground—you'd miss de recliner and no doubt, boi. But de worst of de worst was my chest. A freezing rain had fallen on us at some point, and I was soaking and sick as a ferret now. Much as I hated to do it to anyone, I yanked Zeke's halo. Oh, de drop. Terrible *evil* drop. From de looks of it, his was as bad as mine.

Cold ran through us—couldn't move my fingers. We huddled, propping each other up, a meagre house of cards shuffling itself through de woods. We'd avoided using de map function on our halos to find our way, just in case beady eyes were with us. Somehow, just by our wits, we hauled our sorry hides up to de kitchen entrance by late afternoon, wheezing like a pair fit for de knacker's yard. Not a minute too soon: lightning storm was building, and hail de size of knuckles were just starting to pelt down.

Bogdana saw us coming and flung open de door. I felt better as soon as she touched me, bundling us both into de warm room and fussing round and wagging her finger and telling us off in Polish and English. Home. I heard de word *pneumonia* being flayked bout de place. Even warming up hurt, but it was a different species of pain, a sign we'd be grand in de long run. I sucked down mug after mug of tea, grateful for it as if I were a proper Irishman come in from a day of building a wall or digging a ditch. I let de mug burn into my palms. My lungbags heaved—a sea of sludge shifted round under de breastbone. Scary things moved in de deep.

"Dying, Boggy!" I moaned.

"Idiot!" she snapped, stirring up some homegrown remedy. "Sleeping in woods! I should let you rot right there on your chair!"

De tenderness was lost on Zeke. He had his thinking face on—dead stare into space. You could nearly hear de little hamster wheel in his skull turning fast and squeaky. Suddenly he stood bolt upright.

"I need to borrow a coat and shovel," he announced, all man-of-action. Where'd he get de energy?

"Ah, give it a rest willa Zeke?" Hurt to talk. Throat was seizing up. Had a frog in it.

He leaned right into my face, whispering so low I could barely make it out: "They might already be there… digging our prize out from under us." I hocked a Dublin Bay oyster into my hand, felt de pulp slither in my grasp.

"Oh Jesus," I moaned. "Dat's not good." My condition didn't put in nor out on Zeke. He was up and off, looking for a shovel.

"Will ya siddown!" I called feebly after him. Thunder cracked overhead—His Nibs wasn't goan nowhere, boi. *Bed*. De word, de idea, draped itself round me, a luvvly blanket. "Boggy, I'll take my tea and medicine upstairs," I croaked, and drifted off, one foot in de ghost world, de other causing de stairs to creak and groan under de weight of skin and bone.

Twas all I could do not to wail *Poor, poooor Tayto* as I hauled off my damp clothes and slithered into some ragged peejays Boggy had fetched. I was fully into dem before I clocked dem as my dad's. Here I was, a half-corpse in a dead man's sleepwear. My hands stuck out de sleeves: nottin like his hands. Mam's hands really, only longer. Left de peejays on—too tired to be rooting round for something else. Stole a scanse into my trouser pocket and saw de two halos, curved and patient. Pure temptation, boi. I'd a powerful notion to light up den and dere, and just ride out my sickness. But it seemed too cheeky in a household where halos were verboten. Besides, Sol and Bogdana kept popping in on me to see how I was—another reason to stay in de here and now. De attention was making me half purr to myself, like a dirty moggy lifted indoors from de sleet to a master bedroom. Sickness feels different when yur watched over. I even liked how Sol didn't knock when she came in. Made me her poorly pet, ailing in my basket. Cos who knocks to visit a pet, like?

She sauntered in with another cup of Boggy's medicinal brew.

"To Lily de Pink!" I toasted, and slugged de lot. Gawd, stuff tasted luvvly. Bogdana was great. De Polish were great, weren't dey? People were bloody great. My bed cradled me ever closer. Sol performed some ritual over me. Looked like a cross between an Indian dance and a cop directing traffic when de lights break down. I axed her was it voodoo. She said naw, she didn't believe in hocus-pocus. But she liked rituals. She said it was like a greeting, or farewell, or any other formal thing. *Brings order, a sense of decorum*, she said. Not quite control, but… she couldn't explain. It's like grace, I said. She shrugged. Well, Tayto's up for it, I said. If it did even one hug's worth of help, I'd take it.

As she ministered to de sick, I got a chance to gaze at her some more. Say you charge—what?—a euro a pop for access to a Crown. You know a billion people will want it. Sher, isn't dat a billion yoyos tucked in yur back pocket right dere? Dat's not being greedy now, dat's just sums. Wish I knew de first thing bout business. Or law. Or managing Escher portfolios, or whaddevver it is razor droids do at a stock market to shave profit. All dat stuff was double-dutch. I'd never even had a wallet. Ah sher, you'd pick it up, like. Everything's learnable when you give a toss. Sol was doing a slow turn, hovering her arms over my legs. She was thorough, give her dat. My throat was feeling so much better I figured I'd float de notion of wealth with her and see what she did with it.

"Money's de root of all evil. Do you reckon some broke fiens came up with dat one?"

She paused, den went back to her dance. "Private property is a problem," she mused. "As soon as you have more than you need you're taking it from someone else."

"Says yur wan in my folks' house."

"No one was using it. It was rotting."

"I'm only pulling yur leg, girl!"

"Everyone needs a place to live. I'm not saying there aren't basic needs. But private property is a slippery slope. The most addictive drug there is."

"And what would you know bout addiction?"

"Not much. That it's something to be avoided."

"Yeah, but if, say, you'd invented something—or discovered something—dat improved de world... made life better for people... wouldn't it only be right you got a dose of de easy life yurself?"

"Where is this coming from?" she axed, stopping and staring at me.

"Ah no, please, don't stop! I think my legs are feeling better for it." She obliged. I was relaxed enough to keep talking. "Just hypothetical, like. If, say, I came into a load of credit, wouldn't it be a good thing? And say I were to give you a slice, what would you do with it?"

"Well, first, I'd drape myself in diamonds and fur."

"Serious?"

"Look," she stopped and sat on de edge of de mattress. "It's grotesque to turn the Scythe into a good thing. But it seems just as wrong not to take the chance to wipe the board clean and start again. Start a fairer game. One where massive personal wealth isn't the overwhelming objective."

Twas funny—shoot something like dat up a flagpole and old Dirt-Poor Tayto, the humble spud, would have saluted. But not

Rich-As-Fudge Tuxedo Tayto. No, dis fella didn't like de sound of it one little bit. I didn't even have de Crown yet, nor a cent squeezed from it, but I could already see myself as one of de Big Game Players (Wayke version), cruising to one of our meetings in a black limo. Stormtrooper Bram outside with his shockstick, whacking back nutball idealists like Sol as she waved her crappy homemade sign outside my tinted window. *Robin Hood-lums have to be kept down*, I'd explain to my driver, and he'd nod, his own eyes and thoughts private behind tinted glasses.

I wasn't up for going to dinner dat evening, but Eoin brought a sample platter from de table right to my bedside. I said he'd make a fine butler, and he hadn't a bog what dat was so I told him. He nodded and told me he was Bongo's butler. Den he dashed off to fill his pet's water dispenser and kibble bowl. Dat's one lucky bunny, I said again, and horked into my munch.

I rose de next day feeling better dan I'd done in living memory. Tell ya, a good night's rest is yur only man. Of course, without my halo I'd had rakes of stoopid dreams. Grateful to wake up and get away from de mattress. One dream returned on me during brekkie: I kept trying to look after Bongo but I couldn't do a thing for him—dere was no water for his bottle, no kibble for his bowl. I was hunting through de house, getting more and more frantic. At one stage I was out in de fields on my hands and knees, rooting round for anything at all to give him, but it was slim pickings. I was ripping up doc leaves and all sorts of crap, stuffing dem through de mesh of his hutch, but he wouldn't look at it. He appeared worse and worse for wear. I turned de dream round in my head as I turned de bugs round in my mouth. Zeke had snuck off like a thief in de night, and I got a strong notion I should go check on him, bring him some water and nosh if he was digging. Hunt him down like a dog if he'd done a runner with my inheritance.

I was faster finding de shroom dis time, but I still got a bit lost. Over de course of my wandering it swung from nippy to feverish hot. I found Zeke topless, waist deep in his trench in front of de shroom, digging away like it was his mother trapped below. He'd a child's tent set up wonkily a few feet away.

"Why are yur tits out, y'wally?"

"Hot," he spat. I touched his forehead—he was burning up.

"Yur on de way out," I said. He grunted out a laugh and hacked into de stiff, still half-frozen earth. "Stop, Zeke. Here, have some water. Eat, willa?"

He slumped down in his trench, took a few reluctant bites of protein cake and supped his water. I'd some of de medicine broth in a flask but he took one slug and spat it out.

"Zeke, boi, you need to come back to de house. Yur not looking de best."

"Sure. I'll just leave all this completely unguarded."

"Whatcha think of de cakes? Bogdana showed me how to bake. I made dem, like. Myself."

He said nottin.

To be fair, I took a bite of my cake and it wasn't up to much. Think I'd got de bug-to-sugar ratio off. When I sampled dem in the kitchen I must've been too excited to notice. First time I'd cooked anything. It was like… what? Being an artist. A potter, who molds and den fires a yoke with heat and—art. Hot and flaky. Well, my wayking art was a beginner effort, dat much was certain. But he could've been nicer bout it.

He had de spade, so I grabbed de shovel and we flayked into de dirty bastard earth together. It's pure violent, digging. But parently dat's how clueless nobs dig, cos after only a few minutes I was royally flahed, with a new round of feckin blisters! Vicious ones, palmside of my knuckles. Here I was swinging de long shovel like de big man, and wasn't I only fucken myself.

My back hurt. Needed a sit down, sup of uisce. Perched on the edge of de hole, my brow covered in sweat, my cakes tasted better now. Zeke kept digging. He had de spade, de proper digging doodad, and worked like a man possessed. He was a machine. Beautiful, in a way. De little bits of fat on his hips jiggling as he hit in, and den he'd *whoosh*—feck de dirt away and plunge in again. A man sparing no energy for de walk home. A man without a home. He was digging like a criminal tunnelling his way out of de lowliest prison imaginable. He stopped, turned to look at me. Didn't say a word, just stared. I got up and took a few more timid digs at de soil. Twas getting rocky. My blisters sang in shrill feckin falsettos of pain each time de shovel impacted. *EEEEEE!* Whack. *EEEEEE!* Whack.

Naw. Couldn't take much more of dis. I tried to wrap my mind round visions of byors hanging off me cos of all my wealth and fame. *Dirty* byors. Clever girls. Groups of women, coming on to me in a block. Nottin doin. Wasn't used to fantasizing bout Waykean stuff. Sher, yur still you. Pair you up with anyone, doesn't change de fact of Tayto's body and mug and spud-grey matter between de ears. Who'd be with me? Not me, boi, for all de tea in China. A Tayto in a fancy suit is still nottin but a tangy cheese-n-onion flake.

I dug anyways. If Yogi had a message for me, I wanted it. If dis was his weirdo way of sharing it with me, so be it.

Neither wealth nor women could get me through de blister sting, but den I found myself thinking bout my dad's peejays, and my being reduced to wearing dem, for some reason it really helped me belt into de dirt. Any pain dat came was welcomed. I whacked in till I bled. And when I saw de deep tears on my hand, and some blood trickling down de wood handle... ah, I decided to call it a day. I left Zeke in de hole, his body bent double, sweating milk, gouging away like de clappers into stones and roots, and all sorts of mean-spirited crap.

Got back to de house to find Bogdana not one bit happy. Turned out some looderamawn in de next townland had been caught impersonating de dead—*haunting*. Some will let it slide, or even welcome it, like, but dere's a certain element'll beat you down for dat sortuv carry on, so Bram and a few other armed neighbourhood peacemakers had tromped over to see to it no one got cudgelled, and some manner of law and order was in place.

Huh. Better you dan me, boi. Mobs need to cudgel a body from time to time, more so after de Scythe. Any excuse. Wouldn't fancy getting between lynch parties and deir payoff. D'y'knaw, you'd nearly miss de coppers out here. Dere's a few cops can be right bolloxes, specially to de most harmless fiens, like saints, but dey're good enough lads for stopping a ruck. Now de trains were up and running, you'd have to spose some guards would come back to de sticks. Sher, aren't most of dem culchies in de first place?

But Bram was a rock of sense. He'd never hurl himself into a situation he couldn't handle. Funny auld procession: de haunters, chased by de punishment mobs, who are hounded by de self-appointed sheriffs. Twas pure play-acting from start to finish. One bunch of randomers go, *Shag dis—I'll play at being someone else.* And de neighbours want in, so dey play hard chaws who'll sort yur man out. And den another gowl goes *I'll sort ye all out, I'm de Law.* Dodgy community theatre, boi.

I wished de Dutchman well. More power to yur shockstick now. Break a few legs and come home in one stern piece. But Boggy was less philosophical. *I know my baby will come while Bram's gone. I know he'll get hurt this time. I know-I know-I know.*

"Sounding a shade hysterical dere, Boggy-girl," I said.

She slapped de back of my head. "Do not use 'hysterical' at me!"

"Alright so." *Jayz, dat was pure hysterical.* "He'll only be gone a few hours. What are de odds you'll lay an egg in dat time—" And I thought she was taking de piss, cos didn't she start to groan before I had all my words out. She gripped my arm. "Ahhh, balls. Is it…?" She gritted her teeth and nodded.

I offered to leg it after Bram but she suddenly seemed pure calm and focused: "No, he is committed to saving that idiot man. Don't leave! We can do this ourselves."

I didn't share her confidence, like. I helped her waddle round de yard, and mad quickly de contractions went from mild to fierce on her. Who knew walking would be de job for it? I thought you had to lie down. Tell ya, I wanted to lie down. Naw, she kept pacing and sometimes squatting. Big, impressive breaths. Tiny Bogdana was turning into a strongman right in front of me! And Eoin, too—despite his mother goan primal, de little fella was all business, fetching dis and dat and generally being a proper little man about it. Sol decided to ignore Bogdana and went off to drag Bram back. I didn't make too much of a fuss as she left, cos I'd no want to show her a chicken-flavoured Tayto, but as she shut de door I nearly whimpered after her. De penny dropped: I'd been roped into my very own improv show. Role of midwife.

We made our way up de stairs to my parents' old bedroom. Boggy stripped naked and squatted deep over a towel laid next to de bed. She reached far and wide like she wanted to crush de whole mattress. I was too terrified bout my new job to be much troubled by de sizeable knockers just unleashed. I got Eoin de Orderly to squeeze Boggy's hand and stood up, thinking of de halo. Dere's a tutor program you can access for emergencies. You half-dome, like you would if you were puzzling, and get full medical procedures fed to you. I don't like half-doming for anything but puzzling. Doing something important on a half-dome is pure awkward, like you've had novocaine shot into yur limbs and dey don't work so great. It's a good idea but a bad program—needs a rake of bugs worked out. Still, I wanted de halo. Morale, like.

"I know tis contraband, but I've a halo, Boggy. For getting instructions. No bodder now, I'll just fetch it—"

I was half out de door but she shot me down. She'd talk me through de important stuff. I offered her a halo in place of anaesthetics. Naw! Wanted to be "present." *Mad byor.*

Right you be, says Dr. Tayto, squatting down behind his patient and cracking his knuckles, no idea what to expect next.

"When yur ready so," I announced, trying to hold de voice steady.

Never gave much of a coggle to hatching before. Hadn't a notion of having a sprog myself, and even if I did it wouldn't be me delivering it. In fillums de whole affair looked like a nasty business, alarms goan off all over de gaff, and everyone shrieking to high heaven. Dere was a fair mess alright, but de scene wasn't loud-dramatic like that. It was more or less quiet. And pure weird.

First, dere was de huffing and puffing. I tried to huff and puff along with her, but it made me even more lightheaded, so I went back to holding my breath. All dat huffy-puffy made it seem we were millions of years back in time, in a cave maybe, not humans yet, doing something I didn't understand. "How dilated?" she kept axing, and I pretended not to hear, until at last I yelled *Alright so!* But de only way I could go near her lady business was to close my eyes and guess.

"Dunnaw, maybe… dis wide?" I held my fingers up to show her. More huffy-puffy. She fucken growled. And not long after, de pushing started, and I couldn't finish my midwifery without looking… dere.

I tried not to faint. Something was poking out. A head, she said. Well, take her word for it, but twas more like a black dog's paw creeping out from powerful quicksand. "Dat's no head," I mumbled, and felt crawsick as soon as I opened my gob.

"It is, it is," she gasped. "Touch it."

"I will in me *hole*, girl!"

But dere wasn't room for delicate sensibilities, cos someone had to catch de black paw pointed at me. Baby noggin didn't feel like bone—more like porridge, la. I yanked my hand back, pure scared I'd prod right into de brain or whadevvor.

Animals, I thought. Gawd help us, we're nottin but animals who squeeze out more animals. I wanted to flayke out of de room, at least cover her bare arse with a fancy rug. Something with complicated patterns on it dat took a load of skill to make. Or better yet: machine-made. A shield from our animalness. *Her* animalness. Dat growl.

"It's coming," she groaned, human woman again for a second. "Catch it," she panted, like it took all she had to say a few words.

Now, like?! Didn't even think, I just cupped my hands under like a panhandler sieving a stream for gold, with only one of my eyes open, and de other squeezed shut in case dere was splashing involved. I yelled whatever I could think of dat sounded right— *Push, Boggy! Nice wan! Dowtcha girl!* Finally she told me to shut up and let her concentrate. So I crouched behind her, my back roaring in pain on account of de recent digging. Each *Hhhnngh* sound from momma saw de black soggy paw push a bit closer into de world, and den sink back into de blackness again. Disgust and fear were taking a rearseat to impatience now. Aching back on me! Was all I could do not to shout *Just c'mon willa!* but I kept schtum, hunkered down like de Bomb was about to drop.

And drop it did. A purple bald monkey exploded into my hands like it'd been fired down a chute. Tiny scrunched face like it'd tasted something nasty, well put-out bout being here with us.

A… girl.

Boggy scooped her up to her breasts. Eoin was suddenly by my side.

"Yuck," he mumbled. He handed me a bowl. "For the placenta," he explained.

Goan to fuck! I thought I was just cutting de cord and *sin é.* Tayto out! But naw. Had to wait for de sloppy sequel. Aw, and what a monster it was. It slithered out a few minutes later, missing de basin I'd laid down. Twas all I could do to hoist it quicksharp and slap it in de bowl. In spite of myself, I couldn't take my eyes off it. Now *dat* was an alien. Dark purple and blue, with a sortuv pale tree creeping up de spine. Wispy branches. *Kill it,* I thought. *Kill it with fire.*

"C'mere to me. Dis yoke in de basin here…"

"Don't throw it out," Boggy said, kissing de new byor's tiny slimy head again and again. "We're eating it."

"Course ye are," I sighed, de walls spinning round me. But was I done? Not on yur life, boi.

Now I'd a pair of clamps in my hands, and I'd to squeeze de umbilical cord to cut it. Felt like squid. Twas fitting really, cos de specimen connected to it looked like it had hauled itself up from de briney deep. I dug in with de blades and de rubbery cord wiggled round, reluctant to part ways. But Dr. T hacked through it, boi! Pure perverse, d'y'knaw? Like I'd scored one for de Wayke. One more poor little gome shaking and frail, trying to keep warm and out of trouble.

Boggy hauled herself onto de bed, and laid the baby on her naked skin. De strongman was gone—she was pure gentleness now. After a while she wiped de baby down and wrapped her in a blanket. She handed me her parcel and closed her eyes for a quick kip.

I held de newcomer—ridiculous small thing. Like something you'd find curled up in a cabbage, abandoned by dodgy elves. I found myself laughing, her nibs looked so pissed off! Boggy woke and told me to chuck her into some kinduv toaster oven by de wall. Had a quick check to make sure she wasn't delirious, and toaster oven yoke it was. I fired it up and a gentle orange glow wrapped de baby up like a sun shining on de only planet in its solar system. She smacked her lips, as if to say *Dat's more like it now.*

Eoin crawled into bed with Boggy. I left mom, son, and oven-fresh daughter alone in de room, and gatched down to de kitchen to wash my talented life-giving hands and grab some munch. Stomach was all over de shop. In de glory of my top-notch delivery de whole crawsick vibe had vanished, and now it seemed like de right thing to do was eat. I threw some honey-glazed locusts into a bowl and sat at de dining table. Didn't take a bite, like, just stared at dem— crispy little legs and all!—cos I couldn't stop grinning. Dr. Tayto to de rescue, pulling a rookie into de world. In all my scaping I'd never done anything so… Holding a teeny alien in yur hands, and de beady eyes blinking open and taking you and de whole circus in, and her goan *Ah come off it. Put me back into de nice comfy nowhere, like de drop before de manky body falls into harsh bright Wayke.* But you say *Naw, girl. Rise and shine. Time to wakey wakey and meet de family.* And it was probly de stress, but at de word "family" I could feel myself getting pure maudlin like an alley drunk. My arms started to raise, and didn't I catch myself launching into a spot of grace, like? On my own. Not even hungry, really.

Bram and Sol launched in de door and I drew my hands back to my locusts, fiddling with deir crispy legs.

"Well?" Bram axed. He seemed nervous and small—not a bit like a lad who'd march off to break up a donnybrook. Sol was sortuv hiding behind him too—no one firing up de stairs, like. Dr. Tayto considered his report.

"De mother is doing well. She's resting at present. And de baby girl is—"

"A girl," blurts Bram. Him and Sol hugged. Den dey thumped upstairs.

"Yeah, go on up," I said after dem. "Don't mind me, sher. Amn't I only peachy."

I finished my snack and waited a bit, but no one came down with a cigar for me or nottin, and I know enough to give people space. I grabbed a jacket, packed some heavy blankets, food and water rations, and strolled off to find Zeke. Give him glad tidings bout de baby, and maybe check in to see if we were coronated yet. Coronationed? Corona-ed. Fucken crowned, whadevvor. What a day dat'd be: a baby born and de Crown risen up from de soil, all in one afternoon. But naw, I found Zeke down on his arse trying to dislodge a big bollox of a stone. He looked a sight but I'll tell ya, he was making savage progress.

"Yur making great goshka of de digging!"

"No thanks to you," he grunted, wriggling a smaller stone free.

"Well now," I smirked. "I've been a bit busy myself today." He said nottin, just picked up his spade and started hacking again. "Go on, guess," I prodded. Still nottin. "Delivered a fucken baby, la!" Didn't even look up. Let him off, sher, he's just odd. "These hands, boi. These... life-giving hands." I wiggled my fingers at him. "Speaking of—brought you some sustenence." He took a swig of water but ignored de food. "It's Bogdana's cooking dis time, not mine. Daycent stuff." Sound of de blade slicing into darkness. I sighed, climbed down into de hole, and hefted up de shovel.

Before I left de dig I made sure Zeke's tent was set up proper and packed with blankets I'd brought from de house. He must be freezing his nads off here at night. How was he managing? Maybe I could borrow de baby's toaster oven for de poor daw. I wanted to see him curl up in a warm glow, smacking his lips, finally comfortable.

I heard a thump and stuck my head outside de tent. No sign of yur man. I stepped out fully and scansed round. Dere he was, slumped at de bottom of his attempt at a pit. I lepped in and shook him, slapped him in de face. He came to with a banshee shriek so loud dat I shrieked back nearly as harsh.

"You collapsed, boi!" He nodded, no bodder on him, like some auld fella told he'd just dozed off on de couch. Den he brushed me off, and went to get his spade. "Whaddya doin?!" I shouted. Dis whole day was just too much. I'd lost track of what a normal day might be, but I wished I could have one. Maybe harvesting bugs with Sol. Have grace and grub with de family come evening. Spot of halo before bed. D'y'knaw? No growling naked Polish wans, no catching babies, no chucking bloody sea monsters in a bowl, and definitely no visiting woodland zealots.

I yanked de spade off him. Wasn't hard—Zeke's eyes were half back and rolling in his skull. His soft tekka hands were in tatters, la. Blisters burst and re-burst. Looked like a torture victim.

"D'you hate yurself, is dat it?" I said. He was swaying, so I gave him a fanny-weak dawk and he focused. "Yur losing it, boi. Yur coming back with me." Dat got his attention. He stiffened, den he picked up his spade and—thought he was goan to brain me for a second—fecked it like a javelin straight at de hole's heart.

"IT'S HERE!" he screamed. Den he just slid down de wall of his pit and buried his face in his hands.

I stood still, not a bog what to do. Finally I sat next to him, not too close, like.

"Alright. You don't want to leave. But you've to promise me now you'll eat something. And drink yur water." He nodded. A thought occurred—no idea why I didn't coggle it before. "C'mere, do you want de spare halo?" I figured he'd hop at dat. At least I'd know he was getting a bit of rest. But instead of a nod, I got another scanse at dat fucken hunted look.

"No! No more halos. Understand?"

"Alright, calm down willa."

"I must purify myself."

"Whazza now?" And he stared off into de distance and went into de worst kinduv loony choons chant I couldn't even follow, bout how he'd never been a good man, and some weird stuff didn't make a lick of sense, but de upshot of it all was how his suffering here in de pit was called for before he found de Crown. No scaping till de Great Scape. Kept using de word *pure. Sweat hunger pain makes pure! Pleasure's a saboteur... Endure to ensure...to procure... Body is broken. Then ready. Pure!*

And I felt my heart breaking den, cos Dr. Zeke Zohar was neither family nor friend, but he was a fellow saint. He'd tended de same sacred garden I had, and tended it well. And I'd shared a stretch of bóthar with him. But I reckoned it was time to part ways, at least for now. I'd lost faith in his treasure map. Truth be told, maybe I'd even lost a bit of faith in de treasure itself. Or was I starting to be more scared of finding it dan not finding it? What would such a yoke do to you, even if it worked perfectly? Can you come back from de promised land? After an eon of being a god, wouldn't dropping back into de Tayto packet be a kinduv... punishment? And for all his blather, maybe Zeke de Zealot was right: you should break all bonds with de world before using de Crown. And I'd something with Sol now, and Boggy, and de new baby—even Bongo!—dat I wasn't in a rush to leave.

Zeke was ready, boi. Maybe he should wear it first... assuming it was hidden under dis monster joke of a tree or a shroom, or whadevvor it was altogether. But I wasn't holding my breath for a happy ending for him. I reckoned dere was no healthy man coming out of dis pit dat wasn't healthy goan in.

I rose, stretched my sore back, which was getting sorer and stiffer all de time, and reminded Zeke bout de blankets in de tent. Sun was setting. He was still rhyming to someone bout purity when I bid him goodbye. Walked through de trees to de family back home, pushing Zeke out of my head, all thoughts on de new baby I'd delivered pretty much single-handed. Maybe dey'll name her after yours truly, I thought. What'd be a byor version—Tay*ta*? C'mere to me, it had a fine tangy ring to it.

Got back to de house in record time, but something was off. Still no sign of celebration from upstairs. After moping round in de kitchen long enough, I went to tap on de bedroom door, see how de nipper was. Sol came out, pure quiet. Said something bout de baby "not flourishing." Not flourishing. Sounded like a flower trying to sprout from under a rock. Something dat couldn't open up. I nodded like I understood and, not having a bog what else to do, went down to eat dinner.

No one joined me. I sat at our circley table. Almost automatically I found myself raising up de hands and saying grace. Dunnaw why—it all seemed pure stoopid to me, dis hokey-pokey dance, but I just got de notion it would make de food taste better. Habit, d'y'knaw? Like dat dog, and yur man with de bell... and de name like a dessert.

Everyone was still in Boggy's bedroom. Still hadn't been called for a visit, so I wished dem goodnight from out in de hall. Got a muttered reply. Twas cold tonight—I was freezing my spuds off. I curled into bed and went out fast.

A pale white tree appeared from de dark, glowing—de only light in a black world. Slowly it lit all round it, till I could see I was deep in an ocean, drifting over a deep trench. Streaming out of de crack were all dese purple jellyfish, all with glowing trees on deir backs. Dey kept rising, one straight after another in long coils, floating up to some greater light above. And I wanted to get up dere too, but I couldn't move. I was anchored by something. Wasn't too keen on dese jellyfish. Pure monsters, la. Disgusting. *Let dem burn de roots*, I thought. *I'm here for de flower.*

I woke to de sound of crying. Crying's too soft a word. Dis was angry, vicious. Twas like being woken by an acid bath. Air was freezing. May as well have been no house at all, no walls or roof, just me lying naked outside. I pulled on a second jumper and squeezed tighter under de covers.

Twas Boggy crying, and something told me dere wasn't much to do but keep away. Even with everyone here, de house felt empty. De baby. Sol's words circled in my head like an old screensaver—felt like de were mocking me. *Not flourishing.* All I could think of was a dead flower, uprooted, lying on cold bare ground. *You did dis*, de screensaver in my head said. *You cursed dis family. You curse every living thing you touch.*

De crying sound went in cycles, wailing up to a freakish pitch, den dying down like it might end, only to swell again, angry at itself for letting up for a second.

I was no physio, I only play-acted as one in de Gerries. So whenever a client started de death rattle I'd be out of de room quicksharp—leave it to de big Latvian gurney fiens to deal with it. Always de imposter. Now here I'd been play-acting de family member, saying grace and eating at de roundy table, but in Boggy's hour of need I wouldn't console her for a king's ransom. *Keep back,* I thought, muttering it to me and her at de same time.

I think de whole house was scared, cos at one stage de alarm went off. De insect swarm kicked in, all dull roar. Heard Bram swear in Dutch and stomp downstairs. A shockstick snapped *CRACK* and de alarm sputtered dead. But now we were back to de woman's keening, and a part of me wished he'd left de alarm on. Kept feeling I was listening to someone have surgery without knockout juice. She wouldn't stop, just kept building and falling.

Shut up, I started to think. *Yur a dentist's drill in my head. Nottin I can do to help. I helped already and it didn't help. Maybe de baby's dead because I helped wrong.* And, dere's only so much a body can take, isn't dere? So I dug out my halo and lit up. And for a while all de Wayke's siren swarms and dentist drills fell away.

I kept to Yogi's room. Some neighbours came to pay respects. At least, think dey were neighbours. I heard dem downstairs and didn't recognize a single voice, but what does dat mean? Maybe dey were imposters, coming to thank deir grand protector, Bram. Maybe everyone round dese parts was an imposter now. Why be yurself anymore?

None of de commiserators stayed long. I kept wide of everyone till de burial, which was queer early in de morning. Bram had a small hole dug into de soil of de beanstalk, and de family gathered round it together. I stayed a few feet behind, trying to give respect by not acting like twas my family, my loss. But I was close enough to see her. Dey were burying her without a box. Naked, curled like she was still cosy and warm inside Boggy. Or like a pale prawn. Bogdana laid de body in de hole and den she started to vibrate, and Sol held her firm. Bram was blank, scooping soil over de corpse with his hands. Finally he planted a seed—dunnaw what kind.

Standing behind dem, even a few yards, I felt like a ghost, dere-but-not, unheeded, watching a family grieve. No one could see me. A set of eyes outside time. For all my saintly ways, I'd never felt further from my body dan staring at dat little fresh-dug mound…

All around, insects buzzed from flower to flower. Airborne sex, I thought. De beanstalk heaves with possibilities.

Eoin was clutching Bongo and looking round like he was bored, or wondering what to do. Bram turned to glare at de boy.

"Why don't you cry?" he suddenly barked. Even I, a spectre, flinched. "That's your sister in the ground!"

Eoin mumbled something bout Bram not crying either. Bram launched off his knees and snatched de rabbit.

"How about I kill this rat? Maybe that will wake you up!" He dangled Bongo by de scruff. De rabbit wriggled and kicked, well shitted out. Eoin was crying now alright, begging his dad not to hurt de crayture. Sol and Bogdana pleaded with dad. But dere's no pleading with dad, is dere? Once he knows de good from de bad, wheat from chaff, sheep from goats. Once he's made up his mind to inflict justice. De kid wasn't de only one shaken awake by Bram. Even watching him cover de babe with dirt, I felt nottin. I was a wraith, spying from just outside de world. Something bout Bongo wriggling, silent and helpless in Bram's fist, had my heart pounding now. Wayke, clicking its fingers. *Got yur attention again, langer? I've a hole in de dirt for each of ye. Fucken* justice, *boi.*

Whadevvor peace of mind de funeral was meant to pull off, it didn't work. Small wonder. Bogdana was hollowed out. She kept to her room. It was like we'd put her in de soil out back too. But it was Bram had me more worried. He stopped harvesting and tending de beanstalk. One day he went off and returned, stocked up on all de factory food crap he was killed ranting against: bags full of carbo-nosh bars and bright PEP drinks. He started swilling everything down at a rate woulduv had a sloth doing somersaults. But naw. No effect. He was an old machine, de kind with moving parts, shutting down bit by bit. Every pouch he polished off, you could see him trying and failing to keep de cogs whirring. Dere was a weird glue covering de works, gumming it all up. Some weird glue over everything, wouldn't come off.

I'd a mind to flee after de funeral. Families are tangles—no one needs it. But where to go? Join de shovelling hermit in de woods? Sit in Spillane's lounger plotting profit margins with de froggies?

Nightmares came for me every night. Real bad ones, stalking over de fields with stilty spider legs. It got so bad I took to lighting up from dusk till dawn. Yogi's room was my kwery, and my old habits were on me like a warm but smelly blanket. Days blurred. One morning I dropped into de Wayke to find Sol in front of me.

"Jayz, you frightened de fucken—"

"What's it like?" she said. Wasn't a question, more of a demand. Dis was all I needed: Bram kicking in my door, desperate for a bit o'pep, leddering both of us with a shockstick, trying to shatter me like he did de alarm system.

She was holding de spare halo with both hands: a virgin begging me, St. Tayto, to lead her faithfully into de Scape. I couldn't get my head round what her life was like now, with de home breaking apart piece by piece in a quiet wind. *Dat's homes for ya*, I wanted to say. *Need to take out insurance.* But she'd come to me for help, to learn haloship. How could I say no?

It felt weird to be teaching. I'd been lighting up so long, right from de first days of Joov, couldn't get my head around not knowing how.

"Tis dead easy," I said. "Nottin user-friendlier dan dese yokes. Just lie back, don it, and close yur eyes like you fancy a daydream."

"I don't need to do anything?"

"Naw, it's simple as nodding off, but instant. And de Scape's pure vivid—you've loads more control over it dan a dream." She was nervous. Wasn't sure if I was allowed, but I reached out and took her hand. She didn't pull away or slap me or give me de guzz eye. Just squeezed back. I told her first time she goes in, she'll be pure awkward finding her feet. I mean seriously, some people find it a balls building a body for de first time. Dere's a knack to it, like. You click to it fast enough, but until dat part of yur brain gets used to conjuring a vehicle (some saints call it a vector), you can feel at sea, and get woeful fear, or de gawks can kick in—even if you've no stomach. But minds are addicted to having bodies, so you can weave one up, and for some reason de one you weave will suit you better dan de one you got in de Wayke lottery. Yur first new body is usually something familiar, a kinduv spirit animal, say. Or something you'd recognize from life. Most folks say dis new skin *fits* better. Dat fitting-better is de real virgin high. *I've found my true body!* De joy is so big and whoop-dee-doo it almost feels like panic.

But de better you get at playing, you can shed de physical trip if you want, and dissolve into deeper realms—pure abstract stuff. Some maths and physics fiens go dere straight off, right out de gate. We used to call it earning yur wings. No idea what young fellas say now. Not boddered to find out either.

We lay back on Yogi's mattress. I squeezed her hand again, my way of saying *I'll be with you de whole way, girl. No worries at all.* Sol gave me a weak smile, den closed her eyes. De band lighting over her hair claimed her Scape virginity. De Wayke would never feel as natural to her again. For a second I felt a twinge—a sortuv guilt. Like I was leading her into temptation, a scrawny cheese'n'onion devil. I shook it off—you don't drop from de Wayke unless you've already had yur fill of de First Slap, as our old psych-art teacher Macca used to call it. I dove in to catch her.

You wake in cramped space. Muted light. A feeling of being trapped. You wriggle furiously—the walls are giving way as you struggle. Victory feels certain. You are on the brink of escape. A crack—you can glimpse out. Your limbs extend to force the opening wider. Six black legs.

With a final thrust you are free of your chrysalis. Something large is unfolding awkwardly behind you. A set of wings. They beat, unsteady, rhythmless at first, then faster, easier, beating time. Now you cannot remember life without wings.

Everything bristles with life. Vivid signals track through the warm air. The world is a network of pulsing signals. Spring into flight.

The speed and ease of insect flight is ecstatic. Navigate this buzzing vertical city. It is familiar. Out of the chaos, you sense her trace. Over there, that set of dazzling wings. Sol-butterfly. Flit to her leaf.

This is the greatest moment of my life, she wants you to know. Why did no one tell me? Why did I wait so long?

You're here now, you reassure her. And then there is nothing but the spiral of your flight together. Fusion. You sense a greater pattern. She is recreating one of her flight mandalas from the beanstalk. Her recall is prodigious. Weeks' worth of flight data, layers of detail, from species' growth rates to pollination activity, all manifesting around you. She is gifted beyond compare—phenomenal..

She is recreating one of her flight mandalas from the beanstalk. Her recall is prodigious. Weeks' worth of flight data, layers of detail, from species' growth rates to pollination activity, all manifesting around you. She is gifted beyond compare—phenomenal.

Her mind is wondrous. Her consciousness and the mandala

are one. You want to fly near her forever, worshipping such a being. The halo was made for her. You find yourself in a loop, a mantra, unsure what it means: She is the haloscape... the haloscape... She is the haloscape.

Butler rabbit struggles from a chrysalis, brushes himself down.

"Begging your pardon, sir," he lifts a paw. "Peripheral systems are lodging multiple trauma reports. It would seem you are being assaulted."

It is hard to drop away from paradise when there is no pain. You tell Sol you will return. You drop.

Probly de worst drop of my life, and dat's saying something. Pain, boi. Bram was standing over me, raining blows down on my face and gut. I tried to cover up, but he'd some talent for getting past my limbs and dawking a daycent target—like de dodgy rib de crows had walloped a while back.

"Fucken STOP, willa?!" I managed to bark out. He hauled me up to his face.

"What did I tell you? Halos are banned in this house! I don't want my daughter a useless saint waste of space like you!" He slapped me once more and fecked me back on de mattress. Den he yanked both our halos. Sol came to with a shriek. Must be some shock to have yur virgin voyage cut off like dat. And what a deep trip too. She squirmed, trying to get her head round being a human female ape again, sprawled on a lumpy mattress in a cold farmhouse bedroom in Cork. Bram went to clout her too, but she was so confused she didn't even flinch. He stopped short. Den, cruel as a Crow, he snapped our halos in two. I winced as if he'd snapped some vital bone or nerve in my own body. He seemed to be hunting for words, but in de end he just fecked de halo fragments in our faces and stormed out.

"Are you okay?" she axed. I could tell from her expression de answer was no.

"Who beats up a sleeping saint?" I heard my voice shaky, bleaty like a sheep. But even behind my shock and pain I felt guilt. I'd given her de keys to a new world, but I'd locked her out of her old one for good.

Sol was doing more wincing dan me as she slathered antiseptic onto de cuts round my eyes and cheekbones. I didn't mind so much—I'd had worse, like. De way I looked at it, maybe I'd broken his rule, but Bram was in de wrong. Plain and simple. He'd had a conniption, overreacted, and now we could call it quits. Might even snap him out of his humpiness. Never know—some people just need to bayte up a saint to get dem back to working order.

Between cringes at my injuries, Sol was gushing bout her first Scape. *How could it all feel so much realer than real life? How do you get better at it?*

I tried to explain as well as I understood it. When you light up, you commune with a larger system, part A.I., part crowd source, depending on de sort of stuff yur into, like. And yeah, tis weird how doing it helps you slip off yur old notion of what you are, but at de same time you become more... yurself, d'y'knaw? Shag it, I could never talk good halo banter. For me, twas always in de doing. Leave de tek natter for de dossers in Trinity. A byor like Sol would figure out de angles soon enough. I told her she was handy out, de knackiest byor—or fien!—I'd ever seen at first light. *Yur a genius*, I wanted to say. But dat word gets lobbed around too much. And having known one genius in my life, I didn't want to jinx anyone else with de label. She smiled anyway. Knacky was good enough. Meant something to her, I spose. Den she went back to smearing stingy gel on my lumps and bumps, wincing with me all de way.

To be fair, now, I never made any grand claims to understanding Bram—but what happened next struck me as out of character even for a dedicated oddball like him. He walked out into de fields with a bow and arrow. Where'd he get de hunting gear? Not a bog on me. When he returned after a few hours, he had a dead fox slung over his shoulder. I watched him from different windows as he set up a fire. Were we having BBQ? He chucked de furry fecker into a steel bowl and lowered it into de flames. No BBQ so. He stood dere, watching de corpse's hair sizzle, den de fat went up in a flash, den muscle blackened, and finally de bones were left. He shook de skeleton onto de yard and watched how it fell out. Just stared at it for yonks, like twas a troll's riddle, or a hobgoblin crossword puzzle.

Dat man needs to get back to routine, I thought. Maybe if Sol showed me how to harvest, and he saw us farming again, he might... dunnaw. *Snap out of it.* Don't want to use dat shitty phrase talking bout depression. Anyone who's been to Joov or de Gerries, or any kwery up and down de length of de country, is no stranger to glimpsing de black dog. And to be fair to Bram, I never buried a—I never lost what he just lost. But come off it. Burning foxes isn't on, boi. Bram hunkered down lower, and turned his ear to de bones. I'd swear he was listening.

And den it all happened fast. De family was packing up what little possessions dey had. A mangy local donkey arrived, complete with rickety cart didn't look like it'd make a half mile down de road. Bogdana was stuffing clothes and random pots into a backpack in our kitchen.

"Story, Bogdana? Ye goan on holiday?"

"No, Tayto. Moving."

"Moving *out*, moving?"

"Yes, Bram has considered everything, and says this is time to move."

"C'mere to me. Not to talk bout Bram behind his back, like, but I don't reckon he's been axing de right people. Bit worried bout him, la. *He was burning a—*"

"I agree with him, Tayto. We never meant to stay here so long. It is not our home. And this house… it just feels wrong. Please wish us well."

"But… what bout de beanstalk? Yur just goan to up and leave it?"

"Bram has germ cultures to grow another skin. It's not difficult. We can be set up in a few weeks. Besides, I think he needs a break from insects. We all do."

I wasn't so sure Sol needed a break from her insects. Seemed more to me like she was having her wings ripped off.

"So, you'll just wander round killing rabbits and foxes with yur archery kits? Dat's de plan?" I could feel a weird rage rising.

"Look," she said, staring out de window. "Spring flowers." And I scansed out, but I didn't see shit worth staring at.

Eoin and Sol fecked de last bags onto de cart. De donkey slapped his long schlong up against his grey belly, pure bored with waiting. If he'd a cab meter at least he could watch his fare goan up. Naw. He schlapped his schlong again.

I didn't lift a finger to help. Just lent against de side wall and watched from a distance. Dey won't get far. Tis a short madness. Dey'll get halfway down de road and Bram'll claim tis some kinduv drill, or a trick on me. Or de weather isn't looking too good for a move right now. Who moves in such changeable weather anyways? Drizzly bastard of a season to do anything. Donkey's on his last legs. Whole thing was a joke.

And suddenly de cart was loaded. I didn't come out to say goodbye, but Eoin found me. He'd been crying, big red eyes on him.

"Dad says there's no room for Bongo on the cart. I said I could carry him in my arms but he still said no. So I have to leave him here in his hutch. Will you look after my rabbit please?" *Fuck saaaake.*

"Uh, yeah. Course."

"Thank you very much, Mr. Tayto," he said. And he suddenly hugged my hip.

"No bodder, boi."

"I'll miss you, Mr. Tayto." He was looking right at me, waiting for something.

"Don't worry bout Bongo," was all I could say. "Bongo'll be fine, alright?"

Sol found me a few minutes later. Small bit of acne breaking out on her forehead. She hugged me, but I shook her off, fairly stroppy. Whoever was operating my body, he was a right gowl and no mistake.

"I'll find you in the Scape," she whispered. For a second I felt a lift, a flicker of hope. But it fizzled. Saints as talented as Sol vanish in de Scape. She wouldn't even recognise herself in a year. She'd either be plugged into some brainiac hive solving problems, or psychonauting her way through inner space. No tiptoeing through de feckin tulips with fiens whose farmhouses she squatted in once.

"Scape's a big place," I said with a shrug. "We'll see."

I watched her lift Eoin onto de cart. Once on board dey both waved at me. Kept my arm down. De family moved off den, Bram leading de ass down de road with a tap of a wooden switch.

"Please don't leave me," I said, pure quiet. But it was already like dey'd never been. De squatters were as gone as my own parents and brother. Gone as de people who owned our house before my folks got it. Inside, de walls were blank—pale faces of de sick. Windows were tongueless, big stoopid holes gaping into de Wayke.

Chapter 11: Deeper

Bram left a rake of pep pouches lying round. By afternoon I'd drained most of dem till I was half-demented, pottering round de gaff, poking and sniffing like an abandoned pet hedgehog pumped up on amphetabean—and other essential oils and vitamins.

Pep. Hated de stuff, but I wouldn't stop guzzling it. Even started wiggling my hedgehog hips as I snooped, cracking open pouches and sliding open kitchen drawers. Dusty old recipes for cake.

Living room. Staring at Mom's prized collection of crappy figurines and the Made In Timbuktu stickers on deir feet. Something bout dose figurines always made me sad as a kid—*why collect dis soppy shite? Can't play with dem, sher. Just sit on a shelf, big baby eyes on dem, la.* But now I felt like busting my hole laughing. Kids with baskets. Being trailed by a duck. Fishing with Grandpa. Two fiens hugging. Nobbers! Cracked open a pouch and sucked it like venom from a snakebite.

Up in Yogi's room I gazed over de pages of his torn-out notebook alongside a mirror. Fucken Leo da Vinci fucken fucker, hah? Equations all over de place. What's a fucken equation? Squiggles on one side, and another tangle of gibberish over de fence. What's it to do with getting some munch, or finding a couch to rest yur bones? Sweet F.A.I.

But in de margins he'd tucked away little sketches, and dey were beautiful. Little gems glinting up at de big caveman head on me. Pictures—I get pictures. Hard to believe just a pen point and a scrap of paper could do dis. A cloud of ink dots assembled into dead-on details of leaves or petals. Earthworm mouths. Zoom-ups of beetle legs. Life sprouting out of nottin but dots.

As a sprog I was a dab-hand at drawing, but drawing is one thing. Drawing is in de hand, and de hand is a grand con artist. I wanted to know where Yogi got dis talent to just… *see* stuff. How'd he learn to slow down enough, to squint close enough, to draw all dese little doors back into de home world for me? What sort of Will'o'de'wisp was he at all? Leading me into or out of de natural order of things?

Does genius sprout from de pebbledash? He didn't get it from dad, I'll tell ya right now. Auld Man was a gome, let's call a spade a spade. Always narky bout nottin. And mom—too quiet to know if she was smart. Always reading, if dat means anything. Reading made my neck sore. Dey were always making you do it in school, like dere was vitamins in it.

Here and dere in his notes, I'd catch a snatch of de readable. Flints and sparks of childhood. Random ideas. Something of himself, mam and dad, old pets. It's like Yogi wasn't sure what kinduv brother would be here to read dis, and left layers of message behind, from de pigshit simple all de way to… gawd knows what it meant. I couldn't unlock de deeper stuff. Just shy of having de right eyes. And to be fair, his handwriting was woeful—worse dan mine, and I barely knew how to hold a pen anymore. For all de careful curves and crosshatches and dots of his sketches, once Yogi went from pictures to words twas like de Tasmanian devil took de wheel. Some fien worked up to frenzy—too many ideas to follow for one poor pen and its measly black trail, a squid tied to a propeller, spraying ink in every direction. Looking at page after page of whiplash writing and gorgeous image, side by side, was like listening to a DJ mashing up hummingbird dance choons with snail make-out music. I touched de crinkly sheets, wondering why a freak like Yogi would use paper at all.

And den it hit me. He wasn't sure there'd be a Scape left by de time I got here. He couldn't even trust dere'd be electricity. Cos we never know when de old familiar wallpaper will come peeling off de walls, and our parents slide out of sight forever, and de tentacle arms of de Wayke, in de form of Joovs or Gerries, pull us from one another and everything we know. We never know when de flood will come, or how hard we'll find it to swim against de currents. Or whether we'll even try to get back to our source, our little spot by de riverbank where we first came blinking into de light. And now

I had a message in a bottle, and I hadn't a bog what Yogi wanted anyone to get from it. But he wanted some sortuv message passed on. So he used paper to record himself, and maybe dat was why I had a hard time concentrating. Something bout paper. So bleak and old. A dead pale thing. Like Ruth's skin back in de Gerries. *Home Sweet Home.*

I upped and went for a hedgehog wiggle. Cabinets and drawers, mostly empty. Waiting for gangs to burgle de gaff. Probly wouldn't mind me—just think twas odd to see a hedgehog knocking bout with a pep pouch. Dey'd shrug and keep scansing for pearls, or a daycent rain mack.

Wiggled and supped my way out to de yard. Boring. Tore into de beanstalk, and felt de sticky hot air wrap round me. Not sure what to do with de place. Could I farm it? Dere were tutorials in de Scape, but it looked like hard work. Lots of little chores, all de time. Hassle, like.

Hedgehogs don't like hassle. You've only to take one look at dem to know it. And dead right too. Go 'way with yur hoe and yur sweating. Sod off with yur irrigation and soil pH. Go 'way with yur teeth trying to eat me. I'll ball up and spine ya, boi. Taking it handy, me.

Shut my eyes and listened. All de living, rippling things. How do you maintain de skin? Dat part was knacky. And if you did nottin, dis vertical farm would dissolve—rotting away from within, torn apart from outside by weather and small nibbly animals.

Picture it: big raw space where dere used to be a towering garden. Like waking up one morning to see de town giant has left. Snuck out in de night.

Whizz of wings round my head.

I opened my eyes. A tiny shoot was already sprouting from de fresh dug soil where de baby lay. Still no idea what kinduv plant it was.

Probly didn't matter.

De hedgehog went to check on de rabbit Bongo. No word of

a lie, twas nearly as hot outside de beanstalk as in. You'd nearly miss de regular seasons, like, from back-when. But I was glad to be free of de cold for a bit. I fed de thankless, twitchy scut— nyom-nyom-ing into his munch, not even a nod of *Cheers for dat, boi. Nice wan.* But what can you do? Dey're pure spoiled, modern youngsters. Found myself wondering if he'd survive abroad in de wild. Prefer it even? Settle down in a grand sprawly warren with a nice dirty doe who's mad for it—not be living a monk's life cooped up in a hutch. De hedgehog was a wondery crayture altogether. All wonderment and spines and tiny paws. Could Tayto survive in de wild, he axed himself? Sher, hasn't he been dis whole time?

De hedgehog wondered should he chase after Sol.
Ah, not another fecken adventure. Paws feel mad tired and small.
He launched into one more pouch—a little pep. A little lift.

De hedgehog found himself wiggling down de road—all business. Evening crept on, but it just got warmer and warmer. No sense to it.
He came to a fork in de road, and peeked beyond into de Awful Field.

Dad showed Tayto de place as a kid. A simple plot of land you'd barely notice. Back before de Church said *Limbo? Sher what's dat?* men would come here at night to bury unbaptized babies. Only men. Only at night.

All de way from de 1200s or dereabouts, when monks were howling in deir abbeys, right up to de last century. Generations of men, digging away under moonlight, dumping seeds dat'd never take root. Keeping de duds as far from de family plot as possible.

May as well have been launching dem into space.
And, said Dad, lowering his voice like it was a secret, a grown man was buried here.
A man "beyond redemption." Dose words.

De hedgehog scansed out over de field with beady X-ray eyes, pierced under de soil, and dere he was: suicide man. Lying flat on his back, long and full-grown. And all round him, curled like white stars made of bone, a constellation of babies.

A fork in de road. In de culchie mind, one stream of dead would go off into some kinduv heaven, and de others to hell. But here, at de fork, dese infants who didn't know up from down float off into limbo. An infant crying forever for its mother, no clue why it's been abandoned.

De hedgehog reckoned dat's where demons come from—not hell. Tis abandoned children in limbo, neglected too long, grown mad with impatience and de want of a hug. Rocking babies in Joov, breaking from de long rigid chair, stalking back to de Wayke for whadevvor dey can get.

Beyond redemption. What does it even mean? Weren't dey all lying here together, de "innocent" and "guilty," no difference in de end? Nippers too young to accept a belief, and one langer who rejected it. Dose who couldn't survive, and some bloke who'd said *feck dis* to life.

When Tayto came here with Dad life was normal and dere was a family. Twas weird looking at de field now, after so many years. After de Scythe swept up Mam. And den Dad—lost, angry Dad—decided he was beyond redemption too. And den Yogi got led off to special ed.

Three desertions in a row—de Wayke making a point to do it bit by bit instead of all at once.

Slow, lazy. Like slaps in a fight between a bouncer and a schoolkid.

No one sure who started it. No one stepping in to break it up.

Deep down, de hedgehog wondered, Tayto must be fundamentally bad or so many important people to up and leave him.

Getting warmer still.

He wiggled onward. Wasn't far to de faery fort. A strange space—de surface of an auld vinyl record. Deep grooves to keep livestock in and raiders out. And de trees make it so dark. An unlucky hedgehog could wiggle inside and wander in circles forever.

It plays strange music, dis record. Plays it backward.
Can't work out if tis soothing or creepy.
Either way, you get into it. Hard to leave a faery fort.

Dey say you need someone to help you find yur way out sometimes.
A man beyond redemption.
Sher, speaking of de devil—dere was someone to help him out of
de fort! Hadn't he to check on Zeke Zohar, de poor nervy bollox?

Luckily, Hedgehog had packed provisions—water and de last of de
insect bread.

And a few more pounches of pep.
For good measure.

Getting closer to de shroomtree in de woods, things were leaning
funny. He checked de pouch instructions: *Restrict use to two a day.*
8,333% RDA of vitamin B12. He blinked. Sher, dat couldn't be right.
No bodder. It was all working out so far.

He was floating now, like Will'o'de'wisp—no need to use paws.
Plus de provisions bag felt almost weightless on his spiny back.
How bad?

A chuckle escaped him. Was he turning into Zeke? And as he got
closer to de tree and its dry moat, close enough to see down over
de lip of de fresh-dug trench, which stretched nearly in a full circle
around de tree, he saw his old buddy lying on de ground.

At last, he thought. *He's having a bit of a liedown.*
But what was dis near his feet? An open cardboard Tayto box.
And what was bedecking his noggin?

A harder chuckle again. De langer had dug de wrong way round
de shroomtree.

Dere were only two choices, right or left—had he turned anti-
clockwise he'd have found it in de first few shovels-full. Some

bolloxes have to do things de hard way, spose.

Zeke's soft hands were torn to fuck. He was shrunken—dead of thirst? Like you'd see in kweries before de age of butlers. Was dat a slight smile on Zeke's face? Hedgehog tugged de Crown off, held it in his shaking paws. He was wondering good and hard now.

Maybe you can't sip a drop of infinity.
One taste and yur swallowed whole. But how bad?
Why be a spark when you can be a sun, raging for eons, warming worlds?

Why bodder with dis piddly corner of de universe, dis pokey little skull balanced on a frame?

Sun was setting. He held de Crown in his hands...
Somebody should let Bongo out of his hutch.

A call from de round dining table: Grub's up. Chatter of family, all axing where's Tayto.
C'mere to me, everyone needs some Tayto. Tisn't a meal without Tayto. Dere's loads more tangy stuff to come, but first we need Tayto. C'mon and give us some Tayto, willa!

He wheeled round, sniffing de air, beady peepers trying to spot a pair of green eyes staring from a slit, or something stalking through de trees, well-dressed and frightening.

Nobody. Nobody. Alone.

In de bottom of de hole, Hedgehog faced a choice: Burrow deep into de roots, or clamber out and up into clearer air. He froze. What is a fork in a road?

De sun was setting. A moon was high.

About the Author

Colm O'Shea is a professor of writing at NYU's Tisch School of the Arts. His short story "A World Apart" was selected by Singapore University's Centre for Quantum Technologies 2022 flash fiction competition, and his poetry has been anthologized in *Voice Recognition: 21 Poets for the 21st Century* (Bloodaxe) and *Initiate: An Oxford Anthology of New Writing*. His book on sacred/morbid geometry in Finnegans Wake, *James Joyce's Mandala*, is available from Routledge.

He lives in Beacon, NY, with his wife and four children. Visit him online at: colmoshea.com

Curious about other Crossroad Press books?
Stop by our site:
http://store.crossroadpress.com
We offer quality writing
in digital, audio, and print formats.

Printed in the USA
CPSIA information can be obtained
at www.ICGtesting.com
CBHW032325010424
6241CB00014B/62